Praise f THE BOOK WOMAN'S DAUGHTER

"For those who loved *The Book Woman of Troublesome Creek*, author Kim Michele Richardson offers another fine evocation of the often cruel conditions of rural Appalachia in the last century and a powerful portrait of the courageous women there who fought against ignorance, misogyny, and racial prejudice. Steeped in an intimate knowledge of the traditions and lore of the region and written with a loving eye to the natural beauty of the landscape, *The Book Woman's Daughter* is a brilliant and compelling narrative sure to please readers already familiar with Richardson's work and to win her a well-deserved host of additional fans."

—William Kent Krueger, *New York Times* bestselling author of *This Tender Land* and *Ordinary Grace*

"A mesmerizing and beautifully rendered Appalachian tale of strong women, bravery, and resilience, told through the eyes of a new heroine reminiscent of Harper Lee's own Scout Finch."

—Ron Rash, *New York Times* bestselling author of *One Foot in Eden* and *Serena*

"In Kim Michele Richardson's beautifully and authentically rendered *The Book Woman's Daughter*, she once again paints a stunning portrait of the raw, somber beauty of Appalachia, the strong resolve of remarkable women living in a world dominated by men, and the power of books and sisterhood to prevail in the harshest circumstances. A critical and profoundly important read for our time. Badass women at their best!"

—Sara Gruen, #1 *New York Times* bestselling author of *Water for Elephants*

"Fierce, beautiful, and inspirational, Kim Michele Richardson has created a powerful tale about brave, extraordinary heroines who are downright haunting and unforgettable."

—Abbott Kahler, *New York Times* bestselling author
(as Karen Abbott) of *The Ghosts of Eden Park*

"Kim Michele Richardson's *The Book Woman's Daughter* sets us deep inside Kentucky's rugged Appalachia in the early 1950s and gives us Honey Mary-Angeline Lovett, a sixteen-year-old as fierce and brave as her mama, Cussy Mary. Their world is cruel with its prejudice, and Richardson is not afraid to peel back its ugliness and take us there. But, like the best writers in not only this generation but the ones past, Richardson gifts us readers with something extraordinary, a way back."

—Bren McClain, multi-award-winning
author of *One Good Mama Bone*

Praise for
THE BOOK WOMAN *of* TROUBLESOME CREEK

"What Richardson has written is a novel about the best of us. And the worst. And has done so with magnificence."
—Bren McClain, multiple-award winning author of *One Good Mama Bone*

"Richardson's latest work is a hauntingly atmospheric love letter to the first mobile library in Kentucky and the fierce, brave Pack Horse librarians who wove their way from shack to shack dispensing literacy, hope, and—just as importantly—a compassionate human connection. Richardson's rendering of stark poverty against the ferocity of the human spirit is irresistible. Add to this the history of the unique and oppressed blue-skinned people of Kentucky, and you've got an unputdownable work that holds real cultural significance."
—Sara Gruen, #1 *New York Times* bestselling author of *Water for Elephants*

"This is Richardson's finest, as beautiful and honest as it is fierce and heart-wrenching. *The Book Woman of Troublesome Creek* explores the fascinating and unique blue-skinned people of Kentucky and the brave Pack Horse librarians. A timeless and significant tale about poverty, intolerance, and how books can bring hope and light to even the darkest pocket of history."
—Abbott Kahler, *New York Times* bestselling author (as Karen Abbott) of *The Ghosts of Eden Park*

"Emotionally resonant and unforgettable, *The Book Woman of Troublesome Creek* is a lush love letter to the redemptive power of books. It is by far my favorite Kim Michele Richardson book—and I am her huge fan. Cussy Mary is an indomitable and valiant heroine, and through her true-blue eyes, 1930s Kentucky comes to vivid and often harrowing life. Richardson's dialogue is note-perfect; Cussy Mary's voice is still ringing in my head, and the sometimes dark story she tells highlights such gorgeous, glowing grace notes that I was often moved to hopeful tears."

—Joshilyn Jackson, *New York Times* and *USA Today* bestselling author of *The Almost Sisters*

"Kim Michele Richardson has written a fascinating novel about people almost forgotten by history: Kentucky's Pack Horse librarians and 'blue people.' The factual information alone would make this book a treasure, but with her impressive storytelling and empathy, Richardson gives us so much more."

—Ron Rash, *New York Times* bestselling author of *One Foot in Eden* and *Serena*

"A rare literary adventure that casts librarians as heroes, smart, tough women on horseback in rough terrain doing the brave and hard work of getting the right book into the right hands. Richardson has weaved an inspiring tale about the power of literature."

—Alexander Chee, author of *Edinburgh* and *Queen of the Night*

"With a focus on the personal joy and broadened horizons that can result from access to reading material, this well-researched tale serves as a solid history lesson on 1930s Kentucky. A unique story about Appalachia and the healing power of the written word."

—*Kirkus Reviews*

"This gem of a historical from Richardson (*The Sisters of Glass Ferry*) features an indomitable heroine navigating a community steeped in racial intolerance. In 1936, nineteen-year-old Cussy Mary Carter works for the New Deal–funded Pack Horse Library Project, delivering reading material to the rural people of Kentucky... Readers will adore the memorable Cussy and appreciate Richardson's fine rendering of rural Kentucky life."

—*Publishers Weekly*

"Based on true stories from different times (the blue-skinned people of Kentucky and the WPA's Pack Horse librarians), this novel packs a lot of hot topics into one narrative. Perfect for book clubs."

—*Library Journal*

"Readers will respond to quiet Cussy's steel spine... And book groups who like to explore lesser-known aspects of American history will be fascinated."

—*Booklist*

"Richardson has penned an emotionally moving and fascinating story about the power of literacy over bigotry, hatred, and fear."

—*BookPage*

"A powerful yet heartfelt story that gives readers a privileged glimpse into an impoverished yet rigidly hierarchical society, this time by shining a light on the courageous, dedicated women who brought books and hope to those struggling to survive on its lowest rung. Strongly recommended."

—Historical Novel Society

ALSO BY KIM MICHELE RICHARDSON

The

BOOK WOMAN'S DAUGHTER

a novel

The

BOOK WOMAN'S DAUGHTER

a novel

KIM MICHELE RICHARDSON

sourcebooks landmark

Published by Sourcebooks Landmark, an imprint of Sourcebooks
P.O. Box 4410, Naperville, Illinois 60567-4410
(630) 961-3900
sourcebooks.com

Cataloging-in-Publication Data is on file with the Library of Congress.

Printed and bound in the United States of America.
LSC 10 9 8 7 6 5 4 3 2 1

For Joe,
Always my secret weapon.

"Show me a family of readers, and I will show you the people who move the world."

—Napoleon Bonaparte

Kentucky

They still call her Book Woman, having long forgotten the epithet for her cobalt-blue flesh, though she's gone now from these hills and hollers, from her loving husband and daughter and endearing Junia, her patrons and their heartaches and yearnings for more. But you must know another story, really all the other important stories that swirled around and after her, before they are lost to winters of rotting foliage and sleeping trees, swallowed into the spring hymnals of birdsong rising above carpets of phlox, snakeroot, and foxglove. These stories beg to be unspooled from Kentucky's hardened old hands, to be bound and eternally rooted like the poplar and oak to the everlasting land.

One

The bitter howls of winter, uncertainty, and a soon-to-be forgotten war rolled over the sleepy, dark hills of Thousandsticks, Kentucky, in early March, leaving behind an angry ache of despair. And though we'd practiced my escape many times, it still felt terrifying that this time was no longer a drill.

I remember when I was twelve, and the shrill air-raid alarm sounded in the schoolyard as we were dropping books off at the stone school over in Troublesome Creek. The teacher yelled out to Mama, "It's a duck-and-cover drill," and then rushed us all inside, instructing everyone to crawl under the desks and cover our heads. It had been scary, but I still felt safe under the thin, wooden lip of the school desk.

Today, at sixteen, I realized how foolish it was to think that a little desk could protect anyone from a bomb—how difficult it was now to believe that hiding would somehow save me from the bigger scatter bombs coming.

I shifted my feet on the stiff, frozen grass umbrella'd under the Cumberland Forest, breathing in the cold as Mama helped me into her heavy coat. In every direction, hoarfrost crowned the forest surrounding our cabin, its gray crystals shimmering through pines, hickories, and oaks, as the twining psalms of chickadees and warblers announced the morning. Overhead, a turkey buzzard glided low, scanning for dead flesh. I shivered as the ugly bird dipped lower and lower.

"You must hurry," Mama chided for the second time, a pull of the cold escaping her breath. "He'll be coming up here to escort us to court anytime now. Remember everything we told you. Everything we practiced."

From the side of our cabin, the hood of a lawman's parked automobile poked out behind a thicket of chokeberries, the first rays of sunlight flashing off headlights and polished chrome.

"I'm frightened, Mama."

"That's not a bad thing, darling daughter. It'll make you more cautious."

Two weeks ago, my parents hid me in the cellar when the law showed up to arrest them for violating miscegenation laws, after a peddler happened upon our family and remarked back in town about Mama's strange blue color. Papa hired counsel, bond was posted, and yesterday word came of a revocation hearing while I stayed hidden in the cellar. Today they would go in front of a judge because of Papa's parole violation on his 1936 banishment order and for daring to marry a woman of mixed color—a blue-skinned Kentuckian.

After Papa got out of prison, we'd moved over to Thousandsticks from Troublesome Creek, and our family had been living in secret here for the last twelve years.

I saw the fear in Mama's eyes as she reached for the scarf. Her hearing was also set for today.

Hiding inside after the lawman arrived last night, I peeked out the curtains and saw him watching from his automobile to make sure Mama and Papa didn't flee the county before the hearing. He'd stayed all night and was out there right now sleeping in his official vehicle.

"Mama, I don't want to leave you and Papa. *My home.*" I swiped at my eyes with the cuff of her scratchy wool coat.

"You're not safe here." She wrapped a knit scarf around my neck.

"I want to stay and wait for you and Papa to come back after the hearing. I'm nearly grown, almost seventeen—"

"It's too dangerous, Honey Mary-Angeline," she said, including my middle names she and Papa christened me with years ago when one of the saddlebag preachers stopped at our small cabin hidden near the forest. Mama asked what name I'd like to take and I had said *Mary*, for her middle name, *Cussy Mary Lovett*, the distinguished Book Woman of these ol' hills who'd worked for the Kentucky Pack Horse Library Project when I was little. Then I asked if I could have two, and added Angeline for my first mama.

Angeline and my first papa, Willie Moffit, had been Blues, too, but neither of them knew it, Mama had told me later. Angeline died in '36, right after she birthed me. Mama never said much about my first papa, only that an accident caused his demise. By the time I turned six, I had lost most of the methemoglobinemia, the gene disorder that the ol' doc over in Troublesome Creek said me and Mama and the Moffits had.

Doc explained that Mama's parents, the Carters, like other clans 'round the country, were all kin to themselves, same as the royalty in Europe. Only difference, we didn't have us a family tree like most folk. Instead, we'd gotten twisty vines that knotted, wrapped, and wound around each other. And although my hands and feet still turned a bruising blue whenever I got scared or excited, only those parts of me took on the strange color.

I was grateful I could easily hide the affliction. *Affliction*. A hard word for me to swallow, but it wasn't nothing compared to hearing how Mama had been treated. How the law ripped her and Papa apart on their wedding day, calling them immoral and sinners and worse. Mama said I was only three months old when the Troublesome Creek sheriff had beaten and arrested Papa and threatened to lock Mama up, too, and throw me into the Home of the Idiots on that October day in '36.

Lifting my palms, I watched the tint of a robin's-egg blue rise and spread with a darker tinge outlining them. Nothing as dark

as Mama's color that covered every inch of her. I thought of
the fright, scorn, and horror that would appear in others' eyes
when they glimpsed Mama's ink-blue skin. The embarrassment,
shame, and sadness leaching into Mama's.

Once, when I was six years old, we were buying apples
inside a store in Tennessee when the man behind the counter
called Mama an ugly name and ordered us out. When I saw
the hurt pooling in Mama's eyes, a blinding fury like no other
rose inside me. Unable to tamp it down, I threw my apple
at the shopkeeper. He snatched up a thick wooden broom.
Mama apologized to the angry man and scolded me as she
rushed us out the door, shielding my small frame while taking
the brunt of the shopkeeper's battering strikes and raging
curses.

Mama received eight stitches on her scalp. After that, I learned
to keep quiet and lower my head—learned what a Blue had to
do to stay safe.

I looked over at the lawman's automobile, my stomach
stitched in knots. Mama's hands trembled as she reached into
my coat pocket, pulled out a pair of gloves, and handed them
to me. She'd been knitting these to hide my blue skin and to
keep me, the last of our kind, hidden from the rest of the world.
Papa, wanting to contribute, had stitched me black leather ones
to switch out. They were my armor, a shield against folk who
hunted the Blues.

"Can I go to Tennessee and visit Papa's kin instead?"

"Great Uncle Emmet's place is bursting at the seams. There's
fourteen in the home and they can't squeeze in another soul. I'm
sorry, Honey, there's no one else."

She flipped down the thick collar on the coat and straightened
it. "I packed your brown journal. You be sure to keep writing
those pretty poems of yours."

I nodded, feeling the tremble on my chin. The journal was
my favorite and what I wrote down all my poetry in.

"Papa's packed your .22 for the journey," Mama went on,

fussing with the bulky leather-wrapped coat buttons, pausing to wipe away a tear.

I glanced at our mule, standing to the side and out of sight from the law, and spotted my rifle poking out of the rawhide scabbard.

"Take Junia and ride straight to Troublesome, and don't stop till you reach Miss Loretta's," Mama said, her voice thickening.

The next county over was thirty-some miles away, but with all the rough terrain, narrow mountain trails, and countless switchbacks, it might as well have been three hundred.

"Straight to Loretta's," she said again. "If you meet any trouble, find Devil John."

Moonshiner Devil John was one of Mama's old library patrons who also lived over in Troublesome Creek. He'd been visiting us here in the Cumberland for years.

"Mama, I love Retta, but she's got to be one hundred years old. How will she care for me?"

"Ninety-one, and you'll help out Miss Loretta, and she'll keep you safe till we can all be together again." Her words were swollen in grief, pained.

"Yes, ma'am, I will," I whispered.

"Listen to your mama, li'l Book Woman." Papa stepped outside, his bright eyes now troubled and dark. He raked his fingers through thick brown hair, peeked at the law's automobile, and dropped his voice to a whisper. "You need to hurry. He'll be waking up any time now, and we dare not let him see you here. Remember, your mama has sewn a little emergency money into the lining of your coat. Be gentle with old Junia, and she'll see you safely there."

"Ol' Junia never minds me like she does Mama," I said stalling. "Can't I stay just a bit longer—"

"We talked about this, Honey. Your mama and I have been accused of breaking the law. If the judge finds us guilty"—he stole a glance to Mama—"there will be a punishment."

I tugged on Papa's coat and squinted up at him. "But won't your lawyer fight it? What—"

"Shh. We have to be prepared. Slip on those gloves now," he said more sternly, more slowly, making me latch on to his every word.

If my folks were found guilty and taken away, the court could send me to the orphans' home until I turned eighteen or, worse, to the House of Reform where the children wear chains and toil from sunup to sundown on the farms till they're twenty-one.

"C'mon, Honey," Papa said. "Let's put the pannier on Junia and get you home to Loretta."

"Papa, what should I say if the law comes after me?" I glanced out at the automobile and pulled my gloves on.

"Right now they only know we have a daughter, but they don't know where you are, Honey, or what you look like. And they won't find you where you're going. Mr. Morgan shares the same office as our attorney, Mr. Faust. He's signed up with the courts to represent you and is working on the legal papers to get you a guardian. You remember Bob Morgan, don't you?"

"Yes, sir."

"Just don't say anything except that you want to talk to Mr. Morgan if anyone asks. He'll help you."

I clung to Mama, afraid. That I could lose them both because men would punish my parents for loving each other was terrifying. And I knew somehow that going back to Troublesome was going to be *troublesome* for me.

"*Mama.*"

"My darling daughter, you'll be safer there." Mama wrapped me in a hug. A moment later, she said quietly, "When we went back to your grandparents' cabin last fall to visit and clean the cemeteries, you'll remember we stocked the root cellar with food."

"Yes, ma'am, I remember."

"Your papa took some more victuals over last month. Key's in your pocket. Don't lose it. And you be sure and share everything with Miss Loretta." She gave one last hug, then kissed my cheek. "I'll send word when it's safe. If all goes well, you might be able to come home tomorrow at first light." She drew back and gave me a small, reassuring smile. "I'll come straight to you. I promise."

But there was no promise to be had in her worried eyes, the darkening blue flesh of her face betraying the words. "Mama," I said, chasing down the ghosts of childhood to return to a safer place—any place other than where they were going and where I was being sent. I searched their faces. "Mama, Papa, I love you."

Mama laid her head against mine. "I love you, darling daughter."

Papa pulled us into his embrace and spoke softly: "I love you. Ride safe, li'l Book Woman." He drew back, kissed my forehead, then pulled us close once again. When he released his hold, he turned back toward the automobile. But not before I saw a small tear fall from the corner of his eye.

"*Papa*," I whispered, my heart breaking, the ache deep, my love and the pain of losing them cutting even deeper.

"Be quick, Honey," he said hoarsely, keeping his back to me. "You'll return when we come for you, or when we send word it's safe." Once more he peeked out at the automobile, then snuck quietly over to Junia.

There was a sober finality in our brief goodbye, and we all felt it. Our future together was about to be erased, the same as in 1936 when the sheriff over in Troublesome erased my papa and mama's marriage and then the courts banished him from entering Kentucky again for twenty-five years. What was coming loomed bigger, bolder, and the fear seized hold, punching hard at my bones.

I hugged him once more and climbed atop Junia, then rode her out on the narrower trail on the other side of the yard, away from the lawman and his automobile, the cold winds lashing at my stinging wet cheeks, the pounding of the beast's hooves raging in my chest, stoking the anger and sorrow inside.

When I was at a safe distance but could still make them out, I climbed down. From behind a grove of trees, I stood beside

Junia, peeking over her withers, waiting, and then watched as the lawman sauntered up to the cabin. In a minute my parents stepped out the door.

Mama stood helpless, clasping her hands while Papa talked to the official, their conversation lost to the wilderness. Several times, the lawman shook his head, his face darkening to a mottled red. With each shake it felt like a knife piercing, and I held my breath, watching until Junia swished her tail and a rumble threatened to leap from her chest.

"*Shh*," I hissed. But it was too late. The ol' girl pinned back her ears as the man took a step toward them. Mama cowed, raised an arm protectively over her face, and tried to back away. But the lawman latched hold and twisted her arm up behind her back, pinning her tight against the automobile. Mama tilted back her head and, with deep, guttural anguish, howled into Junia's startled whinny, drowning the beast's fury.

I didn't need to hear the crushing snap to know he'd broken her arm.

Again, cries pulled from the mule's chest, and I quickly put my hand on her muzzle. "Quiet, Junia," I warned, not taking my eye off my parents.

Papa grabbed the lawman by the shoulders, pulling him off Mama, but the man spun around, whipped out his billy club, and struck Papa hard upside the head. He crashed to the ground on both knees, cradling his face with both palms. Shouts lifted as the lawman handcuffed him and knocked him over onto the cold ground. He gave a swift kick to Papa's side and turned back to Mama.

Junia pawed the earth when she saw the man shove Mama into the back seat of his automobile.

Calling out for Papa, Mama banged on the window with her fist.

I wanted to scream and curse the man. Instead I clamped my hand over my mouth, watching in horror as tears streamed from my eyes.

Junia lifted her muzzle and bawled into the sleeping woods, and I ducked lower, barely peeking over her withers.

The lawman stopped and turned our way. My gaze dropped to my .22, then fell back on the man, and my breathing hitched as I shifted toward the scabbard.

He took a few steps forward and cupped a hand over his brows, searching. My gloved palm slid over the shoulder stock. Seconds later, he dropped his arm and turned away.

Quickly, I tugged Junia deeper into the trees, climbed atop, and rode the mule hard toward Troublesome Creek.

Two

With every mile, my courage dwindled and the doubts loomed larger. Finally, I stopped in the moss-blanketed forest to see if I was being followed, the swirls of fog ghosting up into the slices of morning light, our shadows growing longer on frosted pine-needled paths. My despair settled deep with each step, separating me from them. I placed a hand over my heaving chest, the panic like a tempest inside, escaping through cold breaths.

I rode another mile before Junia slowed down. Every few minutes the mule would look back yonder to home, to Mama. I couldn't help but look back longingly, too, hoping they would return today, praying the court would release them.

"Ghee up, Junia. C'mon, ol girl, *ghee up!*" Junia poked along despite my pleas and loud urgings. Dropping my whole weight into the saddle, I kicked my heels against her sides.

She swung her head and sassed back with a spray of garbled brays.

A light dimmed in me; the despair and helplessness had set in. "I miss them, too, but at this rate we won't be there till dark." I slid off, stuffed my gloves into my pocket, and grabbed the reins, tugging the beast along. "We've only gone about six miles, but we have at least twenty-five more ahead," I told her as we walked the forest paths, stepping carefully over and around logs, on the lookout for critters.

The sun finally broke through the fog, the push of an early

spring calling out to the hills. We rested by a brook for an hour as I tried to take my mind off my parents by soaking it all up. Patches of tender green shoots, blossomed coughwort, and showy toadshade sprang up from the earth. Moss and rotted wood perfumed the air. Mama had insisted on teaching me about nature, made me pay close attention and treasure it all, most especially during the coming of spring. It was a necessity, a means of survival for all Kentucky folk, but especially for us Blues, she'd said.

I pulled out Mama's pocket watch from underneath my coat. The silver timepiece twirled on a leather string, catching a glint of sunlight that escaped through the fogged, tree-forested crown. It had been her great-grandpa's in France, and she'd passed it to me last July when I turned sixteen. I pushed down on the pumpkin crown and released the latch. The tiny, glass-bubbled case opened, the porcelain face showing it was 9:12 a.m. I snapped the timepiece shut and tried to ride Junia again.

Five hours later, I rode alongside Troublesome Creek, the steady clip-clops of Junia's hooves murmuring as we crossed trickling creek waters and rode up into pine-treed mountains. We passed a woman and child walking the path. She toted a basket brimming with roots and other herbs. A moment later, a white turkey skittered across, its stream of loud gurgles trailing behind.

A man carrying a fishing pole called out a friendly greeting. "Honey Lovett, it's been awhile since I've seen the Book Woman and her daughter."

"Sir, good day." I nodded as we passed one of Mama's old patrons.

In a few more minutes, Junia halted and brayed out warnings, then calmed. Tightening the reins, I looked between her tall ears and saw the ol' moonshiner, Devil John, and his horse. I couldn't make out the other person riding alongside him.

"Devil John, sir, it's me, Honey," I called out, relieved to see the family friend after all this time. I nudged Junia over to the moonshiner and a woman riding a fine horse, sneaking peeks at the stranger.

"Honey," Devil John greeted me, tipping the black floppy hat with his calling card, a raccoon dick fastened to its front, his invitation to let folk know he was selling the shine—though it was known he didn't partake of the spirits himself.

"Didn't expect to see you or Cussy here till at least May. I was fixin' to journey over to Thousandsticks to drop off some hardware supplies for your pa and visit your family in a few days." He rubbed his long, gray beard, studying me.

We always looked forward to seeing Devil John. Several times during the year, me and Mama came back over to Troublesome to stay a couple of weeks during the fall and for almost two months in the summer. We would weed the Carter cemetery, visit her patrons, and then tend to the small grave site of my family, the Moffits. We'd spend a lot of time with Retta and some of Mama's other folk who'd been on her book route while Papa busied himself traveling to Tennessee on timber business.

I never understood why we hadn't moved out of the state— why Mama chose to stay in Kentucky. There'd been talk of moving to Tennessee or north to Ohio, but the notion got tamped down just as quick as it arose. Mama'd said she hoped to continue her important library work in Kentucky one day, and she couldn't bear to let her family's cabin go to rot and the Carter and Moffit cemetery go to seed. Troublesome was her home, her kin and ancestors' home, she insisted. And like Papa had remarked from time to time, sometimes with a wistful sigh: *This ol' 'Tucky land sure makes a man yearn for it and want to flee it altogether. And you can sure 'nough have yourself one foot on foreign soil, but the other is always pointed home.*

But today Kentucky had become our prison. And for the first time, I felt its shackles and choking ropes on me and my family. I looked away, thinking about my parents' brutal beatings this morning, trying not to let the sorrow reach my eyes.

"Everything okay over in Thousandsticks?" Devil John looked over my shoulder, expecting to see Mama.

"Mama's not with me today, sir." I glanced over at the woman who was studying a map of sorts. "She sent me back to visit Retta, while she, uh, takes care of things back home." My voice strained a bit and Devil John raised a brow. I couldn't tell him family business in front of a stranger, even though he was close friends with my parents and we never hid anything from him.

He turned to the woman beside him. "Miss Grant, this is Honey Lovett, the daughter of our decorated book woman, Cussy Carter Lovett. Cussy worked for our Pack Horse Library Project here and delivered books to us."

The woman looked up from the paper with sketching on it. "We had the same project over in Somerset, my hometown. Hi, call me Pearl, and I'm pleased to meet you, Honey." She smiled easily and lifted a hand, jangling her silver bracelet full of charms. "I love a good book and I'm going to need a lot where I'm going."

"Troublesome has itself a fine borrowing branch now," I told her quietly, liking her already because she loved the books.

Pearl didn't look much older than me, but her eyes said different. They were playful and spirited, yet held an edge of something troubling, maybe even a hint of sadness. I admired her hair, a stylish, short haircut full of soft curls like the Italian movie star I'd seen in some of the magazines Papa brought home from his Tennessee trips. Her riding britches had a lot more life to them than mine, and her tall, leather boots were stitched with fancy embroidery to match her gloves. I glanced down at Mama's old hand-me-downs, the three-dollar, leather-bitten boots, and pressed them closer to Junia wishing her fur would swallow them. Still, the young woman seemed friendly.

"Pearl's our new fire-tower watcher," Devil John said. "She got lost back on the path when I happened upon her. Thought I'd show her to the lookout."

Pearl shrugged sheepishly and held up a curling map. "Pie got us turned around about four miles back after we crossed the creek and my directions got wet." She petted the handsome piebald's spotted white and red neck, stroked his long strawberry mane.

Admiration and respect surged through me. It could be a dangerous job manning the fire tower, and all alone at that. I wanted to find out more about her.

"You say you're headed to Miss Loretta's?" Devil John asked.

"Yes, sir, on my way to Retta's right now."

"I still have to make a stop back in town. Since you'll be passing the fire tower, would you mind showing Pearl the rest of the way?"

"Happy to take Pearl for you, sir."

"Much obliged, Honey." He turned to Pearl. "You're in good hands. I'll bring up that trunk you mentioned earlier, once it arrives in the morning."

We journeyed through the woods while Pearl chatted about her job, distracting me from my thoughts of home.

"The ranger said I'll have every Sunday off and at least one weekend off a month. Where do folks go for fun?" she asked.

"When R.C. was the lookout, he used to take his fiancée to the picture show over in the next town. There's a train depot about four miles from the tower that'll tote you there."

"We have us a fine movie house in Somerset. It's called the Virginia Cinema and I loved going. Last month, Mother took me to see *Singin' in the Rain* with Gene Kelly and Debbie Reynolds. Oh, but it was grand!"

"I read about it in the newspaper. Mama promised to take me if it's still playing." I quieted and snapped the reins, urging Junia onward. I knew the chances of seeing the musical were slim now.

At the foot of Hogtail Mountain, I stopped and climbed off Junia, motioning for Pearl to do the same. "It's narrow ahead. We'll have to walk most of the way from here."

"It doesn't look much wider than a bicycle path." Pearl laughed.

"Some spots are easier than others. Mama used to bring me up here all the time to see R.C. and Ruth. We were real tickled to learn about his promotion."

"Last week, my uncle brought my horse over to R.C. so he could be here when I arrived. I met R.C. at the ranger station this morning when I picked up Pie and the maps. Met him and another ranger named Robbie Hardin." She frowned at the mention of Hardin.

"Sure is something, you being appointed a female fire-tower lookout, and so young." I stopped to study her a bit closer. Pearl must've sensed my curiosity.

"I just turned nineteen. Graduated high school last year and spent the summer working part time over at the Big Knob lookout in Pulaski County. As soon as my boss told me there was an opening here for full-time work, I applied. How about you?"

"I'm from here and I've always wanted to be a book woman like my mama."

"You can't be more than fifteen. You have plenty of time to get your librarianship."

I looked away, thinking about the House of Reform and agonizing over whether to fib to this new acquaintance. It didn't feel right, but neither did the whole day. "Eighteen," I lied, worrying that I might have to keep lying to strangers if my parents never came back for me.

Pearl stared down at my coloring hands. "Are you okay?"

I realized I'd forgotten to put back on my gloves after checking my timepiece. "Fine, it's nothing but a disorder that flares up once in a while. It's been a long day already." Quickly, I turned away and led Junia along the mountain path. "Watch your step," I called back to remind Pearl, digging into my pocket for the gloves.

"What's Somerset like? I've never been," I asked while we walked.

"Small town. Nice enough. We live near Lake Cumberland and spend a lot of time boating and fishing on the lake."

"Sounds nice. I've seen pictures in the local magazines, and it's sure a pretty lake."

"Yeah, but nothing like these beautiful knobs you have. I can't wait to explore it all."

"Spring is always special. I'm in town for a while and can show you around one day." It wouldn't be long till warmer winds were here. Soon the forest would cast aside its sleeping blanket and perfume the air with its riches. We traveled up the twisty, mud-packed paths, the scents of fresh earth rising with each step taken.

"Already graduate high school?" she inquired as we rounded another switchback.

"Never been." I was glad she was behind me so I couldn't see her face.

"*Never?* However did you manage that?" she asked with a big question in her voice.

"A lot of kids can't attend. Some are taught at home and others just drop out or don't go because they aren't close enough, or don't want to live at the Hindman Settlement or Caney Creek Schools. And a lot of folk don't want their children taught by the fotched-on women either, yet others say they are some of the best teachers in the world. Mama said the fotched-on women make these ol' hills a better place. But she insisted on teaching me from home and believes she gave me an education better than a lot of book-read folk."

"What's '*fotched-on* women'?"

"Well-to-do outsiders they *fetched* into our hills to teach in the settlement schools."

Junia suddenly stopped, pinned back her ears, and brayed into the tree-soaked hills. A thin, piercing scream vibrated up, and I spied a startled bird limping toward the side of the path, dragging its wing.

"What is it?" Pearl leaned over my shoulder. "What the devil is wrong with that ailing creature?"

"That mama bird"—I poked a finger toward the thrashing

critter shrilling on the grassy bank nearby—"ain't ailing. The killdeer's trying to draw us away from the nest she's built on the path."

Pearl whistled. "Just when I thought I'd seen it all in my last job. There's so much I've yet to learn."

"You will, and the critters will teach you something new each day."

Together we peered up the rocky path and spotted an indention with three black-speckled eggs tucked inside.

Dropping Junia's rein, I sprinted up to the nest and stepped around it. "C'mon, Junia, there's room to pass." I walked back to the mule and then up to the nest, sidestepping around it again. "Ghee up," I ordered. But the ol' girl weren't having none of it. Instead she bellowed in singsong with the shrieking killdeer, causing so much racket I had to cover my ears.

Finally, I grabbed Pearl's horse, leading it around Junia. The horse backed up, pawed at the hard earth, and I lost my footing, nearly falling off the mountain. Junia screamed out haws and snorted loudly, biting and nipping at the poor mount's hide. The mule was determined to be in charge of this trip, and she wasn't about to let Pearl's horse take the lead.

"Pie, whoa, whoa," Pearl ordered.

"Junia," I cried out. "*Whoa!* Stop or you're going to throw us off the mountain." Junia took another nip of Pearl's mount as we passed. Pie reared and bumped against me. Stumbling, I fell and busted my chin as he dragged me past Junia, leaving my face scuffed, lit afire by rock and clay, my legs dangling over the mountain. I gulped down scents of wet pine and rotted leaves, while I fought to scrape the air and lift myself to solid footing.

Again, Junia sent a thundering warning to the horse, the echoes lost to a still-sleeping forest.

"Honey, don't move," Pearl called out. She wedged past Junia, giving a firm tug to her halter. "*Halt*," she scolded and lightly bopped the mule's nose.

Junia snorted, then quieted.

Pearl rushed over to me. "Honey, let me get Junia so you can grab her lead."

Sweat trickled from my brow, stinging my eyes. Again, I thrashed, struggled to find footing, digging my boots into the rocky mountainside, clawing at grass, rock, and debris, the smell of fear rising off my chest. Finally, I dared to peek over my shoulder and looked several thousand feet down into nothing but brush and craggy rock.

Quickly, I buried my face into the hard ground, my breaths coming fast and short. Junia ambled over, sniffed my hair, and I let go of one hand and blindly groped for her rein. Slipping down a little farther, I scratched the earth and rock with my boots and felt one loosen, a scream collapsing in my chest. The mule nudged my back, and I latched onto her rein, holding on for dear life.

"Back, back," Pearl said gently to the mule.

Junia moved slow.

Pearl grabbed my other arm, and together she and the mule slowly dragged me back onto the path. I crooked my neck and looked back, twisting my legs. Then one of my boots fell off and went tumbling over the steep, rugged cliff, bouncing off razor-sharp rocks and prickly limbs, until it was swallowed up by the mountain.

I panted, looking up at Pearl from the ground, a little embarrassed, wanting to cry but trying desperately to be brave in front of the courageous woman.

"Obliged, Pearl." I grabbed her outstretched hand. "If you weren't here, I would've been falling till next season." Standing somewhat shaky, I touched my hurting chin and sighed as I brushed the dirt off my coat and britches. One button was missing from Mama's coat. I looked around the mud-leaf path and found the old leather button and slipped it into my pocket. "Junia, we're going to have to find my boot before we go home."

Junia snorted and moseyed past the nest and a screaming mama killdeer.

Pearl chuckled. "Does she always win?"

"It's wise to let her," I said. Then we both fell into fits of laughter, my worries masked behind a flood of snorts, giggles, and guffaws, the tearful laughter hiding the sorrows of the morning.

After a bit, Pearl said, "Are you sure you're okay? I can go on from here and let you get home to clean up and rest."

I gulped down the last of my hilarity, wiping my eyes. It felt good to finally have a taste of laughter and even better to share it with someone.

"Go on, Honey, I bet you're tired. I can manage."

Between the horrors of this morning and the long ride to Troublesome, *rest* was just what I needed, and for a moment, I was tempted to accept.

Junia sidled up to me, sniffed my face, then laid her big head over my shoulder, keeping a mistrustful eye on Pearl and her mount. "I'll be fine as long as Junia behaves."

Pearl admired her a moment while I stripped off the other boot and stuffed it inside my pannier. "Junia, huh?" She scratched the mule's floppy ear. "Wherever did she get the name, Honey?"

"It's Biblical. Mama said it's just a word or two, but from a part of the Bible that says maybe there was a female apostle." I stroked Junia's gray muzzle. "C'mon, apostle girl, let's get to the tower and then go find my other boot."

Pearl reached around in her bags and after a moment dug out a pair of red velvet house slippers. "Here, you can wear these until you find your boot."

"I can't. They'd get ruined."

"I have another pair and won't be needing them. Mother insisted on trying to pack two of everything." She laughed, her eyes bright and cheery.

Grateful, I wrestled the slippers on over my thick socks. Snug, but at least they would keep my feet warm.

Testing, I took a few steps and frowned, feeling the mud sucking at the fine slippers. I dared to look down.

Pearl soothed a skittish Pie, pretending not to notice.

We took several more switchbacks leading up to the lookout with me leading the way, hugging the cragged rock face, Junia slow-poking behind me and Pearl, and Pie bringing up the rear.

Every few feet, Junia would stop and gaze out into the distance as if searching for Mama. My eyes would follow, too, hoping it was all a mistake and that Mama would come riding over the next ridge to take us home.

At the top, Pearl gasped. "Home, finally!" She spotted the large shed for her horse and the outhouse beside it, pointing, soaking it all up. Hay and horse feed had been toted up and were stacked under a partially covered lean-to.

Pearl looked out at the forest, inhaling the fresh air. White skies crowned the brown tops of the forest below. Faraway, I could see a curtain of mist slumbering over the darkened hills, heading our way. It looked like snow, and I inhaled, tasting the breaths of its crisp promise. Nearby, a crow cried out into a distant bird's chattering, and below, a forest critter's thin wailing carried into the breeze.

"Eight landings and one-hundred-thirty-three steps to the trapdoor," I told Pearl as we tied our mounts at the bottom. "Used to be only eighty-four steps, but they had a fire in the cab that destroyed it. They decided to rebuild and raise the cab higher."

Pearl cupped her hand over her eyes and stared up at her new wooden home atop the winding steel stairs with its metal catwalk encircling it. "It's perfect," she said.

I couldn't help but wonder why a woman would want to take on the dangerous job, much less want to live here alone.

As if hearing my thoughts, she said, "I was born to do this job. To be able to live as close as you can get to your Maker, in His mighty nature. Ever heard of Hallie Daggett, Honey?"

I shook my head.

"I read about her work years ago. She became the first female fire lookout of the Forest Service in 1913. Spent fifteen years on the job working at the Eddy Gulch fire tower in the Klamath National Forest. That's way up at the top of California. And I want to be just like her, only spend my next *thirty* being a lookout." She laughed.

"That's something." I stared at her a moment, even more impressed that she knew what she wanted for herself and was determined to get it.

"Seven men put in for this appointment, but R.C. said I was capable as any of them because I had manned the fire tower back home. Also, I passed the eyesight test with flying colors. Two of the men had poor eyesight and only one had the formal classroom training for becoming a fire lookout like I'd had. R.C. said none of the applicants had formally studied topography like me. The Forestry made me spend an eight-hour grueling day hiking the forest, and another hour running up and down the fire-tower steps with the men. There were only three of us left."

I was flabbergasted that she had won the appointment over so many men and overwhelmed with admiration. Somehow, I felt close to her, and a kinship I'd never known before took hold. If Pearl could do all that, maybe I could survive on my own too.

"The men didn't like it much and grumbled to the bosses," she said. "Some said it wasn't fair for a female to steal a man's rightful paycheck. But some of those old boys didn't know how to even locate a fire, much less tell the difference between a sleeping one or sheep dust or a fog puff." Pearl laughed.

"I'm glad you got it," I said, meaning it.

She sighed happily. "*Home.*"

"C'mon, I'll help you carry the bags up before I head out to Retta's place."

"Thanks. Is Retta family?"

I couldn't tell this brave girl that she was my babysitter. Instead, I said, "Loretta Adams is a close friend of my family."

Pearl dug into her pocket and pulled out two small keys on a chain and jangled them, smiling. "R.C. gave me the padlock keys this morning. I can't wait to see my cab! I'd like to have you over once I settle in."

"I'd like that," I said, needing a friend more than ever. And with one as smart as her, I could learn a lot by being her friend.

I took one of her panniers and we trudged up the old metal steps, the tower slightly swaying, the stairs rumbling protests as we climbed toward the top. We stopped a moment and Pearl searched the mountain-layered horizon. I pointed out the snow curtain, sheets of white heading toward Troublesome.

When we reached the last landing where the metal platform under the cab led up to the trapdoor, Pearl whisked out a cry.

I peered over her shoulder. Someone had taken a hacksaw to four of the metal steps and cut them off, making it impossible to reach the trapdoor that led up inside the cab.

She cried out once more and pointed to the trapdoor and the half-broke padlock on the outside latch.

I stared at the ugly words scrawled across the door in red paint. *PUT BACK ON YOUR APRON & GO BACK TO YOUR KITCHEN—BITCH*

I gasped and uttered a curse, an anger rising for the horrible man who did this.

Pearl grimaced and put a clenched fist to her hip. "I bet it was Robbie Hardin. At the station this morning, he tried to coax R.C. into betting how long I'd stay. Wondering aloud how fast I'd hightail it down the mountain and back over to my cozy kitchen in Somerset when the first storm came in, or when I faced my first wild creature."

"The Hardins always had a mean streak in them," I said, remembering the whispered talks between my folks about how Mama's librarian supervisor, Harriett Hardin, had been responsible for getting my papa jailed and then banished from Kentucky.

"Well, I'm not going back to *any* kitchen," she spat out. "I'm here to stay. Stay."

I put a comforting hand on her shoulder.

"*Stay*, dammit!" She raised the words to the forest, pounding a fist atop the steel railing, sending out her battle cry, and in it, I heard the screams of my mama, felt the pain she and Papa had suffered earlier.

And then whether it was because she was overwhelmed or exhausted from the trip, or maybe both, she cried and howled her curses to the heavens.

I stared down at my mud-soaked slippered feet, wringing my hands, wanting to help and be a friend to her, needing to curse and wail my own sufferings. Finally, I said shyly, "If you want, Pearl, you can stay at my grandparents' cabin until the ranger station can weld back new steps. There's plenty of room and I can help settle you in. Retta won't mind me coming tomorrow. It'll be fine," I said, though I knew from my folk, nothing was ever completely *fine* in Troublesome.

"That's real neighborly, Honey, and unless there's a motel, I'll have to take you up on it." She swiped a palm across her damp eyes.

"No motel here unless you want to rent a room above the Company store… That's if there's any vacant."

"Thank you, your family's cabin will do just fine."

Below, Junia called out a low haw. I peered over the railing, studying the beast. She lifted her muzzle and gave three short bursts. Her ears were parked stiff, not relaxed, her stance shifting and worrisome.

Mama taught me long ago: *Look at the beast, the bird, the wild dog, the critters, and listen closely because God spent all their might on the ears so they would have protection. And that safeguard is what ensures ours.*

I searched the forest below, looking for any movement or sign of something amiss. I couldn't help feel that someone was watching back. Again, Junia raised warnings, and I glimpsed how her always-distrustful eyes were now watchful for our protection.

Glancing up at the trapdoor, I knotted a fist, disgusted with the cowardly welcome Pearl had received from the men. Again,

Mama's piercing screams echoed in my head, and I felt an angry tear slip down my jaw and vowed somehow to fight like this brave fire lookout.

"Let's go, Pearl. I still need to find my boot, and it's coming on bad weather and dark soon."

Three

I'd lost Junia.

Though I'd found my other boot that fell from the mountain path, when I slid off the ol' girl to put it on, Junia lit back off toward the east—Thousandsticks and Mama—without a warning, taking my other packed boot with her. It seemed I was destined to have no more than one shoe at a time today, and inwardly, I cursed my foolishness.

I dropped my boot and chased after her, my curses hoarse and strangling, my calves tight and burning. If something happened to that mule, Mama would never forgive me. I wouldn't neither. Junia was ornery, but she was also my protector and childhood pet, a legend in these parts. When I was seven, I'd been playing out in the yard when Junia let out one of her war cries and sped toward me. Confused, I jumped up, then spotted the snake slithering my way. Junia stomped down furious and fast on the ol' copperhead, kicking it over into the woods. The same with the mama bear and her two cubs that wandered too close to me a few years later. Junia had risen up on her hind legs and protested so loud the windows rattled, chasing off the frightened bears.

Pearl caught up with me, carrying my boot. "Oh, Honey, I'm sorry. She is trouble with a capital T. How do you put up with her?"

Breathless, I rested my hands on my hips and took several deep breaths. "My folk will be upset if anything happens to her, Pearl." Neither of them had ever so much as taken a switch to me, but I would take a hundred lashings rather than witness the sadness and disappointment in their eyes if something happened to Junia. "*Junia!*" I hollered. A light snow began to fall, and I grew frantic. "JUNIA!"

"Climb on up. Let's go find her," Pearl offered, pulling her coat collar up around her ears. "Maybe Pie can catch up with the old girl."

"Much obliged, Pearl." After this morning, I appreciated her kindness and was greatly relieved to know I wasn't completely on my own.

"But first, can you take me by Devil John's? I want to let him know what happened so he doesn't haul my trunk up here and leave it where it would sit out in the snow. Maybe he can also send word to R.C. for me."

I worried a moment that we wouldn't be able to catch up with Junia.

"Is it far from here?" she asked.

"No, but let's hurry." I couldn't let her trunk get ruined after she had her home vandalized. Likely, I'd catch Junia back in Thousandsticks waiting for Mama, and for as long as it took. I was sure I'd find her there, but what I wasn't so sure of was whether the law would find *me*.

We smelled woodsmoke from the Smiths' cabin minutes before we got there. I knocked on the old wooden door and Devil John's wife, Martha Hannah, cracked it half-open, holding a baby. Three young'uns poked their heads out behind the skirts of her worn duster, pushing the door open wider.

"Honey," she said, surprised. "Devil said you were home. Didn't expect a visit so soon. Come in and have some warm food." She sat the baby down behind her on the floor.

"We're in a hurry, ma'am—"

One of the little ones yanked on her skirts. "Colleen, *Colleen*," Martha Hannah yelled over her shoulder. "Come get these gran'babes so I can talk to our company. Lawsy," she flipped back one of her silver braids, smoothed down her skirts. "My whole life's been nothing but the babies. I get one batch good n' grow'd, and another set of 'em finds their way in. Lil cockleburs they be." She laughed and swatted a little one back inside.

"Ma'am, we ran into some trouble over at the lookout. Is Devil John around?" I asked.

Martha Hannah looked at Pearl. "Trouble? You must be the young firewoman Devil told me was lost. Welcome."

"I'm Pearl Grant. Nice to meet you, Mrs. Smith, even under these poor circumstances," Pearl said politely.

"Devil had some 'portant business to tend to after dinner," Martha Hannah said, her eyes darting between our faces.

She didn't say moonshine business, but it was there just the same as the foxtail, clover, and nightshade growing in these hills. Moonshine was farming for some, a living, an existence to keep shoes on the children and bellies fed.

"Ya sure ya can't come in and let me fix y'all some supper? Fine stew, I have," she said. It was tempting. I could smell it cooking, the delicious gravy with scents of onion and other herbs wafting out the door.

"Obliged, but we need to hurry, ma'am."

"I'll have Carson fetch him."

I glanced over my shoulder, looking up at the white, starless sky, the spitting snow. "It's Junia. She took off, and I fear she may be heading back toward Thousandsticks. I hope to find her before she gets herself into trouble." Or worse, the both of us.

"That sweet apostle sure has seen her share with your dear mama," Martha Hannah said knowingly.

"If you'll let Mr. Smith know someone vandalized the lookout stairs and that I'll be staying with Honey here, I would appreciate it," Pearl said. "Tell him I can get my trunk later."

"Lawsy, I'll send Carson right now. *Carson*, git out here and go fetch your pa!"

The couple's twenty-three-year-old son poked his head out the window. "Pa done took off for Knoxville to meet Allen on some business 'bout an hour ago. Oh, hey, Honey."

I smiled and waved a hello.

"Carson, get on your coat, saddle up, and go catch up with your pa," Martha Hannah said.

Carson ducked his head back inside.

"Hoping he can also get word to the ranger station for me, Mrs. Smith," Pearl said.

"I'll make sure he tends to it for ya." Martha Hannah nodded.

Birds hurried to their nest, pulling on the mantle of darkness. Snow dropped a little heavier and it looked as if it might get worse.

"Much obliged, ma'am," I said. "We best be on our way. It would be great to find Junia before she gets to Thousandsticks. Otherwise, we might be stuck there for the night."

"If I know'd Junia like I do, she's already there, Honey." She chuckled. "I'll let Devil know you're headed that way and send him over to check in with ya and our new lookout," Martha Hannah assured us.

Pearl started to object. "I don't want to trouble him any further—"

Martha Hannah dismissed Pearl, shaking her head. "I insist. We take care of our Kentucky daughters. Ride safe, girls. We have us a big snow a'comin' in."

∾

Together we rode Pie, stopping occasionally to call out and search the paths for any signs of the mule. With each step closer to my home, an uneasiness took root. I hoped that Junia would be safe and my parents had been released and I'd find them there. I knew I was taking a chance, and the warning about the children's prison weighed heavily.

We arrived back in Thousandsticks a little after one in the morning. We heard the ol' mule before we saw her. Junia stood near the porch, her whinnying rising into the lonesome night song of whip-poor-wills and thrush. Still, something was wrong, with Junia out here alone and especially untethered like that.

I dismounted and flew up the steps, grabbing the porch lantern and matches off the wooden rail, calling, "Mama? Papa, Mama, are you back?" The door was unlocked. Inside, I lit the lantern and held it up. "Mama, Papa, Pa—" I choked, my heart sinking with each break of breath. Slowly, I moved into the kitchen and then into their small bedroom and to my loft above, calling out for my parents, the only family I had left in Kentucky, the world. "Mama, Papa?"

Outside, Junia's worrisome ramblings rose as she tried to summon her beloved Book Woman.

Again, I walked around the cabin feeling helpless and scared, the cinch in my throat tightening, the old puncheon floorboards groaning with every shaky step. "*Mama?*"

"Honey, is everything okay in there?" Pearl called from the yard.

"They're really gone," I answered as I came out, not wanting to believe it, but finally realizing it was true. "*Gone.*"

"Honey, Honey—"

"They were taken earlier and I hoped they might have returned." I hurried past her to the barn and flung open the door, searching. Papa's ol' Ford truck was there, but I was surprised to see his horse was missing. I could only hope that maybe, *just maybe*, my folk were free and coming for me.

The snow came down fast, in large, powdery flakes. I walked over to Junia, pressed my face into the mule's trembling flesh.

Pearl put her hand on my shoulder, and I glanced up at my home and shuddered as the truth grabbed hold that Mama was right.

I wasn't safe here.

Four

After I built a fire, I sat down at the table and waited for Pearl to tend to my wound. "Mama and Papa had an illegal marriage," I said as Pearl dabbed Mercurochrome onto my busted chin, still hurting from its brush with the rocks earlier. It stung, and I quickly fanned my face as the antiseptic set the injury afire.

Pearl bent down and blew on my chin, taking away some of the pain. "Mother used to do that after she put the medicine on my scrapes," she said.

"Mine still does," I said, wishing she were here to do it tonight.

"Why was the marriage in trouble?" Pearl asked as she sat back down at the table and looked at me thoughtfully.

"It was a union that went against the moral supremacy of the Kentucky man, God, and miscegenation laws, or so folk around here thought," I said quietly.

Pearl shot me a puzzled look.

"The law separated them in 1936 on their wedding day because of mine and Mama's blue color. And I guess because the law thought I was born out of wedlock and fornication had been committed. But after my first parents died, Mama and Papa got a copy of their marriage license that the town sheriff had destroyed. When I turned five, we had to travel all the way to Washington, DC, to find a judge who would recognize their marriage and let them officially adopt me."

"Back home, Mr. Sawyer tried to marry a woman from China and was fined and jailed. So it's marrying outside your color?" she asked, still somewhat confused.

"Yes, the mixing of any color is not allowed in Kentucky, the law says." In the candlelight, I searched Pearl's face for any hint of disapproval, but her eyes were kind and invited me to say more.

"Doc said we have methemoglobinemia, a gene disorder." I tucked my hands under the table, folding them on my lap. "All of us, my first folk and my mama now. Though my papa isn't one of us blue-skinned folk, he was punished just the same. And imprisoned for over three years and banned from Kentucky for twenty-five more."

Pearl's eyes widened and she firmly shook her head. "There ought to be a law against ignorance like that. Those type of ugly people need to be whipped with their own ugly sticks."

"Being different here in white or black Kentucky puts you on the lowest rung. Heard talk over the years about an old preacher in Troublesome who hunted anyone unlike him and his congregation. The folk with odd markings." I stood up and went over to the window. "Mama said he attacked her and Junia one day on the book route."

"What happened?" Pearl asked quietly.

"She escaped with Junia's help. Preacher had already drowned other different folk in baptismals down in Troublesome's cold creek waters, declaring them sinners and that the odd peculiarities the devil had marked them with were proof. A young Melungeon girl who couldn't be cured of her fits with herbs and tonics and two of the Goodwin triplets were drowned after the preacher told his flock the birthing of three was beastly and surely the sign of Satan's seed. There was the albino boy and the three-foot-tall man who'd grow'd an extra nipple. My kind and untold others, he raged against."

"The man is an ill-bred lout and sounds like Satan himself!" Pearl hissed.

Pulling back the curtain, I looked out, searching for shadows in the blackness, squinting my eyes for any law sneaking around. I hope Martha Hannah got word to Devil John, because I would feel much better if he were here.

"That preacher up and disappeared one day," I said, turning back to Pearl. "No one gave much attention to the matter."

Pearl nodded. "Father always said only the miserable, cowardly, and ignorant will stand on the backs of the meek to make themselves feel powerful. Got his due, I'd say, a righteous dose of Kentucky justice."

I peered out the window once more into the darkness, the snow coming down hard, leaving me trapped. I thought about my parents' warning about coming back. Shivering, I briskly rubbed my arms and said, "Looks like we're not going anywhere right now in this weather. I should get us something to eat."

After a quick, late supper, Pearl helped me clear the table and carry the dishes over to the sink.

"It's been a hard day," I told Pearl, "and I'm sorry I made it harder. It's nearly three in the morning, and I suppose Devil John isn't coming out in this weather. He's probably trapped in same as us. I'll sleep in my parents' room, and you can have my bed up in the loft."

"I'm just glad you don't have to be here alone," Pearl said. "Besides, I'm grateful for a place to stay until the Forestry can repair the steps."

We washed up the supper dishes and talked a little bit about her people back home, her job, and the town of Troublesome.

Pearl looked around the cabin and asked, "Is there television in these parts?"

"Television?" I said, astonished, then added, "I've seen pictures of them, but ain't *never* heard of anyone in these hills having one yet. Not a single living soul."

"I'll miss that the most, I suppose. Mother bought one the first year she went to work for the Palm Beach factory sewing men's clothing."

I'd never heard of a woman taking a factory job, and when Pearl caught the surprise on my face, she shared more.

"My father was the clothing inspector at Palm after the war, and when one seamstress retired several years ago, Mother got on." Her eyes grew distant and a sadness climbed across her face. She suddenly waved a hand like she was dismissing a small bother.

I was shocked into silence by her mama working and making a lot of money. *Two* parents working in a factory. She had to be really rich, and I was suddenly embarrassed by our modest cabin, its homespun curtains and hand-braided rugs. "What did you see on the television set?" I asked.

Excited, Pearl leaned in and told me, "My favorite is *Your Hit Parade*. There's all kinds of singing and dancing." She wriggled her shoulders and snapped her fingers as she sang a snappy advertisement jingle by the cigarette company that I had heard a few times on the radio.

"Be happy, go lucky,
Be happy, go Lucky Strike.
Be happy, go lucky,
Go Lucky Strike today!"

I grinned and hummed along.

"They sing it at the beginning of *Your Hit Parade*. Oh, *I Love Lucy* and *Life with Elizabeth* are funny programs. I'll really miss those television broadcasts. The movie actresses Betty White and Lucille Ball are hilarious, and once..."

Distracted from my worries, I hung on to every word, trying to imagine the cheerful people inside the screen talking, dancing, and singing to make the audience happy.

After I dried the last dish, we turned in for the night. I tossed in the bed, drained, but my mind racing to the darker, worrisome places that fear brings. Burying my head into the pillow, I let the folds of fabric swallow the quiet sobs until I was exhausted in both spirit and bone, the nightmares breaking my slumber throughout the night.

We stayed one more night because of the snow, with me tirelessly checking out the windows, praying for the skies to clear.

"See anyone?" Pearl asked over my shoulder.

"No one will be out in this weather," I said with some relief, my breath fogging the cold pane before I let the curtain fall back.

"I wonder if Carson told Devil John about the fire tower. I hope he doesn't have to ride all the way over here on my account."

"You can depend on Carson, and I'm sure Devil John will report it to R.C. as soon as the weather breaks." My eyes went to the window again. With Papa's horse missing, I still held out a thin hope for word from my parents, or their lawyer, even for them coming home.

On the second morning, the skies cleared and the sun came out, and we decided to pack and leave. Several times, I peeked outside, worrying.

Anxious to get back to Troublesome, I whipped up a small batch of biscuits for us, while Pearl made the beds and fed Pie and Junia. I thought about Mama and Papa and what the lawman might do if he got hold of me. Pearl was busy fussing over Pie, rubbing him down and checking his hooves. "Let's hurry, Pearl, it's safe to move about now that most of the snow has melted," I called to her from the porch, my voice sounding thin and pitched, worried others might have the same notion.

"Pie has a stone stuck in his hoof and a loose shoe. Do you have a shoe hammer?"

"Papa has his farrier shoeing tools hanging above the workbench in the barn."

It was almost noon by the time Pearl finished tending her horse, and I locked up the cabin.

Just as I mounted Junia, a strange automobile appeared far in the distance with another rolling in behind it, plumes of wet,

snowy slush and debris rising in their trail. They were headed
our way. My mouth went dry as I tried to swallow.

Junia shook her head and brayed loudly, baring ugly brown
teeth.

Pearl nudged Pie closer to me. "Do you know them, Honey?"

"I'm not sure."

"Maybe they have news of your parents. What else could they
possibly want?"

I narrowed my eyes. "I fear they're wanting something more.
Me." I choked on the word, feeling it lodge in my throat.

Pearl glared at the automobiles rambling toward us. "But
you've done nothing."

Don't take much for a Blue, I remember Mama telling Papa
when she thought I was out of earshot. "I'm a minor, and I
won't be seventeen till July."

Pearl frowned.

"I'm sorry I had to lie to you, Pearl." I looked away, feeling
bad I'd done so.

"With everything you've been through, I understand. But it's
not against the law to be a minor."

"Shouldn't be against the law to love someone either. But
it sure ought to be against the law for men to decide who you
can and can't love." Quickly, I slipped my gloves on. Taking a
breath, I gripped the reins and stiffened in the saddle. I shifted,
wanting to chance it and run off. Would they catch me? Hurt
me? *Don't take much for a Blue...*

"You've done nothing wrong, Honey," Pearl said again,
glowering at the automobiles, courage straightening her spine.

I drew strength from it and righted my own.

Junia pricked her long ears, wheeled around, and softly whinnied toward the woods behind us, a trail of cold escaping her
breath.

My eyes followed, and I cupped a palm over my brows and
then I saw him.

Five

Devil John and his horse broke through a grove of trees, cantering toward us. The moonshiner joined my side and watched the automobiles approach from atop his horse, resting an arm on the scabbard holding his .30–30. "Martha Hannah told me you girls stopped by. Would've been here sooner but for the snow. Also, I got word from your pa's lawyer. Let me know about your folks' arrest," he said low. "Glad I headed out as soon as the weather cleared. Guessing them folks had the same thoughts." He jutted his bearded chin toward the vehicles.

"We'd been trapped by the weather, too, and were just leaving. Why are they here, Devil John?"

He sat up straight. "'Bout to find out."

"What will we say to explain why all of us are here?"

"Little as possible," he said, his mouth tightening as he looked ahead.

A mature woman stepped out of the first automobile. She had on an expensive wool coat, matching beret, and dark shoes. She reached back in and grabbed her large, shiny pocketbook and hooked the straps over her arm. The sheriff slammed his door and walked over to her.

Junia paid no attention to Devil John's mount. Instead she bit at the air and pawed at the grass, kicking a leg toward the lawman and his female companion. "Halt, *halt*." I jerked on her reins.

The sheriff whispered something to the woman, then called out from a distance. "Miss, you best calm that obstinate beast down, lessen you want me to do it for you," he warned, placing a hand over his holster.

"Back, *back*," I ordered Junia as she heaved under my weight. I climbed off, seized the halter, jerking it aside to force her back. When I had Junia safely behind me, I stepped in front of her.

The mule calmed a bit and rested her heavy head on my shoulder, keeping a wary eye on our visitors.

"It's okay, ol' girl, shh," I soothed, stroking her muzzle.

Devil John said, "Sheriff, I'm John Smith, a friend of the retired Pack Horse librarian, Cussy Carter Lovett. Please state your business, sir."

The sheriff pointed to the woman who then stepped forward.

"Thank you for meeting me over here, Sheriff," she said to the lawman. "As I told you on the telephone, I'd hoped to take care of this a few days ago but the snow shut down the courts, leaving everyone homebound."

The lawman wagged his head. "It sure was a frightful mess. I didn't get my automobile out of the ditch till late last night."

"Mr. Smith." She turned to Devil John. "I'm Mrs. Geraldine Wallace, the Leslie County social worker, and I'm here on official government business." She rummaged through her pocketbook and withdrew some folded papers.

I moved closer to Junia, cursing the snow under my breath, wishing I'd left sooner.

The older woman looked to Pearl and then over to me. "Which of you girls is Lovett?"

No one answered.

"Honey Mary-Angeline Lovett." Mrs. Wallace looked at us again and then up at Devil John sitting on his horse. "I have a court order dated and signed this morning, March 6, 1953, from the honorable Judge Roy Taylor after the girl's parents were found guilty of violating Kentucky's miscegenation laws a second time. The court ruled that the mother be sentenced to two years in prison. And the father's parole was revoked. He'll do another two years."

Any hope of them coming home was gone. My hands and feet latched onto my rising fright, and I didn't have to see them to know they were coloring, the heartbeats pounding in both palms, each arch on my foot thumping, my itchy flesh darkening under knit cloth and leather soles. Any second now I feared the color would betray me, bleed out onto my gloves, socks, and shoes, revealing me. Holding tight on Junia's reins, I clasped my hands behind my back.

The woman snapped the papers and gently cleared her throat. "Upon my recommendation and given the immoral life the juvenile has led living with those...those *animals*," she spat out, "those fornicating devils that tried to destroy the moral decency of our Godly, law-abiding good folk, the court hereby declared that the minor, Honey Mary-Angeline Lovett, age sixteen, being orphaned and without any known living relatives, be taken into custody and remanded to the Kentucky House of Reform until *it* reaches the age of twenty-one—"

It, she'd called me. I wasn't even human to them. An angry tear sprang up, and I lowered my head and quickly blinked it away as a fury thundered inside me. Pearl edged Pie closer to me.

"Furthermore, it is hereby ordered that Honey Mary-Angeline Lovett work the farm and—"

Kentucky House of Reform. The children's prison. A roar licked at my ears, her words dizzying me as my world was crushed, my life robbed. For the first time I understood how a heart could break, how it felt, and I placed a protective hand over mine. It ached for the loss of my parents and the punishment I was about to receive. So much so that I feared my heart would leap out of my chest, shrivel up, and rot on the cold Kentucky ground.

The woman took a step toward us.

Junia shifted, and I grabbed hold of her mane and felt her muscles shuddering, the dangerous neigh rising from her chest, calling for a storm.

The social worker inched closer, close enough to snatch my arm if she had a mind to. Junia toe-hopped, swished her tail as if flicking the woman back. The woman took another step, and one more.

Then the mule passed noxious gas and shrieked out two warnings, blowing her hot, smelly breath into the older woman's face, sending her and the sheriff reeling backwards and pinching their noses. Mrs. Wallace dug into her coat pocket and pulled out a handkerchief.

My eyes watered, and I choked on the smell. Pearl coughed several times, then fanned a hand in front of her face and leaned over, closer to Junia's ear, and whispered, "Whoa. You did yourself proud, old apostle gal. That would peel the paint off Heaven's door."

"Mr. Smith," the woman called out to him, her voice muffled, pressing the handkerchief to her nose and wet eyes. "I'm here to take one of these girls into custody, and if you won't tell me, I'll take them both. One way or another, one or both of these girls will be shackled tomorrow and digging rock come sunrise—"

Devil Smith held up his hand. "Ma'am, I know you have yourself a job to do, but I need to get my daughters home in time for supper and chores. It's a long ride through them hills." He looked down at me and then over to Pearl atop her horse and said loudly, "Lettie and Colleen, I reckon we won't be dropping off supplies this week for Book Woman. Let's get home 'fore your ma starts frettin' our whereabouts."

I looked at our full panniers, realizing we had put them back on the mounts this morning, and was grateful to Devil John for his quick thinking.

"Can you prove they're your daughters, Mr. Smith?" the sheriff asked, polite enough.

"Not unless you want to follow me home 'bout thirty-odd miles yander over them hills, and *not* as the crow flies," Devil John answered.

Oh, what was Devil John up to, I wondered. No moonshiner

would ever lead a lawman into his holler—and no lawman would ever find a 'Tucky hootch peddler that didn't want to be found. *No sir.*

"You'll need yourself a sturdy mount. No roads where I live, only trails, an' some still likely to be snow-packed," Devil John advised. "Be happy to have my woman feed ya supper though. She put on a pot of leather britches this morn'. Reckon we'll have some skillet corn bread, too, and a tasty apple stack cake afterward. Mighty good fixin's she whips up."

The lawman swiped a finger over a wet mouth and looked at his wristwatch, annoyed.

I lifted up a silent prayer and hoped he wouldn't want to miss his dinner back in town.

From behind, someone hollered "Pa, Pa" and sprinted toward us.

It was Carson.

My heart sank, and I felt a tremble crawl into my hands, afraid he'd give me away.

"Pa, I got a ride partway in Mr. Brown's wagon." He ran a hand across his head, smoothing down his tousled brown hair. His cheeks were spotted pink from the run. "Had to run the rest," he said, out of breath. "Ma sent me to fetch ya home. One of the babies took to the colic again. It's real bad, and she needs ya to call on one of the frontier nurses."

The sheriff wrinkled his brow. "Boy, come here," the sheriff ordered. "I have a question for ya. Come on over here. Righ' here, righ' now."

Carson hesitated and looked up at his father with questioning eyes.

Devil John nodded his permission. "Go on, Son, do as the sheriff asks."

"Yes, sir." Carson lowered his head and walked doggedly over to the lawman.

The sheriff put a hand on Carson's shoulder, bent his head to the young man's, and pointed his finger at me and Pearl. "Now, boy, I want you to tell me who these girls are and their names. Tell me the truth now, or you could get arrested for obstructing justice and lying to a lawman. Yessir, go straight to the hoosegow." He shot a suspicious eye toward Devil John.

I tried to swallow, but the fear seized hold, almost strangling me. The afternoon sun shone bright, and I put my fingers under the scarf and tugged, loosened and stretched the knit yarn, sliding it off my neck and into my damp gloved hand.

Pearl bent slightly over Pie, muttering something I couldn't hear.

I stepped back to Junia's side, placed a firm hand on her withers, and took a deep breath. The ol' mule shuddered, feeling the bother. I pressed my dry lips together, waiting for the worst. It would only take me a fast Kentucky second to jump on her back and run. *But what if poor ol' Junia stalled? She couldn't outrun a bullet if the sheriff decided to shoot me.*

"Speak up, young man!" the social worker screeched.

Carson raised his arm and pointed at us. "Why them's my sisters, Lettie and Colleen Smith. And, dang it, Colleen"—he wagged a shaming finger at me—"Ma's none too pleased with ya today for taking off without doing your chores. Me neither. Second time this week ya done gone and left a pile of dirty laundry."

My cheeks warmed as all eyes fell on me. I felt the blue deepen, itch at my hands and feet. I peeked down at them, making sure the color hadn't leached out. "Real sorry, Carson. I'll help ya with your chores the rest of the week. *Promise.*" I tucked my head like a scolded pup.

The sheriff looked over to me and Pearl, then back to the boy and over to the social worker. He narrowed his eyes, lightly scratched his neck.

An uncomfortable silence batted around in the crisp March winds. A crow squawked overhead, then the sheriff frowned. "Let's go, Mrs. Wallace. Our work here is done. The snow's put me behind in my official duties as it is. And now my dinner's getting cold," the sheriff grumbled, hitching his utility belt up over a ripe belly. "Girl's probably stowed away to long-lost relatives in West Virginny by now! Good day, Mr. Smith."

Devil John said, "Let's water our mounts and get home, young'uns."

Mrs. Wallace's angry eyes darted back and forth between me and Pearl, then steadied on mine, narrowing.

I crossed my arms, tucking my gloved hands under them, fearing any minute she would rip them off and out me as a Blue.

She looked again at Pearl before locking eyes with mine.

I met hers with coldness, determined to do whatever it took to stay free and escape the horrid chains she was determined to put me in.

Six

When the social worker finally tore her gaze away and turned toward the automobile, my hands shook so violently that I dropped Junia's reins. Pearl slid off her horse and handed them to me. "They're leaving now, Honey."

I nodded, unable to speak, the fear still clinging to me like the sweat dampening my forehead.

We led the horses and mule over to the springhouse in silence as the automobiles drove off, their tires slapping away at the snowy slush.

Finally, Devil John said, "Honey, Evan Faust told me he picked up your pa's horse and would tend to it for you. Said Bob Morgan was assigned by the courts to be your lawyer. He'll be in touch soon. Your folks' attorney know'd you'd been sent to Troublesome, so he wanted to get word to you that the law was coming to try and take you to the House of Reform."

"Sorry, but I never made it to Retta's," I said.

"Figured as much after talking to Carson and Martha Hannah. I went up to the fire tower and inspected the damage to the stairs." He frowned. "Then I thought I'd go over yander to Loretta's 'fore coming here, but no one answered the door and I didn't see your mounts. Even went over to your grandpa Elijah's cabin. Then the snow came in and shut everyone in."

"We aimed to get to the ol' Carter homestead, but Junia had other thoughts."

He studied his son a moment. "Sure am glad Martha Hannah had me tote Carson along—in case we ran into trouble, we'd be able to give double back."

I glanced at his rifle and dared not think of the kind of trouble he might've given back. Devil John was a decent, loyal man, but not someone you would want to cross.

"We planned on trying to get ya back to Troublesome, then I heard the automobiles. I dropped Carson off behind the trees and told him to listen to whatever happened when them two vehicles drove up. To send word back to my Martha Hannah should something happen here." Devil John struck out his finger toward Carson. "Son, you were supposed to stay put back yander, run home if anything happened to me or the girls..." He paused, and I knew he was thinking whether he should fuss at Carson or drop it. "Reckon ya did all right."

The young man beamed. "Just heard ya'll talking to the law and what all they said, Pa. Wanted to help our Honey Mary-Angeline, our True Blue, same as her ma's always helped us," he said, using the nickname he'd given to me when we played as children.

"Real smart, this one is," Devil John said proudly. "Cussy and her books is what did that for us and a lot of folk. Real sorry this is happening to your family, Honey." He looked at me and Pearl, then dropped a sly grin. "That sheriff's never been to my holler, so he has no idea 'bout the rest of my brood, what they look like, how old they be, or how to find my place. And I know'd that ol' boy was lazy and too hungry for his dinner to try and find out."

"Much obliged, Devil John. I'm indebted and appreciative. And Carson, I owe you a basket of clean laundry."

"A week's worth ought to do it," he teased.

"If you hadn't come along, well..." I cringed at the thought of wearing leg chains and digging rock for five years at the old children's prison. To Pearl, I said, "Thank you. That was brave and kind." I smiled appreciatively.

"I couldn't let that horrid woman drag you away."

My heart warmed because her eyes told me she meant it.

"Try not to fret," Devil John said. "I'm sure Bob Morgan will be filing a custody order over in Knott County for you to stay with Loretta. Those were your folks' wishes. So until you get that guardianship, you'll want to stay put where you're safe."

"I'll head to Retta's first thing tomorrow after I settle Pearl in at my grandparents' cabin."

Devil John stroked his beard, mulling it over.

"I'm happy to look after her," Pearl said. "If I can be tasked with looking after the whole forest, I imagine I can protect Honey and her sneaky skunk-in-disguise of a mule."

"It's harmless enough, sir, and the old homestead has kept me and my people safe for years," I pushed.

"Reckon you're right," he admitted. "Pearl, someone will send word once the stairs are fixed. I stopped at the ranger station on the way over here, and they're getting welders out to the lookout sometime this week, latest, next week. R.C. sends his apologies and hopes it won't make ya retire your appointment."

"It won't, Devil John. And I'm prepared to mete out trouble to protect another troublesome woman"—Pearl grinned at me—"a *sister* in these old hills."

Somehow, the cloak of sorrow and loss and years of living in the forest with nary a friend was lifted a little. There was a great-uncle on Papa's side down in Tennessee we'd see a few times a year, and the kids back in Troublesome I'd play with on my visits. But I never stayed long enough to get real close with any my age, except Devil John's lot. To think, I might now have a friend *and* a sister. "*Sister*," I said, my heart nearly bursting with hope.

"Reckon we can never have too many troublesome women where we're headed. Saddle up," Devil John said.

Seven

We rode into Troublesome under a star-dusted sky, the cold March air nipping at our backs. Junia knew the way, and if it hadn't been so blustery, I might've dozed off in the saddle.

When we reached my grandparents' cabin, Pearl lit the stove and stacked a few logs in the fireplace, while I hung quilts over the drafty windows. In a few minutes, I went down into the root cellar to get victuals for supper. Below, I placed the lantern on a table and the room lit up.

The cellar brimmed with food, and I marveled over the canning jars of every size, stacked on shelves that climbed to the ceiling. There were peas, butter beans, roasting ears, mustard greens, sweet potatoes, turnips, jams, and more. Papa had brought in sacks of flour, crocks of smoked apples, and barrels of kraut. Dried berries and persimmon, and strings of pumpkin; leather britches hung beside large hams, pork, sausage, and venison. All smoked and salted, the meats would easily last through this year and the next.

Hungry, I grabbed a peach leather strip and chewed on the sweet candy treat. Mama made the best. I'd help her prepare and cook the peaches with brown sugar or honey, and then we'd spread the thick peach sauce outside on large, clean cutting boards and leave them in the sun a few days. Once it was good 'n' leathered, Mama would cut them into strips and hang them up inside. I wondered what her supper would be tonight.

I plucked up a large basket off the cold dirt floor and placed a quart jar of stew inside. I scanned the preserves and selected apple butter and a smaller bag of flour. Tomorrow morning, I would fry up thick slices of ham with redeye gravy and biscuits, along with baked smoked apples.

I finished off the peach leather, snatched another strip for Pearl, and hurried upstairs.

Setting the basket on the table, I said, "You got yourself a good fire going."

Pearl only stared at the flames with a sadness puddling at her feet. I wondered if she was homesick like me, or if it was something more.

Not wanting to pry, I told her, "I've got us good victuals and something extra for you." I handed her the peach leather. "You must be starved."

"What is it?"

"Candy treat."

"Before supper?" She raised a sly brow.

"I reckon it won't bother us having dessert first." I laughed and then stopped, mindful of what Mama would say. It wouldn't be allowed, and I drew a sharp breath, missing her love and my parents' protection. I thought about Bob Morgan, hoping he'd get my guardianship before the state caught up with me.

After we ate, Pearl helped with the dishes. Then I put clean linens on the iron bed that was tucked into the corner while she checked on our mounts.

It was late, and I was eager for bed, so I could get an early start to Retta's. Climbing the loft, I called down, "I'm heading out early." I was anxious to see Retta, to finally feel safe. "I'll try to get back in a few days. And I'm going to stop by the library. Want me to check out some books for you?" I knew a book would carry her away from any gloom.

"Oh, a good book would be perfect. If there's any newspapers, I'd take those too."

"Good night, Pearl." I climbed the last rung, comforted

because I'd found someone else to talk to about books and maybe in time lots of other things, relieved because I'd soon have a guardian who would keep me out of the children's prison.

On the way to Retta's, I stopped in town at the Troublesome Creek Library branch.

Inside, I studied the bulletin board. Someone had penned an advertisement about a new litter of pointer hunting dogs available for a fair price at Timothy Garvey's place. Another posted: *Get a dozen eggs for only 65 cents.* Someone else was looking for a mechanic's helper or gas attendant over at the filling station, and there was a post about missing eyeglasses. Another board had a posting for an assistant librarian, and I studied it.

March 2, 1953
WANTED, ASSISTANT OUTREACH LIBRARIAN
We have an opening for a respectable, steady, young
female rider to deliver books and reading material in
Knott County. Weekends off. Pay $98 per month. Reply to
Eula Foster.

I thought about Mama. She would've loved doing it again, and I was surprised to see the pay was raised from $28 to almost $100 now. Sure was a lot of money, and I envied the person who got it. I was tempted to apply, but I knew I had to get Retta's guardianship before I did anything.

A man stepped up behind me, and I moved aside as he left a new advertisement on the board. *March 7, 1953, 1 room for rent over the Company store. Kitchen and bath privileges. See Mr. Edgar Franklin.*

Browsing the new books section, I spent a half hour trying to guess Pearl's favorite reads, once in a while looking up to peek out the tall windows, making sure the sheriff and social worker over in Leslie County hadn't decided to come snooping around over here in Knott County.

From behind, someone said, "Ray Bradbury's *The Golden Apples of the Sun* is a real grabber filled with twenty-two stories." I spun around. It was Eula Foster, the director of the library and the woman who Mama had worked for long ago. They'd started out on the wrong foot, but Mama won her over in the end. Mama claimed it was the books that changed Miss Foster. She always said the printed word could soften the hardest of hardened hearts.

She was not so lucky with another librarian, Harriett Hardin. After Eula Foster found out the horrid things Harriett did to my folk, the director called Harriett a seed spreader, a cultivator of ill will, and eventually got rid of the disgraceful librarian by transferring her over to Marion County.

"Hello, Miss Foster."

"Honey, it's good to see you. You're back early this year. How are you and your mama doing?" she asked warmly.

"Ma'am, we're doing just fine," I lied. "Mama sent me ahead to visit with Retta. I wanted to take some books back with me. I'll likely be here a while." Then because it felt safer, I picked up Bradbury's book and changed the subject. "Hmm. A real grabber, you say?"

"Oh, my, I enjoyed it," Miss Foster gushed. "We were lucky to get an early copy from the big library in Lexington. I think 'The Fruit at the Bottom of the Bowl' may be my favorite." She tapped a finger to her lips, thinking. "But I so loved 'The Pedestrian' too. And there was the wonderful short story called 'The Golden Apples of the Sun.' The anthology collection is some of his finest work!"

"I'll take it. Much obliged, Miss Foster," I said.

She nodded, pleased. "Well, good day, Honey. I need to get back to work." I watched her slip into her small office behind the checkout counter.

I added Robert Hichens's novel *Strange Lady* and a novel by Barbara Pym, *Excellent Women*, that sounded humorous.

I moved over to a table and found a recent combined Sunday edition of the *Lexington Herald* and the *Lexington Leader*, along with an older edition of the *Louisville Times*.

In the magazine section, I picked up *Hit Parader* and admired a picture of a woman named Betty Grable. I flicked through the magazine and set it back down. The cover of a smudged, tattered *Life* magazine caught my eye. The pretty woman named Janet Leigh was scantily clad in a ruffled lace dress exposing a large part of her breasts. I scanned the library to make sure no one was looking.

It looked to be what Mama and the older librarians always called an excitement read. I was surprised that the magazine had been shelved and thought for sure it would've been banned by the elders in the community. Yet, here it was in my gloved hands, with the bold, nearly bare-chested, beautiful woman staring right back at me. The title down to the left read: "Janet Leigh: A Marriage and A New Career."

Again, I darted my eyes around the library, making sure no one was watching. I had to read this excitement read about this pretty lady. Mama always said, *You grow readers, expand minds, if you let them choose, but you go banning a read, you stunt the whole community.*

Quickly, I hid the *Life* magazine in my pile of reading material and hurried to check everything out.

Librarian Mrs. Martin came over to the counter, and I handed her my library card. "Get you some good reads today, Honey?"

"Yes, ma'am," I said, itching to leave.

Miss Foster came up behind her and said, "I'll check Honey out, Mrs. Martin, if you'll go help Mr. Wilson. He's looking for a good detective novel for himself and a nice read for Elizabeth. Maybe show him the latest by Rex Stout." Miss Foster picked up my reading material and straightened it. "Let's see what treasures you've found today, Honey. I can remember Cussy bringing you in, and you couldn't even reach the counter. The years have flown and you grow taller each time I see you. You must be, what, sixteen, seventeen, by now? Not too much younger than your mama when she first came to work for us," she chatted on.

I could feel my face warm as she separated the reads. What would she say about the magazine? But when she came across the *Life*, the librarian didn't say a word. Instead, she continued stamping the checkout cards for me. When she was done, she neatly set the material to the side and handed me back my card. Suddenly, Miss Foster wrinkled her brow. "Oh my, I almost forgot." She inspected my reading material and placed a palm over the stack. "Please step into my office a minute so I might have a word with you, Honey?"

My face burned with embarrassment. *Would she scold me for wanting the excitement read or, worse, ban me from the library?*

"It'll only take a minute." She stepped over to her office door and held it open, waiting.

I looked around, searching for a distraction, anyone to help me. A few elders browsed books. Another was seated at the table while Mrs. Martin helped Mr. Wilson select his books.

"Promise it'll only take a few minutes," Miss Foster said.

I walked around the counter to her office, my heart thumping so hard I feared it could be heard.

Once inside the cramped room, Miss Foster shut the door and seated herself behind the desk. "Have a seat, Honey." She pointed to the chair across from her, shuffling papers and moving a stack of books to the side.

Turning behind to a narrow table, she picked up two books. "I ordered these for you after you mentioned how much you loved the poetry books last fall. And I recall Cussy telling me you write some fine poetry. You must because you have excellent taste in reading material. Most excellent. Just like Cussy."

Grateful, I took the books from her, studying the cover of *The Poetry of Ezra Pound*. "Thank you, ma'am. I'll take good care of these." I smiled, relieved she didn't scold me.

"Let's finish checking you out," she said, pleased with her selection.

Outside, I packed the reads inside the pannier and patted Junia's shoulder. Devil John called from across the road in front of the farrier's building. He walked over to me. "My horse threw a shoe coming down the trail, and I'm waiting for a new one from the blacksmith. Glad I caught you when I did. You've saved me a trip."

"What is it? Have you heard news from—"

He raised a hand. "Everything's fine, Honey. Your father had a visit with his lawyer, Evan Faust, and also Bob Morgan. They had him fill out a form and sign a letter saying he gave custody to Loretta Adams. Next, Bob'll file the application for guardianship with a judge here. He wants ya to meet him on the steps of the courthouse, March 12 at twelve thirty. Get this mess fixed so you'll be safe."

"Thank you, Devil John." I threw my arms around him and kissed his cheek. The ol' moonshiner blushed.

"Hope you'll understand that I can't be with ya in the courtroom that day. My questionable standing in the community might harm your chances of getting a favorable result."

"Yes, sir," I said, knowing moonshining would not be looked favorably upon by the law.

"But I'll be waiting for ya outside on the steps. You keep yourself on the lookout for any trouble." He pulled a card out of his long leather coat. "Here's Bob Morgan's telephone number. He said call him anytime."

I slipped it into my coat pocket.

"You can use the telephone booth inside the Company store." He pointed across the street. "Be at the courthouse next week and on time." He tipped his hat and was off back to the farrier.

"Let's hurry, ol' girl." I mounted Junia and rode her out of town, down rutted, black-stained paths left from the big wheels of coal trucks. I couldn't wait to see Retta.

Eight

On coffee-painted paths smattered with rotting penny and butterscotch-colored leaves, I rode up to Retta's, worrying if she'd still be willing to take me in. She'd watched me for years while Mama tended her book routes, and Retta's cabin always felt like my second home. I needed her now more than ever and wanted her to fuss over me like always, wrap me in a quilt, then settle us in with some hot tea, molasses bread, and quiet conversation.

Scents of mud and fresh waters wafted as Junia forded a trickling stream. It was like coming home again and made me long for the days when I was a child rocked to sleep on Retta's lap.

A noon train whistled through the blue hills. Kissing my teeth in short bursts, I pushed Junia to hurry through the woods.

After I tethered Junia to the porch, I knocked and the door creaked open. "Retta?" I peeked around the frame.

Retta sat at the table working on a new quilt, the sunlight streaming through her homespun curtains, the warmth spreading from the rays and a lit fire.

"Iffin that's Honey Mary-Angeline, I've been a'waitin' for ya, child." Retta squinted through her glasses at the sunlight streaming through the open door. She stuck her needle into the pincushion and pushed the fabric aside.

"Yes, ma'am, it's me!" I rushed over to her and fell into her welcoming embrace.

"My prettiest petunia," she said in a soft warbled voice, using the name she'd called me since birth. "Such a sight for these old eyes. My poor child, you and your folks have been through a lot." She grimaced. "Looks like you're needing some ointment for that scraped chin."

"No, ma'am, it's fine. I put medicine on it this morning." I hugged her and stepped back from the chair. She removed her glasses and rubbed her eyes.

"Have your eyes been ailing you again, Retta?"

"Same as always." Retta fussed with her white bun, smoothed down her worn, crumpled skirts.

"Reckon you should fetch Doc to give you another eye exam."

"Soon." She grabbed my hand. "You've grown almost as tall as your ma." She picked up an envelope and frowned. "There's a hearing next week about your guardianship."

"Yes, ma'am, I know."

"Your parents asked me to take care of ya until they can again."

"Yes, ma'am," I said quietly, taking a seat beside her at the table. "The state wants to send me to the children's prison. If I could stay, I promise to help you with chores, do whatever you ask. I can even get a job, Retta, so I can pay you fair for living here, and—"

She held up her old hand. "Nonsense, child. I won't accept money for taking in *family*. Next week I'll wear my Sunday best and have Alonzo tote me to the hearing in his horse-drawn wagon. Iffin the man is sober."

Her nephew rarely was.

Relieved, I let out a long silent breath. "Much obliged, Retta. I'll be glad when it's all over." I looked over to the little iron bed that I used to nap on long ago.

"Put on the kettle, child, and I'll fetch us a fine supper." Retta stood.

"Need help?"

"I could fix this dish blind." She chuckled, easing herself over to the woodstove.

After I put on the water to boil, I let Junia graze before leading her into the small stall across from Retta's cabin.

I couldn't help thinking about Mama and Papa. Would they be in shackles now, cold on their prison cots with only a frayed sheet of burlap to warm them? I pushed back the dark thoughts and grabbed my books.

Inside, Retta cooked a meal of fried ramps, potatoes, and sausage. With our bellies full, I washed her dishes outside at the pump. Then we worked on one of her quilts and chatted.

"I saw a bulletin where the library is extending an outreach program back into the hills. Toting books same as Mama and other Pack Horse librarians did back then."

"It was a good program all right. How I loved your mama's visits."

"I have some good reads that I checked out, and Miss Foster gave me two poetry books. I can read one to you."

"No need to read them foolish government books to me, child. Your mama always tried, but I'd make her read my Bible instead," Retta said firmly, but I could see a smile tickle the corners of her mouth as she looked inward, recalling the fond memories.

I looked down at the wobbly table, knocked on it, remembering how Mama said ol' Retta would make her use one of the library books to prop the shorter leg up until Mama was done reading Retta's Bible. Despite Mama telling her otherwise, Retta got it stuck in her head that the government would think she was cheating Mama's time, their time, if she didn't somehow have one of the Book Woman's reading materials in her home. When they finished the visit, Retta made Mama take back the table prop.

A shelf hung from the wall with several children's books Retta had ordered for me over the years. She caught me looking at it.

"Well, a child's got to learn the children's books, and her

nursery rhymes as well, her prayers. Especially my girl," she excused, fluffing her skirts. She pointed a gnarled finger at me. "*Books'll learn ya,*" she said, her ol' eyes twinkling with mischief and merriment.

I laughed, remembering it was my favorite saying as a child while carrying the children's books around the yard, riding an old stick pony, pretending to be a Kentucky Pack Horse librarian.

Candlelight flickered; scents of piney woodsmoke cozied the cabin. I dipped my needle in and out of the fabric, laddering tight stitches up the quilt, agonizing over my family being ripped away from me.

After a few moments, I set aside the quilt and picked up the poetry book Miss Foster had given me, losing myself in the pages. *Books'll save you*, my troubled heart knew.

Nine

Through the fog-soaked mountains, I made my way toward the Carter homestead to drop off the library loans for Pearl before I headed down to the Troublesome courthouse, relieved a little that Mr. Morgan had scheduled the hearing over here in Knott County and out of Leslie County.

Pearl had left a note saying she was going to meet R.C. about the steps and would be back later if they weren't fixed, adding an invitation to come by the fire tower to have dinner with her on Sunday if she didn't return. I shuddered, thinking about the ugly words the men left on the door, and marveled at how brave and determined Pearl was to keep her job. Soon, I stiffened in the saddle, straightening my own spine, searching for the courage to face today.

Junia trotted through wooded paths of budding dead nettle, toothwort, and bloodroot, fording icy-cold waters and following the creek into town with nary a fuss or bother. It was like she knew how important this day was for me, for her.

In town, I led the mule onto the courthouse grounds and tethered her to a post in the grassy side lot used for horses. Junia gave a tired whinny and I lingered beside her, hugging her neck, stroking her nose.

The postmaster strolled past and bid me a hearty good day, but I barely heard him, as worried and eaten up as I was by what was coming next.

I climbed the courthouse steps and peeked inside the building. A uniformed man sat at a desk, reading his newspaper. I crooked my neck around the jamb. The halls were quiet, and I reckoned everyone was having dinner. Outside, I tapped my foot on the concrete, anxious for Mr. Morgan's and Retta's arrival. Every couple of minutes, I pulled out the timepiece. Twelve seventeen. *Where could they be?*

I looked over the stately courthouse steps and down at the town. Coal miners on their dinner breaks milled in front of the Company store owned by the coal company, some sitting on benches in front of it, smoking and exchanging gossip after a long morning down in the mine. Squinting against the sun, I cupped a hand over my eyes and saw one of the miners off to the side standing alone. It was hard to make out who it was when the men came out of the mines looking the same, their faces and clothes blackened with coal dust. Then the one standing alone removed the helmet and long, dark hair spilled out.

It was Bonnie Powell, one of the students from Mama's schoolhouse route from long ago. I babysat for her in the summer and a few other times. The young woman had lost her husband to a mine accident last year, and I'd sat her son for a full week while Bonnie took her training and education classes for the coal position.

I spotted ten-year-old Wrenna Abbott, the great-granddaughter of the granny woman, Emma McCain, her long, dark curls sun-streaked and tangled, her small, heart-shaped face etched half-woman, half-child. Emma, the elder midwife and respected healer, had been doing her best to raise the wilded child. Wearing an oversized tattered coat over her flour-sack dress, Wrenna walked determinedly through the streets with a bone-white rooster following at her heels. The rooster shrilled its warnings, charging anyone it thought might get closer.

One coal miner pretended to lunge at the girl, riling the bird further. The man hooted and threw a rock at the squawking rooster, missing. Another called out, laughing, "You couldn't hit the side of the barn if it fell on your sorry ass."

I winced and turned my attention to the girl.

Wrenna stopped and picked up the bird, snugging its head into the crook of her arm. She stared icily at the coal miner. He choked back his laughter and turned away.

A few horses passed with their riders, heading toward the farrier, their gaits slightly off. Devil John's son, Carson, held the post office door open for a pretty girl I'd heard he'd been courting since last fall. They stood and chatted outside a few minutes, and I watched as the two flirted with each other, their eyes smiling and cheeks rosied. Normally, I'd tease him a little, like his sisters always did when he found a new girlfriend, but looking at the two like that felt different, more intimate, and I turned away feeling like an intruder, wondering if there would soon be talk of a wedding.

At twelve forty, Retta arrived in Alonzo's buckboard wagon. I raced down the steps and thanked her nephew. Alonzo said he'd wait while I helped Retta carefully up the steps, letting her pause as we climbed the thirty-six stairs to the top. I seated her on the big concrete ledge outside the courtroom doors.

Minutes later, a shiny apple-red Chevrolet pulled into a parking spot below. A man jumped out and waved up at us, calling out a greeting to me. Mr. Morgan wore a smart, brown business suit, polished shoes, and a matching fedora with a fancy speckled bow on the wide grosgrain band. Carrying a briefcase, he called out my name and took the courthouse steps two at a time.

"Good morning. Visiting over in the next county this morning, didn't expect to be running so late. Honey, how you doing?" he asked before turning to Retta. "Miss Adams, thank you for joining us today and for giving Honey a home."

"Can't give her what's always been hers." Retta shot me a crooked smile and dusted lint off her coat.

He lightly squeezed her arm before turning back to me.

"How are my folk, Mr. Morgan?"

"They're doing just fine and send their love. Now today there will be a short hearing. Judge Norton will be presiding. He's a fair man."

"I know'd Buddy Norton well," Retta said, pressing a fussing palm to the side of her white bun, carefully tucking loose strands under it.

"The judge will decide whether to grant our application for guardianship. Ready?" He held open the courthouse door for me and Retta.

I hesitated. "And if he won't?"

"We'll cross that bridge when we get to it. Until then, if he asks you anything, just tell the truth. And if you don't know, say so. We'll sit together at the counsel table. You'll stand when the bailiff announces the judge and stand when the judge asks you anything. Just follow my lead." He swept out an arm for us to enter.

Retta grabbed for my hand, and we walked together down the hall, slipping past two men chatting on the pay telephones and a few others milling around waiting to use them next, the smoke ghost-tailing into their wired conversations.

Inside the courtroom, Mr. Morgan led us to the long wooden table in front of the judge's bench and seated us in the chairs. Across from us, a small man in a drab business suit sat at the other counsel table with a large brown folder in front of him, writing in a notebook.

Mr. Morgan went over and greeted the man. "Hello, Dan, it's been a while. How're Marie and the boys?"

Smiling, Dan stood up and shook Mr. Morgan's hand. Then they dropped their voices. Several times the men glanced over at me.

When Mr. Morgan came back, he said, "That's Dan Greene, he's the Knott County social worker here today. Like me and Judge Norton, he'll be looking out for your welfare, deciding what's in your best interest as well."

I looked at him nervously, wondering how the men even knew my best interest.

Retta commented, "Humph. Sure takes a lot of men to decide one li'l girl's best interest."

"Sure does," I worried. And there was something scary about it all but I didn't quite know why. The room was stuffy, the walls littered with large pictures of even stuffier old men. Light-headed, I helped Retta out of her coat, then took off mine and laid them both across the back of my chair. I plucked at my bodice, my armpits sticky and uncomfortable.

Retta had insisted on sewing me a new dress, using a dark-blue-checked homespun fabric. I worried about the color matching my hands, and asked for pink fabric instead, but Retta shushed me, insisting the dark color was more respectable. She fussed a week over the pattern, measuring and making the long-sleeved dress perfect, adding two inches more than the length called for, making me strip down to my undergarments to check the fit all over again, and then several more times, all the while saying, "We have to make a good 'pression on the judge."

She had inspected the dress again this morning, making sure everything was perfect, studying every inch of me. By the time I'd escaped her nervous chatter and critical eye, I realized half-way to the courthouse I'd left behind the matching gloves she'd sewn.

I fiddled with the Peter Pan collar and smoothed down my long skirts. Stealing peeks around the courtroom, I quickly crossed my arms over my chest and tucked my hands under to hide the color.

Mr. Morgan pulled out papers from his briefcase and placed them neatly in front of him. A woman came in from behind the judge's bench and took a seat at the table below it, inspecting her papers.

A few minutes later, a bailiff entered the courtroom and said, "Everyone stand. The Honorable Judge Norton presiding."

I stood up, weak-kneed. Retta gripped my hand.

The judge came in, and when he was planted on his perch, the bailiff said, "Please be seated."

He was a young judge who shot us nary a glance as he shuffled through his paperwork.

Judge Norton said, "Before we get started, there's an order out of Judge Roy Taylor's court over in Leslie County. That order states the minor child, Honey Mary-Angeline Lovett, is to be taken into custody and turned over to the state, where she will be transferred to the Kentucky House of Reform. Mr. Morgan, is there any reason I shouldn't do that?"

Retta stood up and shook her head. "Because she's coming home with me is the reason, Buddy Norton."

Mr. Greene made quick notes on his paper.

"Miss Adams, you will please refrain from outbursts," the judge warned, furrowing his brow.

Mr. Morgan eased Retta back into her seat and said, "Yes, Your Honor, there's strong reason. That's why I filed an application for guardianship with your court."

"This is most unusual," Judge Norton commented. "Why didn't you take this up with Judge Taylor? The girl should be bound to the House of Reform—"

"Humph." Retta scowled at the judge, then tsked loudly. "To think, Buddy Norton, I made your ma's wedding dress and then sewed your layette not five months later when you came along," she said gruffly.

"*Order!*" the judge and bailiff chorused loudly, startling me.

Retta lifted a stubborn chin, trailed her fingers up to her bun, and mumbled something low.

Mr. Morgan leaned across me and whispered into her ear, then stood.

I chewed on a nail till Retta pulled down my hand. My eyes locked with hers, pleading for her to remain silent.

"Your Honor," Mr. Morgan said, "these are unusual circumstances—"

"This smacks of judge-shopping to me, Mr. Morgan. Tell me why I shouldn't deny without prejudice and have you file over there?" the judge quipped.

Mr. Greene narrowed his eyes at Mr. Morgan, then wrote something down.

My throat was dry. I pinched the skin on my neck, struggling to swallow.

"Your Honor, I'm here to represent the child's best interest. This is an unusual matter. Miss Adams resides here, and this is Miss Lovett's birthplace, the home of her family, her ancestors. Under our law, it seems that the court which has jurisdiction over the guardian and the ward has jurisdiction. This would be the court to enforce any future orders, as needed. If the court will please look at the letter inside the file, it will explain." Mr. Morgan seated himself and briskly organized his papers again.

The courtroom quieted as the judge opened the file. Thumbing through the pages, he pulled out a sheet and scanned it once more.

"Okay." The judge peered over the paper at the lawyer. "I have an application from you to award the guardianship of Honey Mary-Angeline Lovett to Miss Loretta Adams. Also included in this file is a letter from the father stating in case of incarceration he requested that Miss Adams would be the legal guardian. Is this correct?" he asked.

Mr. Morgan half stood and then sat back down, "Yes, Your Honor."

"Mr. Greene, does the state have any objection?"

The man stood up and turned, studying us for a few seconds, concern stitched across his brow. Finally, he looked up at the judge. "Your Honor, Knott County Social Services is only concerned that the proffered guardian is qualified…and that the guardian remains so." His eyes fell on Retta, questioning, as he tucked his tie and sat back down.

"Hmm. But we still have Judge Taylor over in Leslie County granting guardianship of the minor to the state." The judge looked directly at me.

I squirmed in my seat, wiped the perspiration from my upper lip.

"Your Honor," Mr. Morgan said. "Surely the court wouldn't object to the minor being raised by someone who loves her. I visited the father, and he agreed that Miss Adams would be the ideal guardian. We would hope that you will honor the parent's wishes—"

The judge lifted his hand. "Mr. Morgan, I'm not inclined to be swayed by an inmate's wishes. Also, before I rule on this, I have to contact Judge Taylor over there. In light of the father's letter and Miss Loretta Adams appearing in front of me today, agreeing to accept guardianship of the minor, he still may not—" He paused and called out to Retta, "Are you willing to accept guardianship, Miss Adams?"

I glanced wildly at Retta.

Retta popped up from her chair and said, "Yessir, Buddy Norton. I've been tending to Honey Mary-Angeline here since birth. Changed many of that child's cloths, same as I did yours when your mama came to visit."

The judge looked down at his paperwork and gently cleared his throat at the mention of diapers, and I felt my own face heating from embarrassment for both of us.

"What about you, Miss Lovett?"

"Sir, Your Honor?" I stood up with knocking knees, my indigo-blazed hands gripping the table for support. Alarmed, I locked my hands behind my back, hoping he hadn't seen them, wishing I had my gloves.

"Are you in agreement?" the judge asked somberly. "Are these your wishes, Miss Lovett?"

I looked at him, surprised. Not once since my folk were arrested could I remember anyone asking my wishes. Retta nudged me. "Yes, sir, uh, Your Honor, sir. Miss Retta's like family sure enough." I sat back down before my legs failed me, folding anxious hands into my lap, hiding them under the table.

The judge nodded. "Well, I still need to hear from the Honorable Judge Taylor. We are in recess while I call him. Bailiff, Miss Lovett is not allowed to leave the courtroom."

"Yes, Your Honor," the bailiff answered and pinned bored eyes to mine.

As the judge stepped off the bench, he turned to us and warned, "If Judge Taylor isn't in agreement to rescind his order, my hands are tied." Then he disappeared somewhere into the back.

Terrified, my eyes searched Mr. Morgan's. If the lawyer was concerned, he didn't show it. Instead, Mr. Morgan jumped up and said, "I'm going out in the hall. I have some telephone calls to make about another case. You wait here like the judge said."

He gave a nod to Mr. Greene who joined him. The Knott County social worker shot Retta a troubled glance as he passed.

I looked into Retta's worried eyes and folded her old, soft hands into mine.

"You're freezing, child." She briskly rubbed my hands.

"Retta, in case they take me to prison, our root cellar is full with enough food to last several seasons. You have Alonzo ride all of it over to you. I'll need someone to tend to Junia." It broke my heart to think about the ol' girl all alone or, worse, sold off to a meat-packing plant because she was too ornery to get along with most.

"Nonsense, child." She released our hands and tucked a strand of hair behind my ear. Her eyes were fierce, but her touch gentle. "They're gonna have to fight my ol' hide if they dare try and take you anywhere." She squared her shoulders, plucked at the collar of her fresh, clean dress, then shot the bailiff a mean eye.

Unconcerned, the deputy turned his back to us when a lawman poked his head through the judge's back entryway. The two struck up a conversation.

Sunlight streamed through the windows, puddling on the walnut plank flooring, streaking across our wooden table. I placed a finger on the table, tracing the old grains, the wood soft and indented. I wondered how many others had rubbed their worriment into the table, polished it with their remorse and sorrows.

I looked at the bailiff and then back over my shoulder at the door, counting the steps that could lead me to freedom— agonizing over how fast I could make it out the door and to Junia. I chanced a peek back to the bailiff chatting with his fellow worker. I was sure he'd beat me like the lawman over in Thousandsticks did my parents, or worse. *Worse* always had a way of finding the Blues, I'd been told, and for the smallest infractions.

I'd seen the notes in my grandparents' old Bible, heard the whispers between my folks. Several Blues had been hanged. A great-uncle had been thrown down a mine shift after standing up to a man who put his hands on his wife. Another was buried alive in Darby, a sinkhole that later turned into a pond. More were used in the coal mines and suffered "accidents" like my grandpa. There was 1936, Mama and Papa's wedding... For a moment I felt like I would be sick and put a palm to my sticky brow.

Retta must have noticed because she turned around and searched her coat pockets and handed me a piece of angelica root. "It'll settle the nerves some, child. Never leave home without having my angelica or peach-tree bark."

I popped the root into my mouth and slowly chewed. Satisfied, Retta pressed her hand over mine. In a few minutes, my stomach settled and I stared up at the black-rimmed clock above the judge's bench, watching the red second hand inch slowly around. Against the wall, a cast-iron radiator hissed and spit, its steam rising.

A full ten minutes passed before Mr. Morgan returned and sat down next to me. He glanced at his wristwatch, then took notes on a sheet of paper. Mr. Greene settled in at his table shortly after.

Another twenty minutes, and I looked over my shoulder to the door. I wanted to go check on Junia. Kiss her soft muzzle and say goodbye. The thought of losing that ol' girl, the only living thing I had left now, struck deeply.

I took the root from my mouth and put it inside my coat.

"Mr. Morgan." I tapped his shoulder. He looked up from his papers. "Sir," I whispered into his ear, "I know Mr. Faust took in my papa's horse. If they take me, could you care for Junia until I'm free? I can pay." I held up my coat partway. "Mama sewed money inside the lining. You can have it all—"

Before he could answer, the bailiff moved away from the doorway. Judge Norton stepped in, his robe swishing into the weary air as he climbed the steps to his bench.

We all rose and then sat back down as Judge Norton mumbled, "Be seated."

I wrung my clammy hands beneath the table, twisted until my knuckles were hurting.

"Thank you for waiting," the judge told us. "I had a devil of a time getting hold of Judge Taylor. He was in a hearing. When he telephoned back, I advised him of the current circumstances and the wishes of Miss Lovett and her father. I also let him know Knott County has no objection, per Mr. Greene's earlier statement. But—"

"*Retta.*" I rested my head on her shoulder, squeezed my eyes shut, waiting.

"Shh, 'Tunia." Retta kissed the top of my head, grasped my hands, and I latched on, pressing against her cool, dry ones.

Judge Norton continued. "Judge Taylor was not too pleased hearing Miss Lovett had fled Leslie County to escape apprehension. A bit agitated, in fact. The Leslie County state social worker even more so, Judge Taylor said."

I opened my eyes and gawked fearfully at the Knott County social worker.

Mr. Greene tightened his mouth, hearing the judge's words, then frowned and dropped his head to the notebook.

Retta stiffened and shot out an indignant *humph.*

I squeezed my eyes shut, fighting back tears.

"But," Judge Norton said, "after I explained it, he agreed that it was in the best interest of the minor to rescind his order and release Miss Lovett into the custody of Miss Loretta—"

Retta cried out a hoarse, shaky cheer.

"Application of guardianship for Honey Mary-Angeline Lovett is hereby granted," the judge continued.

My eyes flew open.

"Anything more, Mr. Morgan?"

"No, Your Honor. Thank you."

"Court's adjourned," the judge said, standing.

Mr. Morgan repeated, "Thank you, Your Honor." He collected some paperwork from the clerk sitting below the judge, then came back to our table, smiling. "Congratulations," he said to us.

"Thank you, sir. Mr. Morgan, when can I visit my parents?" I needed to see them, had to know how they were doing, let them know how I was doing.

He took out a sheet of paper and wrote on it, then handed it to me. "Here's the addresses and the times for visitation, Honey. Make sure you leave all personal items outside the prison."

"Yes, sir, thank you," I said, wondering how I'd get a ride.

"You telephone if you need me." He grabbed his briefcase and stood. "Oh, and one more thing, Honey..." He dug into his pants pocket, pulled out a shiny nickel, and dropped it on the table. "Buy that old Junia an apple on me." He winked, then walked over to Mr. Greene and shook his hand.

Outside on the courthouse steps, Devil John and Martha Hannah were waiting. "Honey, you're safe now," the moonshiner declared.

"Safe." The word rose in a breathless shudder, and all I could think about was seeing my folk to make sure they were too. "Devil John, is there someone I can hire to drive me to see Mama and Papa? Mr. Morgan says they're up in Pewee Valley and La Grange. I have to see my folk."

Devil John stroked his beard, thinking. Martha Hannah lit up. "That'd be Amara Ballard, the newest frontier nurse on Old Trace Road. She has herself a dependable automobile and is always travelin' to Louisville and La Grange for medical supplies.

She's bringing serum to inoculate the gran'babes next week. I can ask her."

"Thank you, ma'am," I said.

Retta was tired, and we said our goodbyes to the Smiths.

I couldn't wait to see Junia. "I'll meet you back home, Retta."

Retta held my hand, reluctant to let go. With teary eyes, she drew me into her embrace and said, "My prettiest petunia is finally coming home."

Mr. Morgan and Mr. Greene strolled out of the courthouse together. My lawyer paused in front of me and whispered, "One last thing, Honey. Mr. Greene advised you'll be under the watchful eye of the court until you turn eighteen. Don't think I have to worry about this, but you and Miss Adams need to be model citizens and not break any laws. We don't want to have the order rescinded. Don't go getting into trouble, and you'll be just fine." He smiled and patted my shoulder before joining a watchful Mr. Greene.

Rescinded. I looked back at them worriedly, wondering just what Mr. Greene meant. How could I possibly break the law, much less, dear Retta? *Don't take much for a Blue...* The words swirled around my mind, and like my folk, I knew to remain guarded and on the lookout for those who would harm our kind.

Ten

Alonzo brought quail over to Retta's that he'd hunted last fall, and we dipped them in butter, wrapped the nine li'l birds in jowl bacon, and roasted them on a spit in the woodstove. I helped mix up chestnut corn bread and roast sweet potatoes.

Saying the blessing, her nephew thanked the Heavenly Father for the food and my safety and added a prayer to watch over my folk, tipsy after bringing in a bottle of liquor to sip from, but not forgetful of his Maker.

Retta scolded him with her eyes when he reached for his third drink.

"Auntie, it was a mighty fine spread tonight." He belched loudly, accidentally knocking over his glass while going for his fourth.

Retta scowled, and I jumped up to fetch a tea towel.

"Well, now," he said, pressing his hands against his shirt pockets fattened with his glasses and pens, a comb, a matchbox, a tobacco tin, papers, and other oddities—his life poking out of the bulging fabric. "I best let you ladies retire and journey on back to my home," he said drunkenly, swaying a little as he stood.

"You need any help, Alonzo?" I asked, worrying if he could make it down the path without falling off the mountain.

"Obliged, Honey, but it ain't more than five minutes down, and I'll be tucked in tight as a tick 'fore you can holler my name and it comes boomerangin' back." He chuckled.

Alonzo left, and me and Retta retired to her robin's-egg blue and white metal glider on the porch.

Under a quilt, I snuggled up to the old woman and laid my head on her shoulder like I used to when I was a little girl. The porch lantern burned low; scents of woodsmoke, tired cooking oil, and spent sparkle from our supper lingered. A lone coyote called from the hills as the lantern cast warm light across the wooden slants.

Retta's cat, Pennie, mewed as she jumped onto the porch, rubbing her long whiskers against the quilt. I scratched her cream-colored head, listening to the cat's purring contentment.

Retta went inside and came back out with a dish of meat scraps for the cat. Greedy, Pennie chewed loudly and licked the plate. The cat cleaned her whiskers, then headed over to Junia's stall.

After a few minutes, I sat up and said, "Retta, what would you have done if that judge sent me away?"

"Humph, that boy would've know'd better than to try. An' iffin his ma ever found out, she would fuss him into the next county, iffin I didn't boot him there first. Humph," she said again, fluffing her long skirts. "Boy done got too briggity going to them fancy stone schools and big universities for the book-read. Well, I'm a moonlighter an' I went and got my readin' an' writing smarts too. Up at the ol' Moonlight Schools, an' lawsy, do I know'd a thing or two I could teach *him*."

"Retta, you never told me you attended the Moonlight Schools. What was it like?"

"It was long 'fore your time, Honey. I think I started going in 1913. But as ya probably know, the Moonlight Schools were held at night and only when the moon was fat an' bright, so me an' other folks could learn our letters, read an' write. Walk safely up them ol' moonlit paths to the one-room schoolhouse to meet my teacher, Miss Sundie Ball." A secret glimmered in her eyes, and she raised a finger and said:

"The heights by great men reached and kept
Were not attained by sudden flight,
But they, while their companions slept,
Were toiling upward in the night."

"'The Ladder of St. Augustine,'" I said, remembering Mama'd told me the night schools began around that time for the uneducated, elderly hillfolk and the Kentucky men going off to fight in the Great War. It was vital to free folk from illiteracy, to save those imprisoned by its bondage, she'd said.

I traced the pie-crust pattern on the seat of Retta's glider, trying to picture Retta and the others hobbling along the moonlit paths. For a moment, the notion made me sad, and I envied those who'd gone to a real school. It felt like I'd been robbed, cheated out of a chance to be like other students. Even ol' Retta had been given that.

Retta said, "The moonlighters know'd ol' Longfellow well. His was the very first words they learnt us to write... Ah, 'Tunia, it's getting late, I need to go to bed now." She stood, unsteady, flailing an arm.

"Retta, what's wrong?" I jumped up and took a firm hold of her.

She winced. "It'll pass, child, these ol' bones are jus' tired. Ain't used to so much big to-dos, and all in one day."

Worried, I searched her face. She waved away my concern and shuffled her tired bones to the door.

I followed inside. "Retta, let's get you into bed. I'll put on the kettle and fetch you a fresh bedpig." At the foot of Retta's iron bed, I pulled out the foot warmer from under the covers, unscrewed the lid, and emptied the water from the pottery-shaped pig off the side of the porch. I collected more wood for the stove and fireplace. In a few minutes the kettle whistled, and I filled the bedpig up with hot water and slipped it back under her covers.

I helped Retta over to her bed and tucked her in. "Thank you for everything, Retta." I studied her sweet sleepy face and kissed the old woman's cheek as she drifted off.

Several times, I noticed Retta wince in her sleep. Growing uneasy, I lifted the back of my hand to her forehead checking for fever and then sat a while watching her breathe.

Eleven

Three days later, I climbed the fire tower as the March winds knotted into wisps of fog around the little wooden cab in the sky. Scents of an awakening forest sweetened the air after its winter slumber. Somewhere in the hills a dog barked, and another answered back. A lively tune slipped out from the cab as I knocked on the trapdoor.

The music stopped and Pearl opened the wooden trap. "Come up, Honey. I'm glad you made it over. I'm cooking a gourmet dish, and I made enough for two." She waved a dish towel, motioning me up.

I took the stairs up the platform and stepped inside.

"Smells delicious."

"You just missed R.C.," she said, standing over the stove. "Whoever did the steps wrecked my cab up here and destroyed the new radio."

"I'm sorry. Did R.C. find out anymore?"

"No, he dropped off one of his old radios from the station and this new padlock for the outside latch." She pointed her fork to a shiny, big lock on the counter. "He wanted me to be able to use it on the inside latch at night and the outside one when I needed to run errands."

"R.C.'s smart like that," I said.

"Make yourself comfortable. You can sit anywhere."

The cab was spotless with a few scattered rugs. A potbelly

cozied beside a cooking stove, both warming the cab. I set my leather satchel down on the floor and slipped off my coat, folding it over a chair.

Her narrow wooden bed had been placed across from the table, the tick mattress spilling some of its corn-husk stuffing. It was unmade and I moved over to it, admiring two old stuffed toys strewn across it. I touched the cloth baby doll with its sweet hand-painted face, studied the faded flowery seersucker dress and frizzed yarn hair. It looked like the stuffed body had been stitched up a few times. A worn, dark-brown horse with a soft golden mane, tail, and matching button eyes rested close by.

I remembered my cloth baby doll that Mama had sewn and the stuffed teddy bear Papa had bought for me in Tennessee.

Pearl came over and scooped them up, mumbling low, "Let me move Arlie and Mr. Cleveland, so you can sit." She blushed and stuffed the toys under her pillow and quickly pulled up the sheets and quilt. "Mother insisted on packing them. Sorry for the mess. I got busy with the Osborne and forgot to make my bed this morning." She smoothed down the covers.

A small chifforobe sat beside her bed. I peeked around the dresser to where a door stood half-open. A leggy, wooden washstand holding a pitcher, bowl, and chamber pot had been squeezed inside the closet.

In the center of the room, an Osborne Firefinder rested atop a large wooden table next to a black rotary-dial telephone. I bent over and peeked through the sliding peephole of the Osborne and took the sight handle, lining it up with the crosshairs.

At the stove, Pearl glanced over her shoulder. "Oh, I see you know how it works."

"Yes, R.C. taught me and Mama." I looked at all the ledgers. There was one for Fire Reports, a second for False Fires, and another that said Weather. I picked up one for Lightning Strikes and scanned another thick one labeled Maps. "Sure is a lot of work recording everything and fighting fires."

"I don't mind," she said. "It's real important to keep track of it all, and it helps me when I go scout out any campfires or sleepers from lightning strikes. When berry-picking time is here, it'll keep me extra busy. We get a lot of fires when people are in the forest and leaving behind trash."

I straightened the ledgers back up, then ran a fingertip across the top of the telephone while peering at the numbers printed on its white round face.

Pearl turned around and raised a fork above the lard-spitting skillet. "Go ahead, Honey, you can telephone someone if you like. R.C. had it installed last week."

"I've never talked on one. Don't even know anyone who owns a telephone," I said, amazed. "Maybe the town doc. The only ones I've seen up close are the pay booth inside of the Company store and the two pay telephones hanging on the wall in the courthouse hall."

She turned back to her skillet. "We'll call my mother later, and I'll let you say hello. Have a seat."

My hand lingered on the dial and I frowned, thinking about Mama and Papa. If only I could speak to them now. Pick up the telephone anytime like Pearl and hear their voices.

I rummaged through my bag and pulled out a string of smoked apples and some peach leather wrapped in cloth I'd picked up at my grandpa's cabin.

Pearl brought over a plate of fried strips of something I didn't recognize and set it between her chair and mine.

I pushed the bag toward her.

"What's this?"

"Mama says never show up empty-handed and always welcome a new home with a sweet treat," I said shyly, unwrapping the candy to show her.

"Thank you. I loved those peach leather sweets." Pearl placed a fork and plate in front of me and put another setting down for herself. "I'll get our drinks," she said as she opened the small icebox by the stove. She pulled out two Coca-Colas and pried off the tops with a church key.

The cold cola was a rare treat. Once a year on Mama's birthday, Papa took us all down to Knoxville in his truck to eat at Regas Brothers, a fancy city restaurant. He always ordered me a tall glass of Coca-Cola and had the waitress put two cherries atop.

Pearl put the bottle in front of me, sat down, and passed the plate of food. "Caught me a rattler near my woodpile down there and got him with my ax. Thought I'd skin it and have us a treat."

I admired her bravery. "Mama used to have a tasty batter for the ones Papa brought home." I took a bite, and after swallowing, I said, "It's really good."

"Gene, my boss over at Big Knob, showed me how to cook them."

After we ate, I dug out the newspapers and Barbara Pym's *Excellent Women* I'd picked out for her. "Here you go. And, I've got some good news. I'm free now. The judge said I can stay with Retta."

Pearl looked at me closely. "That is good news. Does that mean—"

"Yes, I won't have to worry about Mrs. Wallace finding me and throwing me into the children's prison, as long as Retta will have me."

"Oh!" Pearl jumped up and went to her pantry. "We'll truly celebrate!" She pulled out a bottle of blackberry wine and poured some into two small jelly-jar glasses.

She handed me one, then raised her glass in a toast and said, "To your freedom." Pearl raised a finger. "Let's telephone Mother." I took a small sip and set the glass aside. It was the first time anyone had given me drink, and I worried what would happen if someone found out.

I fidgeted with my hair and the buttons on my blouse as she dialed. Then she placed the earpiece between us. I took a breath and heard a rumbling ring followed by another, then a woman's voice say, "*Hello?*"

"Mother, it's me," Pearl said. "I have someone here who wants to say hello."

The woman answered back, "Who's on the line? Is that you, Mrs. Barry? Oh, hold, Pearl, one of the Barrys is on the party line again. Mrs. Barry, please hang up, it's for me... Hang up, it's my Pearly! Mrs. Barry?" There was a short pause, then a loud click. Pearl shoved the earpiece into my hand.

All I could do was stare at it, my hands darkening, washed in blue. But if Pearl noticed, she didn't say anything. "Put it up to your ear, and speak into the bottom here," Pearl whispered, tapping the mouthpiece.

"Oh! Hello, hello, this is Honey Lovett, Mother, uh, Mrs. Grant, ma'am, from Troublesome Creek, Kentucky."

Pearl's mother said, "This is Elizabeth Grant, Honey, over in Somerset." I stared out the windowed room, across the vast hills, forest, and streams, imagining the countless miles, then looked at the earpiece and back to the windows again. "She's in Somerset," I said to Pearl and turned around slowly, stretching the coiled cord, gazing out the sheets of window glass that climbed up the cab's walls, the fog outside ghosting up and over the woodlands and creeks. "Clear over in Somerset, Kentucky, Pearl, and talking to me like she's standing right here." I pressed a palm over my mouth. "*Somerset*," I said, muffled.

Pearl laughed, gently lifted the telephone back to my ear.

"Honey," Pearl's mother chatted on, "I want to thank you for giving my Pearly a place to stay while her cab was being repaired."

"Yes, ma'am, Mrs. Grant, anytime." Dumbfounded, I handed the handset back to Pearl, my mind dizzy from the thought of talking to someone that far away. I slid sweaty hands down my britches and leaned my head closer to Pearl's, listening.

Never before had I understood when Mama told me about the first time she'd seen an aeroplane flying overhead. I felt the same way about this telephone.

I glanced around at Pearl's icebox, stove, record player, and telephone, pondering it all. The Wonders. And other than in magazines, I'd never seen such, the likings of machinery tethered to a mind like that, and I gasped, realizing the notions were just that.

From below, Junia brayed into Pie's sudden neigh. Pearl said goodbye to her mother and hung up the telephone, rushing out to the catwalk. I followed and saw her eyes fearfully searching the trees. "Mother is sending my .410, and if I catch him breaking in here again, I'm going to pepper his hairy ass with birdshot." Her jaw twitched.

Twelve

While Retta napped Sunday afternoon, I would read a few pages and pause when she'd jerk in her sleep, troubled by the amount of time she was spending in bed, worrying she was in pain.

When she finally stirred, I went over to check on her. She'd been sleeping a lot lately. "Retta, *Retta*." I gently shook her shoulders, then laid the back of my hand on her forehead. *Cool.* She roused long enough to flutter her eyes and turn over. I frowned. *How much was too much sleep for a ninety-one-year-old woman?*

Later that evening, Retta staggered out of bed holding on to me. She stayed up for a supper of corn bread, hot tea, and even more unusual, little talk. Soon, she was back in the bed, waving away my worries. "Don't fret none, child. I'll be good as new by morn'."

I needed to find Doc or one of the frontier nurses and ask them to come check on her.

On Monday morn', I fried Retta up some sage sausage and boiled corn for hominy with a jar of pinto beans I'd brought over from my root cellar, then dressed to go to town.

I picked up my coat and found the hidden zipper and reached inside and pulled out some money. I counted out five one-dollar bills, tallied them twice, and stuffed the rest back inside, and wrote down the directions for the nurse to find Retta's home.

"Child, travel safe," Retta said, holding onto the porch beam.

"And you"—she shook a stiff finger at Junia—"take care of my Honey, you cantankerous ol' cuss," she warned.

Two hours later, I knocked on the nurse's door. No answer. Again, I gave several thumps and waited, trying to peek inside the curtained windows. Likely, she was off tending to sick folk. And when I checked over at Doc's, I didn't get an answer there either.

Resigned, I climbed atop Junia and hurried back to Retta. When I rode into the yard, I was surprised to see the cabin dark and the clay chimney smokeless.

After I put Junia in her stall, I rushed inside. The room was cold, and I called out for Retta as I lit a lantern and slipped out of my gloves and coat.

Retta rasped back, and I rushed over to her bed. "Retta," I said, peering down at her, feeling her forehead and cheeks. She looked pale.

"Did you fetch the doc, child?" she asked weakly, pulling the covers closer to her chin.

"I couldn't find anyone, but I will, Retta. First, I need to get you warm." I put my coat back on, went out to the well, and pumped water into a bucket. Once I had it safely inside, I gathered kindling from the porch. Lighting the stove, I asked Retta if she'd had anything to eat. Her silence told me she hadn't, and I looked for any dirty dishes that might've said otherwise. The sink was spotless.

I filled the kettle, then pulled out the cold bedpig from under her covers.

"I'll have you warm in a minute, Retta," I whispered. "I want you to drink some hot tea before I go. Then I'll take the lantern to town and try to get hold of Doc, unless you want me to go for the granny woman, Emma McCain?"

"No, child," she said tiredly. "These ol' bones is needing more than the herbs and tonics, I fear."

"I'll go straight back out, Retta, as soon as I get you settled in."

Pulling the chair across the room, I sat down and helped her with the cup. She took a sip and I urged her to drink more.

When I had her bedpig warmed, I slipped it back under the covers, then took the quilt from my bed and laid it atop of hers. "I'll be back, Retta, as soon I can." I kissed her cheek.

Junia seemed to sense the urgency and sped on the paths. The winds chafed my face as the lantern light danced across dark woods and any slinking night critters.

"Hurry," I urged Junia. "*Hurry!*"

It took two hours to get to Doc's. I tied Junia to the white picket fence outside the yard, extinguished my lantern, and raced up the wide porch steps. "Doc," I called out banging on the door. "Doc, it's me Honey Lovett."

In a minute, the porch lights on his big house came on and the door swung open.

It was Millie, Doc's second wife, and the Swedish woman looked none too pleased as she tied the belt on her fluffy robe.

"Ma'am, I'm sorry to disturb you, but I need Doc. Need him to tend to Loretta Ad—"

She shook her head. "*Doc är inte här, han är i Natti.*"

"I got money." I pulled out the bills I was going to give the nurse.

She pushed my arm away. "*Natti.*"

"Natti?" I puzzled. "Natti what—?"

"Natti!" the woman shouted, and I jumped back. "*Gå och se gräns sköterskorna som rider på häst. Häst!*" She pointed beyond my head. "*Läkare i Natti.*"

"Natti?" I stretched my neck, looking past her, inside the house. "Doc," I called out. "It's me, Honey Lovett. Loretta Adams's taken to the bed and—"

Millie snorted, then grabbed something off the table in the hall beside her. She stepped over the threshold and shoved a matchbook into my hand. "Natti." She scowled.

I looked down at the matches with the advertisement for a tall-towered building named The Terrance Plaza Hotel somewhere up in Cincinnati, Ohio.

"*Natti.*" Doc was away. My heart sank, and I dropped the money into my coat pocket. Millie must've seen my despair because she said it softer, "Nur, *nurses.*" She pointed behind me. "Rider. *Ah-Amara Ballard.*"

"The riders. Frontier nurses," I whispered.

"*Ja.* Old Tw-trace." She snatched the matches out of my hand, slipped back inside, and slammed the door. In a second the porch went dark.

Once more I pointed Junia toward Amara Ballard's, urging her to go fast, hoping this time the nurse would be there.

When we got there, she still wasn't home. I sat down on the stoop and waited for over an hour, worrying she was not going to be back anytime soon, maybe not even tomorrow or the day after that. I looked up at the stars, stood, and knocked again though I knew it was useless.

Reaching into my coat pocket, I pulled out the bills and note, then found a small rock and carried it to her door, sitting the stone atop the money with Retta's address and directions.

I dusted off my hands and said a prayer the nurse would come, another that Retta was safe.

I arrived back at Retta's a little past nine, surprised to see her sitting at the table with a cup of tea, mopping her last bite of corn bread across a plate of molasses.

"Doc's out of town, Retta, but I left a note for the frontier nurse. You feeling better?" I kissed her cheek.

"A li'l better, child. Had me a bite of dinner, then brewed some hawthorn berries."

Retta knew a lot about herbs and remedies, more than Doc even.

She pushed back wisps of hair and patted her sloppy bun, gave me a wobbly smile that never lifted into her eyes. "Hawthorn pert me right up."

Hawthorn. I knew the herb well. Mama'd taught me it was used for ailing hearts—*failing hearts.* I studied Retta, worrying.

Retta glanced at my darkening hand. "I'm pert, sure 'nough, child."

I quickly swallowed my fright and nodded. "Let's get you another cup of tea."

Thirteen

I was up most of the night checking on the old woman, peeking out her curtains into the darkness, watching for the wide sweep of the nurse's lantern.

At sunrise, Retta called my name, rousing me from my deep slumber. "Child?" She stood over my bed, one hand on the head-rail. "Child, get ya some breakfast 'fore you head out to Junia."

I raised up on my elbows and saw she had a plate waiting on the table.

Yawning, I rubbed my eyes. "Retta? Retta, you feeling better?" I quickly kicked off my covers and stood.

"I'm feeling much better this morn', Honey. Go on, child, take yourself out for fresh air an' a ride after you eat."

Relief flooded over me and I hugged her carefully. I couldn't imagine what would happen if she got worse. "I'd rather stay here today." I went behind the hanging curtain in the corner and slipped out of my long gown and into britches and a flannel shirt.

After breakfast, I let Junia out to graze, cleaned her stall, then inspected the mule's coat and shoes. Inside the cozy home, the quiet morning slipped into a quieter afternoon, and later, the day chased the last hours of light into shadowed, tired, soot-baked walls and cobwebbed corners. I sighed.

The nurse wasn't coming. But Retta seemed to be feeling much better today, so I put on the kettle and made us tea.

I sat at the table mending aprons with Retta, glancing up from my stitches to make sure she was doing well. In a moment I saw she'd fallen asleep, and I reached over and gently took off her glasses, placing them in front of her.

"Let's get you to bed," I said, standing, waking her up. "Me, too, Retta. I'm tired."

Retta gave a sleepy, toothless grin as she pushed herself away from the teacup and pressed her palms down on the table to stand. "Ya don't get to be tired till you is ninety-two young, child, and not a day sooner." She wagged a finger.

"Ninety-two, Retta?"

"Sunday." Her eyes were tired but playful.

Her birthday was March 15, and here it was already March 17 and I'd forgotten and spent the day with Pearl. I began to lay down an enthusiastic apology and well wishes across the room when she shushed me with a dismissive hand.

I hugged the ol' woman and said "Happy birthday," sad and feeling badly that her nephew, and now me, had missed it.

"Ninety-two and not going anywhere!" Retta exclaimed. "I got me a girl to finish raising."

Wednesday morning, Retta fussed and insisted she was better, then shooed me out of the cabin. She watched from the porch as I climbed atop Junia.

"Retta, you sure you'll be okay?" I snatched glances at her as I rode over to the cabin. "I can stay."

"Go on, ride safe, child, Alonzo's takin' me to town. A girl only gets one chance to grow up, an' I want mine to have the very best." Retta waved, then pointed a gnarled finger to Junia. "Keep my girl safe, ya obstinate beast."

"I can ride into town with you."

"No, child, you need to get out and exercise Junia some. Have yourself a bite of youth. I'll be back this afternoon."

"Yes, ma'am. I think I'll ride over to the fire tower and visit the new lookout." I hoped the visit would be welcomed because it would be nice to talk with my new friend again.

We rode slow, taking our time. I was trying to think of something nice I could do for Retta for a belated birthday surprise when I spotted it ahead. "Whoa, girl." I climbed down and tied Junia to a tree. I pulled out a knife from my satchel, then walked through some maidenhair fern over to a clump of grasses.

Ramps. Me and Retta liked to collect them, and here the oniony treat was, popping up early. I cut off the broad leaves, wrapped them in twine, and then hooked it to my saddle. Retta always fried them in a li'l bacon grease, then seasoned the tasty greens with salt and vinegar. Tonight, I'd cook up some apple dumplings and butterbeans to go with them.

I moved to another patch, running my fingers over the leaves. Retta said you had to be careful and make sure you were foraging the safe ones, not the deadly lily of the valleys. I inspected to see if the plant had a bulb. Satisfied that it did, I tore the leaf and sniffed, inhaling the onion and garlic scent.

It was rumored Marigold Hall over in the next holler killed her husband with the poisonous lilies after receiving one too many visits from a frontier nurse to fix her broken, bruised body. The nurse noticed fresh lily cuttings on the table the day the couple's cabin burned down and would remember the odd resemblance later. She'd arrived to stitch Marigold's forehead. In a hurry to nurse the woman's battered face, she paid no mind to the poisonous plant.

And when Mr. Hall came in lit from the shine later that evening, demanding his supper, Marigold prepared a feast for him—a fine spread of his favorites: pork shoulder and cabbage, cooked-down greens and corn bread dipped in pot likker just the way he liked it. Solemn and shy, Marigold had told the sheriff how grateful she was for their last meal together.

I stood and wrapped the ramps and wiped my hands on my britches.

"Let's go, Junia. Oh—" Several feet away, I spotted eyebright, and went over and dug up the herb, then carefully packed it in my pannier. These were perfect for making Retta an eyewash to soothe her ailing eyes.

From atop the lookout's circling catwalk, Pearl waved and hollered down to me. "Oh, Honey, it's good to see you. Come on up." She slipped back into her cab.

I trekked up the winding stairs. The trapdoor was open, and I climbed up inside.

"I'm glad you're here," she said.

"Retta went into town and I thought I'd drop by," I said, a little out of breath from the stairs.

"Well, since you're here, have a seat. I'll fix us something to drink." I slipped off my coat.

She pulled out a pitcher of tea from her icebox and poured two glasses. She glanced down at my gloved hands. "It's okay, Honey. You don't have to hide who you were meant to be."

A blush warmed my face, and I pulled off the gloves, grateful.

Pearl set the drink in front of me, then peeked at the Osborne and took a seat. "I could use a friend. Can you stay for dinner?" She fidgeted with one of the buttons on her blouse and kept glancing out the windows. Finally she got up, peered out the glass, and cranked open one of the small glass window frames. The bottom half pivoted out, while the top half swung into the cab, letting in the sweet mountain air.

"I have to be back early," I said, concerned about Retta. "What's wrong?" Pearl seemed a bit agitated. She'd put the ax beside the trapdoor.

Pearl frowned and plopped back onto her seat. "My telephone lines were cut the other day, and my woodpile was set on fire. Poor Pie got so scared, he broke out of his stall and fled to the hills. Took me most of the day to round him back up, and part of the evening to soothe him."

"Oh, how awful! Who would do that?" I looked at the telephone.

She picked up the receiver and pressed it to her ear, then slammed the handset back down. "Still dead. I'm sure it was Robbie Hardin. I heard Pie making a fuss out there and looked down just in time to see Robbie's red cap as he slipped off into the woods." Pearl crossed her legs and kicked one up and down, annoyed. "Had to use that old rusty radio to call R.C. Barely works." She jerked a thumb over her shoulder to where the radio sat.

"Real sorry, Pearl. What did R.C. say?"

"He thinks Robbie is angry because his cousin didn't get the job. He said he'd have a word with him. Other than that, unless he caught him, there was little he could do. Same as the sheriff said when R.C. brought him up here."

"Hardins are rabid mean," I whispered.

"Why I brought the ax up until I get my .410." She sighed and stood. "I made a lemon cake. Would you like a slice?"

"Looks delicious, but not today. Retta's been ailing a bit, and I want to get back home."

Junia brayed outside. "Ol' Junia's tired. Me too. Thanks for the tea." I pulled the satchel into my lap.

Pearl handed me the newspapers and book she'd borrowed from me, and I stuffed them inside and stood.

"Hold on, Honey, I'll grab my coat and walk you down. I want to feed Pie his oats and brush him."

I watched as Pearl lead Pie out of the stall. She rubbed his muzzle and patted his spotted neck, running a loving hand across the silky mane. "Handsome boy, Pie. Such a strong beauty," she talked sweetly to the horse. I watched Pearl's worries disappear with each stroke, softening her taut face.

She tied him to the landing and inspected his legs. Pie turned and quickly untied the rope with his mouth and tossed it back at her. Pearl put her hands on her hips and laughed.

Surprised, I clasped a hand across my mouth, giggling. "Oh, Pie, I sure hope you don't teach Junia this trick."

Pearl petted him. "Okay, one short ride, boy, to check for campfires, and then I have to get back to my lookout," she warned, wagging a finger. Pie flapped his lips over Pearl's cheek. "*Ah.*" She moved back and rubbed her red cheek. "Chaffed again. I should know better by now, but I do love your kisses," she said, chuckling.

I knew Pearl had to be lonely up here without family or friends. I missed my mama and papa something fierce. But I had Retta, and Pearl had no one but me in these parts. I smiled, thankful to Retta for saving me from the clutches of the prison.

"Ride over to Retta's for dinner Sunday. Retta turned ninety-two. I'm going to make her a celebration meal and you're invited."

"Ninety-two, that's remarkable. Love to meet and toast your dear Retta," she said with a grateful smile.

Ninety-two. Pearl said it sweetly, but her words drew a worry. "Best hurry home. See you Sunday, Pearl."

Fourteen

Puzzled, I stopped and stared ahead. Junia brayed loudly and swished her tail. Something was wrong.

A strange horse was loosely tethered to the post on Retta's porch, grazing. Junia kicked sideways and called out bossy neighs. The horse glanced up. Bored, it lowered its head back to the grasses as I tried to steady the mule.

When Junia was settled in her stall, I climbed up the wooden steps. "Retta, I picked some herbs and ramps." I dropped my bag on the porch, creaked open the door. "*Retta?*"

The young woman greeted me, wearing a dark-blue jacket with *FNS* embroidered on its sleeve and a pair of matching wool britches. A nurse's cap rested on her head and a stethoscope hung from her neck.

She put a shushing finger to her lips. "Miss Adams is ill," she barely whispered. "I'm Amara Ballard from the Frontier Nursing Service. I've been nursing her. Are you a relative?" she asked.

As far as Retta was concerned and the court decreed, I was. "I'm Honey Lovett, and I live with Retta. I left you the money and a note to come." I peered over her shoulder.

The nurse nodded, understanding. "She's in grave condition; her heart is failing, Honey. I'm sorry but I've done everything I can." Amara stepped outside.

I gripped the post and gasped. "She was fine this morning. What do you mean her heart is failing? *Please help her.*"

"I'm truly sorry. There is nothing more I can do—"

"Please, I have money," I whispered hoarsely, the tears strangling as I tore off my coat and reached inside the lining. Amara touched my shoulder and I saw the helplessness reflected in her eyes.

"She's all I have left. The only one in the world. There must be something you can do to make her well again. *Please*, Nurse Amara," I said, shoving the coat into her hands. "Take all the money, just save my *Retta*," I half sobbed her name.

"I'm sorry. She's been calling for you. Go in and visit with her, Honey, I'll wait out here a while." She handed me back my coat.

Inside, I rushed over to Retta's bed, knelt down, and grabbed her hand in my gloved one. "Retta, it's me. It's me, Honey! *Retta*." I waited for her response, but I found none in her limp hand. I tore off my gloves. Pressing her hand against my cheek, I rubbed and kissed her fingers. "Retta, it's me, your petunia."

From behind, a chair scraped against the wooden floors. Someone placed a hand on my shoulder. "*Honey.*" I got a whiff of his whiskey-soaked clothing and breath. I looked up into her nephew's reddened eyes. Alonzo said, "She took a spell in town after we came out of the bank. Brought her home and put her straight to bed. She's been waiting for you, Honey." He studied Retta. "Auntie, Honey's come home," he said, clutching a paper in his hand. "I have to go now, but I'll be back tonight."

I stood and stepped back, knowing Alonzo wouldn't.

He bent over and kissed Retta's ashen forehead and whispered a sparse prayer, then glided the back of his rough hand down her cheek and said a final goodbye. I watched as Alonzo hobbled out the door and on to one of his monthly tears around town.

"Retta," I whispered urgently, going back to her side. The old woman fluttered her eyelids, then opened them. She raised a crooked finger and I drew closer.

"It's me, Retta."

"Iffin that's my prettiest petunia"—she coughed weakly—"fetch me my glasses, child."

I searched the one-room cabin and found them under fabric

stacked up on a chair. "Here, Retta, let me help." I put them on her, making sure they didn't pinch her ears or nose.

"Child, get me the dress in my chest over there." She motioned toward a large trunk.

"Retta, you need to rest in your gown—"

She shook her head. "It's 'portant I dress."

"Yes, ma'am." I opened the lid and pulled out a deep-burgundy velvet dress and held it up.

"That's it," she said hoarsely. "Help me into it, child?"

I wondered why Retta would want to wear this now, but I didn't want to upset her by questioning her. "Yes, ma'am." I sat Retta up in the bed and carefully dressed her. The dress was beautiful with long sleeves, a smocked bodice, and a fancy sash. I buttoned up the back, admiring the twelve tiny buttons covered in velvet. "Sure is pretty on you," I said, tying the sash.

"Sewed this 'un to kick up my heels with the angels," Retta said as I gently laid her back on the bed.

My eyes blurred, and I took her hands in mine, looked into her weak, red eyes, and said, "It's a fine dress you sewed, Retta. *Beautiful.*" My voice broke and a sob slipped out. "This workmanship is better than any I've seen in magazine advertisements for store-bought, Retta."

She met my eyes. "Don't be sad, child. Ain't long for this world, but I can leave it now, knowing you're safe an' ya have a home." She swallowed hard to catch her breath. "Signed over my deed to Alonzo and tol' him you're to always have a place here. He's promised to honor my wishes and pass the deed on to you when you come of age to own real proper-tee." She swallowed the last word.

The candles flickered, and the light chased webbed shadows around the darkened cabin. "Retta, thank you, but don't say such. You have to get stronger," I whispered, looking around for anything to comfort her. "Want some tea? Can I read to you?"

She lifted a weak, toothless grin. "I still like mine best. Fetch it for me, child, like your sweet mama always did."

"Yes, ma'am." I picked up Retta's Bible from the table, dragged a chair over to her bed, and read.

The frontier nurse slipped back in and checked Retta's pulse as I waited across the room. The nurse looked at me and sadly shook her head. "I'll be going on to my other patients. There's a family in the next holler that's been struck with the fevers, and another whose children have come down with the worms. Are you okay to sit with her, Honey?" Amara asked.

I looked back over her shoulder at a frail Retta swathed in her fine funeral dress and choked out a *yes*.

"Just keep her comfortable and warm," she said kindly as I followed her onto the porch, the damp of fog and darkness cloaking the tiny cabin.

"I will. Obliged, Amara."

"The Smiths said you were looking for a ride to the city?" Amara asked.

"I need to visit my parents in La Grange and Pewee Valley prisons."

She looked at me strangely.

"I need to see them again. I have money—"

"Happy to have the company. I'll be leaving next Saturday for Louisville at dawn. Meet me at my cabin."

"Much obliged."

She squeezed my shoulder. "I'm sorry about Miss Adams. We're in short supply of medicine and medical help here," the tired young woman said. "Makes it damn difficult with the poor diets most elderly are keeping in these hills. It won't be long now. I'll check back in tonight. She's to be buried with her folks alongside her sister at their old homestead cemetery down the trail, her nephew said. Just keep her comfortable. My best to you, Honey. I'm very sorry."

I squeezed out a thank-you.

Then she was off with her lantern and bag, her tall nurse's cap casting a monstrous shadow across the yard.

Back inside, I put the kettle on to brew sassafras tea, one of

Retta's favorites, then pulled out her bedpig and freshened it with steaming water. Smoothing down the quilt, I gently tucked her in. "You warm enough, Retta? Can I get you another cover?"

"Drink, child," she replied, her voice gravelly.

I offered Retta a few sips of tea, then read some of the marked Scriptures from her Bible for several hours, peeking over the book in between pages.

Retta suddenly reached for my hand and swallowed hard. "Child, I–I want you to have my Bible. I—" She was having trouble breathing now. "I tol' 'Lonzo it's yours."

"I love you, Retta." I kissed her hand.

"It was…a'might easy…lovin' you," Retta rasped and her eyelids closed one last time.

I leaned over and whispered, "Retta." I patted her hand and rubbed briskly. "Don't go."

She moaned and took two rattled breaths, then spent one last.

"Don't die." I gripped her limp, graying hand, pressed it to my damp cheek. "Please don't leave me, Retta."

Fifteen

Outside, blustery weather pushed over the old mountains and licked at the weather-beaten boards as I covered Retta's lifeless body with her quilt.

I walked out onto the porch and lifted up my sorrows to the mourning winds, my heart heavy, shattered in grief, the loneliness unbearable, smothering.

Retta had been as close as kin, what remained of any family I had left. A hope that Retta would replace the loss of my parents and help the healing was now lost to the old lands. I tightened my bruise-colored hands over the splintered porch rail, leaned over, and wailed to the trees, cried for dear Retta and my family taken from me.

From the stall, Junia hawed and kicked at her door, raring to break free and see me. Exhausted, I straightened and walked over, pressed my cheek against her neck and stroked her muzzle. Junia whisked out a trembling bray. She was all I had left now, and her big solemn eyes and worrisome ramblings told me the girl knew we only had each other.

Pennie jumped up onto the ledge of the Dutch door, purring, butting her head against Junia's face, and the ol' mule let her. I was surprised how quickly their friendship had developed but grateful the cat consoled her.

I turned to Retta's darkened cabin, the nightfall crowning the hard day and harder times sweeping in. "We have to go down the mountain and find Alonzo," I said, saddling Junia.

When I got to his tiny cabin five minutes later, it was empty and he was nowhere to be found. I banged on the door one last time, my fist darkening from my anger and dismay.

A curse slipped off my lips. I headed back to Retta's, not knowing a lick about burials or funerals but reckoning it was up to me to handle it all. At the table I rummaged through the lining of my coat and pulled out the bills, then folded them into my pocket.

Nurse Amara slipped in later to let me know she'd send the funeral wagon up tomorrow afternoon, then gave solemn condolences before wearily going on to her next patients.

In the glow of candlelight, I sat and read Retta's Bible, praying for her, and for me and my folk, dozing off as the pulls and sighs of the long night shifted into the fatter hours of slumber.

Several times, I jerked awake thinking I heard someone crying. Rubbing tired eyes, I found my lashes wet. It weren't long till my lids grew heavy again, my tears dried, and the leaving hours of night called me back asleep.

The next morning, Junia neighed outside and I raised my head from the table. Sunrise filtered through the windows and skated in between the cracks of ol' weathered boards, haloing over Retta's bed of eternal slumber.

I sat at the table, thinking. If I went to town and told folk of her passing, it could bring the law down on me. And without Retta, I would surely be sent to the House of Reform. But Retta deserved to have her friends pay their respects. I was torn and tapped the worrisome thoughts onto the table.

As Amara promised, the funeral wagon arrived a little past noon and the men carefully placed Retta in a pine coffin.

I grabbed my gloves and Retta's Bible, looked around one last time and quietly closed the door. Following the four men in the wagon, we rode toward Retta's family cemetery.

The men dug hard and fast, and after they lowered the cheap pine box into the ground and filled the hole with dirt, one of them, a young colored man, came over and removed his cap.

"Ma'am, I'm Leon Payne. Me and the fellers wondered if there was anyone other than you?" He pulled out a handkerchief and wiped the sweat from his brow, looking around the small graveyard.

I'd hoped her nephew would come, but the ornery man had gone on a tear. I wondered if Amara had published the news to others. It was as if the world didn't know Loretta Adeline Adams existed, scratched out a life to make a difference—a talented seamstress to many in these hills, mother to her nephew, nanny to me, and loyal friend. She deserved better for her ninety-two years of service to others, and the guilt of not letting others know last night weighed heavily on my heart.

Talk traveled fast in the small town, and even faster when it was bad news. I prayed Retta would forgive me for not telling folk, but I had to try to keep myself from going to prison. Somehow, I had to get out of the ugly grip the state held on me, and if this allowed me more time, it meant another day of freedom.

"Ma'am, is there no one else?" Mr. Payne inquired again. "I'm happy to wait. Send one of the fellers into town to let the townsfolk know about her burial so they can come out and pay their respects."

"No, sir, just me. And she asked for a private burial," I lied. Pulling out money, I passed him fifteen dollars for their labor and another ten for the box and added four more dollars. "Is this enough, sir?"

"Sure is, thanks." He pocketed the money and said, "I sometimes ride a ministry circuit. I'd be honored to say a prayer, lift Miss Adams up into her Heavenly Father's arms."

"Much obliged, Mr. Payne." I turned one last time, searching past the smattering of crumbly headstones for him. Likely, Alonzo was passed out in his bed, or a town alley.

The men gathered around the fresh-dug grave and took off their caps and bowed their heads as Mr. Payne recited Corinthians 15:51–57. "'Death is swallowed up in victory... O death, where is thy sting? O grave, where is thy victory?'"

Mr. Payne gave a fine eulogy, one that honored Retta, and I was grateful. When the man finished, he sang a dirge, slow and quiet. The other three men joined in, lifting the sweet, mournful song into the hills.

I peered up to the blue endless skies and mouthed, *Don't leave me, Retta, Don't go.*

After the song, Mr. Payne came over and laid a comforting hand on my shoulder. The other men passed in front of me, dropping whispered condolences.

When they were gone, I stood alone over her fresh grave. "Retta, your prettiest petunia will always miss and love you. Thank you for reading to me every day when I was little, for your love." I kneeled down. "Mama, Papa, I miss you. Come home soon. *Come home, I need you.*" I struck a fist to the earth, delivering my demand. Time passed, shadows stretched longer as my grief grew and sat lodged like a live stone in my throat that my sobs couldn't loosen.

In a while, Junia called out softly. I looked out to the ancient hills and said one last prayer, then scooped up a handful of the Kentucky soil and tossed it across her grave. "I love you, Retta. Go dance with your angels."

Sixteen

Back at Retta's, I fed Pennie on the porch, then went inside and collected the linens. After I'd washed them, I tidied the home, trying to stay busy, trying to forget that for the first time in my life, I was all alone. They were all gone now, and the thought gnawed at me and brought on a fresh sheet of tears.

Retta's home was a fine one nestled here up on a ridge. My grandparents' cabin was in the dark holler surrounded by the rotted breaths of dampness, moss, and lichen. But I ached for home from time to time—ached for the loving family who had driven out the darkness with light.

I was grateful Retta had seen fit to share her home with me, told Alonzo to let me stay. I wiped down the worn table, dusted the wobbly legs, smiling at the wedge of pine Retta had used to prop it up. Straightening the split-bottom chairs, I ran my hands across the woven seats Retta had painstakingly made from bark strips. I picked up her worn cobbler's apron, admired the lace and tight stitches, pressed it to my face. How many times had I sat at her feet, watching her fashion one thing or another? I stared at a small photograph of us sitting on her nightstand. I was seven, standing beside Retta on the porch in a dress she'd sewn for me. I studied her big, wide grin and soft, comforting arms around me.

Neatly, I folded the apron and hung it over her chair. The grief spilled out again. How I missed her! I slowly scanned the room, soaking up the details. Retta had left her love, her life, and the small cabin drew breath from it in her homespun curtains, doilies, hanging woven baskets, and quilts.

I pulled an ol' hanging copper teapot off its hook. It was so heavy, it slipped out of my grip and crashed to the floor, spilling out silver dollars. Surprised, I scooped them up, dropping the coins back into their container. Lifting one up to the light, I studied the sitting Liberty gazing off in the distance, rubbed the date, and did my arithmetic. I picked up another coin and then several more, looking at the year on each. All were stamped 1861. Retta's birth year. Had her papa brought these from Texas and been saving them for his daughter?

I fed the last silver dollar back into the teapot and placed it on the table. I didn't know how much a gravestone would cost, but surely with the coins and my money inside my coat, Retta would get a fine marker. Maybe even one with a pretty angel looking down on her.

When I was through cleaning, I sat down on Retta's stripped mattress and stared out the window, the March day unusually warm. Several turkeys strutted into the yard. Clean sheets hung on the clothesline, rippling in the afternoon breezes. Somewhere in the hills, a train whistle sounded two blows.

It was as if the world would not pause for anything, not even for death. I pulled open the drawer on her nightstand and saw Mama's last letter to her, asking her to take guardianship of me, and I found myself growing fearful.

What would happen to me now? I pressed a knuckle to my mouth. Would the state come and shackle me, throw me into the House of Reform once news of her death spread?

Judge Norton's face flashed across my mind, and a fear clutched hold. I jumped up and escaped outside, struggling for breath, shaking. In sixteen months, I would be eighteen. *Could I stay hidden in these hills for that long?*

Afraid to leave Retta's, I fretted the next morning about the judge, hoping no one would ask about her. I struggled several times with announcing the news, or keeping quiet about the burial. My mind went to the hearing, and I thought about Retta sassing the judge. Thought about how close I came to being shipped over to the Leslie County social worker who would throw me into prison in a blink. *Surely, Retta would rather see me safe.*

The kettle whistled, and I poured a cup of tea. After a bit, I looked over on Retta's shelf lined with the children's books she had bought me when I was little. I pulled them down, thinking of my collection at home. They were my favorite reads that always brought a great comfort no matter how old I was. I pored over the illustrations, sipped on the verses. Soon, I was safe, back in Retta's embrace, home and in Mama's arms, reading about Mei Li and the adventures of *The ABC Bunny.*

I jumped up when I heard the knock, almost kicking over my chair. I'd been so lost in the storybooks, I hadn't heard Junia's warnings.

Again, two more knocks and a third, more loud and urgent.

Slowly, I cracked open the door, and a man and woman in tattered clothes greeted me. The woman's coat was threadbare, and the man wore none, but a knitted cap. I searched for their mount and couldn't find one. Red mud clung to their shoes, and they looked like they'd walked a long way.

"We're here to speak with ya, ma'am, 'bout Miss Adams," the man said.

"Come in," I said, somewhat shaken but relieved it wasn't the law, rushing over to the table and pulling on my gloves. I glanced back over my shoulder. "I have a nice fire going."

The man nodded, stepped over the threshold, and the woman followed, her eyes downcast as she entered the home.

Amara must've published the news. "If you're here to pay your respects, I can show you Retta's grave, Mr. and Mrs. uh—"

The man removed his hat and cleared his throat. "Ma'am, Miss Lovett, I'm Howie Spencer, and this is Mrs. Spencer."

I searched their eyes, but neither would meet mine.

Mr. Spencer pulled out a paper. "We own this place now." He held the document up to me, and I chewed over the legal words, my heart pounding in my ears.

Staggering back, I gripped the table for support.

"'Lonzo sold it to us yesterday," Mr. Spencer said into his wife's nod.

The couple looked like they didn't have two nickels to rub together, much less money for this tract of land and a home.

"We done went to the county clerk, recorded the new deed today. Got 'Lonzo's signature notarized all legal. Real sorry, ma'am, 'bout Miss Adams passing and all."

His wife stared down at her feet, bobbing her head in testament, sneaking glances at me.

A new grief latched on and shook, and I lifted a glove to my mouth in surprise and anguish.

Mrs. Spencer drew her eyes to my bare feet. Alarmed by my color, she gasped and recoiled, taking several steps back.

"Well, er, good day, ma'am," Mr. Spencer said, sneaking glances, too. Putting back on his cap, he took his wife by the arm. "Jus' thought we'd tell ya we's taking possession on Monday. That'd be Monday at noon, ma'am." He darted his eyes greedily around the room, taking stock of his new possessions, then hurried out the door and right past Alonzo without a greeting.

Alonzo stood there under a half-broke thorned locust, head buried in his hands.

I ran over to him. "Is it true? Alonzo, is it true? Alonzo, please, tell me it's not..." I shook the small man's shoulders. "Dammit, tell me!"

He raised his ruddy face and nodded tearfully. "I'm sorry, Honey. Lawsy, I'm so sorry, child. W-what have I done? Lord... Dear Auntie, I'm sorry. Please forgive me. Didn't mean to disrespect your wishes, but I sorely needed the money." He whimpered, folded his hands in prayer, and looked up to the heavens. "Please forgive me, Heavenly Father." He hiccupped and wiped his nose on the back of a calloused, dirt-stained hand. "Lord knows I tried to rustle up what I needed. Even sold off my two chickens, but it weren't never enough. My ol' wagon down the hill an' that nag of mine wouldn't fetch nearly enough. Sorely needed the money to pay off debts, buy some victuals an' stuff."

"*Stuff*. You done went and pissed your aunt's home away. My home! Damn you, Alonzo." Furious, I stared at the man blubbering in front of me. "Dammit."

"*Please, please…*" He reached for my arm. "Honey, can you forgive me?"

I slapped his hands away and backed up. "I've lost everything, Alonzo, everything," I spat out. "And now I could go to prison because of it. *You*." Angry tears blurred my eyes, and I swiped them away on my scratchy knit glove.

"Please, Honey. Please jus' give me your forgiveness an' show mercy on my poor, wretched soul."

"How dare you ask when you didn't show it for her?" I said through gritted teeth.

He lowered his head. "Please jus' understand. Honey, forgive me."

Tired, disgusted, I stared at him hard, the anger draining me, and because I knew ol' Retta would, I patted his back and choked out a weary *yes*, gulping down more hot tears. The ol' man sobbed into my shoulders, reeking from his last night's tear.

"Let's get you inside, Alonzo." I helped him into the cabin like I'd seen Retta do so many times before.

I made coffee and a quick dinner, trying to sober Alonzo up. The man was ashamed and could barely meet my eyes as he shoveled down the bowl of beans, mopping up the last juices with a roll.

Finally, I broke the silence. "Retta was all I had, Alonzo."

"When my sweet bride passed twenty-four years ago, Auntie took care of me." He dipped his bread again in the bowl.

I looked out the window. "Will you marry again?" I asked quietly. "Retta always hoped you would."

He pushed the bowl aside, rubbed his hand tiredly over several weeks' worth of whiskers and thought a minute. "I ain't through grieving her jus' yet, Honey. She's worthy of more. A lifetime." Alonzo's agony rested on his slumped shoulders.

I let the stillness wrap the air as we sipped from our cups, remembering my own grief, and now the fresh grief of losing another, and knew he was right.

Retta told me once that Alonzo's wife, Lily, had been a midwife. She was riding home during a night of heavy rains when her buggy's wheel broke off as she crossed the creek. They found her body several miles downstream. Alonzo never forgave himself because he was working late and couldn't take her to deliver the baby.

"Alonzo, it hurts to lose the last of Retta like this." I glanced around the room.

"What can we do?" he asked.

"Fetch your horse and wagon, and I'll start packing Retta's belongings so you can take it all down to your cabin. That way we won't be losing everything of Retta's." With his home being so close, I knew it wouldn't take him long.

Alonzo nodded and gulped down the last of his coffee. "Yes, we'll save what we can of Auntie's. Real sorry I sold the home, Honey. Well, I don't think there will be room to take the beds, but you're welcome to a pallet on my cabin floor if you like."

"I'm going back to my grandparents' place," I said, the gloom filling me, the loneliness pressing in.

"As you wish." He shot up from his chair. "You be sure an' keep whatever heirlooms you like."

I nodded somberly. The copper teapot was still on the table, and I was mindful to hide the money from Alonzo and save it for Retta's marker.

I packed the pannier with my books Retta had bought for me over the years, along with the Bible she passed on, then folded her quilts and fabric, stacking them by the door for Alonzo to pick up later.

Sunlight streamed through the curtains, bouncing off the two delicate gold-trimmed, white teacups as I wrapped them in old newspaper. Her papa had carried them and his Bible from Texas where he'd been a preacher before settling his family here in 1857. She never once fussed about me drinking from them, even though my tiny hands were clumsy when I was toddling about. I clutched them to my chest, remembering, then packed them carefully inside my pannier.

I opened the door and leaned against the jamb and inhaled fresh pine air. I would go back to the holler where Mama grew up and my family settled, where my feet were first planted and where I could be away from the law.

It was all I had now.

Seventeen

I had just finished sweeping the floor when Junia bawled several warnings. I swallowed hard, then parted the curtain and dared to peek out Retta's window. With everything happening, I'd forgotten about my dinner invitation to Pearl.

"Come in." I opened the door, and we stood there for a long moment, looking at each other but not saying a word, not being able to hide my sadness. Finally, I uttered, "I'm sorry I can't offer you anything. I'm on my way back to my homestead. Retta passed on Wednesday," I blurted out, knowing it would be stacking another lie onto our new friendship if she didn't hear it from me first.

"Oh, I'm sorry, Honey. How dreadful!" She set down the bottle of blackberry wine she'd brought and gave me a small hug.

"This place was sold, and I'm just packing up the last of it." I looked around the almost empty room, satisfied that Alonzo had managed to get everything but my bed and the table down to his cabin. I folded my quilt and hugged it in my arms along with some of Retta's old scarves.

"What will you do?" Pearl asked, worried.

"I need to get over to my grandparents' place for a while."

"Let me help. There's a new relief ranger staying over at the base camp for my lookout replacement. He said I could take an extra day off if I wanted. Happy to keep you company," Pearl said with a comforting smile.

"That would be nice, thanks, Pearl. I could use the company about now." I was warmed by this new friendship. And I could feel the grief halved and the loneliness lifting from my heavy heart as I squeezed her hand in gratitude.

"I can stay as long as you like," she offered. "My relief man is at the base and won't go anywhere till I return."

"I'd like that. And I remember when the lookouts had to share the tower with their reliefs when they had time off. They finally built the base cab a couple of miles away from you a few years ago."

"I'm glad no one is sleeping in my bed or going through my things while I'm gone. Had enough of that with whoever broke in. And I think my relief wants to spend extra time with his girl, because when I rode Pie over there to tell him I was leaving, I saw one playing house. Helping him hang his wash on the line. And the man didn't look like he was in any hurry to leave." She grinned and lifted the pile from my arms, her charm bracelet tinkling in the shaft of a sunbeam. "Here, Honey, let me carry that."

I picked up the photograph of Retta and me and stood at the threshold looking around one final time. Pearl came over and softly shut the door. Taking me by the hand, she walked me out into the yard.

Retta's cat cried and circled me, mewing for her mistress. "You best come with us," I told Pennie. "You'd only be supper for a fox or coyote if you stay." After I mounted, Pearl lifted the little cat into my arms. At first, I thought Junia might fuss, but she just shook her head and snorted.

We rode down the path, winding around the trails into the forest, both of us quiet in our thoughts. I inhaled and took a deep breath.

"What was Retta like?" Pearl finally spoke.

I smiled, remembering how much unlike the ol' woman was from everyone else. "Retta was something else." I recalled my fond memories, forgetting the sad and troubling ones.

"Mama saved my beautiful layette Retta sewed me," I told Pearl. "Retta had ordered expensive satin to make my gown and matching jacket and hat. She embroidered it and added lace to all the pieces, even my bloomers. Always dressing me up like I was her dolly."

"Because you were her *favorite* doll baby and the one she loved," Pearl said.

I told Pearl about Judge Norton's early layette set that Retta sewed, and the ol' woman's boldness in the courtroom and how she'd sassed the judge.

"Oh, Pearl, I was so frightened that she was going to get us both thrown in jail."

"I wish I could've seen her!"

We both fell into a fit of giggles, nearly falling off our mounts as I recounted all of it. I scratched Pennie's head and readjusted her on the saddle as my laughter finally stilled.

Soon, we arrived at my cabin with me still chattering away, my nerves lit from the past week, the worry of facing court again heavily on my mind.

Pearl climbed down Pie, reached for the cat, and said, "You sure have some wonderful memories."

"Yes, I really do." And I was grateful she'd encouraged me to share them.

We unpacked and carried my belongings inside.

"Want to stay for supper?" I asked.

"Only if you sit and let me cook it."

"I'd be obliged, Pearl."

"I'll feed the mounts and Pennie and be back in a minute," she said, picking up Pennie and nuzzling the cat's tiny head with her chin. "Let's get you fed, sweet girl."

An hour later, Pearl raised a second glass of her blackberry wine over our supper of potato soup and fried cornmeal mush. "To Miss Retta." She dipped her spoon into a bowl and asked, "Will you stay here?"

"I want to, but"—I grimaced—"the law might not let me

once they find out Retta has passed. As easy as that freedom came, it has been quickly stripped away."

"Laws written by men don't protect females much." Pearl sighed.

It was the first time I thought about it, and I suddenly realized it was true, remembering Retta's comment in the courtroom about the men and my *best interest*.

I picked up my spoon, played with my soup. "Just sixteen months until I'm legally an adult, according to the law. But if the children's prison or that social worker gets ahold of me, well, they can keep me another three years on top of that."

"You wouldn't get out till you're twenty-one! We can't let that horrid woman try again. Can't you just stay hidden here?"

"I have a little money saved, but I'm going to need to find work," I said, setting down my spoon, worrying the thought.

"What type of work?"

I thought about Bonnie Powell, spending long shifts in the mine, crawling across hard rock and smothered by dampness and rock dust. "Not many jobs around these parts but coal mining."

"I've seen a few female miners around."

"Bonnie Powell works it. She said the men don't like women working down there with them though. They claim the females are trying to steal their paychecks, and their wives claim the women are trying to steal their men. But all the female miners want is the same chance as the men, to keep a dry roof over their heads and food on their table for their little ones."

Pearl wrinkled her nose. "Surely there's something else."

"I've got to get work and support myself, have enough money to keep this place up. It's the only thing that can keep me from the children's prison." I looked around the cabin and spotted the pile of books I brought from Retta's. She'd fussed about the books, but like Mama, she made sure I had as many as I wanted.

For a moment, I shut my eyes and felt both Mama and Retta at my side, their gentle hands on my shoulders. Their presence was so strong that I jumped up, startling Pearl.

"What is it?" Pearl asked, flying to my side.

"Books, Pearl! The books." I laughed. The realization that the librarian job might still be open struck hope. "The library is hiring an assistant outreach librarian and needs a Pack Horse librarian. Maybe I can see if the job's still open."

"It would be perfect," Pearl admitted, excited for me. "You were made for the job."

"It would keep me in the hills and away from the law's prying eyes. Steady work and weekends off."

"Oh, maybe we could get together my next weekend off! I can have you up at the cab for dinner, dancing, and records. It will lift our spirits. We'll have a pajama party! It's been a while since I've had one. Let's do that, Honey. My next weekend off is April 11."

"Never had one, but I've read about the parties and seen pictures in the magazines. I'll bring the books," I offered, then quieted, a little embarrassed, wondering exactly one did at a pajama party, hoping she didn't think of me as too backwards.

"Books and magazines sound dreamy," she said.

It did sound dreamy and reminded me of the Norman Rockwell painting I'd seen in *The Post*. The one that showed three pretty girls dressed in frilly, colorful dresses off for a fun day on the town. A fun party was something I'd only read about. To be able to live it lifted my spirits. To escape, feel the freedoms of my young life, be sixteen for a moment even, an hour, a day, would be a respite like no other. Still, I wondered if any of that would happen, if the law found out I'd lost my guardian.

"Mother is sending me a package next week," she said. "She ordered me some Avon, and we'll do your nails, if you like."

"I remember Mama curling my hair with strips of fabric. When it dried, she'd brush them out into soft ringlets." I looked around, a flood of sadness coming over me, longing for them. The books we shared around the woodstove, our evenings on the porch. I pushed away my bowl, stood, and walked over to the window, playing with the soft folds of fabric Mama had sewed.

Pearl came up behind me and touched my shoulder.

"I miss them all so much," I whispered, the anguish nearly suffocating the strained words, the rawness of fresh grief over Retta's death weighted like rock on my heart. I took a deep breath. "Maybe I can get the librarian job. Having it would be in many ways like having my mama here. Having us both here and *free*."

Eighteen

We talked on the porch until the night creatures' chorals descended into the darkness, swallowing our sleepy voices.

When I climbed down from the loft in the morning, Pearl's bed was neatly made and she was gone. A loaf of fresh bread wrapped in a tea cloth rested on the table. After I ate, I dressed quickly, then hurried to town. Passing the Company store, I glimpsed a few women chatting in front of the building, but mostly the town was quiet for a Monday morning. I nudged Junia into the back parking lot of the library. Inside, I scanned the bulletin board and whisked out a breath, relieved to see the post. I snatched the job position off and went to find Miss Foster. When I learned she was out on an errand, Mrs. Martin invited me to wait for her at a table, saying Miss Foster had to approve any hiring. She left to help a patron check out material.

With shaky hands, I read the advertisement again, smoothing out the wrinkled flyer.

WANTED, ASSISTANT OUTREACH LIBRARIAN
We have an opening for a respectable, steady, young female rider to deliver books and reading material in Knott County. Weekends off. Pay: $98 per month. Reply to Eula Foster.

Ninety-eight dollars. More than enough to keep food in the belly and me away from the watchful eyes of the law. I stared at the post and reread it again.

Worried, I picked up a magazine and tried to scan an article, but my eyes were drawn back to the door and windows. An hour later, Miss Foster came back and I blurted out her name. The librarian led me to her office, a finger to her lip, reminding me to stay quiet. Inside, Miss Foster said, "What can I help you with today, Honey?"

"Ma'am, is the position still open?" I pressed my gloved hands together and held up the flyer. "This one, ma'am."

"Hmm, let's see." She moved some paperwork around on her desk, pushed a stack of books aside. "I'm not sure. I approved one hire after Evelyn Scott's oldest girl expressed interest and was going to fill out the application, but I don't know if she's done so. Have a seat, Honey," she invited warmly, "and I'll go ask one of our librarians if they've seen any paperwork come through."

I sat down and wrung my hands in my lap, staring at the closed door. The cramped office closed in on me, and I worried the threads of fabric on my gloves until I unraveled more string, making a mess of Mama's fine needlework.

When Miss Foster finally returned, I couldn't help but jump up. "Ma'am?"

She stared at me a moment, then wagged her head and sat down.

Slowly, I sank back into my chair. The librarian went on. "It's the darnedest thing, but Mrs. Martin interviewed the girl just yesterday and found out she didn't own a mount and had never ridden before, which won't do for this job. No, it will not do." She seemed to puzzle over the matter.

No, I knew it wouldn't, and I wagged my head in agreement, waiting a few seconds before I spoke. "Ma'am, I know I could do a good job if you hire me. Junia knows the paths, and I've rode the book routes with Mama many times while she dropped off the reading materials. Please give me a chance, and I'll work hard for you and the patrons. Just like my mama did." A desperation braided the words, squeezing out my plea.

"Do you have your mother's permission?"

"Mama agrees," I lied, knowing she would if she knew about the job.

"Let me go check further with the other librarians. I recall Ella King inquiring about the position. Mr. King died in the mine accident in February, so we'd need to consider her first, you understand."

"Yes, ma'am," I said, solemn.

The librarian stood. "I'll be back shortly."

I felt the air leave as she left the room, and again my hands became restless inside the gloves.

Minutes later she swept back into her office. "Honey, Ella is moving over to Jackson to be with her parents. There was another applicant, an English woman who settled here last winter. But our library chairs would never let a foreigner take food off the table of a Kentucky woman."

I nodded, knowing the Pack Horse Library Project began as a way to put the poor Kentucky women to work, and there were still too many hungry folk in these pockets desperate for jobs.

Eula's eyes grew sad and took on a distance. Then she picked up the pen, tapped a paper, and said in a grave, watery voice, "We must always, *always* remember Caroline Barnes...what those from *far off* did."

"Yes, ma'am." I recalled Mama mentioning Mrs. Barnes many times, how hunger killed more Kentucky hillfolk than any deadly influenza. The sickly mama had staggered nine miles into town to save her twelve babies from starvation only to die of the pellagra in the street. Many lives were lost, Mama'd said, and while the poor folk here died from lack of food, the rich from far off got fatter.

I leaned in close and whispered, "Miss Foster, I *need* this job."

She pulled herself from her thoughts, set down the pen, and

moved papers around, straightening her desk. "If you have time to wait, Honey, I'll get your paperwork together, and we'll make it official. We sorely need an outreach librarian again, and we've gotten in enough funds to revive our little Pack Horse librarian project that ended here in '43. There are still inaccessible families up there, and others who just can't make it down to our borrowing branch."

"Yes, ma'am, I can wait. Much obliged, Miss Foster. Junia will be happy to return to her routes," I chattered, my excitement nearly shaking the picture frames off her walls.

"Grab something to read outside, and when I collect all the paperwork, I'll call for you."

Twenty minutes later, she invited me back in. After I filled out the paperwork, she handed me a list of the names of patrons on my route and their addresses.

"You can start tomorrow if you'd like," the librarian said, pleased.

"Yes, ma'am, I'd like that a whole lot."

"Your outpost that houses the reading materials will be the same as your mama's, the boarded-up church down by the creek. It's still standing."

"Yes, ma'am, I remember." I thanked her several more times.

"Paychecks will arrive at your outpost, and you can cash them at the bank or the Company store. Assistant Librarian Oren Taft will get your reading material out on Tuesday mornings. Oh, weekends off, but should you find you can't cover the route on a certain day, you can make it up on those days off. Just leave a note for Oren to give to me. Your only duty is to get the reading material into the hands of *anyone* wanting it."

Relieved, I inhaled the scent of book-and-paper-soaked air. Bringing the written word to others would keep me free.

"Thank you for your service, Honey. It'll be a godsend around here," she said and sounded like she meant it. She picked up something from her desk, then pinned the official name tag onto my coat and gave me back the flyer from the bulletin board. I looked down at my name and the title she'd typed out neat and correctly.

HONEY LOVETT
ASSISTANT OUTREACH LIBRARIAN

A door jingle announced my arrival at the Company store, rattling the Coca-Cola sign that showed a happy young girl reading a book on the floor and raising the bottle to remind folk to *Serve Coke at Home.* Another advertisement hung above the Champion mechanical kiddie ride showing a beaming Santa Claus toasting the holidays with his cola. Next to the dark-brown horse, a man fed coins into a cigarette machine while a young'un dropped money into a red bubble-glass gumball stand.

I made my way around the rack of bib overalls, coal miners' britches, and shirts and stepped around a group of huddled men discussing the latest news, weather, and work, their murmurs lifting into wisps of cigarette smoke. I found a basket of apples beside the bread rack and egg bin, and then inspected several and picked the shiniest.

Up at the cash register, I set the fruit on the counter. A boy about my age picked it up, sneaking glances at my name tag. "Honey Lovett, huh? Don't believe I've heard the name. You from these parts?" He pulled out a tiny brown sack from underneath the counter to bag the apple.

I was sure he was someone I hadn't seen before, yet he looked familiar. "My mama, Cussy Carter, was a book woman for the Pack Horse Library Project, and my grandpa Elijah was a miner."

His eyes widened. "My gramps worked with Elijah Carter! Yours saved his life in the mining accident back in '36. Gramps gave away your mama, at her wedding to, uh—" He snapped a finger, trying to remember. "She was the Pack Horse librarian and he—"

"Jackson Lovett, that's my papa," I said, surprised, remembering my folk talking about Mr. Moore.

"Good folks, my family always said. Are you taking over your mama's government route?" He pointed the apple to my name tag.

My cheeks warmed, and I turned away, digging into my pockets, fumbling for a coin with my awkward gloves on. I pulled one off to grip the money. "Yes, and the WPA no longer funds it, but the library is going to revive the service and pay me wages." I lit a shy smile and plunked down a coin, snatching my arms to my side, wanting to get out of there before I ruined it all with my loud-talking blue hands.

His eyes were friendly, and he didn't seem to notice. "I'm Francis Moore from Straight Creek. My folks moved here last year to be closer to kin and get work. I'll have to tell Mama to sign up for the route."

"I'm happy to have you on the route. *Her*." I blushed even deeper and felt the heat traveling over every inch of me.

He inspected the apple, then slipped it into a bag and handed it to me, pushing the nickel back toward me. "The Company can't sell this one. It has a bruise." His eyes teased.

"Much obliged. My mule will appreciate it," I told him, pocketing the nickel and sneaking in a few more glances of him.

"See you, Honey." He came around the counter and held open the door.

I practically skipped out, lighthearted as I was, but stumbled on busted concrete and fell awkward against him.

Francis caught me, and I straightened and backed away, nearly falling toward him again from the worn, crumbly pavement in front of the store. Though I always knew to be careful on the old town sidewalks, it was like my feet suddenly had a mind of their own and wanted to ruin my graceful departure.

"Need me to walk you over to your mule?" he asked, pleasant enough.

Again, I could feel the warmth creeping into my face. "No,

uh, it's just that this sidewalk has gotten a lot worse." I lifted up the small bag with the apple. "Obliged. See you later, Francis." I moved away before my feet could betray me again.

Francis stuffed his hands into the pockets of his britches and watched me a moment, his face ripened with concern, amusement, and other strange, inviting curiosities.

I cast my eyes downward and hurried over to Junia, not looking back, dare I stumble again or, worse, see his face change. I'd witnessed that change to an uninviting or fearful look in many people over the years when their eyes fell on Mama or caught sight of my hands.

I took out a pocketknife from the pannier and sliced the apple for Junia. The ol' girl ate while I talked about the cute boy I'd just met. "Oh, I acted a fool," I whispered. "A *clumsy* fool. But he had the most handsome face," I told her.

Junia snorted, her signal that she was done with the apple and done with my chatter.

Once we were safe in the woods, I jumped down, grabbed the flyer, and let out several hoots, twirling in circles.

Junia hee-hawed into my cheers and flopped her ears, content. Twice, I kissed her on the soft muzzle and scratched her limp ears.

"Can you believe it, Junia?" I kissed her again. "They're going to pay *me* to deliver my favorite thing—books. Books!" For the first time in days, a hope and happiness latched onto my heart, and I laughed and spun around until I was dizzy, drunk from the new job and, more, meeting a boy.

I spun wildly around once more, my head tilted upward, arms outstretched toward ancient pines, breathing in the scents of their unbridled growth and freedom until Junia snorted an annoyed warning and bumped me with her long pokey nose, making me fall onto the leaf-rotted path on my knees.

When I arrived back at my cabin, I was surprised to find Devil John, Carson, and Mr. Morgan sitting on the porch. Uneasy, I slid down off the mule, circled around a talkative Pennie, and pulled Junia past their mounts over into the stall. Carrying my bag up to the porch, I looked at the men, their faces pinched with what I could see was worriment. And I knew that worriment was dropping down on *me*.

"Mr. Morgan." I sat down my satchel. "Why are you here?"

"Hello, Honey." The men stood, and Mr. Morgan pointed a finger at me. "As your court-appointed lawyer, I'm here about you today. About your guardian passing. John was gracious enough to accompany me to your home."

I winced.

"I'm sure sorry to hear about Miss Adams, and I'm sorry for what this might mean for you." He frowned.

Carson and Devil John murmured their condolences.

The whole town knew about Retta, and I'd been a fool to think I could hide her burial and stay hidden. I swallowed hard, darting my eyes between the men. "Yes, sir."

"Without a proper guardian, the judge could easily make you a ward of the state," Mr. Morgan said. "Send you to the House of Reform."

"What can I do?" I asked, the panic gnawing at my belly as I peeled off the gloves and stuffed them inside a coat pocket, the fright staining my hands.

A silence filled the forest but it was deafening like tree frogs lifting their chorus in the darkness.

Devil John leaned toward me. "Might have figured another way to keep you safe." He nudged Carson's arm with his elbow.

I looked back and forth between the two.

Carson blushed and pulled out a small bouquet of pennywort and bird's-foot violets from behind his back, pushing them toward me.

"What's this, Carson?" I took the posy and uttered a *much obliged*, thinking maybe it was for Retta's passing.

But Carson just stood there with something more in his eyes. There was a strange, uncomfortable look in them, but I couldn't be sure and immediately drew back.

Devil John looked at Carson and wiggled his finger toward me, giving a quick nod.

Carson led me out into the yard. He took off his floppy leather hat, twisting it around in his hands, then softly cleared his throat. "Honey, uh, um, I'd like to marry ya." He shot me a wide smile that never really made it to his eyes. "Will ya marry me?"

A gasp slipped past my teeth. I had known Carson my whole life, but never once had I given thought to any romantic notions or a marriage to him. And Papa would never allow me to wed so young.

Devil John said, "Be mighty proud to have you as our daughter-in-law. Martha Hannah too."

Exasperated, I turned to Mr. Morgan, the joy I'd captured earlier meeting Francis and getting work, souring in my stomach. "No, Mr. Morgan," I barely whispered.

Mr. Morgan said quietly, "It's true you'd be safe, and the law could not interfere between the union. The court would simply declare you an adult. And the state would lose its control. I'm sure your father would give his written consent for such a union—"

"But, I'm a Blue!" I raised wriggling flushed hands. "The law says we're mixed, and I can't marry whites."

"Not with these." Devil John dug into his pocket and pulled out delicate white gloves with lace trims. "Martha Hannah whipped these up, and we'll get a justice over yander in the next county to marry ya. Hardly anyone here knows you're a Blue. Your mama always saw fit to keep your hands covered with gloves. Keep ya safe like that."

Carson nudged me farther into the yard, away from the men, and whispered, "I'd take good care of ya, Honey."

"Carson, I—" I fidgeted with my collar. "I'm grateful, but I can't." I frowned as the disappointment flooded his face. "This was your papa's idea and it feels like, well, like charity." I pressed the flowers back into his hand.

"Honey, no, it's not. I swear it's mine and mine alone. Marry me and let me keep ya safe," he urged.

Shocked, I stepped back, shaking my head. "It's not like we're kids anymore, Carson, fishing and playing in the creek. I don't want to play house with anyone—with you. I just don't love you that way." I thought about my parents, the great love they had for each other, the way it always shone bright like a flame that never went out. I wanted that. "Carson, I'm sixteen and I haven't even had a chance to find out about love yet." I turned my head, thinking about Francis, his smile. "I want that chance." Embarrassed, I crossed my arms.

"I could think of worse things than to marry me. Am I that bad that you'd rather go to...to *prison*?" He bit down on the word.

Surprised by his harshness, I stepped back. Peering down at the bouquet he held, I begged for the right words to come.

"Is it because I'm the moonshiner's son, Honey? I can get work in the mines." He dropped his voice to barely a whisper, glanced back at his papa. "I'll work that dirty rock, be a dirt-digger and dig myself two graves, whatever it takes to keep ya free."

"*No, Carson*," I hissed low. "Our families have been friends forever. You're good folk."

"I could be a *good* husband." He looked over his shoulder to Devil John.

"I'm sorry," I said.

"But you're already sixteen," he whispered, reminding what some in these parts might suggest to a girl in danger of becoming an old maid.

"I don't need to catch a man before my next birthday, Carson. And I'm not marrying someone whose happiness belongs to another. I've seen you with Greta Clemmons."

He frowned, knowing it was true.

I looked Devil John straight in the eye and said with all my might, "I'll be an adult in sixteen months. And I have a respectable job that pays good money." I whipped out the job post flyer from my coat and held it up, then tapped on the pinned name tag. "I have a home and means to support myself." I swept my arm toward the cabin. "And without taking charity, Devil John. If the laws says I'm old enough to marry at sixteen, why can't it declare me an adult when I have a home, a job, and can fend for myself?" I shifted my stare to Mr. Morgan. "Why, sir?"

Mr. Morgan's eyes met mine while he also pondered an answer.

The men were quiet as my eyes searched their faces, the question loud but hanging quiet between them. Carson wrung the floppy brim of his hat and snuck glances at me, his face miserable and reddened—I guessed from failing at the task his papa had set before him.

Finally, Mr. Morgan said, "Honey, can we go inside and talk in private?"

"Yes, sir."

"Honey, wait." Carson reached for my hand. "I don't want to see ya sent away to that damn prison. I'd be honored to have you as my bride," he said, a pained smile lifted on his lips.

Carson was as fine a man as any, one who still had his sweet ways and boyish smile—the look a youth holds before manhood and the ol' Kentucky land and the hardness latch on and wither it.

"I'm really sorry, Carson," I said, picking up my satchel.

"Devil, I won't be long." Mr. Morgan opened the door and motioned me inside.

I glanced at the ol' moonshiner and, seeing his disappointment and worry pinched across his face, hoped he wouldn't think me too ungrateful.

Slipping inside, I dropped my bag by the door. Mr. Morgan followed, and the old wooden floor groaned under the lawyer's weight as he peeled off his coat and handed it to me. I hung it on the peg, offering him something to drink.

"Coffee if you have it, Honey." He eased into the chair, perched his elbows on the table, watching.

I lit the woodstove and put on the kettle, then pulled out Mama's ol' copper and glass bubbled percolator from France, filled the burner with kerosene, and lit it after adding the water and coffee. When it was done, I poured his coffee and my tea in Retta's cups and placed them on the table.

He took a sip and said, "You've got a comfortable place here."

I looked around, proud that I had cleaned it and made my bed before leaving this morning.

"Tell me more about your job," he said.

"The library hired me to revive their outreach program. I'm a librarian assistant, and I'll bring the books up in the hills for folk who can't get into town. Same as Mama did long ago. And it pays $70 more than what she made."

He rubbed his chin, studying me. "Spreading literacy is quite an important job. Respectable. A big responsibility, too, in these hills." He tapped the table with his fingers. "It's too bad the law bars a minor from owning property until they're of age. I know Miss Adams would've wanted you to have hers because she told me." He frowned. "Passed Leon Payne this morning, and he told me you took care of Miss Adams's funeral and paid for it. Praised how collected you were despite doing it all by yourself."

Uncomfortable, I worried my stained-blue hands, rubbing the worn wooden table with a palm. "Yes, sir. Alonzo, well, he was indisposed. I mean to get her a stone marker too. With some coins she left and my pay coming, she'll be taken care of in her eternal rest." I thought of Retta up there twirling in her fancy bold dress, dancing with the angels.

"Fine thing, Honey." He took another sip of coffee, set the china cup down. "Talk in town said Alonzo sold Miss Adams's home, despite her wishes that you'd always have a place to stay. They say Alonzo came into town inebriated, blabbed it all, and told others how you helped him pack up her personal items so he wouldn't lose them."

I picked up Retta's delicate cup and said quietly, a tremble in my grip, "We didn't feel it would be right for strangers to have Retta's personal things. Alonzo and me thought they should go to family and loved ones. I took my quilt and these cups and a few other thing. It's what Retta would've wanted."

"Back to Carson's generous offer. Now Kentucky does not object to marrying off its child brides, and I know you don't take to the idea of marriage, but—"

I set the teacup down, rattling the saucer before dropping my hands into my lap. "No, sir, I do not."

"Honey, is there anyone who could be your guardian?"

"Maybe Pearl Grant could. She's the new fire lookout and is very responsible."

"How old is Pearl?"

"Nineteen."

"The court would never allow it. Can you think of anyone over twenty-one?"

"Only Devil John, and I suppose there's Alonzo," I said, more in a moan.

"As your court-appointed attorney, I have to keep your safety, well-being, and best interest at heart. I couldn't recommend Alonzo, and the courts wouldn't grant John guardianship." He pondered it a few seconds. "Let me see what I can come up with. Maybe we can find you foster care. I'll speak with a few ministers in the area."

"What's foster care?"

"Families who look after children who are orphaned or who've lost their parents."

"Strangers? But my parents ain't lost, Mr. Morgan. The courts took them from me, is all." I looked down at his hands, then up to his face.

He followed. "No, Honey, it's highly unlikely the court would grant a single man guardianship over a young lady." He raised his ringless finger. "Better head on back to the office. In the meantime, we still have one option. *Carson.*"

"The law will send me to prison if I don't marry? Take away my freedom?"

"Something like that, though it's a bit more tricky. But, yes, that's the gist of the matter."

"*Freedom*." I turned the word over in my mind. "Here, Mama and Papa's was stolen *for* marrying." I shook my head. "I don't want to go to prison, or be punished with marriage. I just want my freedom, Mr. Morgan."

Mr. Morgan stared at me for the longest moment, mulling over something in his own mind. "Let me get back to the office and work on it and also talk with a few ministers."

"Would I have to marry?"

"I'll know more soon."

I followed him out the door. From the porch, I watched as the men got on their horses.

Carson rode over, looked down at me, then off toward the mountains. "Honey, we've sure missed having a book woman in them hills. Be nice to have books in the cabin again for me and my little nieces and nephews. Ma would really like that." He looked at me thoughtful, and bent over with an open palm. "Be like ol' times, True," Carson called me by the nickname he'd given me.

"Ol' times." I stepped up to his mount and took his hand, warmed by his kind proposal today.

"The offer's still there, Honey, and I would honor ya everyday, build us a good home and promise only you my heart." He released my hand.

"Obliged, Carson. But the books are the sanctuary for my heart. And like you, I want to decide my own marriage should I ever find someone. I'll carry the books up to Martha Hannah and the babies. Right up to your cabin window, same as Mama did."

His eyes were understanding, and he tipped his hat and followed the men out of the yard.

I stayed outside till dusk arrived, filling the skies with an endless blackened blue, and the loneliness and worries chased me back inside.

Nineteen

Freedom. The word rattled my thoughts. I was relieved there might be a chance of getting it without marrying. Yet, I puzzled over the law, why it was so unfair and cruel, and was disgusted by the thought that Kentucky men would send their young to a children's prison if they couldn't be married off as a child bride.

I hoped I'd made the right decision about Carson and that it wouldn't hurt our friendship. He had said *like ol' times,* so maybe he meant it and we could get back to those times of just friendship.

From a shelf above the woodstove, I pulled down Mama's old courting candle my grandpa had used during her courtship. I played with the iron-forged rattail, moving the taper up and down. This made me wonder how many times Grandpa Elijah had set the timekeeper for a lengthy visit from the expected courter and how many times Mama had cheated by lowering it to chase off any unfavorable suitors she thought might be coming. Mama had said she'd thrown it out in the yard when Papa came calling, but he'd plucked it up to save for me. I couldn't help thinking about how my papa would've set the candle for Carson, and I dared compare it to Francis, worried why fathers around these parts still did this to their daughters. Studied on why men decided it all.

Turning it around, I tapped the spiral iron taper, reflecting on the conversations that must've swirled over and around it. Though

Mama'd said she chosen Papa of her own accord, how difficult it must have been having your father determine your lifelong happiness or misery. I walked over to the trunk by the bed, opened it, and buried the courting candle underneath a stack of quilts.

I took a collection of poems off our bookcase and warmed as I read the inscription to Mama from Papa on their wedding day, fondly remembering their devotion to each other and their deep love for the written word. I traced the words to the Yeats poem "An Isle in the Water" that Papa had written along with his salutation: *For my dear bride and book woman, Cussy Mary Lovett, October 20, 1936.*

I was grateful to Carson, but even more appreciative for the librarian work. A job and money—and the books—meant I could at least survive, and do it on my own. Surely Mr. Morgan would find a way.

Flopping down onto the kitchen chair, I peered down at the list of patrons Miss Foster had given me. After studying it, I grew excited and began to work on a schedule for my route.

Monday would be the best day to visit the stone school and three other patrons nearby, Oliver Baker the beekeeper, granny woman Emma McCain, and homebound Mr. Prine. On Tuesday, I'd go to the outpost and pick up the reading material and shelve the older loans. Wednesday, I would drop off loans to the Flynns, Evans, and Cecils, then add Devil John and Pearl as my last stops.

I tapped the pencil on the page, thinking. There was librarian Oren Taft's Tobacco Top community. Nine families lived there, and they were known as holler dwellers, some of the poorest in the hills. Mr. Taft was working at the library full time after moving his wife closer to town. I would be delivering reading materials to his son on Thursdays.

Coal miner Bonnie Powell, frontier nurse Amara Ballard, and the Gillis family would be scheduled for Friday. I paused as I wrote down the last name. There were quite a few families named Gillis, and I wondered which one this was.

By the time I was through shining Mama's boots to wear on my first day at work, it was time for bed and I rushed outside to feed Pennie and Junia.

After a quick breakfast, I wrapped two sausage patties and a fried apple pie, adding two carrots for Junia to have on our first day at work.

Eager to be out riding the hillsides, Junia moved at a steady pace. It was like she sensed my new life had awakened her ol' one, feeling the hope and promise that the books would bring us.

In the woods, chimney smoke curled into the fog, feathery, revealing the camouflaged nests of small ghost homes. When Junia saw the boarded-up church by the creek, she neighed and whinnied. "Whoa, ol' girl." I tried to slow her down. But she sped up even faster, remembering the outpost and her rider from back then.

The mule stopped in front of the chapel door and lifted her nose, sniffing. Junia snorted and searched with her big eyes and pinned-up ears. She swung her head to the left, then to the right, and scouted some more, her ears still pinned straight. Again, she looked around, baring her teeth as if struggling with her next move. From the vine-wrapped crumbling chimney, a single dove cooed soft and then louder twice more before flying off, its flapping wings thrumming through the trees.

The ol' apostle girl heaved, swished her tail, then let out a slow rippling haw, a muffled chord of cries that I'd never heard before. The sound came from deep within her, dull and long, past the reaches of flesh and muscle, traveling directly from an abandoned heart.

I climbed down and scratched her ears, trying to soothe her. "Junia, I'm sorry but she's not here." I patted her neck. "You'll have the book route again and make her proud." I sighed, aching for Mama, for all of us. If only she was here to see it. "I miss Mama too," I whispered.

Junia's big eyes popped even wider when I mentioned her.

Slowly, I moved down along her side to her rump. "I need to unload the pannier and satchel of food and take it inside, ol' girl. It's our first day on the job."

As soon as I lifted the bags, Junia was off, neighing and hawing, racing toward the east. "JUNIA!" I dropped the bags and chased after her, both of our screams lighting the nuthatch, chickadees, and warblers from their nests, the leaves singing in protest.

"*Junia!*"

Breathless, I stopped a mile later alongside the mouth of the creek, bent over, and rested my hands on my thighs. In a minute, I called out for her but heard only the prattling trills of birdsong, and no Junia anywhere in sight. I kicked a rock, scattering dirt and debris, angry at my foolishness for letting her run off a second time. I blinked, searched around me again.

I ran for another mile, stopping to scan the woods and call for her. Exhausted, I began walking, fearing I might have to walk the thirty miles over to Thousandsticks.

A few minutes later, I heard her indignant screams and barking haws.

Mr. Taft, the librarian, led Junia behind a horse, a sunny grin on his weathered face.

Junia kicked forward, nipping, trying to get a piece of his steed.

"Oh, ol' girl, you scared me something silly." I ran up to them, my eyes blurring from tears. "Mr. Taft, I'm much obliged for your help, sir. She ran off at the outpost." I looked her over for any scratches and scrapes, checking her hooves before pressing a cheek into her fur. "You'll be okay, Junia." I ran my hands, up, down, and under, searching like Mama'd taught me.

"I was on my way to drop off the loans to you at the outpost, and I figured the gal ran off. Caught her just as she screamed past, and riderless at that," the librarian said with a chuckle.

"She misses Mama." I took her reins, relieved.

"Yes, your mama's been sorely missed in these parts." He looked off and I could see he was thinking about her, his book woman from long ago. He was a dear patron, and Mama had helped Oren Taft get the library job. "Let's get your reading material to the chapel," he said. "I have to get back down to the library and work the desk. My boy will meet up with you Thursday."

"Mr. Taft, much obliged for your help today, and I'll be there to meet him. Junia—" I started to scold as I mounted but stopped. I didn't have the heart to go on. The poor mule's head hung cheerless, her sides quivered with an ache brought on by the loneliness that only loss brings.

"I miss her and Papa too." My own heart was heavy, the weight of the hard Kaintuck land and even harder life and folk pressed in, smothering.

"Honey"—Mr. Taft studied me a moment before speaking quietly—"books can help soothe all matters of the heart. Your mama taught me that." He nodded. "I remember her loaning me a tattered book by a fella named Rabindranath Tagore from way across the big pond. Far from these ol' blood-soaked knobs and our whisperin' blue hills. I recall one of his passages she'd quoted for me: 'Faith is the bird that feels the light and sings when the dawn is still dark.' I'll be mindful to try and find you some of his works, if you like."

"Real pretty, Mr. Taft. I love reading the poetry books."

The librarian followed us back to the outpost. I tethered Junia to a tree and then helped him unpack the reading material and take it inside.

Before he left, he handed me a note. "Miss Foster asked me to pass this to you. There's a few more requests for book drops. Miss Foster said she'd be much obliged if you can fit the folks into your schedule. And there are also requests for certain reads from your patrons."

My patrons. The words lifted my heart. "Obliged, Mr. Taft." I took the paper and glanced at the names, surprised to see Francis and one other patron whose name I didn't recognize.

He set down the lantern on the table. "Keep the light for your outpost." He dug a cookie out of his coat pocket and passed it to me. "This will keep Junia near and doing your bidding. My woman mixes up a batter of oats, carrots, apple, and molasses, then bakes 'em and cuts 'em into cookies for my steed."

Then he was off and out the door, whistling, as his horse crossed creek waters to head toward town.

I stepped off the porch and grabbed my small satchel. "No more trouble from you today," I warned. Junia stared into my eyes looking innocent, though we both knew different. I broke off part of the oat cookie, and her ears flopped with pleasure as she tasted the sweet ingredients.

"You like that, Junia?" She nudged my hand for more. "I'll bake you some but only if you stop running off." I scratched her neck, fed her the rest.

Back inside, I looked around the small church. Except for a scarred wooden table with a chair and some makeshift shelves, the outpost was empty, full of cobwebbed corners and years of grime and ghost sermons.

Tucked back on a shelf, I found one of Mama's old scrapbooks, a precious book that she and the other Pack Horse librarians used to make for their patrons when the books were hard to come by. I blew on the cover, wiping away the dust with my arm.

Mama had talked a lot about the Pack Horse Library Project that the Kentucky Federation of Women's Clubs created in 1913. The program expired the next year after the benefactor, a Kentucky coal baron, passed away. But in 1934, the Kentucky women suggested it be revived under President Roosevelt's Works Progress Administration. It ran till 1943, when the funding stopped.

I recall how surprised I was to learn that the president paid the librarians $28 a month, and only that. Before Mama got Junia, she had to rent her mounts from Mr. Murphy, paying $7.25 a month. With no books or money to buy them, she and the other librarians had to scrounge around for their reading materials.

But the librarians were determined and sent out a cry for donated books to the Boy Scouts, PTAs, and other groups. Soon penny funds were started, and cast-off and tattered books and magazines and newsprint arrived. And while they waited for new reading material, the scrapbooks became treasures.

A corner of the cardboard cover had been nibbled off by a mouse, and the wet woodlands had ribboned most of the paper. Opening the faded blue, lined notebook, I carefully turned the delicate pages full of cutouts from old magazines and newsprint. There were many colorful birds in flight, cheerful flowers, recipes, quilt patterns, and household tips that had been pasted in, along with notes written beside them. Many times, Mama had set me at the table with the paste jar to help make them for her patrons. On the last pages, I read the poems and prayers Mama had handwritten inside with her fine penmanship. Missing her, I closed the scrapbook and set it back on the shelf.

Inside a closet, I found old cleaning supplies, and swept and dusted, sneezing in between. Done, I toted a bucket out to the creek and filled it with water to mop the slanted wooden floors.

It was an office as grand as Miss Foster's. It was *my* office. Outside, birds welcomed the new day, their songs lifting, carrying across the sighing woods into ol' grandmother mountains.

Proud, I took a moment looking over my work before I continued scrubbing. When I put the broom and mop back in the closet, I noticed a stack of newspapers on the top shelf. I climbed onto a chair and retrieved one to inspect, wondering if I should toss them out or save them in case someone might request an old newsprint. I examined the 1943 paper and set it over on my table to read after I finished.

Several hours later, I sat down at the table and separated the reading material, poring over the books, magazines, and newsprint and organizing them for the coming days, while nibbling on the dinner I'd packed. It was comforting and somehow it was like Mama was here sitting beside me. I closed my eyes and exhaled, remembering the times she had graced this building, carefully poring over the books to make sure each patron received the perfect read.

When I finished my work, I skimmed the old newspaper, pausing on a death notice someone had circled in bold black ink about a man named Byrne McDaniel. It noted a court case the Kentucky man was involved in long ago:

> In a landmark court case, Byrne McDaniel won his
> emancipation when he left home at age twelve after his
> father failed in his duty to give him a parental home
> and instead forced him into labor by making him go out
> into the world to seek his own fortune. In 1909, when
> Byrne was fourteen, the court ruled to grant the young
> minor his adulthood...freeing the child, for all period of
> its minority, from care, custody, control, and service...
> Byrne served honorably in WWI and was awarded the
> Silver Star medal for gallantry in action... Byrne credited
> his emancipation... He was a deacon at the White Oak
> Church, and practiced...will be remembered for...

Emancipation, I turned the word over and thought about my own freedom as I read Byrne's accomplishments and life services.

Many times, Mama had said books helped her survive, gave her a freedom like no other in these hills. And sitting here in the quiet where she used to sit, books gave me hope for my own.

I reread Byrne's obituary, my finger running under the words as I soaked them up before tucking the old newspaper into my bags.

Freedom. It was all I could think about. I picked up a book and rubbed its worn cover, fanned through the pages, marveling over the power you could get from books.

Excited, I packed the rest of Mr. Taft's loans inside the pannier, thinking about my freedom, knowing somehow the books were the key.

Twenty

I found the door half-open when I arrived home, and a loud ruckus coming from inside.

Alarmed, I slid off Junia, pulled out the rifle from its scabbard, and snuck over to the porch, the gun snugged to my shoulder.

Quieting my breaths, I lifted a boot, and nudged the door open wider. Broken dishes, scattered pots, pans, and split bags of flour, sugar, and walnuts were littered across the floor, the contents spilling out everywhere.

Then it ran toward me.

Junia screamed as the wild raccoon bolted out the door right past me, hissing and screeching. My legs near buckling, I steadied myself against a porch beam watching while Junia drove the creature from the yard, and a yowling Pennie flew out of the stall, joining the chase.

Breathing hard, I recalled a couple living in the next holler. How they were awakened during the middle of the night after a rabid one crawled down their chimney and tore off half of the sleeping woman's face.

After I rounded up Junia and cleaned up the mess, I baked Mrs. Taft's cookies, hoping I could train the mule to be more agreeable and keep her from running off. Soon, the sun dropped low and I lit the lantern and built a fire, digging out my journal to read the poems I'd written and addressing a note to Mr. Taft asking him to leave a few poetry books at the outpost.

Tired, I looked over my list of patrons for tomorrow, then donned my nightgown. It was one of Mama's and I ran my hand over the frayed threads, rubbed the soft fabric against my cheek, grateful she'd packed it for me.

I picked up the newspaper I'd carried home, pulled the lantern closer, and once again read about Byrne's emancipation, my mind turning.

At dawn, I slipped on my coat and gloves and climbed atop Junia for my Wednesday route. Mr. Cecil was the first drop-off. He was a widowed coal miner taking care of Charlotte, his thirteen-year-old daughter, Miss Foster had said.

After I left the loans, I turned onto the Smiths' path and rode deep into the woods until we came upon the moonshiner's cabin.

Laughter and squeals of young babes skated out the cabin as Junia rode straight past the empty clothesline and up to Martha Hannah's open window.

"Honey." Martha Hannah placed a palm across her breast. "It sure does these ol' eyes good to see ya riding in here like your ma did." She leaned out and scratched Junia's head. "You too, ol' girl." She reached around and grabbed a half-chopped carrot for Junia.

Junia snorted her thanks and gobbled down every bite, poking her head inside for more.

Three sets of curious eyes peeked over the windowsill. Junia moved her mouth over their heads, tousling hair. The children shrieked and fell back giggling.

I turned partway around and dug inside the pannier for the material.

"I brought you some children's books." I handed her *The Runaway Bunny, April's Kittens,* and *Bear Party.* "Here's a *Sports Afield* for Devil John and *Woman's Day* for you. And there's some pamphlets from the health department and the latest flyer from the Company store." I passed them through to her.

"Thank you, Honey. Sure is nourishment for the soul. And Devil will 'preciate his new magazine."

Carson strolled through the yard. "What'd ya bring me, Mary True and Blue? Or are ya here to finally wash that week's worth of dirty laundry you promised me over in Thousandsticks?" he teased. His face was boyish, and his eyes were lit with amusement.

I laughed, remembering him wagging his finger at me in front of the sheriff and social worker. "It'll have to wait, Carson, and it looks like I forgot your book. I'll fetch you a good read next week. Promise. Maybe your papa will share his till then."

"You can read to the gran'babies." Martha Hannah leaned out of the window and told him, "Git in here and help me with 'em so I can git my supper on."

"Aw, Ma, I was just going over to visit Greta," Carson said, sneaking glances at me.

"Greta seems nice," I said, looking down, remembering his proposal.

"You were right, Honey. She's the one, and I aim to marry her next year," he whispered. "But like I said, the proposal still stands if it'll keep ya outta prison."

I nodded, warmed by his offer.

"Hurry up, Carson," Martha Hannah ordered.

"See you later." I smiled.

He grinned and shot up the steps.

I said goodbye to Martha Hannah and headed toward the fire tower.

Grateful for the job, I found the week flew by as I waited on word from Mr. Morgan. In no time it was Friday and we journeyed to Bonnie Powell's, one of the first of three patrons on today's route, the cool morning growing into a warmer afternoon, leaving me to unbutton my coat.

An old woman with a brindle dog following behind her walked out of the yard as I tied Junia to the splintered porch propped up by worm-eaten stilts. The tired-looking cabin had seen better days, its roof sagging, the blackened boards rotting and bulging from the sides. I dug into the pannier, sneaking peeks at the widowed young woman coming out.

Bonnie pushed open the tattered screen door, smoking a cigarette, her bib overalls covered in coal dust, the miner's helmet still resting atop her head. "See ya tomorrow, Grandma," she called out to the woman. "Oh, Honey, thanks for putting me on the route." Bonnie walked down the steps, dropped her cigarette, and stamped it out with a dirty black-dusted boot. "My cousin, Francis, told me, and I signed up right away, hoping for the books."

"I didn't know he was your cousin," I said but could see some resemblance now that she mentioned it.

"Yeah, good kid, he's eighteen, two years behind me. We've all missed your mama's route—missed you, too, sweet pea." She pinched my cheek affectionately, then walked over to Junia and stroked her. "Hey, ol' apostle, you 'member me, girl?" She kissed the mule's nose. Junia flopped her big ears, pleased. "'Member Bonnie? 'Member me?"

It was hard to forget Bonnie. The last two summers when we'd visited Troublesome, I sat her son while the young couple went to Knoxville for a night out on the town, or met up with another couple for an evening at the Moose Club.

When I'd first knocked on the door years ago, Bonnie had opened it wearing nothing more than a bullet bra and corselet she'd ordered from the Frederick's of Hollywood catalog, her hair done up in big curlers, her feet covered in canary-yellow satin slippers.

Bonnie loved to talk, and I enjoyed listening to her friendly chatter. Impressed by her beauty and sweet nature, I'd sat at the kitchen table fascinated while she drew on cat eyeliner and painted her lids with a dusty sky-blue eyeshadow, rouged her cheeks and brushed her lips in bold pink hues. When she was through, she did the same with me, leaving me speechless over the amount she used—and leaving my folk unsettled with pleas for cosmetics.

Today, Bonnie's eyes were weary, and it looked like she'd been crying. She moved toward me and peeked over my shoulder inside the bag.

"Want to see what I have? Lot of good ones in here today, Bonnie," I said, proud of my selections, moving aside to give her a better glimpse.

"Sure would. Come on up to the porch, sweet pea. Grandma just put the baby down 'fore she left. Sorry." She stopped on the steps, kicking aside an empty pack of Lucky Strikes. "Haven't had money to buy a proper porch chair."

"How's Joey Junior?" I asked as I carried the pannier up to the porch. We took a seat and sat huddled together on the top step next to several three-welled glass ashtrays overflowing with cigarette butts.

"He's a'growin' just fine. Heard about Miss Adams. Real sorry to hear she's passed. She sewed the baby a fine layette before his birth. Sorry I couldn't attend the funeral, but the Company bosses wouldn't have let me off anyway."

I picked at lint on my coat, feeling guilty no one had because I didn't run into town and announce it.

Bonnie took off her helmet and tossed it onto the porch boards in back of her.

I drew in a sharp breath when I saw all her beautiful hair had been cut into a boy's cut. But Bonnie kept pulling out books and reading material like she hadn't noticed my surprise.

She lifted up another book, *Hitty, Her First Hundred Years*, by Rachel Field and illustrator Dorothy Lathrop, and pressed it to her chest, smiling. "I 'member Book Woman bringing this to the schoolhouse. Your mama read it to the class a lot of times. It was my favorite."

"That little wooden doll sure got around," I said, trying not to stare but fondly remembering Mama holding me in her lap and reading it to me many times.

"'Member Hitty meeting Charles Dickens?" Bonnie lit another cigarette. "Oh! And the time she snuck out to go to a concert with a boy? Reckon, Book Woman reading you all the stories is why you're a smart book woman today." She looked out into the brown bare yard stitched with cowslips and dandelions, twisting her small, gold wedding band around her finger.

I nodded weakly, thinking about Mama.

Bonnie rummaged through the bag, looking for other reads as she spoke quietly. "Some of the miners did it." She grabbed a fistful of short hair from her head and let out a long sigh. "A few of 'em are mean like that. They sheared off my hair today after one of their roof jacks blew out last week. Said it was bad luck having a female down in the mine and next time they'd tar me."

She pulled out a pamphlet from the health department, set it atop of Field's book and another book called *The English Teacher*. "They dragged me back into the dark belly down there, wrestled me to the ground. Tried to fight 'em, but there were too many. See?" She pulled down the collar of her stained shirt revealing scratches and bruises on her neck and chest. "One of 'em stuffed the cut locks into my mouth to keep me from screaming, nearly choking me to death. Lucky it was only a haircut. They said next time I'd lose worse."

Gasping, I shook my head in dismay, cursing under my breath. "I should go get the nurse."

Bonnie shook her head and made tiny spitting noises as if the hair was still gagging her, then scraped her tongue with her teeth, picking at the tip with a fingernail.

"Real sorry, Bonnie. Let me get Nurse Ballard for you," I offered again. "She's on my route today. Not too far from here, right after the Gillis drop."

"Don't matter." Bonnie shook her head and swallowed hard, digging back into the bag, looking for something else to read.

"'Cause I can't quit. There's no other work 'round here and I need to feed me and my baby. So, I told one of the boss men 'bout it, and he grabbed me by the front of my overalls and whispered, 'Some advice for ya, Bonnie: Try'n be more like Big Dessie, or them ol' boys are gonna keep piling on the trouble. And I got me enough trouble down here without the female hysterics adding to it. It's that or I'll boot your scrawny ass onto the hoot-owl shift.'"

I curled my fist, my knuckles lit in hot blue anger.

"Now Big Dessie ain't big anywhere but here." Bonnie cupped two hands out in front of her breasts. She pressed down on her chopped hair, worrying it with a palm, then twisted the loose wedding band around her finger again. Dropping her voice low, Bonnie picked out another book, studying it. "Big Dessie used to wear the bib dungarees like me, but now she struts around in tight britches and a chambray shirt unbuttoned clean down to her navel. *Keep the men perk and happy. It'll keep you happy—and keep food on your table,* she warned."

I clenched my fist tighter. "Bonnie—"

"Know what else ol' boss man said?" She snuck a glance at me, took a puff off her cigarette, and went back to the books, searching. "It's important things we women need to tell other women."

I warmed at that, grateful she saw me as an equal, appreciative another woman had said it.

She stopped, searched my face. "You know I've always shot it to you straight, sweet pea, and ol' Bonnie ain't going to dip the *straight* into honey. 'Cause sometimes it has to come from the dog-shit pile it came from and be called for what it is. Okay, sweet pea?"

I whispered a faint *yes*, but was afraid to hear what Bonnie was going to tell me next.

"Boss man done tol' me them good ol' boys work real hard, and it lifts their spirits some when a pretty female dresses up nice for 'em—said them boys make a mighty sacrifice while digging themselves a second grave for the Company kings, and it's the least I could do... Then he let me know I could have myself an *easier* job, operating the shuttle carts instead of shoveling the heavy, muddy slop back onto the belts. Same as Big Dessie."

I pressed a hand over my mouth, horrified for her.

Bonnie reached into my pannier, thumped another book onto her stack of picked reads. "Them ol' boys always a'grabbin' my breasts—crotching me with their stank, coal-dirt fingers, digging into my privates when I climb into the cage to head down into the damp mine and then on to the shuttle cart. *Eight times, their filthy, scaly fingers pierced cloth, dug into my flesh today.* Can't afford new bibs so I gotta get out my sewing kit again."

I lowered my head, feeling her shame that belonged to others—the menfolk.

Bonnie slammed down another book, tapped her cigarette ash, slightly spread her legs, examining her dungarees. She blinked hard and mumbled a curse.

I touched her arm, seeing she was worn and beaten down.

She quieted, but in a minute said hoarsely, "Damn, I *want* my man, my *good* man." It came out in a low, long aching grind, a guttural caterwauling that had settled deep in her chest. "I *sorely* miss my sweet Joey."

She pulled out the leather cord hidden underneath her shirt, and kissed a dangling five-cent coal scrip that had belonged to him. Joey always carried around a bunch of the Company coins and would always slip me a few extra nickels after I sat for them.

"He was a good man, your Joey was." I put a hand on her shoulder, my heart breaking for the young, widowed mother, her grief weighing like stone.

She rubbed the scrip across her mouth. "I can still taste his kiss," she whispered. "I taste it every day, sweet pea. Ya know, a girl should marry a man whose last kiss can stay on her lips forever." She reached over and tucked back a stray lock that had fallen in my face. "*Forever and ever.* That's what I did, sweet pea."

My thoughts went to her cousin, wondering what his kisses were like, and I felt myself reddening.

Again, Bonnie fiddled with the thin wedding band, gliding it around and 'round her finger before dropping one more book onto her loans with a brutal slap. "Dammit, them sonsabitches are gonna have to kill me, 'cause I ain't never, ever gonna be another Dessie peddling my pussy in a dark drift."

Inside, the baby startled and whined.

Bonnie stood up with her books and reading material, a rebellion in her small parting smile. She sighed and looked over her shoulder, then flicked the cigarette into the yard. "Guess Joey Junior's not gonna nap today. Thank you, I'll take these, Honey." She turned toward the door, but not before I saw her soaked eyes latching onto mine—her testimonial warning to me and other women stamped across her dispirited face.

Twenty-One

We followed the creek and stopped at a shady spot to let Junia graze and have a drink while I thought about Bonnie, studying on what books I could give her that would make her life easier, happier.

For a few minutes, I sat on the mossy bank eating a cold meat sandwich I'd packed, watching the creek waters gasp and ripple over rocks, their airy song rising into the woodlands' boughs of budding trees. My thoughts pulled to my life over in the Cumberland, Mama and Papa, what we had and what we'd never have because of their love. I pressed a finger to my mouth, wondering if I would ever have a chance at love.

My mind drifted to Byrne's sudden adulthood I'd read about in the newspaper, and I knew if I was to ever have a chance at anything, I had to find a way to earn mine.

Junia plodded over to my side and dribbled water on my head and brayed. I followed her wide eyes. Two young boys carrying fishing poles hurried toward us. I dusted off the crumbs on my hands and slipped back on my gloves.

"Ma'am, you're the new Book Woman, aren't ya?" the taller boy called out. "I'm Pete Duncan, and this here is my brother, Franklin."

"Hello, Pete and Franklin," I said, standing, smoothing away the droplets of water on my hair, dusting off my riding britches. "I'm Honey Lovett, the assistant outreach librarian."

"Sure glad to run into you. We heard about the new book route. We'd be wanting ya to include us, ma'am. We're only five minutes across the creek, the little, white board house with the two goats in the yard."

Junia hawed, and the boys' eyes rounded. They took a step back. "Mama and us love the books, and we can read jus 'bout anything ya give us. If it ain't much trouble, Book Woman."

"I'd be happy to schedule your drop on Fridays," I said.

"Thank ya, ma'am," they both chorused.

Prying, I asked a little bit about them so I could choose their reads. Pete was twelve and enjoyed detective novels, while Franklin told me he was going on ten and liked any books about dogs and nature. I listened while the young'un proudly trilled birdsong his papa had taught him. Franklin called out to the catbirds, finches, and warblers, and I marveled and clapped when they separately answered back again and again.

Thrilled to have more patrons, I said goodbye and rode off toward the next book drop.

A few minutes later, Junia stopped suddenly and straightened her ears. I crooked my neck to the right and left, hearing shouts and hollering sifting through the trees.

Alarmed, I dug my heels into the mule's sides and rode her into the yard up ahead.

A woman stood by the well screaming, waving her hands back and forth. A clothesline full of cloth diapers, linens, and britches billowed in the breezes behind her. A soiled sheet lay on the ground beside a turned-over laundry basket.

I called out, "I'm the Book Woman, what's wrong?"

"It's my boy, Johnnie Gillis." She bobbed her head and ran to the well. "Help me, Book Woman! Over here, over here."

Junia snorted and sidestepped, trying to turn us back.

"Halt," I commanded and climbed down, grabbing the trembling mule's rein and tugging her over to the well. "What is it?" I said breathless.

"It's my Johnnie. He's done fell into the well. I thought I'd use the clothesline since it was warm. Only took my eye off him for a minute to hang my last sheet. Help me, oh Lord, mercy, help me. My husband's gonna be real mad," she pleaded tearfully. Her cheek was bruised, and she had a cut above her brow. "Help me, Book Woman."

I peered over the well and saw the small young'un, shivering, gripping the rope and an ol' bucket sitting halfway in the water with the other. He couldn't be more than two years old, three at the most.

"Get him out!" she hollered. "I'm not strong enough. Bring him up on that rope." She jabbed a finger to the tight, knotted cotton wrapped around the crank.

I looked inside the well and then to Junia, and back again. "Don't let go, Johnnie, we're going to get you out. Hang on." I tethered Junia to my waist and tried to crank up the rope holding the bucket, but the boy was too heavy or stuck. If I pulled any harder, I feared the line would snap or give away, sending him to a watery grave.

Mrs. Gillis moaned and began shrieking. Junia toe-hopped and tried to break free of my grip, almost pulling me down to the ground.

"Halt, halt." I spun around, and Junia stopped pulling. Memories of Papa rescuing a stray pup from a well, how he'd pulled up the scared dog with a rope and his horse came to me. Daisy had lived a long life with us after that. "Mrs. Gillis, do you have another rope?"

She pressed a shaky fist to her mouth.

"A rope, Mrs. Gillis?"

She pointed toward the shed. "Yes."

"If you go get it, ma'am, it will help."

She ran off, stumbling twice, her twisted long, green skirts tripping her.

I rubbed Junia's muzzle and spoke softly. "We got to get the young'un out, and I need you to do that, ol' girl."

The boy whimpered, and I bent over the well's concrete lip

and said, "I'm going to come down for you, Johnnie. You just hold on real tight." Johnnie, straddling the bucket and holding on with all his might, stared up wild-eyed with fright. I took off my coat and gloves and threw them onto the grass, remembering Papa doing the very same.

Mrs. Gillis came running back with a long rope. I tied it to Junia's saddle horn, Papa's hands seeming to guide me, again speaking quiet to the beast, then I wrapped the rope around my chest and under my arms, securing it with a tight granny knot.

"Mrs. Gillis, Junia's going to lower me into the well so I can get your son out. I need you to tell her when to pull forward and backward." The woman was trembling now, and her tears came hot and fresh. She kept looking over her shoulder toward the path.

"*Hurry*. Johnnie can't hold on much longer. My husband'll be home any time now."

"I'll try, ma'am."

"Get him out!"

"Mrs. Gillis, ma'am, can you do that for me, help the mule?" *Keep me from crashing to the bottom*, I thought, the words seeping out in my sweat. I placed her hand on the rope tethered to Junia's saddle, and she stared over at the well, breathed out a warbled *yes*.

Then I pulled Junia toward me and slowly climbed atop the well, took a breath and lowered myself over the side. "*Forward*," I said, as I inched my way down into the well. "*Forward!*"

Junia obeyed and allowed me to get closer and closer to the whimpering child. "Hang onto the rope and bucket, Johnnie. *Forward, forward, Junia!*" I commanded.

"*Forward*," Mrs. Gillis parroted.

My hands grew sweaty and weakened, but I'd bound the rope real good to one of them, and it held. I prayed the mule would be able to get us out, prayed the rope would hold, prayed Johnnie could hang on a bit longer—and prayed Mrs. Gillis would get us through this.

It grew darker as I made my way down and my body blocked

the sunlight, the mold and dampness tickling my nostrils, seeping through the fabric, wetting my perspiring flesh. Then my foot touched the bucket and I scrunched down closer until my legs were below the bucket. Getting within an arm's length of the boy, I told him to grab my neck. The soaked boy latched on, nearly strangling me, and I coughed, scooped him up into the crook of my arm, choking, gripping him tight, trying to straighten us up so we'd have a clear passage out.

"Hold on, Johnnie. Back, back!" I called desperately from the bottom to Junia, my words echoing off concrete.

Mrs. Gillis sobbed out my calls to the mule, and I heard her curse the beast, and the muffled strikes and returned brays as she beat on her.

"No, Mrs. Gillis. *Noo!*" Johnnie whimpered and I pulled the boy's quaking body closer to me. "Shh, it's okay, Johnnie." Then more urgent. "Easy, back, easy, Junia."

"*Pull. Her. Back.*" Mrs. Gillis hollered at the mule.

"Easy, ol' girl." Again, Junia did what I begged, and we moved slowly to the top. When our heads poked out over the wall, Mrs. Gillis came running from Junia and snatched Johnnie out of my arms. "*Ma-ma-ma,*" the child blubbered.

"Steady, Junia," I said climbing out of the well. Once my feet hit the ground, I shuddered as I untied the rope under my arms and dropped it onto the ground. "Is he okay, ma'am?" Cranking the leather bucket, I tethered it tight.

"No worse for the wear, Book Woman, just bruised and scratched." Mrs. Gillis walked up to me, toting Johnnie on her hip. "Thank you mightily," she said tearfully. "You saved him—me. That ol' well's been dry a couple of years and we've since put in a spring pump. But it still fills some during the heavy rains and snow melts we's always getting. Even more this year." She rubbed his wet head, kissed his cheek, while the young'un sucked earnestly on a thumb.

I let out a sigh of relief, brushed down my wet britches, stomped the water out of my boots and inspected my shirt.

There was a rip in the collar and sleeve, and it was missing three white buttons from where Johnnie had clung to me, or I had scraped them off on the way up or down. Mrs. Gillis's kelly-green dress looked like it was missing buttons too and a few inches of eyelet trim along her waist had been torn off.

The three of us just stood there looking at each other, our eyes darting to the well with the bucket snugged up to the spool. We stayed quiet a bit, thinking about what could've been and what hadn't been. Everyone around these parts knew the stories about children gone missing only to be found in family wells.

After a moment, Mrs. Gillis said, "I'm sorry about striking your mule. I got scared. Forgive me. Please call me Guyla Belle." She leaned toward me. "Guyla Belle Gillis. I'm from North Carolina." She reached out with a trembly hand before giving a little curtsy while she gripped Johnnie.

"Honey Lovett, Guyla Belle," I answered, then bent my head down to Johnnie. "Your new book woman at your bidding," I said, tossing a smile, relieved the boy was going to be fine.

"Book Woman saved you from the well. Say thank you, hon," Guyla told him, stroking his hair and cheeks.

"Buk uman saved me well, tank ya," he said, then pointed at me and repeated it louder.

"Book Woman, let me get you a towel and some dry socks for your troubles. Stay right here. I'll be right back," Guyla said, picking up the rope.

She came back out in minutes with Johnnie wrapped in a blanket and an apple for Junia. "Sure wish I could give you more."

"Much obliged. It's more than enough," I said, putting the apple in my pannier. Shivering, I dried off my clothes as best I could with the ragged towel, taking off the wet boots, the cold air biting my flesh.

"Here, let me take your socks," Guyla said, reaching for them. "I'll wash and dry them and have them ready for you next week."

"If it's not too much trouble, I'd appreciate it, Guyla Belle. I'll do the same with these." I pulled on the dry socks and damp boots and sighed, grateful for the warmth. "Let's get your reading material, Johnnie. I have a fine one in here."

"I'll feed you the apple later." I caressed Junia and whispered a thank-you in her ear, then reached inside my pannier and pulled out *Andy and The Lion*. But when I tried to pass it to him, the boy's eyes scrunched up as he glimpsed my dark-blue hands. He crinkled his reddening face and wailed and covered it, burying his head into his mama's shoulders as if he'd seen a big, scary lizard's hand.

Instantly, I lowered my arm, embarrassed by the color, shamed and saddened it had spooked the young child—that I was the cause of his tearful fright. Once when Papa took us all to the Knoxville restaurant, a waitress had dropped her tray of dishes when she saw Mama. Another had gasped upon seeing me slip off my gloves. We were finally seated in a dark corner by the kitchen where we waited for a good twenty minutes for a waiter to come over and take our order, and that was only after Papa talked to the manager.

If Guyla Belle noticed the coloring, she was too polite to mention it, because she rocked Johnnie on her hip, whispered soothing words, trying to quiet him. "Shh, Johnnie. Book Woman saved you from the well. Say thank you."

Obedient, he babbled, rubbing his eyes, "Buk uman saved me well."

Hesitant, I held up the book again. He took it, rubbing his gums across the hard edges. "And maybe this one for you, Guyla Belle." I handed her a sweet romance.

Guyla Belle clutched the book. An automobile door slammed in the distance. Her eyes widened in fright and she barely whispered, "Please don't say anything to my husband, Honey. Shh, Johnnie." She grabbed his book, tucking the loans under her arm.

A moment later, Mr. Gillis walked wearily into the yard, dirty and tired from his mine shift, toting a six-pack carry case of Falls City Beer and his lunch pail. "Damn, I miss my ol' truck I had last year. Had to catch a ride with Toby today. One of these days, I'll save enough to buy his old pickup so I won't have to be waitin' on rides," he said with a long-winded sigh.

I was taken aback somewhat. He was the same man who'd teased little Wrenna and her pet rooster outside the Company store. His hand was scratched and blood-smattered.

"You're hurt. What happened, Perry?" Guyla Belle asked worriedly, inspecting the wound.

"Man can't have himself a cold one in peace. Damn Abbott bitch's rooster done nailed me outside the Company store. She's a quare one all right, and I'm gonna ring that gawdamn bird's neck if I ever catch it."

Junia snorted and toe-hopped.

"Damn, forgot my miner's helmet again. Left it in Toby's truck." He set the beer down and took off a red Texaco ball cap with the star hardly recognizable, dropping it and his lunch pail beside Guyla Belle, then pulled little Johnnie into his arms. "What's wrong, son?" The boy peeked at my hands and wailed once more.

"Johnnie had a-a li'l accident, Perry, but he's fine, just a scrape. Uh, Book Woman, here, is dropping off—" Guyla Belle rushed her words, hugging the books to her chest.

"Quiet, woman," he barked. "What's all this frettin' about nothing, son?"

Guyla Belle opened her mouth, but Mr. Gillis raised a palm as if to strike her, and she cowed and stumbled back.

Oh, he was a mean 'un, alright, the type who talked with a fat, hard fist, knocking women in and out of chairs, down stairs, into walls, and down darkened halls. Cowardly men like those who sheared off Bonnie's hair and destroyed Pearl's cab. Disgust and anger rose inside me, and I shifted closer to Guyla and Junia followed.

Mr. Gillis narrowed his eyes when he saw what had his son

upset, and quickly wrapped his dirty arm around the boy, shielding him. "I heard your kind had come back. You're one of them Blues, ain't ya? One of them immoral Blues my pa chased out of the town square in '36."

"No, sir, I'm not immoral—"

"Uh-huh." He wagged his head. "I was jus' knee-high, but I heard all about it from my kin Harriett Hardin. You sign us up for this book route, Guyla?" He shot his wife a hard look, and she lowered her head and melted into the pressed books.

I stiffened.

Junia shifted closer and raised alert ears, laying her head over my shoulder and pinning a big, guarded eye onto the man.

"Wait, is that our towel, Guyla? Did you go and let *her* use it?" Mr. Gillis asked, looking at me like I had grown two heads.

Trembling, Guyla Belle took the towel from me, mumbled an apology. "Perry—"

I placed a protective hand on Guyla's arm, and she jerked away like I'd scalded her. "Mr. Gillis, I got wet on my route and asked your wife for a towel. She didn't want to, but I begged her."

Mr. Gillis's face was ripened with a mixture of fear and distrust, the hate pouring out, deeply anchored to his kin and the kin before that. I could see that the rot had set to its work. And I knew that nothing could ever change it—or his kind. I glanced at Mr. Gillis's son, knowing he would pass on the hatred, keep it alive and rooted in the boy and the boy's children and those children who came after.

"You tryin' to make me catch somethin' and get sick?" He jerked the towel out of her hands, threw it on the ground, and stomped a dirty boot across it. "*Burn it!* And take us off her route, and quit lazing 'round with them damn foolish books you're bent on soaking up in your dim-witted brain. Give 'em back to her, right now. You got chores to do," he said through tucked teeth, kicking the lunch pail at his wife.

It bounced off her shin, and Guyla Belle cried out, dropped her books, and pressed a palm atop the deep gash. The boy rubbed his eyes and began bawling. Mr. Gillis grabbed his cheek and shook hard. Junia shrieked and I jerked on her reins, fearful she would go for him.

"Shut up, boy. Woman, git me a beer and git my gawdamn supper on the table!" He carried his son up to the cabin, the boy's tearing eyes never leaving mine.

A rawboned, tailless dog slunk out from beneath the porch and skittered away. Guyla scrambled to pick up the beer, cap, and lunch pail. "Please don't take me off the route, Book Woman." She grabbed my arm. "He works late a lot of days, and I'll leave an empty milk bottle on the well if it's safe and the loans from the week before," she whispered, handing back the books. "Don't have any kin here or anywhere anymore. Not a soul, I'm a far piece from my home in Greenville. And all I got is them books. I'll keep them hid from him. *Please.*" She limped up to the cabin, looked back at me with pleading, weak eyes before slipping inside.

It was haunting, like looking into Bonnie's eyes. Though I was afraid of him, too, I thought about the brave coal-mining woman and nodded a promised *yes.* Then once again and more determined.

I had to believe the books would give her power—free her from Gillis's mistreatments.

Junia lifted her head off my shoulder, but a sorrow still perched, weighing heavy. I exhaled loudly. "You did real good, ol' girl." I lightly tickled her neck. "Going to give you that fat apple when we get home." I stared up at the Gillis home and felt a shiver latch on and circle my neck, prickling skin.

After loading the pannier, I pulled on my coat and stuffed my damp gloves into a pocket. The door opened and Mr. Gillis stepped onto the porch with a beer in his hand and a pistol tucked inside his waistband. He cut a mean eye to me as he guzzled down his alcohol, then tossed the empty bottle in our direction. "Git on down the path and outta here!"

Junia shrieked at him, and Mr. Gillis's hand moved to his gun and gripped the handle. I tugged on her reins and quickly led the mule out of the yard. Several times, I looked back over my shoulder, making sure Gillis hadn't decided to come after us.

Twenty-Two

Amara Ballard stood outside the horse stall, hands hitched to her hips. "I'm so sorry about Miss Adams's passing, Honey, but it's good to see you again, and under favorable circumstances. How are you holding up?"

"I miss Retta, but I'm grateful for the memories, grateful for your visit," I told her as I slid off Junia.

"Are you still needing a ride to see your parents tomorrow?" she asked.

"Sure am. Thank you. What time do you need me to be here?" I tethered Junia to a tall stump, excited.

"I'll be leaving at dawn if Katherine William's pregnancy doesn't delay me. You can leave your mule in the building over there where I house my automobile, and I'll have one of the boys from town tend to our mounts while we're gone."

"Much obliged, Amara, but ol' Junia gets fussy with the men-folk unless she knows them."

"Smart girl. I'll have one of the nurses stop by. What'd you bring today?"

"I have some good selections. Anything particular you looking for?" I pulled off the pannier.

She swept off her beret and said, "Well, any romance in there? And I'm missing my newspaper from back home. Do you think maybe you can get hold of a copy of the *Louisville Times*?"

I smiled. "I like romances too. We have lots of them, and I

have the latest circulation of the *Times*." I wondered if she liked excitement reads. "I can even bring you a *Life* magazine that has Janet Leigh on the front." I thought about the daring photograph of the movie star, then quieted, feeling I'd overstepped my welcome.

Amara chuckled. "We're going to be good friends."

Grinning, I pulled out the rolled newspaper and handed it to her. Amara looked down and frowned at my dark-blue skin. She tucked the newspaper under her arm and took my hand in hers, examining it.

I snatched it back and put my hand inside my pocket, feeling the damp gloves.

"Honey, are you feeling poorly? Are you unwell—"

"No, it's a gene hitch, Doc said. Methemoglobinemia is what it's called. Most of my kin have had it for centuries." I waved my hand in an overexaggerated matter. "Flares up some when I get riled, or something bad—" I shrugged, not wanting to tell her what happened at Bonnie's and the Gillis's. Bonnie didn't want the nurse to come, and Amara might want to check on the boy. But if Mr. Gillis found out about him falling down the well, I worried Guyla Belle would have to pay for it hard, maybe me also.

"Is there a cure?"

"No cure. Methylene blue can make it go away for a bit. But Mama said some medicines are worse than the cure."

"Hmm, the old drug used for cyanide poisoning. Methemoglobinemia." She pocketed the big word. "I'm not too familiar with the medical term, but I'm intrigued. You'll have to tell me more on the way to Louisville."

I nodded, rummaging through the bag. "Here's a good one. *With All My Heart.*" I gave it to her. "It's a love story about Charles II and Catherine of Braganza."

Amara studied the front and flipped it over to read the back dust cover.

I liked the novel because the princess had an ol' blind woman like Retta who gave her smart advice. "Oh, the author, Margaret Campbell Barnes, was an ambulance driver during the last war in London," I added.

"I'll take it!"

I gave her a flyer from the Company store and some church pamphlets.

Above, a lone bird flew over, lifting its natters as the thinning sunlight swept its last hours into darkness. Junia neighed into the rises and lows.

"It's getting late," I said.

"Are you still living at Miss Adams's?"

"I moved back to my grandparents' cabin because Alonzo had to sell hers."

"That old man sure is a mess," she said. "Thank you for these. See you tomorrow."

"Much obliged, Amara. I can't wait to see them, and I'll pay you for the gasoline."

Thinking about how I'd see my folk erased the meanness of the day and lit a small joy in my heart. I hurried over to Junia, light in my step, and planted a kiss on her muzzle. "Tomorrow, tomorrow, ol' girl, I will be in Mama and Papa's arms!" Junia opened her sleepy eyes and whinnied softly.

Patting her neck, I thought about Carson's proposal and worried if I should mention it tomorrow to my folk. They might push me into marrying him for my safety. Turning it over in my mind, I decided I wouldn't tell them about Carson. Instead, I'd show them Byrne's obituary.

Twenty-Three

I awoke at two on Saturday morning, hurrying to eat and dress, excited to finally see my folk. I remembered gas was about 30 cents a gallon and pulled two dollars out from my coat lining, then packed some dried peaches, sausage, biscuits, and apples, doubling it so I could share it with my folk. Carefully, I slipped it inside Mama's worn leather satchel.

Outside, I carried a lit lantern over to Junia's stall. Sleepy-eyed, the ol' mule ambled out slowly. "I'm going to see Mama and Papa today, so you need to carry me quick to the nurse's cabin." Junia straightened her ears and looked around. "No fussing or poking along, today, Junia. Straight to Amara's."

I wrestled her saddle onto her back and slipped the satchel inside the pannier. Junia bared teeth, quietly nibbling the air. "I forgot your cookies." She bobbed her head, nuzzling my shoulder. I hurried back inside to pack her treats.

The lantern chewed through darkness and the swirling morning fog as we rode away. Soon a light mist came down. I rolled my knit hat down over my ears and burrowed my chin deeper into my coat.

In the distance, dogs barked, their high-pitched exchanges skating back and forth across pine tops. I stiffened. Again their screams shimmied the forest, raising the hairs on the nape of my neck. *Coyotes.* I glanced down at my scabbard and tried to make Junia go faster.

Suddenly, I felt something move around my bottom and creep slowly onto my lap. A shriek escaped in a long-winded quiver, and I shut my eyes, feeling whatever it was lumber across my thighs.

Blowing hard, Junia slowed to a halt.

With a trembling hand, I raised the lantern over my lap and swallowed hard. Exhaling three sharp breaths, I gulped down another and then fluttered my eyelids open before dropping the collected air like a brick.

Pennie. I nearly collapsed at the sight of her.

The cat had stolen away inside the pannier. "Pennie," I squeaked out, stroking her small head, relieved. "I've never been so happy to see you," I told the cat. "But you nearly knocked me off my mount with fright. You have to go back."

Junia snorted impatiently, exhaling puffs of cold air. Pennie stretched and kneaded the mule's withers, purring loudly. The mule's muscles rippled with pleasure. Flopping her ears, Junia nibbled at the air.

I pulled the damp cat closer and turned Junia back to our cabin. When we arrived home, I climbed down and carried Pennie over to the stall. But Junia beat us to it and pounded inside. She wouldn't budge.

I stared up at the dark sky, worrying. We had already lost an hour carrying Pennie home, and I had to spend another half hour fussing over the mule's loud indignant brays. I grew frantic. *Would Amara wait or leave without me?* Finally, I coaxed Junia out with a cookie.

"*Hurry.*" I prodded her with my knees. "Hurry, Junia. I don't want to lose my ride." Hours later, the rain stopped and the sun broke through the misty fog, the skies lightened in hues of lavenders, pinks, and oranges as we rode the paths. Birds trilled their choruses of sputters, chatters, and chirps, calling the new day.

I cut through town and saw the sidewalks empty except for a miner hurrying inside the Company store. Mrs. Martin was headed into the library, and the courthouse was deserted.

When we rode into Amara's yard, I was relieved to see her lights on. I told Junia, "You're going to stay in the building over there." I climbed down and tethered her to the porch, then dug into my pocket for her cookie. "Stay put, ol' girl. I'll be right back to take you to Amara's stall." I kissed her nose, then raced up the steps and knocked lightly, scents of chimney smoke wafting over the small home.

Amara opened the door with a shushing finger to her lips. "Come in, Honey, and get warm. You can hang your coat on the rack," she whispered. I stepped over the threshold, slipped off my damp coat and hat, and hung them on a hall tree beside her door. I stared down at my gloved hands and peeled them off.

A cot sat over by a window to the far edge of the room with someone small bundled underneath the covers.

"Have a seat, Honey, and I'll serve us coffee."

Worried, I sat down at her table, sneaking peeks over to the makeshift bed.

In a few minutes, Amara sat down beside me with our full cups. "I'm sorry, but I have a patient. The boy, Johnnie Gillis, is doing better since I've gave him a shot of penicillin last night for his bout of pneumonia."

"Johnnie," I whispered, suddenly feeling ill.

"He'll be fine, but none of the other nurses are available to sit, so I won't be able to leave today."

I was crushed. "I hope the boy will heal quick," I said, meaning it, though the news almost doubled me over from the ache of not being able to visit my folk. I had to see them and tell them about Retta and Byrne and let them know I was without a guardian.

She sipped her coffee quietly for a few minutes as I fretted it all. When I couldn't swallow any more, I pushed the cup aside.

"Thank you. I best go," I said, thinking of my folk, the sadness smothering in the cramped, sterile room reeking of rot, bandaged sickness, and strange antiseptics.

Amara reached across the table, patted my hand. "I know

it's a long trip down here, but if you'll call again next Saturday, maybe—"

A sudden banging startled us, and I jumped up.

Amara opened the door, a draft of woodsmoke and pine skittering into the home just as Mr. Gillis stepped inside with Guyla Belle following. "How's Johnnie this morn—" Mr. Gillis stopped in midsentence. Catching a glimpse of me, he stretched out an arm. "*You!* What are you doing here with my son? Didn't I tell you not to bring them books around us again?"

I stepped back.

"*Mr. Gillis!*" Amara whispered harshly, glaring at him. "Miss Lovett is a guest in my home, and if you don't lower your voice, I'll have to ask you to leave."

Over on the cot, Johnnie stirred and sat up. Rubbing his sickly eyes, he looked at his mama and then saw me. He pointed my way. Just when I thought he'd start screaming, burst out crying, he piped, "Buk uman well, tank ya," and repeated it again, this time grinning big, wanting to mimic his mama's earlier instructions, hoping to please her.

Mr. Gillis followed his hand.

Guyla Belle's dull eyes filled with tears.

"What's that, Son?" Mr. Gillis asked softly, looking back and forth between me and his son. "I–I fall'd down well, Dad-dee. Well hurt Johnnie bad," the little boy said in a pout.

"Guyla, is the boy saying what I think he's saying? *Guyla!*" he shouted, and took off his Texaco ball cap and swatted her face with it. "Did you let my son fall down that well?"

"*Ma-ma-maa!*" Johnnie began sobbing, pulling the bedsheet up into his mouth and sucking on its corner.

"Our boy done got the pneumonia from falling down that cold well full of winter rains, Guyla?" His wife trembled and tucked her head. Mr. Gillis shot out an arm and backhanded her hard across the mouth, splitting her lips. "He could've drown, woman!"

Guyla Belle staggered backward and fell into a heap on the floor, knocking her head on the brick skirt of the fireplace.

I choked out a scream. Outside, Junia bawled maddening hee-haws, kicking at the porch.

Amara rushed over and knelt down beside Guyla Belle. "Leave this instant, Mr. Gillis."

He curled his lips and raised a fist.

"*Now*, Mr. Gillis. I won't ask you twice," she said icily and darted her eyes to the shotgun hanging across her mantel.

Mr. Gillis's gaze followed hers, and he jerked his head back to his wife, staring hard, his jaw cut hard, rigid.

Amara glanced at me, and her eyes shifted toward the gun.

Dashing over to the mantel, I smacked down an itching hand, ready to grab the shotgun. "Leave, Mr. Gillis."

Mr. Gillis turned toward me, widening his eyes. "Blue devil bitch," he growled.

Then to Guyla Belle he said real low, "Get up. I've got me another sixteen-hour shift comin' down in that devil hole today, Guyla, so I can put food on our table and keep a roof over our heads. I married myself a lazy, good-for-nothing woman, Guyla, who ain't fit to be the mother of my son. And now I'm gonna have to work even more hours to pay for the concrete to cover that damn well. You get my son dressed and outta here, and have supper waiting at midnight when I get off." He looked over to Johnnie, then turned one last contemptuous eye on his stirring wife and stormed out the door.

I hurried over to the threshold. Junia blew angrily, kicked sideways, raring for a piece of him. "He's gone," I said, shutting the door.

Guyla Belle groaned and tried to push herself up, and I ran over to her.

"Help me seat her at the table," Amara said, inspecting Guyla Belle's face, gently running her fingers over her head. "Get some hot water on, Honey. And grab the Mercurochrome beside the stove."

At the sink, I filled the kettle and set it on the hot stove.

When it whistled, I poured water into a wash basin and placed it on the table.

Amara washed the deep gash on Guyla Belle's forehead, and I handed her the bottle of Mercurochrome. I grabbed hold of Guyla Belle's hands as the nurse dispensed droplets of the burning orange medicine onto the open wound. Guyla Belle moaned and sweat popped up on her forehead as she clamped down on my damp hand, her eyes filled with pain and misery.

A while later, Amara had her wounds stitched up and bandaged.

I made tea and set a cup in front of Guyla Belle, but she ignored it, pushing it aside.

"Thank you for pulling my Johnnie out of the well, Honey. I've got to get home now." Guyla stood shakily, walked over to the cot, and kissed her boy. "Let's get your clothes on, Son. Mama's got to get home and get the chores done." She patted the boy's legs and drew back the covers. "Thank you again, Book Woman, for saving my boy. Might appreciative for your service, Nurse Amara."

Amara went over to Johnnie. "I'd like to keep you and the boy overnight, Mrs. Gillis," she said. "Make sure you don't have a concussion and the boy is stable enough to travel."

Guyla Belle shook her head. "If you'll bring me his clothes, we can be on our way, ma'am."

"They're over here, Mrs. Gillis." Amara pointed. "I washed them." She collected the boy's freshly cleaned clothes from a corner stool, set them on the foot of the bed, and began to dress him. After he was clothed, the nurse took his temperature with the thermometer, then shook down the mercury in the glass tubing, sticking it back inside its leather case. Amara said, "I'd still feel better if you stayed, Mrs. Gillis."

"Please stay, Guyla Belle," I said, following them to the door.

"Sorry for all the trouble," she said. "Perry weren't always like this. The coal is the devil, a bad'un, it is. Seeps into good hearts and blackens like the coal ash that keeps finding its way into our fresh-swept rooms."

Johnnie latched onto his mama's hand. I thought about Bonnie down there, the good miners, the sweet boy in front of me hardening to a lump of blackened coal.

"Please bring me them books, Honey, I promise to keep 'em good 'n' hid. *Promise*," Guyla Belle said, the desperation slipping into her quivering voice.

"It's too dangerous for you to go back there," I whispered, laying a hand on her slumped shoulder.

"Dangerous if I don't. I could never leave him. Ain't got no money or family. Only him and my boy in this world," Guyla Belle uttered, holding onto the doorframe with one hand and her son's palm in the other before stepping outside.

"Wait, Guyla Belle."

She turned to me.

I could barely glance at her swollen eyes. She looked lost, the sadness and desperation painful to see. "I'll make sure you get the books."

Gratitude swept across her face. We watched her walk slow and stiff-legged out of the yard, with Johnnie in tow.

"They always go back to those pantywaist cowards, no matter how many times I stitch them up or set their broke bones," Amara said, a bitterness wrenched in her words.

When the mother and son slipped through the trees, I pulled out my timepiece and saw it was going on eleven thirty. I raised the case and asked Amara, "Do we have time?"

"It's a good five hours or more drive, Honey, and we'd never make the visiting hours to the prisons or get to the health center before they close." She touched my arm. "I'm sorry. Maybe you can try and telephone them today. Let's plan on next Saturday."

I stared out into the fog-soaked hills, heartbroken.

"Let me fix you breakfast, Honey. It's the least I can do for your trouble."

"Obliged, but I have food packed. I think I'll go into town and get a few things I've been needing." I wanted to run and escape to a place where I could hurt without others seeing me hurt.

I shut the door quietly behind me and walked briskly over to Junia, crumpling against the mule, burying my face against her shoulder, quelling the sorrows of the morning. The ol' girl didn't twitch, or move in the slightest, and I knew she was hurting as much as me.

Twenty-Four

I climbed atop the mule and rode into a busy town square, grieving with a burning hunger to reach my folk.

Men and women called out their hidey-dos as they went about their Saturday business and morning shopping. I nudged Junia over to the post office where I tied her to a hitching post, deciding to buy stamps to write letters to my folk.

Postmaster Bill waited patiently while I tried to decide which stamps to buy. In the end, I purchased a sheet of the deep-blue, three-cent Women in Our Armed Services stamps, admiring the four brave women who fought in the four branches of the military. I stared at their cheerful faces, surprised they were blue. I puzzled over whether their color was a trick of the artist or whether they were really blue, and I wondered why war would make them so happy—doubting that their four-star generals did anything better than the women here in Troublesome, the miner woman, the frontier nurse, and the lookout. A man in line behind me inched closer, stepping an impatient reminder onto my heel with his shoe. I scooted forward, paid for the stamps and envelopes, and slipped outside.

Inside the library, I lingered over the latest book arrivals before leaving.

When I was through, I stepped outside and watched miners come out of the Company store next door on their afternoon dinner break. Some chatted while others piled into the back of pickup trucks to head back over to the mines. I searched for Bonnie but couldn't find her.

In a minute, Perry Gillis stepped out with another miner, and Bonnie followed seconds later. She had a Coca-Cola in her hand and moved over to the other side, away from the men, sipping her cool drink. She still wore her blackened bib overalls, hadn't followed the boss man's orders yet.

Francis opened the Company's door, peeked outside. When he saw his cousin, he went up to her. I could see that Francis was upset about something because Bonnie kept shaking her head. Then she ripped off her miner's helmet and threw it on the ground, the coal-stained hat bouncing out into the street, her boy's cut poking out like a spent scarecrow at the end of its season.

Her cousin stepped back as if he'd been hit, pointed at her hair. "Who did it? Tell me!" His shouts carried high above the town and into pine-treed hills, his face mottling with anger.

The small group of huddled miners peered over their shoulders. Francis stormed over to them, yelling, "Which one of you filthy dirt-diggers touched my cousin? You best tell me now, or you'll all be getting a piece of me." He raised both fists.

"Francis, stop," Bonnie said, grabbing his arm. But he jerked away. "Francis, *please*—" Her Coca-Cola tumbled to the sidewalk and busted, the jagged neck of the bottle rolling into the streets.

I hurried over to Bonnie's side. "Francis, stop it," I yelled. "Please don't!"

Mr. Gillis shoved the boy away. Francis punched him in his jaw, and then they were tumbling, fighting out in the street. Francis got a couple of good licks in, but Gillis had more might and punched Francis once and then again. The young man dropped to his knees and hit the ground.

Gillis searched the pavement, then slowly bent down to scoop up a large piece of the bottle. I sprang over and kicked it away, the disappointing morning mounted in my hard boot. Gillis screwed up his face at me and reached for the Cola's broke neck.

Surprised at my anger, I stumbled back. Another coal miner grabbed Gillis's arm and twisted his wrist, knocking the sharp, jagged glass out of his hand. Francis stood and staggered and Gillis lunged for him again. Several men came out of the store and separated the two, dragging Francis back inside. "Come on, Son," one man told Francis, "let's get you upstairs to one of the rooms and clean you up." Francis limped inside.

Bonnie snatched her helmet and took off fast.

The other men talked heatedly to the miner in between Gillis's curses.

Worried about Francis, wanting to escape Gillis, I decided to go inside. Maybe I could try to use the telephone and ring my folk like Amara suggested. Hesitant, I waited a few minutes, then pulled a dollar out from my coat pocket and moved closer to the Company store.

Perry Gillis stepped in front of me and blocked the entrance. He leaned into my face and said, "If you bring any more of them filthy books to my home, so much as a page, I'll register a complaint with the library and sic the law on ya for coming between a man and his wife."

I cringed, remembering that I had read somewhere about the old alienation-of-affection law.

He pushed his face closer to mine and I tucked my chin, cowering, knowing if there was one thing the Blue folk had in common with other womenfolk, it was to do just that, duck from a man's hard flying fist. Like all Kentucky women, I knew when to stand and knew when to bow and back down. It was a means of survival that was taught to the very young, instilled in the smallest of girls.

"Listen up good now, gal. Ya hear me?" He grabbed hold of my hair and yanked hard, burning my scalp. My eyes watered as he wound his beefy fingers tighter, knotted, and jerked harder.

A small cry escaped my clenched teeth.

"You stop running your mouth to my woman and stay the hell away from my place!" Gillis blew his stale breath into my face, taking a clump of hair with him as he shoved me backwards. When I finally looked up, he was walking back to the group of miners.

Torn, I stared at his back, breathing hard, shaken, trying to decide whether I should take Guyla Belle off the list. Wincing, I rubbed my scalp. If I lost my job, I wouldn't have a chance of making it on my own. I needed this job and the steady income, and more pay stubs. She'd been desperate for the books, and I wanted to help the woman escape from her misery. If he brought the law down on me, it would be bad and even hurt anything Mr. Morgan was trying to do to keep me out of the prison. I could lose what liberty I had left.

But Guyla Belle had begged for the library material, and I'd promised her. And didn't Miss Foster say it was my job, my duty to get the books into the hands of all readers? Would she fire me if she found out I didn't? I recalled some of the difficulties Mama said she'd faced with folk when trying to deliver books. Some of them were downright dangerous. Still, she stuck with it, determined to grow readers.

I sucked in a weary breath, promising myself to be more cautious and watch for Guyla Belle's dairy bottle.

Inside the store, I waited at the counter for change, staring up at the hanging metal advertisement of the glamorous movie star, Hedy Lamarr, touting an *RC tastes best!* sign nearly naked belly in her blue Bardot two-piece dress.

I sneaked glances of Gillis through the store windows, watching him linger around the men like he was waiting on someone. I rubbed my tender head and rummaged through a display box of wooden spin tops, admiring the colorful toys. A minute later, Francis appeared, his face red and an eye beginning to swell, a dab of orange Mercurochrome dotting a cut down his cheek.

"Honey," Francis said, not looking at me directly, "what can I get you today?" He picked up a wooden top and dropped it back inside the box. "The spinners are a nickel a piece."

"I'm glad you're okay, Francis."

His face reddened. "Sorry you had to see that, Honey, but men like Gillis have to be dealt with or they'll keep hurting women. The men said the book woman kicked the glass away from Perry Gillis. Thanks for your help."

I nodded, embarrassed, gingerly touching my sore head.

"What can I get ya?"

Slipping off a glove, I tucked loose hair behind my ears and pulled out a dollar from my coat. "I'm needing change for the pay phone."

He glanced at my blue hand a second, then opened the cash register. Quietly, he counted out mostly nickels and a few dimes and placed them in my waiting palm, his touch lingering, my hands drenched in blue.

I snatched back my hand and dared to look up at him, pulling back on the glove. But his eyes were warm and welcoming. Jingling the coins, I looked around and behind me, leaned over the counter and whispered, "How do I use it, Francis?"

"Huh?"

"Never used a pay telephone before." I felt my face flush hotly from embarrassment and added, "Never saw the need to until now."

Amusement lit across his eyes, and he called out to someone named Eddie. "Watch the counter while I help her in the back." Francis came out from behind the counter and walked me toward the telephone booth that sat in the corner at the end of the store.

He opened the wooden booth's glass door and stepped in, urging me to do the same. "Okay, here's how it works," he said, standing shoulder to shoulder with me.

My face warmed. Besides the playful tussles with Carter and his brothers when we were young, I had never been this close to a young man before. And the pleasantly odd, swirling scent of boy was dizzying as I tried to curve my shoulders to make room.

"Ya pick up this receiver here like this and then put a nickel in the far-right slot. Right here, Honey. Then dial the rotary.

Telephone book is on the tray here." He raised a finger over the numbers, pretending to turn clockwise, then inserted a fingertip into the circles, spinning the rotary. Again he spun his finger over the dials. "If ya don't have a number, the operator will get it for you," he said.

I looked down, feeling silly. "Op-er-ator?" I said the word slow, stretching the syllables.

"Right here, just dial 0 for operator." He went through the motions again.

I nodded. "Much obliged for your help, Francis, but can you wait outside in case I need you?"

"Sure thing, Honey." He squeezed past me and stepped out, his face just as flushed as I knew mine must be.

I pulled off my gloves, put in a coin, and dialed zero.

"Number, please?" the operator asked.

"Ma'am, this is Honey Lovett in Troublesome Creek, Kentucky. I want to speak to my mama at the women's prison in Pewee Valley, Kentucky, please."

"Women's Division, Kentucky State Reformatory. Deposit another nickel, please."

I fumbled inside my pocket and dropped the coin into its slot.

"Please hold."

"Yes, ma'am, Operator. Much obliged."

Francis had his back to me, hands shoved into his pant pockets, trying not to listen.

Two long rings and a woman picked up. "Women's Division, Kentucky State Reformatory. Mrs. Holland speaking."

"Ma'am, Mrs. Holland, this is Honey Lovett over in Troublesome Creek, ma'am. I want to speak to my mama, please—"

"Prisoners are only allowed to make one telephone call a month if they're housed in the honor wing."

"When can my mama telephone me?"

She sighed, annoyed. "Who is your mother, miss?"

"Cussy Mary Lovett."

I heard her flicking through pages. Shortly, she said, "Lovett has been restricted from telephone calls and outside visits. You're the daughter?"

"Yes, ma'am." I barely breathed, looking wildly around, inhaling stale air.

"We tried to reach her relatives but didn't have an address. Your mother is being housed in the prison infirmary."

"Infirmary, but why?" My legs weakened, and I dropped to the small wooden bench seat and spooled the telephone cord tight in my hand. "What happened to my mama?"

"I'm sorry. You'll need to speak with your attorney about that." I heard a click.

"What's wrong with her? Ma'am? *Ma'am?*" I gripped the small, metal telephone-book tray in front of me.

I stared down at the receiver, lifted it back up to my ear. "*Ma'am?*"

Francis tapped on the glass door and mouthed, *Everything okay, Honey?*

I put on my gloves, and pulled on the brass handle, opening the glass door. "I need to get to Pewee Valley right away."

"I'm off Monday, and I can borrow my pa's truck and take you."

"Much obliged, Francis, but I need to get hold of Mr. Morgan first."

From the front of the store, Eddie called out to Francis. "Mr. Webb needs to be rung up, Francis."

Francis frowned. "Gotta get back to work. If you change your mind and need that ride, just let me know." He stepped away, then turned back to me. "Say, Honey, uh...would you like to go out sometime? Maybe take in a movie at the picture show? Or a picnic down by the creek? Go on a date with me, Honey?" He rushed the words, shoved his hands deep into his pockets, rocking on the balls of his shoes, waiting.

I was more than surprised that he'd asked, and when my answer failed to come, Francis added, "Mama'd be happy to make us up a tasty basket of victuals."

"It sounds fun, but…" I searched for an excuse since I needed Papa's permission first. But I wasn't ready to tell him Papa was in prison. Finally, I told him the truth. "I haven't been given permission to date yet."

"Ask your pa." His eyes were bright and pleading, his smile warm.

"He's not here," I said, wanting to say yes, but not wanting to tell him exactly where my papa was.

Lightly, he leaned over and rapped the telephone booth with his knuckles. "Maybe you can telephone him sometime?" Grinning, he pivoted and walked back to the counter. I watched him snatch glimpses of me as he snapped open a brown bag and began stuffing it with the customer's store goods.

Flustered, I sat down on the small, narrow telephone bench, searching my satchel for Mr. Morgan's number.

Outside the booth, I heard his voice before I saw him. Mr. Gillis and a gray-haired woman who held a sack of groceries huddled alongside a rack of work clothes with their backs to me. Pressing my knee against the wooden bifold door, I cracked it open a bit more, listening.

"I tried, Ma," he said worriedly. "They's working me to my death. Guyla's not taking care of the boy."

"I know'd she was a bad one from the git-go, Son," his mama hissed. "Should've kicked her ass out long ago. You talk with your cousin Robbie?"

"Ain't been able to see him. Coal's been thieving my time. And can't hardly keep my mind on work, Ma, worrying what will befall my son next. Worrying she'll let him get hurt really bad the next time, maybe even—" Mr. Gillis rubbed his face, sniffed. "I need new work that ain't pulling my leg into the grave, and I don't want to lose my boy."

His mama pushed a lock of hair away from his eyes. "I'll talk with Robbie again, have him work on that foolish lookout gal. Meanwhile, you git rid of Guyla."

Mr. Gillis turned slightly to her, seeking what looked like a permission of sorts in his eyes.

She nodded once, then again more firmly. "You get rid of that trash, then it'll be only you and the boy to worry on. Get yourself that cushy forest job like Robbie has. I'll git your sister to help ya sit the boy in the meantime," she said, patting his arm. "Ida won't mind at all helping out her little brother. Get on to your shift tonight, and I'll talk with Robbie and Ida."

The woman turned to leave and our eyes met. Quickly, I lowered my chin to my lap and pulled the booth door closed, rumbling the glass. A chill latched hold of my flesh as she bristled by. I waited until Mr. Gillis's footsteps sounded a few seconds later. Then the store bell jingled, announcing his goodbye.

I composed myself and found Mr. Morgan's card and stood to dial, letting it ring seven times before I hung up. I waited a moment, then tried once more. But the lawyer never answered. I could ride to the outskirts of town where his office was, but I knew that if he didn't pick up the telephone, likely his office was closed.

I thought to try calling Papa, but a man tapped on the glass and pointed to his watch, waiting to use the telephone.

I stepped outside the store, pushing past the gathered miners, wishing the woman at Pewee Valley had let me speak to the prison doctor. *Doctor.* The old mountain doc was our family doctor; maybe he could help.

Greta and Carson were on the corner, their heads bowed in secret conversation, the young lovers smitten with each other.

In the street, Wrenna passed by with her rooster. Gillis still hung around, eating an apple, nursing his wounds as he propped a dirty boot back against the storefront. He pretended to leap for the young girl, stirring a charging fury in the protective pet, the raw, unkind, brutish laughter of the men caroling, coaxing Gillis and the frantic bird on.

Gillis took another bite of his apple and then threw it at the rooster, making the creature fly up and squawk.

For a few seconds, Wrenna stared at him oddly, then sounded a musical *coo-coo*, and the bird hurried back to her side. She picked up the rooster and walked steadily past the men, carrying a small basket of wild berries, poke, and other greens she'd probably picked for her great-grandmother, Emma.

I rode Junia over to Doc's house, hoping he could help me.

Millie frowned when she opened the door.

"Ma'am, I need to talk with Doc."

"*Läkare som äter middag.*" She flicked her hand at me, shooing me away.

I tried to look past her. "Doc," I hollered, "it's Honey Lovett."

Millie wrinkled her brow. "*Middag!*" She jabbed a finger toward her mouth, made like she was chewing, then stopped and gawked at me. "*Lovett.* Book Woman?"

"Book? Book woman, yes." I put a finger on my chest and tapped. "Book woman, Honey Lovett."

"*Böcker,*" she said dreamily, pulling me inside.

Doc came into the foyer with a napkin tucked into his collar. "Honey," he said, surprised. "Come in and join us. We're just having dinner. Millie, set the child a plate."

Millie turned and hurried down the hall, her words floating in the air.

"I need to speak with you about Mama."

"I just got back in town. Come into the dining room; we'll talk about it after dinner." He took my coat and hung it on his ornate hall tree. Doc gestured for my gloves.

I looked down the hall past him toward Millie, hesitating, not wanting her to see my naked hands.

Doc picked up on my thoughts and said, "As the wife of a doctor, she understands we're all different, child. And better for it. Come join us. Millie's fixed a wonderful feast."

Relieved, I pulled my gloves off and he placed them on the entry table. It was hard not to stare at everything in his beautiful home, to sneak glances at the large dark-paneled rooms we passed.

In the dining room, Millie set a fancy china plate in front of me, with polished silverware on linen, neatly on the side.

She sat down beside me. "*Äta.*"

Millie picked up her fork and pointed to the lavish foods in front of us. Then she snatched the linen napkin off my plate and dropped it onto my lap.

It was fine fabric and I hesitated, not wanting to soil it.

Doc took his seat across from me. "Help yourself, Honey, fresh greens, delicious pork, and Millie's wonderful raggmunk."

Millie beamed at her husband, then passed me a plate of what looked like pancakes and jam. "*Ät. Du är för tunn.*"

Doc said to Millie, "*Reta inte,*" then to me, "She's concerned about you not eating enough, and I told her not to tease you." He cut off a bite-sized piece of his pork.

Millie passed me a bowl of food, and I served myself a little out of each dish, not realizing how hungry I was. If she noticed the worry flushed blue on my hands, she didn't say anything.

It was one of the best meals I'd ever eaten, even finer than any of the food at the Regas Brothers' restaurant in Knoxville. "It's delicious, ma'am. Much obliged."

Millie grinned widely, seeming to understand. But when I pushed myself back from the table, she shook her head. "*Efterrätten kommer,*" she said standing.

Doc took a sip of his water and then said, "She's asking you to stay. Don't move."

In a minute, his wife came back with two generous, fluffy cinnamon buns and set them down in front of us. As I took a bite, the buttery, sweet confection melted in my mouth. I patted the napkin over my mouth and nodded my appreciation to Millie.

Millie smiled back, pleased, and began stacking dirty plates.

When I stood to help, she said *"Efterrätten"* again and wagged a finger at me.

Doc said, "Millie will fuss you out of her kitchen if you try and help. I've tried too many times, and my dear bride chases me away."

"How did you meet Millie, Doc?"

He swallowed and wiped his mouth with a napkin, his kind eyes twinkling. "Well, I was invited by a colleague of mine over to the church social in Beauty." He tucked the napkin back into his lap. "Millie was cooking that night, and she served me one of her fine meals. It was so good, I took to attending the socials every month. Gobbling down anything she'd put in front of me to impress her." He chuckled. "Must've packed on ten pounds before I finally asked her out, and another ten before I decided to marry her. Millie makes a ceremony out of our meals, and she likes having her kitchen run just so. Enjoy your dessert, Honey."

After we finished, Doc led me into his parlor and pointed to a seat. I sat down in one of the pastel-green chairs with delicate orange flowers. The rich walnut arms were smooth, and I settled in, the chair gently hugging my backside.

"I'm sure sorry to hear about Miss Adams and Bluet and Jackson," he said, using the nickname he'd given her at birth, declaring Mama was a *fit girl who could turn as blue as the familiar bluet damselfly skinning the Kentucky creek beds when she was born*. "I've been away most of March... Yes, thank you, Millie." She served him a cup of coffee and offered one to me, setting the tray down on the ornate hand-carved wooden table between us before leaving.

"It was hard losing Retta. I miss her terribly. I called the prison today, and they said Mama is in the infirmary. Said I couldn't visit or speak to her. I need your help, Doc."

"What is her condition?"

"They wouldn't tell me," I said, worrying a loose string on the cuff of my shirt.

Doc lifted a white brow. After a pause he said, "Let me go telephone the prison. Stay here and make yourself comfortable while I try to get to the bottom of it."

He grabbed his cup of coffee. After he left the room, I stood and walked over to the mantel, glancing at his photographs atop it, inspecting all the figurines that had been collected. Ten minutes later, I heard the pocket door slide open. Millie stopped him in the hall and whispered something to him.

A moment later, he came back into the parlor and sat down in his chair. I took my seat again.

"First, Honey, Bluet's not ill."

My shoulders relaxed, and I let out a draining sigh.

"I spoke with Warden Marie Sanders and told her I was your mother's personal physician. Seemed like a nice enough gal. She informed me that Bluet underwent a sterilization after the court ordered it several weeks ago."

"*Barren*," I said, shocked, remembering how she talked about giving me a brother or sister one day.

"Eugenics is not uncommon for, um…certain folks, Honey, especially when it involves miscegenation laws."

I stiffened. *Different* folk.

"But Warden did mention some of the prison doctors were curious and wanted to run tests." He rubbed his chin thinking. "Now I didn't take much to that, so I asked her if we could drop by tomorrow and pay Bluet a visit. She said it'd be fine."

I collapsed against the back of the chair. "Obliged, Doc." Finally, I would see her.

"Why don't you take that ornery mule to one of the stalls in the barn, feed it some oats, and I'll have Millie make up a room for you. Wouldn't want you traveling all the way back into the hills late only to have you come back at dark in the morning. We'll leave at first light."

"I need to run over to the homestead and feed my cat first and pack clean clothes for the trip. It shouldn't take but a couple of hours."

"I'll see you then. Ride safe, child." He stood.

I paused as we passed Guyla Belle's. Through the trees I saw her sitting on her stoop. I didn't have time to stop, but maybe I could check on her and Johnnie on my way back and offer her a book that would make her feel better. Junia rode fast and we made it home quick and with extra time to spare.

I unpacked my bags and fed a loud Pennie. Looking through my clothes, I grabbed a clean dress and undergarments, then lingered at the bookcase packed with reads that we'd brought over from the Cumberland cabin for our visits in Troublesome.

After a few minutes of studying them, I hurried up the loft to pore over the stacks of books up there, studying an old dictionary Mama had received from her friend Queenie Johnson. Queenie had worked with Mama a while but left for Philadelphia in 1936 and ended up getting her librarianship. When I turned eight, Mama passed the dictionary to me.

Carefully, I opened the thick book and licked my fingertip, skimming the worn, yellowed, slick pages to the E's until my eyes rested on the word. *Emancipation, n, act of or state of being, etc.; liberation, release, freedom.* I wondered about Byrne McDaniel and how he'd won his freedom.

I closed the dictionary and pressed it to my chest. Somehow, I had to convince Mr. Morgan to get mine.

Setting the thick book aside, I looked over other stacks and plucked up two novels, then climbed down the ladder and stuffed them inside my pannier with my other book returns from Friday's route and the newspaper.

Guyla Belle was still sitting alone on the stoop when I rode into the yard, and I saw she'd placed a dairy bottle on the lip of the well. She jumped up when she spotted me and limped over, her vacant eyes filling with light.

"Book Woman, I thought I'd never see ya again."

"Good evening, Guyla Belle. I wanted to leave you a book, and see how you and Johnnie are doing."

"You're a sight for sore eyes, Honey. Thanks for dropping by." I heard the loneliness escape her ragged breaths. "I'm mending okay. The boy's still running a low fever, but he ate heartily and played some on the porch before I put him down for the evening. He's strong and will likely pert up tomorrow and have me chasing him around the yard." Guyla Belle's face was gaunt. She laughed but it rang false.

I slid off Junia and rummaged through my bag, sneaking glances at the beaten woman, knowing it would be a long time before she would be chasing anything. I wondered what Gillis and his kin were up to and prayed Guyla Belle would be safe, wishing she had a safe place to go.

After a minute of digging around, I pulled out *The Awakening* for her. Chopin's novel was one of Mama's favorites, despite some folk thinking it was immoral and led females down the wrong path, against what men thought best. But I thought being so far from home, Guyla Belle would enjoy reading about Edna Pontellier, the strong Kentucky woman who was living in Louisiana. Maybe the book would help her through her suffering.

"I think you'll like this one, Guyla Belle." I looked around the yard and over my shoulder, hesitating.

She snatched it greedily from my hands. Studying the cover, Guyla Belle flipped it over to read the back, then thumbed through the pages, her eyes hungry for the printed word.

"Guyla Belle, I was in such a hurry, I forgot to bring back the socks you lent me. If your dairy bottle's on the well, I'll get them to you Friday."

"Thank you, Book Woman." She pulled her eyes away from the book. "This one sounds real good. And I'll take good care of it, I promise."

From inside I heard Johnnie call out for her.

Junia whinnied, a warning in its faint rise.

Uneasy, I looked around again, then back at the loan in Guyla Belle's hands, fretting. Finally, I prodded Junia with my knees. "See you next Friday, Guyla Belle."

Doc greeted me at his door, offering to take my satchel.

"Obliged, Doc, but it's not heavy. I only packed my clean dress and a book to read tonight."

"Oh, books." He raised a crooked finger. "Millie said she heard about the revival of the Pack Horse project and that you were hired. She wanted me to ask if you'd put her on your route. She's been hankering for some good books to read lately."

"Yes, sir. I'm the new assistant outreach librarian. I'd be happy to add her to my Friday route."

"Very nice. Now Millie likes good books, was taught to read English when she was a young girl, but just hasn't mastered our language. Rather, she's too stubborn to give up hers." He smiled. "She loves a good historical and also suspenseful novels. Reads the romances, though nothing too racy."

"Yes, sir, I'll remember. Much obliged for you and Millie's generous hospitality."

"Millie is anxious to show you to your room. She has it ready for your visit, and I think you'll find it quite comfortable."

Upstairs, I bounced on a large, fluffy bed filled with pillows and marveled at the fine furniture, the rich mahogany highboy dresser with its beveled mirror and detailed carvings and claw feet that matched the bed's headboard. I pulled off the dusty boots and stretched my bare feet and dug my toes into the Persian rug, admiring the tight weaves in the carpet, the bold colors and delicate floral design.

A few minutes later, there was a knock, and Millie came in with towels, soap, and a gown and robe. She shyly placed it all at the foot of the bed and made a gesture, pretending to wash her face, before pointing to an alcove. When she left, I went over and was surprised to find a sparkling white claw tub, porcelain sink, and inside toilet, all grander than any I'd seen in magazines, much less ever had the chance to use. After I tested the faucets and stopper, I took a long soaking bath and scrubbed every inch of me, the day's hardness slowly vanishing, my tight muscles becoming loose.

In bed, I put my book aside, worried about what they'd done to Mama and fretting for her safety.

Sometime during the night, Millie must've slipped into the room for my clothes, because in the morning I found them laundered and folded on top of the trunk at the foot of the bed.

In the morning, Millie came in with a tray of steaming porridge, baked goods, coffee, and orange juice. "*Äta. Äta*, Book Woman," she said warmly and tucked back her skirts as she left the room.

I snatched a bun off the plate, gulped down the orange juice, and raced around the room to get ready, anxious to see Mama.

Standing next to the automobile, Doc's wife passed me a large, cold, metal milk pail with a cloth lid. I grabbed the wooden handle, lowered it to the ground, and opened it, peeling back the linen. She'd packed it with ice, smoked meats, fat rolls, fruit, and a jar of chowchow and a few other foods I couldn't make out. "Much obliged, ma'am, for your hospitality, everything."

Doc set it on the floorboard in front of the bench seat. "See you late this afternoon, not sure what time I'll be home," he said as he set a small basket with two plates and utensils inside the trunk. He plucked his medical bag off the ground, climbed inside the automobile, and tossed the bag into the back seat.

Millie leaned inside the window and kissed his cheek. "*Hej då*," she rang out and waved to me. "*Hej då*."

I tried to say her words, and she laughed cheerfully when I failed and mispronounced them as *Hey dog*.

"Ready?" Doc asked.

I nodded solemnly, a little scared and burdened by what I might find there, wondering if anyone could ever be ready to go to a prison.

Twenty-Five

We passed through the streets of Troublesome, the town buttoned closed for the Lord's Day. The first breaths of dawn arrived in softened hues of ruby and yellow, sifting through the branches of budding locusts and chestnut oaks and the boughs of soldering pines.

At the outskirts of town on Highway 721, little Wrenna and her rooster walked through tall weeds along the thick-treed banks. As we drew nearer, she stepped out onto the road in a long, breezy sack dress, the yellow ruffled hem ragged and trailing. Doc shook his head and said, "Poor child's always roaming, going nowhere but everywhere."

I turned and watched until her small, weary frame disappeared into the shivering patches of rolling asphalt.

Despite Doc's big, comfortable Plymouth, the narrow, pot-holed roads jostled us. Soon the road opened wider, became new and smoother, and we passed green pastures and meadows with grazing cows and horses.

We talked a little, and I told him about my job and chatted about books, then confided in him about the state wanting to send me to the children's prison.

Doc said, "There's plenty of girls your age with jobs, and a lot are child brides growing families of their own. With you living on your own now, and making a living, and undisturbed, I would think that the court would look favorably on you and leave you alone. You say you were assigned an attorney?"

"Yes, sir. It's Mr. Morgan. He's going to try and help me stay free until I can be with my parents again."

"I know Bob well. Good man. I'm sure he'll do right by you."

I was more worried about what the social worker over in Leslie County would do.

Doc made small talk about the spring weather, home, and Millie, and just when I got up the courage to ask him to be my guardian, he said, "We're going to visit her relatives in Sweden for six months later in the summer. It'll be something else, a grand adventure, but I'll sure miss home."

I stared out the window, dismayed, feeling foolish that I'd thought the newlyweds wouldn't mind being burdened with me.

I turned back to him. "Doc, did you ever hear of a man named Byrne McDaniel?"

He rubbed his hand over his chin, thinking. "Can't say that I know him."

"He received his emancipation when he was just fourteen after he got a job. I'm soon to be seventeen."

Doc held up a finger. "I'm not familiar with the laws. But talk to Bob about seeking it. As I said, there's plenty of young married women around and some widowed living on their own. With you holding down a respectable job, there should be no reason why you can't have it. And why any judge wouldn't grant it." He glanced at me.

I shifted my gaze out the window, worrying that my color and being a female might be the reasons why I couldn't. Worse, I was plagued by Judge Norton's harsh words and fretted about the judge and social worker over in Leslie County holding a grudge.

Doc quieted and turned on the radio, tuning it until the voices climbed over the static. The announcer talked a little about the news, then introduced a preacher named Reverend Daniel Cox.

The man gave his sermon, then other preachers told theirs over the miles falling behind us.

At times, I found myself lulled into sleep and fought to stay awake.

Doc stopped once to have his automobile filled with gasoline. We used the public restrooms and freshened up, then Doc bought us colas. At the counter, Doc pointed to a row of candy bars. "Millie's favorite is the buttercream and orange flavors in the Seven Up bar, and mine is the Chicken Dinner bar there." He plucked up the nut roll and Millie's favorite and placed them on the counter to pay. "The reminder of Hoover's old promise of 'a chicken in every pot.'" He grinned. "I bet yours is the chocolate bar over there."

I smiled and pointed to the Bit-O-Honey bar, and he put the candy next to his and Millie's.

The attendant filled the tank and washed all the windows. When I tried to give Doc gasoline and candy-bar money, he pushed it away, saying, "It's on me. I've been wanting to visit you and Bluet for a while. It'll be nice to see her again."

I tried to recall the last time he'd visited us over in the Cumberland and realized it'd been over a year now.

"Much obliged, Doc," I said, slipping the candy into my bag for later.

We pulled into the prison parking lot, both of us tired. It had taken us almost five hours to get here, and we climbed stiffly out of the Plymouth and stretched our legs. I stared at the ugly gray buildings, spotted the gun towers and razor-wired fencing, and shivered.

"Honey, leave your coat and personal items," Doc said, hunched over from the ride, taking off his coat slowly and laying it across the front bench seat.

Leaving on my gloves, I folded my coat over his and put my satchel on the floorboard, while he grabbed his medical bag. "Can we bring her food?"

He wagged his head, solemn.

"I have a newspaper in my bag."

Again, he shook his head.

Standing at the front gate, we waited as a guard checked us in. Doc showed the official his license, and he inspected the doctor's bag. Then he had me sign my name and who I was visiting. I carefully wrote it down in the visitor slot—the date, March 28, 1953, and my mama's name under the prisoner box—and handed the pencil to Doc.

We walked down the narrow sidewalk to a building that had a sign above the door that read Administration. Doc opened the wooden door and motioned for me to go in. A blast of dampness and disinfectant and other putrid smells hit me in the face as I stepped into the small foyer. In front of me there was another massive barred door with another guard behind it.

A brown door leading somewhere else was on the left side of the room.

The guard sauntered up to the bars and said, "What are you here for?"

Doc pushed past me and said, "I'm here to see my patient, Cussy Mary Lovett, who is in the infirmary. This is her daughter, Honey Lovett."

I nodded, excited to see Mama.

The guard went over to the wall and picked up the telephone receiver. "Have the nurse's aide bring down Lovett."

He hung up and unhooked a big brass key from his belt and unlocked the door. "Come on through the crash gate. Empty your pockets, place your bags and personal items on the table," he said in a bored tone. We stepped inside the small area, and the guard locked the big gate behind us. I stared at the other crash gate in front of us, feeling trapped, penned in.

Doc set his bag on the scarred wooden table and dug out loose change, wallet, and keys. The guard inspected it all and pushed it back toward him.

"Take off your gloves, miss."

Reluctantly, I slipped them off and placed them on the table and stepped back. But the guard didn't pick them up. Instead, he gawped bug-eyed at my staining, dark-blue hands.

Doc cleared his throat, and the guard turned his attention to inspecting my gloves, sneaking glimpses at my hands.

"Uh, I need to get my captain's approval, Doctor." He snuck another glimpse at me, went over to the wall, and picked up the telephone. The guard cupped a hand over the mouthpiece. Hisses, whispers skittered, rising up concrete walls, escaping out the ol' dark metal bars into darkened hallways and tiny darker rooms.

"Blue."

"Infirmary."

"Lovett."

"Doctor." I heard the words escape, each deepening the color of my flesh.

"Hand to God, Cap'n. No, sir, the prisoner's not in the blue room, no, sir. Yes. Ya need to get out here, sir." He peeked over his shoulder at us.

I stared at the guard, bewildered, a panic seizing hold of my chest.

Doc must've seen my puzzlement because he leaned over and whispered, "I've heard from colleagues the blue room is where the guards whip 'em, bruises 'em blue. But she's in a safer place."

Staring up at the big clock on the wall, I watched the minute hand circle slowly, sweeping its last tick into a new hour. From beyond the gate down the darkened hall, I heard squeaking, the sounds of metal clacking, growing closer.

"*Mama!*" I cried out when I saw the aide wheel her up to the crash gate behind the guard. Mama sat slumped in an old wheelchair, barefoot, her wrists bound by leather restraints to the metal arm rails. She wore a threadbare loose robe, and her left arm rested inside a heavy cast from what I knew came from the lawman breaking it. The other limb was spotted with bruising, her eyes hollowed, the blue flesh on her face stretched and skeletal. I ran over to her and knelt down, clutched the bars, pressing my face to the cold steel between us. "Mama, what have they done, what have they done?"

She stared at me a moment as if she didn't know me. Then her eyes filled, and she cradled my face with a feeble smile, searching. "Hon-Honey, you're safe. You're safe, my darling daughter?"

I blinked back the tears and choked out a *yes*.

Mama wriggled her fingers, looking pleadingly up to the aide. The aide frowned and untied one of the arm restraints.

Mama reached out, slipped her bony arm between the bars and touched my face, caressing. "Honey, don't cry. Is everything okay at home? Do you have everything you need?"

"Yes, yes, ma'am, and Junia is fine too," I fibbed, placing a shaky hand over hers, closing my eyes, feeling my mama's gentle touch again. "I love you, Mama."

"I love you, Honey."

"Does your arm hurt much?"

A blank look crawled into her eyes.

Doc limped over, still stiff from the travel. "Let me check your pulse, Bluet." When he'd finished, he inspected her good arm, tenderly touching the veins on her wrists and upper flesh. "Bluet," he whispered, "are they running tests? How long have they been treating you up there? How long have you been in that cast?"

Mama hung her head and tears slipped down her bony cheek as she pressed her hand over her bosom. "They took my necessaries after they performed the sterilization, Doc," she whispered, ashamed.

Doc grimaced.

My hand darkened, and I curled it tight, stood slowly. "You already took enough! Where's my mama's undergarments?" I asked, looking back and forth between the aide and guard. "What'd you do with her necessaries?" I glared hotly at the aide. "Give them back!" I screamed to the guard, fury bruising my raised hand. I lurched toward him.

Alarmed, Doc seemed to regain his spent strength and he grabbed my arm, jerking me back. "Honey, stop—"

Next to a table, the door opened, and a short, thick man walked into the foyer, hitched his uniform britches up. He looked at the aide behind the crash gate and said, "Take her back upstairs, Irene."

"No, no," I moaned. Mama reached inside the bar, softly touched my cheek, tears streaming down her own. I clasped her palm and pressed a kiss into it, placing my hand over hers.

The nurse's aide pulled the wheelchair back, breaking our grip. She wheeled Mama down the hall, darkness swallowing them. "*Mama*," I cried out. Doc latched onto my arm, tugging. "Honey, you must calm down if we're to visit her."

I quieted, swallowing my grief.

The uniformed man with a badge pinned on his starched, white dress shirt stepped over to us. "I'm Cap'n Haeg, and I can't have you hollering in here. Visit's over!"

"I–I'm sorry. I won't do it again. Promise." I raised my shocking blue hands, praying for another chance. "Promise, sir, please let me see Mama."

He recoiled at the sight and took a step back.

Doc said, "Sir, I spoke with Warden Sanders yesterday and she gave me permission to examine my patient, Cussy Lovett."

"No orders on my desk." He waved a palm, dismissing us. "You'll have to take it back up with the warden next week. Enough disruption today."

"Now see here, young man, Warden said—" Doc said.

"I *said*, visit's over!"

Doc shook his winter-white head, narrowed his eyes. "The young girl misses her mother, and we've come a long way, Captain. Please telephone your boss, and she'll straighten it out. Surely you won't deny the mother and child a visit. It's the Lord's Day and the Christian thing to do—"

The captain widened his stance and puffed out his chest, hooking thumbs into the waist band. "In here, I'm God on Sundays, and I say no more visitation."

"Well, *God*, I reckon you'll pay the devil for that sin," Doc said. "I'll be dining with my good friend Governor Wetherby this week. And I'm sure Lawrence will be interested in your mistreatment of my patient. And at your bidding," the ol' mountain doc growled, shoving past him to the table. He stuffed his wallet, coins, and keys into his pants pockets and plucked up his medical bag. "Let's go, Honey." He scooped up my gloves and handed them to me.

I looked past the guards, searching. "Please, I want to see Mama," I whispered, yearning, aching for her. Doc took my arm and led us out.

I stared at the razor-wire fencing until it disappeared, knowing I could be locked behind one at any time. We rode mostly in silence for a good three hours, each of us lost in our own thoughts, me drowning in misery, embarrassed I ruined the visit and wasted Doc's time. Now more than ever, I realized it was just a matter of time before what happened to Mama would happen to me. They'd lock me in chains like a circus animal, strip away the baby making, then use me for a guinea pig. I peeked down at my gloves, plucked at the fingertips. My thoughts drifted to Guyla Belle and then to Bonnie and their own fights to survive.

My mind pulled to my job. I put a knuckle to my mouth, tormented and disappointed. If I was going to make it, I had to fight, and somehow I knew it was not going to be just for me.

Doc rested his elbow on the lip of the window frame, his fingers tapping a worriment of his own across his mouth.

Finally, he leaned into the steering wheel. Peering out, he turned onto a road with a sign that said *Natural Bridge State Park Ahead*.

"I reckon we should have us some supper to keep Millie from fussing. And I figure this place is as good as any, and better scenery than where we just came from. A picnic shelter is just up the road," he said.

I pressed a palm to the window, surprised at the beauty of this place. Massive chestnuts, hemlocks, black oaks, and budding tulip trees canopied the winding road. Everywhere, lush greenery and showy spring blossoms crawled up and down banks.

Doc glanced at me. "Used to bring my Lydia up here every spring."

"Sure is pretty," I said, knowing he missed his first wife who'd passed years ago.

He pulled into a lot where picnic tables were placed under a shelter. Grabbing the basket from the trunk, he handed it to me, then took out the milk pail from the floorboard in the back seat. At the picnic table, Doc pulled out the plates and silverware, then opened the pail, carefully arranging Millie's fine fare between us, and probably like she'd taught him. He glanced over at my hands stuffed inside the hot gloves, as he began filling his plate.

"Honey, there's medicine you can take if your color bothers you. It's called methylene blue."

"Yes, sir. Mama told me the drug was used to treat cyanide poisoning. She said taking it was worse than the temporary fix it gave. That it wasn't a cure, and our color—*any* color—is *not* a poison and doesn't need fixing. Only small poisonous minds. And why I have to wear these for protection." I looked over to where a small family sat having a picnic. Boldly, I pulled off my gloves and dropped them onto our table.

Doc grimaced and pointed to Millie's feast before us. "It's been a long day. Lots of good food. Fix you a plate, Honey," he urged. "We'll discuss Bluet while we eat. A man can't be both smart and hungry at the same time. Now's the time to be smart."

My belly growled, and I knew he was right. Mama used to say something similar when one of my handmade toys would break and I'd get frustrated, shake it or throw it onto the ground. She'd always said, *Can't be angry and smart at the same time. Now, nothing wrong in having the anger, but the two rarely work together. Let's be smart, darling daughter.* And then she'd calmly, and ever so slow, help me repair the busted toy.

Smart. I mulled over the word, trying to decide what the smartest thing for me was. Books were smart. Powerful. And suddenly, I knew my job and the books were my path to freedom. They were everything I wanted and the women on my route needed. An escape, a friend, a lesson, and *liberty* for us all.

"Penny for your thoughts, child."

Sheepish, I said, "*Books.*"

"Bluet always got the same look thinking about her books." Doc smiled and tore a fluffy roll in two and stacked smoked turkey onto it, spreading some of Millie's chowchow relish on top before handing it to me.

"Much obliged." I waited till he made one for himself.

He took a big bite and chewed. After he swallowed, he said, "I'll call her lawyer and ask him to get a court order so I can examine her at the city hospital, also see what medications the prison has her on. Then once I prepare my findings, I'll go to Governor Wetherby and ask for your mother's pardon. If I had known about all this earlier, I could've helped sooner. But I've been traveling so much lately, it's been hard to keep up with the news." He took another bite, chewing slowly. "I think the governor would be receptive to it." Doc wiped his mouth with one of the linen napkins Millie had packed and folded it back onto his lap.

I thanked him and nibbled on my sandwich. It was good, but the food didn't erase the bad taste of the visit, the haunting image of my sickly mama. The scene gnawed at me, leaving little room for appetite. I thought about Mama sitting there without her undergarments, her loss of womanhood. My hands bruised blue, the anger rising, the guilt of ruining the visit with my childish anger smothering.

"Finish up." Doc smacked the crumbs off his hands and stood. "We need to head home. Sooner I can get there, the quicker I can help Bluet."

I took another small bite, my mind pulling back to the books and the dangerous path ahead of me.

Twenty-Six

We arrived in Troublesome as the sun crawled down behind treed ridges, bedding the town, a coal-dusted darkness pulling its shadowed cloak over the ol' Kentucky hills.

Doc opened the passenger door and I climbed out, the breath of grandmother mountains sweet on the face, welcomed after the vile stench of prison walls.

"It's late, child." He checked his pocket watch. "A little after six. You're welcome to stay the night."

"I have my book route in the morning, but I'm much obliged for the offer and for taking me to see Mama." I shrugged on my coat and grabbed my satchel. "Give Millie my thanks and tell her I'll drop off her reading material on Friday." I pecked his cheek.

"She'll be pleased to have new books. I'm going inside to make a few telephone calls. Ride safe." Doc placed a hand on my arm, then walked toward his house.

Reading material. I recalled my own—the newspaper obituary—and our conversation.

I called after him and rushed back to his side. "Doc, could I please use your telephone? I need to call Mr. Morgan."

"Come on in and I'll get him on the line for you."

Inside, Doc picked up the telephone and dialed the rotary, then after a few seconds handed me the receiver.

A woman answered on the first ring, "Morgan Law Office."

"Ma'am, I need to speak with Mr. Morgan."

"Name?"

"Honey Lovett."

"Hold, please. Let me check if he's still in."

Doc slipped out to give me privacy, and I heard Millie talking to him, her voice warm and lifting.

Mr. Morgan answered. "Honey, you just caught me leaving the office for the night. Everything okay with you?"

"Yes, sir, but I'm needing to know if the court is going to let me stay at my home and keep my job? I read—"

"I'm working on it, Honey."

"I need to know something soon, sir."

"Courts are always slow, Honey. You just stay out of trouble and keep doing a good job at your work. I'll see you in a few days."

"Wait, Mr. Morgan. I read about the passing of a man named Byrne McDaniel in an old newspaper, and it noted his important emancipation case… Mr. Morgan, are you still there?"

"Go on, you've got my full attention."

"I'm not much different than Byrne, and I want that. *My freedom. Emancipation.*"

There was a long pause as I waited for him to tell me different, that I was a female and couldn't have what I wanted, to tell me he'd decide what was in my *best interest.*

But instead he said, "I know the 1909 Kentucky case. *Rounds Bros. vs. McDaniel.* You keep collecting your pay stubs. Now let me do some research and I'll get back to you soon. Good night."

"Mr. Morgan—" I heard the click as I was getting ready to tell him about the visit with Mama.

Outside, Junia was eager to be out of the barn, and she sniffed my hair, face, and clothing. *Did she sense that I'd been close to Mama?* It couldn't be. I'd washed my hands at the park facilities before leaving. The mule raised her muzzle, tasting the air, whinnying and hawing softly. "She's not here, Junia. Let's get home." Again, she pressed her nose to my cheek, and I remembered Mama's hand slipping through the bars, cradling.

I lit the lantern and we rode hard toward our holler, comfortable now under the shadowy cover of climbing ivy and dew-treed darkness, the pounding hooves and ancient breaths of the forests bringing new purpose.

On Monday I stopped at the stone school, and Principal Walker bustled out to greet me. "Miss Lovett, what a blessing it is," she said from the steps, "to have the Pack Horse project revived through the library's generous outreach program. I've heard about the wonderful work your mother did years ago when the program was initiated."

"Thank you, ma'am." I reached inside the pannier and walked over to the door and handed her four books.

From inside, I heard a bell clang and Miss Walker turned to the building. "That's the second bell. Maybe next week I can let the students meet you."

"That'd be real nice, Miss Walker. See you next Monday."

I watched her go inside. The sound of children's excited giggles seeped out, and I wondered for a minute what it would've been like going to a real school like that. I'd asked Mama many times to send me to the stone one, but each time the question was dismissed, while Papa would comment I was safer at home. What he meant was I'm different, unlike others, and being *different* wasn't safe for me. But I couldn't help imagining what it would've been like in a classroom filled with classmates learning like they did every day, having their fellowship.

I paused to peek inside the window. A girl who looked my age chatted and laughed with two others, their excitement and untroubled lives etched onto their happy faces. I wondered what it was like being one of them. The girls glanced over and spied me. Embarrassed, I ducked low, scurrying back to Junia.

Later at Emma McCain's small cabin, I stood on the porch with her. She was a granny woman, passing her home tonics and potions and protective stones to the hillfolk up here for as long as I could remember. After I gave her some magazines, she told me to wait while she fetched something. When she came back out, she passed me a small stone, smooth like black ice. "Fer your protection," she said. "Gave your mama one of 'em lodestones long ago."

I turned the stone over in my glove and inspected it.

"That one came from the belly of a white deer two winters ago." She pointed to a tall cross post over by the shed where a gutted deer carcass hung. "I keep a close eye out when I'm dressin' 'em."

"Much obliged, Mrs. McCain. Looks like you got yourself a lot of good meat coming from that one."

"Early Brighton brung it over after I tended to his ailin' son."

I jiggled the stone in my hand. I'd seen a few of the ghost deer over in the Cumberland Forest. The rare albinos were a sight. Folk knew that the lodestones found in unusual critters were special, magical even. I heard the tales of some finding them in the head of the colorful arrow darter, knee of a groundhog, and other creatures. Papa had found one in the belly of a snapping turtle he'd dressed for Mama's soup.

Folk here were funny about their traditions, the signs that called to them, the customs they practiced. I recalled thumbing through one of the Pack Horse librarians' scrapbooks and reading Emma's tips and hearing about others. Remembered a few boys sporting raccoon peckers on leather ropes around their necks after a hunt, believing the bone would be an amulet to excite a girl after the granny witch suggested it to a boy who had failed to attract any females.

There were girls who claimed tucking a four-leaf clover inside their undergarments would bring a rich courter. *And hadn't Retta slept with the eyestones under her eyelids after Emma gave her several.* The healer had promised the BB-sized stones would draw out any foreign substance found in the eyes and give her stronger vision.

Another of Emma's practices instructed midwives to put pepper under women's noses during labor to speed up the childbirth. Bathing the newborn in greasy bathwater prevents illness their first year. And there was the recipe from the ol' granny witch for babies suffering the summer complaint. Emma McCain had written: *To cure the intestinal disease, mash up crawling wood louse and steep them in hot water for a tea for the child to drink.* She believed nails taken from a hanging gallows and used in a town bench were to protect the menfolk from meeting violent deaths. The granny witch warned that sneezing prior to seven brought unfriendly company before eleven.

And didn't I know to wear my dead parents' woven locks that Papa had braided into a mourning ring close to my heart for my own protection and to honor my first parents' deaths by keeping a part of them living. I pressed on the small, coarse lump resting beneath my clothing, their lives snug near my heart.

Mrs. McCain said, "Folks don't 'preciate the ol' healing ways like they used to, now that them newfangled frontier nurses come into our hills to push on them city-slick medicines."

I grimaced, remembering how Retta didn't want the granny woman's herbs or tonics on her deathbed, instead called out for the *city-slick.* I knew it rubbed the ol' woman wrong, losing her customers to the city nurses, and all I could do was nod my head and listen.

Emma's great-granddaughter walked into the yard with her rooster trailing.

"Can't get that chil' to stay put since her parents and grandparents passed," Mrs. McCain commented. "*Wrenna,* come here."

I'd heard their truck had gone over a cliff a few years back.

"Always roaming 'round with Tommie there. Tried to make her wear a special lodestone, but she weren't having none of it and tossed it out into the yard. Ol' Tommie gobbled it down." She gazed fondly at Wrenna, a sadness sweeping into her old eyes. "Reckon the chil's got all the protection she needs with ol' Tommie boy carrying 'round the good energies of the stone and guarding her like he does. He even roosts on her bedpost at night, keeping watch."

Wrenna stopped and looked at me curiously. I watched the rooster tidbitting beside her, foraging for food in the grasses. With an eye on the child, Tommie clucked softly and bobbed his head for Wrenna's attention while picking up bits of seed and dropping them at her feet.

A screaming hawk flew over and Tommie cocked his head, stretched his neck, sending out an abrupt *oo-oo.*

"Whuut-whuut," Wrenna answered softly, searching the sky.

Mrs. McCain chuckled. "'Hens in danger,' he's saying. Last month, an ornery dog strayed into the yard, scrounging for scraps, growling at Wrenna. The chil' called out her warning, and ol' Tommie came a'flyin' from around the tree over there. He fought that snarling mean dog off." Mrs. McCain pointed a calloused, knotted finger at the white rooster. "Yessir, he surely did. Them two's always talking to each other like that."

I admired the old bird's tenderness, protectiveness toward the child, remembering Rudy, the colorful rooster my parents had raised with our chickens. Rudy was always bossing, chasing Junia out of the yard and away from the chickens, and the mule sassed right back with her offended haws and brays, having to wait out of sight till it was safe. Junia eventually learned to tolerate the feisty old bird, even grew fond of it, and in the end let him roost on her backside.

"Would she like a book, Mrs. McCain?"

"I suspect she would. She's practically licked the ink off her favorite that her folks gave her long ago, *The Doll's House.*"

I nodded. Mama had read Rumer Godden's book to me many times.

"She loves to read. And them books help since the schools won't have her. Chil' won't sit still an' won't leave Tommie. Wrenna, *Wrenna Jean,*" the old woman called, "git over here an' let Book Woman give you a good book." She frowned. "I tried the settlement school again last year, but she weren't having none of it, so them fotched-on women said it's best to keep her home."

I breathed in the heady scents of woods and pine and couldn't imagine a wilded Wrenna wanting to leave it for a stuffy, chalk-dusted classroom as free as she was. Nudging my chin over to Junia, I motioned to the girl. "Let's pick out a book for you, Wrenna."

"Book Woman, if ya can git me any of them books by Irvin Cobb, I'd be a'mite grateful," Mrs. McCain said.

"Yes, ma'am, I can bring you several. I noticed *The Thunders of Silence* and *The Glory of the Coming* on the library shelves when I dropped in." Cobb, the Kentucky humorist and author, was a favorite among folk in these parts, and Mama had most of his *Old Judge Priest* stories from my grandpa's collection at our cabin.

Wrenna followed me over to my bags and waited while I looked through the children's books. The girl reached up and petted the mule's neck, and Junia nuzzled her cheek, pressed her big mouth against the girl's head. Wrenna didn't laugh but her eyes were wide and appreciative. Tommie *coo-coo*'d softly and stayed at her side, keeping his head cocked to Junia. The ol' girl swished her tail and backed away, keeping a wary eye on the rooster.

I found two books, Elizabeth Goudge's *The Little White Horse* and *Twig* by Elizabeth Orton Jones. I searched again, thinking about the reads Retta and Mama had bought me when I was about Wrenna's age. There was a wonderful one called *Rabbit Hill* for young'uns who loved animals. It was back at my home in the Cumberland Forest, but maybe I could find a copy at the library.

"Here you go, Wrenna, and I'll bring more next time."

The girl reached up, tickled Junia's soft, floppy ears, then took the books from me, her eyes holding mine, a mixture of curios-ity, innocence, and other things I couldn't see reflecting back.

I searched inside again in case I missed another read she might like, and pulled out the Bit-O-Honey candy bar Doc had purchased, thinking I'd save it for my routes. Wrenna looked longingly at the sweet treat, licking her lips, and I unwrapped the packaging and broke off several pieces of the mixed taffy and almond bits, separating the tiny bars from the wax paper.

I held it out to her and she swallowed, staring at it. "Go ahead and have some. Bit-O-Honey's my favorite."

Wrenna studied me a moment, then dug into her dress pocket. She pulled out several horse chestnuts and a spent flower, then handed me the bud and a seed before snatching the candy out of my hand.

Mrs. McCain said, "The chil's always toting home presents to me."

"Pretty flower and this seed sure is the shiniest one I've ever seen. Thank you, Wrenna." I smiled and inspected the horse chestnut that many thought carrying around would bring good favor.

Hesitant, she tasted the candy with the tip of her tongue, and then took another small lick, her eyes widening with delight.

"Wrenna?" Mrs. McCain said, her voice soft and warbled. "Wrenna Jean, say thank ya to Book Woman." But the child didn't hear. She'd already plopped down in the yard to read with Tommie perched on her shoulder as if he was reading, too, slowly chewing over the words and gnawing on the sticky taffy.

I said goodbye, climbed atop Junia, and pointed her to my next stop, the Moores' cabin. Before I reached their home, I smoothed down my hair and tucked in my blouse, making sure I looked fine when I saw him.

Mrs. Moore insisted I come in. "Francis ain't here, but he and my niece Bonnie done told me all about the new book-drop service and I couldn't wait to sign up."

My shoulders sagged. I'd hope to chat with him away from the Company store.

I stepped inside the small cozy cabin, the panel walls lined with smiling faces of relatives in handmade frames. There were pictures of Bonnie and Francis together in the yard. On a small table there were more photographs. Mrs. Moore caught me looking at them and went over and picked up a small frame. "This is my pa, Howard"—she tapped a finger on one of the men—"and this is your grandpap, Elijah Carter, outside the Blue Diamond mine."

I traced the picture with my finger. Grandpa didn't look much different than Mrs. Moore's papa, both standing in coal-covered clothes, with black-smudged faces and holding their miner helmets in dirty hands. It was the first time I'd seen a photograph of him, and I peered closely, wishing I had spent more time with him before he passed.

Mama kept his old brass carbide lamp that he wore on his miner's helmet atop the mantel. She'd have me light it once a year on his birthday, and then she'd read from the yellowed paper the quote Grandpa Elijah told Mr. Moore to tell her before he died, asking his friend to stand in for him during my parents' matrimony ceremony.

> *"Place me like a seal over your heart, like a seal on your arm;*
> *for love is as strong as death... It burns like a blazing fire,*
> *like a mighty flame."*

"Keep it, Honey, I have others," Mrs. Moore said, taking it out of the frame and handing it to me. She rearranged the photographs and stopped at one. "That's my cousin Kelly Ann Moore." She lifted up a small frame of a woman sitting atop a horse holding books. "She was a Pack Horse librarian over in Straight Creek before she up and married and moved to Texas. Mighty fine book woman she was. And this one sitting on her mule"—she picked up another—"is my dear friend, Laura Adams over in Letcher. Another brave, dedicated Pack Horse librarian who worked the project."

"Much obliged for the photograph, Mrs. Moore." I was

thrilled and couldn't wait to show Mama. Except for the photograph with Retta, there were no pictures of our family, nary a one, and I suspected it was because of the humiliation over our rare color. I pressed the picture to my heart before slipping it into my pocket.

"Reckon I'll be putting up a new one of my niece in her work clothes soon," Mrs. Moore said with a tinge of sorrow, rubbing the empty frame. "Pa always said coal is never really a good neighbor to our people, our land and critters. It rips away the men from their women, leaving behind too many widows."

Inward, I winced, wondering how Bonnie would be dressed today.

Twenty-Seven

The first day of April brought a light snow to the hills, the tender shoots of new life blanketed in a deceiving Christmas-white as a determined wood thrush rang out its roundelay, the flutelike notes calling for spring. And still no word from Mr. Morgan.

Junia rode us up to Pearl's on our last Wednesday drop. I'd been missing my friend these past couple of days and was anxious to see her again. Dipping my gloved hand into my coat pocket, I touched the coins and dollar bills, hoping Pearl would let me use her telephone.

At the lookout, I tied Junia under the first landing, grabbed some books, and hurried up the steps.

Pearl lifted the hatch and I climbed inside. "Here, give me your wet coat, and I'll hang it by the stove." She took the books and set them on the table, then hung my coat. "Coffee, Honey? I just made a fresh pot."

"Much obliged." I slipped off my gloves and rubbed my cold hands together.

She set two cups down and took a seat across from me.

"Any more trouble from Hardin?" I asked, remembering Gillis and his mama's conversation in the Company store, wondering how to tell Pearl. I started to say something, but thought better. I'd tell her when we had the pajama party. Right now I was desperate to call my folk. I glanced at the telephone.

She noticed and said, "It's been quiet. They repaired the telephone. Did you get to Louisville with the nurse?"

"Doc took me, and I saw Mama on Sunday, but only for a few minutes. They had her in the infirmary."

"I'm so sorry. What's wrong with her?"

"She has a broken arm from when the lawman arrested her, and they performed a sterilization. And now she's become a curiosity for the prison doctors."

"They did that, stripped away her motherhood? Your poor mother."

"Mama's only thirty-five, and she and Papa hoped to have more babies one day."

Awful. "Did you see your father?" Pearl asked.

I shook my head. "I wanted to ask to use your telephone to try and call him. I have coins in my coat pocket to pay."

Pearl waved a hand and pushed the telephone toward me. "Call."

I studied the telephone, remembering 0 was for operator. "He won't be able to speak with me. I'd have to give him your number and tell him to ring back."

"That's fine." She handed me the receiver.

I wiped my anxious hands on my britches, raised the receiver to my ear, and dialed zero.

"Number, please," the operator asked.

"I don't have a number, ma'am."

"Ask her to look up the number and connect you," Pearl whispered, resting her elbow on the table with her chin perched on a palm.

"Ma'am, could you connect me to the Kentucky State Reformatory in La Grange, Kentucky, please?" I asked.

"One moment, please."

"It's ringing, Pearl." I stood up and looked out the cab windows, holding my breath.

"Kentucky State Reformatory Administration Building. Clark speaking," the man answered on the fourth long ring.

"Yes, sir, Mr. Clark, this is Honey Lovett over in Troublesome Creek, and I want to see when I can telephone my papa, Jackson Lovett."

"Lovett, Lovett, Lovett, *Jackson*..." he said, papers whispering out rattles as I heard him thumb through the pages. "Here he is. Prisoner Lovett is allowed to make one phone call on Saturdays at 2:00 p.m., miss."

"Saturday at 2:00 p.m.?" I glanced at Pearl, and she nodded a *yes*, tapping the number in the circle on the phone.

"Give this number to him, Honey."

"Uh, sir, could you give him a telephone number for me?" I peered down, the black numbers typed out on a round white circle, my finger hovering over it.

"What is it?" the man asked briskly.

"785–508, sir."

Mr. Clark repeated it, mistaking a five for a nine.

"No, sir, it's 7-8-5-5-0–8," I said, real slow.

"I'll put it in his file." And then he hung up with a loud click, making me recoil.

Had he written it down correctly? I stared out across the hills, the sound piercing like a knife to my heart. Pearl took the receiver and set it in the cradle. "Maybe he'll telephone you Saturday, Honey." She patted my shoulder. "I'll be here all day. I promise I won't go anywhere, not this Saturday or the next, until you get to speak with your father again." She sat down at the table and tapped the chair beside her for me to join her.

"Thank you, Pearl."

"I know you must really miss him, Honey. I dearly miss mine."

"Where is he?" I said, surprised.

"Father got drafted into the army when I was nine. They sent him off to France to fight in the big war. The house was always quiet, and Mother spent a lot of time in her bedroom, closed herself off. Barely cooking or keeping house. I missed him every day. Eight of my classmates lost their fathers over there.

So maybe like Mother, I'd spend hours dreading the knock from the uniformed Western Union messenger, praying he wouldn't show up with the death telegram."

"That's so awful, Pearl. I can't imagine how hard it was fighting in World War II." I sat down beside her. "Papa was in prison during some of that time, but they wouldn't let him join the army after he got out. How long was your papa over there?"

"Too long." Pearl winced. "Father came home to us three years later. With a busted leg...and a busted heart. They'd amputated his leg over there. He was a different man living as a walking ghost. Father used to sit on the porch late at night alone sipping bourbon. Sometimes, when the stump pains would hit his missing leg and it became unbearable, he'd curse, tear off the leather straps, and throw his wooden limb out into the yard. Then he'd scream and wake us up to get it for him. He never was the same, wouldn't talk about what happened, except for yelling out in his sleep. God took what was left of him to a better place in the fall of '51. But really, I lost him long before that."

I thought about never seeing Papa again and how I would have to bear such. "I'm so sorry for the loss of your dear papa, Pearl." I went over and hugged her and felt the grief in her quaking shoulders.

On Thursday morning, April winds rattled through the leaves like angry paper wasps as I made my way to the Tobacco Top community. I passed by Retta's home and moments later saw Alonzo in his wagon.

I pulled up beside him, and Junia sent out two short warnings to the man's ol' horse. "Good day, Alonzo."

"Honey, it's good to see you. I'm off to town." He pressed down his hat to keep the wind from blowing it off, embarrassed to meet my eyes. "Pretty blue skies but a rather windy day," he said.

His wagon was packed with his aunt's furniture, pots, and quilts. "What are you doing with Retta's things?"

He shook his head. "Don't have room, thought I'd sell 'em, unless there's something you want back there."

Sell it for a bottle or two of panther's breath, I thought, but kept it to myself. I slid down off Junia. In the back of the wagon, Retta's beautiful metal glider poked out, and I touched the sweet piecrust pattern, remembering our talks on it.

"Want that, Honey?" Alonzo asked, looking back over his shoulder.

It wouldn't fit on my small porch that was already full with two rockers and a little table. I stared at it a moment, then dug into my coat pocket and pulled out a dollar and some change. "Much obliged. Would you drop it off on Bonnie Powell's porch?"

"Widow Powell?"

"Yes, sir."

"*On et*. Know'd right where it is."

He tucked the money into his pocket and took off, wafts of horse, whiskey, and dirt climbing into the air, haloing him.

Saddened, I watched him ride away with everything I had always known, the very last of my Retta, until I could no longer see his hat and hear the clattering wheels of the wagon.

At the Tobacco Top drop, I tied Junia up next to a tombstone and began pulling out books and magazines for the tiny community that lived eight miles over the pass.

Junia stretched out her neck and blew at our visitor, Mr. Taft's son, Tom, as he stepped off his great-grandparents' crumbling porch, the walls of the small home boarded up, sunken, trailing with wild wisteria, ivy, and honeysuckle vines.

"Honey." He waved. "You sure are a sight for sore eyes. When Pa said you would be delivering the books up here, our hoots could be heard over the mountaintops. It was all I could do to keep my young Iris from following me over here today." He handed me a jar from inside his poke. "My woman grabbed this from the tater hole this morn', said give these blackberry preserves to our bonny Picasso's daughter, our new Book Woman."

"Much obliged to Mrs. Taft. And I remember Mama telling me your papa used to call her that." I grinned. "After Picasso's blue painting of the *Woman with a Helmet of Hair*."

"My folks always said our Maker saved his favorite color for our wonderful Book Woman." Tom pointed upward to the blue skies and then started packing for his trip back.

I thought about Mama in prison, how different she was treated for being *different*. But here I'd grown up watching the good bookfolk welcome her with open arms and shout with joy every time she rode in with her treasures. Now here I was able to bring the books like she had, and my heart filled with pride and love for the printed word. Though Mama and I were the last of the Blues, the very last of our kind, and different from others, the books united every one of us.

Twenty-Eight

From atop Junia, I drew my eyes to the well and tried to spy the glass milk bottle. The yard was empty. Thin grasses poked up between patches of blooming henbit, briar weed, and field mustard. Wet clothing and sheets were pinned to Guyla Belle's clothesline, the scents of lye soap and blooms swirling around the yard. The boy's rusted trike rested on its side. The curtains were drawn on the cabin windows.

Mr. Gillis must be home. I turned Junia back to the road, then chanced another look once more at the well, stretching my neck to get a better sight. I couldn't be sure and I dared not go into the yard to get a closer look, but it seemed like Mr. Gillis had finally concreted it over, and I let out a breath, relieved for the boy's safety.

Then the door creaked open and a small, unkempt woman stuck her head out. "If you're looking for Guyla, she ain't here," she said, her voice full of grave dust.

I nudged Junia closer. "Ma'am, I'm Honey Lovett, the outreach librarian assistant for our branch."

Johnnie squeezed past the woman, and she snatched him back to her side.

"Buk uman." He pointed, his face streaked with dirt, his eyes swollen from crying. "Buk uman an-an-and *Mama*. Well!"

"Hello, Johnnie," I called out, friendly. To the woman, "Ma'am, do you know where I can find Guyla Belle?"

"I'm the boy's auntie, Ida Gillis. Perry's at work and Guyla's done gone."

"*Gone.*" I worried the word. But it was a relief to hear he was working, and I offered her a wobbly smile. Reaching inside my satchel, I said, "Only wanted to drop off Guyla Belle's clean socks—"

"Done took off and left town. Good riddance." She jerked the boy inside and slammed the door.

Good riddance?

Quickly, I dropped the socks back into my bag. From behind the door, I heard the boy wail once before going silent. Then Johnnie's sad face appeared in front of the curtain. Tearful, he pressed his small hand against the old pane.

Junia whinnied softly and sidestepped, turning us around. I looked over my shoulder one last time, then squeezed my legs against her sides. "Halt, ol' girl." Glints of sunlight dropped through the trees, dancing off shards of glass that littered the concreted mouth of the well. I squinted and saw the jagged broken neck of a dairy bottle lying on the ground below it. Under it was the two books I'd loaned her. I climbed down and walked over, sneaking glimpses to the house. My hands trembled as I ran my fingers across the new concrete lid, remembering how Guyla Belle almost lost Johnnie. As ornery as Mr. Gillis was, at least he saw fit to cover it up.

Junia remembered, too, and tapped her hooves nervously, trying to pull me away, struggling to free herself from the reins. "It's okay, ol' girl, Johnnie's safe and won't ever fall down it again."

Dismayed, I picked up the children's book, and spotted *The Awakening* nearby. The pages were ripped and the cover had been violently torn off. I shivered and circled around the well. Two daffodils had sprung up beside it, and a dandelion had pushed itself up through a crack at the concrete base. I studied the strong weed. How it always survived, even against the forces of man and steel. I resisted plucking it up, knowing it would seed year after year, and I bent over, ran a finger over the yellow head, praying that Guyla Belle had the same strength to survive his beatings.

Junia sounded another anxious bray, and I searched the yard once more. Out of the corner of my eye, I saw movement and jerked my head up toward the cabin. My eyes narrowed as I squinted to make out who was there.

The curtains parted a little further, and an outline of someone appeared, then faded behind the fabric just as quick. Could Guyla Belle be in there suffering from another beating, or had she really packed up and left?

I found Bonnie Powell on her porch, sprawled out on Retta's pretty glider, smoking a cigarette, one leg hitched atop it, the other rocking back and forth. She motioned me up.

I grabbed two books and a pamphlet and climbed the steps.

She handed me her old loans. "Hey, sweet pea, will ya look at this. Just came home and found it sitting out in the yard, plain as that. All new-like too. No note, nothing with it." She rubbed her hand alongside the metal arm, traced the pattern on the empty spot next to her. "Nary a dent anywhere," she marveled. "Grandma was out back hanging wash and said she never heard a soul. We carried it up to the porch and it fits perfect." She pitched her cigarette out into the thinning yard, dusted off the ashes that had fallen on her bib overalls.

I was grateful that Alonzo got it here and didn't cheat this time. "It's real pretty," I said, not wanting her to know I'd given it to her, afraid she'd think it was charity.

"Had me another rough day in the mine, shoveling the belt and eating that nasty rock dust. I threw up twice, 'cause I ran out of them vitamin C pills Doc prescribes. Says it helps fight against the sickness the dust causes." Bonnie stretched and massaged her neck, then examined her broken overall strap that was missing its metal button. "Damn men making it even rougher with their grabby hands." She looked out to the yard as if remembering something ugly. "But this sure cheered me up. Can't wait to hold Joey Jr. in it." She rocked the glider with her toe, the squeaky hum breezing the afternoon air.

"He'll go right to bed," I said, smiling, remembering all the times Retta had rocked me to sleep on it.

I handed her two new books, and she studied the covers and then sat them beside her. "These look real good. This one here—" She tapped *Gunnar's Daughter*. "Surprised Miss Foster has it in her library."

"Thought you might enjoy something different."

"Thanks. It was always a treat getting books from your mama's personal collection. They made ya really ponder afterward." She rapped on the metal seat and kicked the rocker into motion with her foot again. "This sure is gonna make bedtime a lot easier on both of us."

I fidgeted with her loans in my lap, slipping off the sweaty gloves, my hands darkening as I rubbed my palm across the book.

Bonnie leaned over, stretched out her arm to pick up a quart mason jar stuffed with sunflower seeds. She poured out a few into her palm and set the jar aside.

Her brow furrowed and she studied the fat brown seeds. "Yessir," she whispered, "gonna make *everything* a lot easier for ol' Bonnie now."

Something strange, almost dangerous lifted in her eyes as she examined the seeds, turning them over in her hand.

Junia trotted past a small group of miners outside the Company store, lifting a hawing caution to the men like she always did when we passed by. A few talked beside their parked trucks, others rushed out of the store as if they were late. The coal miners' shirts and britches were clean, and I knew they were headed to their first shift of the day.

Fretful, I searched the faces for Gillis and didn't see him. Besides the books, I was the closest thing to a friend his wife had. I knew he'd keep threatening me until I dropped Guyla Belle's route and broke off our friendship.

I knocked my knees against Junia, urging her to go faster.

At Doc's house, Millie opened the door. "Book woman. *Läkare. Läkare*," she called over her shoulder, the musical words scattering down the foyer. I handed her two books from my bag, and she studied the covers of *A Stone for Danny Fisher* and *The Hidden Flower*, then pulled me inside. "*Till dig*." She walked down the hall, wagging a finger in the air and leaving me alone in the foyer. In a minute, she came back with a cloth bag and handed it to me.

I peeked inside and saw two oranges.

"*Äta*." She pointed to her mouth and then mine.

"Uh, *eat*, yes, much obliged, Millie. I'll save it for later." I tucked them inside my bag.

"*Böcker*," she said, opening one of the books and walking down the hall flicking a page.

"*Books*," I said, hoping it was the word.

Doc came to the door. "Honey, I'm glad you're here. Come on into the parlor. I'd like to talk with you a moment."

I stared at him, wondering if he had bad news. I'd stopped in a few days ago for word on Mama but no one was home. "Is Mama okay?"

"Yes. Come on in." He opened the door wider and I stepped into the foyer.

"I examined your mother on Tuesday." He led me into the parlor. "Would you like coffee or tea, something else?"

"No, sir. How is she?" I sat in the chair, worried.

"She's fine, but—"

I leaned in toward Doc. "But what? Did they hurt her—?"

"She's fine, Honey. But I spoke with the governor and he let me know it wasn't in his best interest to grant her a pardon at this time."

I groaned. *How could I ever go two years without her, and how could she stay there alive for another two years?* "They stripped her of motherhood! What about my mama's *best interest*?" I snapped.

"You have to realize, child, issues as delicate as miscegenation laws are—Well, now, some issues are political hotbeds and not many elected officials want to confront them. I'm sorry."

My heart sank.

"Now a few of her privileges were restored, at least. And I'm having lunch with the governor next Tuesday and should have more to tell you then."

"Can I telephone her?"

"I don't see why not."

"Much obliged, Doc. I can't bear for her to be in the awful prison one minute more. Is there any more you can do, sir?" I heard his telephone ring in his office.

He gave a sympathetic nod. "I'll keep bending his ear, child. Maybe we'll find a compromise."

Millie poked her head inside the parlor, said something cheerful, and waved a book.

"The phone's for me. And it looks like Millie is pleased with her new reads." Doc stood up and I joined him. "I won't give up. You don't give up either, Honey. You're doing a great job as the new book woman. Bluet would be proud."

I hurried to the Company store, hoping to telephone Mama, rushing past Francis helping a customer at the cash register.

Inside the telephone booth, I took off my gloves, dialed the operator, and waited. But after I deposited the two nickels she'd asked for, the woman said she hadn't received them and demanded more. I had to deposit another three before the operator would ring the number. Finally I got through to the prison, only for them to tell me Mama was in another building working in laundry. Frustrated, I hung up, counting my change.

Francis tapped on the glass. "Okay in there, Honey?"

I cracked open the door. "Fine but the telephone machine took more money than it should have. I had to deposit five coins before the operator would ring the number."

"It acts up like that sometimes. Sorry, Honey. Wait here and I'll go get the key to refund your change."

In a moment, Francis returned with a key. Grinning, he squeezed in beside me. I wriggled closer to the back of the booth, trying to scoot away, watching awkwardly as he opened the box at the bottom of the telephone before counting out my nickels, the scent of boy wild and dizzying in the cramped space.

Francis passed me the coins, the heat of his hand lingering on mine. Our eyes met and a burning hunger lit across his. "I want to take you out soon, Honey," he said in a hoarse whisper. "Spend the day with you." Then he moved in even closer and pressed a feverish kiss onto my lips.

Boldly, I pressed back, pulling into the heady scent of boy.

A rap on the booth parted us. Eddie called out to Francis as he hurried past toward the back, "Truck just pulled in, and I need help unloading."

Embarrassed, I tried to move but Francis was blocking the door.

Francis looked at me, the hunger still bright in his eyes as he fumbled with the door and backed out of the booth. "Go out with me, Honey." He grabbed my hand and gave a gentle tug, then sprinted off toward the back to catch up with Eddie.

Smiling, I pulled my fingers up to my lips, tasting his kiss. For the rest of the day, and tomorrow, and the one after, I was sure I'd check and find his kiss still there. And I thought about what Bonnie said and wondered if Francis would be the one.

Saturday couldn't come soon enough. And I could hardly wait to talk with Papa and ask his permission to date. I arrived at Pearl's cab at noon, two hours before he would call, lighting up the metal stairs like a bald hornet was on my tail, my footsteps clanging across the sleepy forest.

"I'm glad you came early. I could use the company," Pearl said.

"I hoped you wouldn't mind. I'm dying to speak with Papa," I said, breathless from the stirs and my excitement.

Pearl laughed. "I would've done the same. I'm having a bite to eat. Let me get you a plate."

After a dinner of fried liver mush and corn bread, Pearl went down to feed Pie, while I stared back and forth between the telephone and my timepiece snugged beside it. Occasionally, I would tend the Osborne Finder for her, searching for any signs of smoke. I didn't spot the dangerous slow burn of white smolder caused from paper or wood fires. I picked up my timepiece, snapped open the glass case.

Pearl came back up a little before two. "Any word?"

Solemn, I shook my head.

When the little hand moved to 2:00 p.m., I stiffened in the chair and felt my shoulders tighten, inching up to my ears. Then the hand moved slowly, marking 2:07 p.m., and a tiny desperate breath escaped. At 2:24 p.m., Pearl rested a hand on my arm and squeezed. I looked up at her, the worriment latching onto my hands. When the time crawled to 2:27 p.m., the telephone rang, making me jump up from the chair, bumping Pearl sideways.

"Pick up the receiver. Hurry, pick it up," Pearl said, just as excited, jiggling her charm bracelet.

I yanked it off the cradle and pressed it close to my ear. "Papa, papa, it's me, Honey. *Papa?*" I frowned, pulled it away from my head, and stared down at the handset.

Pearl took it from me and said, "Hello, *hello?*" then paused. "Mother, I can't talk. I'm waiting for a telephone call. No, Mother, please hang—" Pearl gripped the cord, shaking her head. "Hang up, Mrs. Barry. Mrs. Barry, hang up your party line! I'll call you back later, Mother. No, Mother, now's not a good time. Later. *Hang up, Mrs. Barry,*" she said through tight teeth before slamming down the telephone and looking at me with apologetic eyes.

Papa would not call, and I grabbed my timepiece, unable to witness the disappointment in her eyes reflected in mine.

"Honey, stay—" she pleaded.

"I have chores, Pearl," I said, embarrassed I'd gotten my hopes up. "Much obliged for your generous hospitality. Dinner was real nice." I put on my coat, picked up the satchel and Pearl's old loans, and opened the hatch.

"Oh, Honey, I'm truly sorry—"

The phone rumbled out one long *brrrng*. Pearl grabbed my sleeve and pulled me back up to the table.

I put the receiver to my ear, and in a small voice breathed out, "*Papa?*"

Pearl's eyes widened, questioning.

"This is the operator, I have a collect call from Mr. Jackson Lovett at the Kentucky State Reformatory for Miss Honey Lovett."

I looked at Pearl and nodded. "It's the operator for a collect call—"

"Hurry and accept it," she said, beaming, bobbing her head.

"Yes, Operator, I accept," I said.

"*Honey*, it's your papa. It's good to hear you again, Daughter." The warmth of his voice traveled across the miles, and I stared out the windows feeling a protective hug.

"*Papa. Papa!*" I lifted a fist to the side of my mouth, soaking up the sunny skies, nearly weeping with joy.

"Daughter." He coughed. "How are you doing? Retta taking good care of you? Staying safe?"

His lawyer hadn't got word to him yet about her passing. I sank into the chair, swallowing back the tears. "Yes," I barely squeaked out, not wanting to tell him I wasn't. Not wanting to burden the happy moment with sadness. "I'm safe enough."

"Old Junia behaving?"

"Junia's doing real good. She misses Mama though."

Pearl slipped out the door to the catwalk's railing. Below, I heard Junia's quiet haws and neighs.

"We'll be together soon," he said quietly, leaving me to strain to hear the next words muffled by his cough.

"Oh, Papa, there's a…a boy. He asked me out and—"

There was a winded sigh, then a long pause.

"Uh, he wants to take me out on a picnic. I'm soon to be seventeen," I reminded.

"Who is he?"

"Francis Moore, Howard Moore's grandson."

Papa coughed and cleared his throat and then said wearily, "Have Loretta meet him, and if she approves, you have my permission."

Frowning, I shook my head and muttered a weak "Okay, Papa."

"You talk with your mama, Daughter?"

"I saw Mama, and I'm coming to see you too."

"How's Mama doing over there?" He coughed again. "Honey?"

"Fine," I fibbed, the lies soaking my hands, a'blazin' them in the blue. "I need to visit you real soon, though."

"It's best you send letters. Prison's not a fit place for a young lady to visit."

"Papa, *please*. I have a ride. A frontier nurse or Doc will bring me."

There was another long pause. Then I heard his heavy sigh. "Daughter, there are no visitors allowed at the prison, only telephone calls."

"Why, what's wrong?" I stood, stretching the cord.

"Some in here have the fevers," he wheezed out. "The poli… outbreak is here…" A man climbed atop his words, booming, "*Time's up, Lovett.*"

I winced, unraveling and spooling the stretched cord around my darkening hand. "Papa, did you say *polio*?"

"Write to me, li'l Book Woman." Clattering and shouts rose from the wires, jarring our telephone conversation.

"Papa?" I stared out the windows, wanting to tell him everything, clamoring for his wisdom and comfort, the words screaming inside, fighting to come out. "Papa, Retta—"

"I love you, Honey," Papa whispered hoarsely.

"Papa, I love—" I dropped back into the seat, a cold numbness crawling over my bones, my sentiment lost in the cruel, hard click of his receiver.

Twenty-Nine

From the window, I watched the two men arrive at the homestead on Monday.

Devil John and Mr. Morgan rode into the yard atop a small wagon just as I was inside packing the pannier for my outpost.

I answered the knock, opening the door wide. "Mr. Morgan, is everything okay with my folk?"

"Fine, just fine, Honey. I'm here about you. May I come in?"

Hesitant, I braced myself and stepped aside, thinking about Papa, the worry of more bad news from the court, the social worker, and law.

"Nice to see ya, Honey. I'll jus' stay over yander by the wagon, Bob," Devil John said.

"Morning, Devil John," I called out before going inside.

Books, magazines, and newspapers littered the table and chairs. I hurried to make room for him to sit, stacking the patrons' reads onto my small bed across the room.

"No need to fuss. I can see you keep a tidy home here, Honey." He shut the door as a breath of the forest escaped inside, lifting into the laundered linens I'd washed just yesterday in a few drops of Mama's rose oil.

"Yes, sir, I was just getting my books together for work. Coffee?" I called out as I placed the last four books on my bed.

"Don't mind if I do."

"There's a batch of beaten biscuits on the stove." I wanted

to be hospitable, so I didn't tell him they didn't turn out and Mama's were better. "Can I get you a plate, Mr. Morgan?"

"Thanks, just coffee," he said.

After I served him a cup, he asked me to sit down at the table.

"You sure are a long way from anybody. Had to get John to bring me over because I thought I'd never find it again on my own."

I was grateful that I was a far piece from town and hoping it would keep me safer and away from the prying eyes of the court.

"How's that job going?"

"It's going well. Folk seem to be real happy to have the service back." I hesitated. "Most folk." I didn't want to tell him about Perry Gillis, in case it caused me trouble with the law.

"That's good." Mr. Morgan took a sip of his coffee and set it back on the table. "I've been thinking about our last visit back in March. And especially about our recent telephone conversation—what you said about your freedom and the McDaniel case. It made me think, and I discussed what you said with a few close colleagues. They thought you were pretty smart. Damn brilliant even."

Pleased with his compliment, I squirmed in my seat, dropping my coloring hands into my lap.

He took another sip and studied me over the rim of Retta's teacup.

"So, Honey, I've had a chance to think over your concerns, specifically your question of why the law would allow you to marry—"

I shook my head, tightening my mouth. "Ain't marrying Carson, Mr. Morgan. It'd be like, well, it'd be like marrying my *brother*." My voice rose, and I jumped up and grabbed the newspaper from the shelf, opened it to the death notices and smacked it down in front of him.

"I want that," I tapped on the old print. "What fourteen-year-old Byrne McDaniel got. *Freedom*."

The lawyer glanced at the newspaper and pushed it aside.

"Honey, I didn't come here to get you hitched to anyone. I came here to say that your concerns are valid and maybe we can do something to get you the right answer—your freedom."

I held my breath, waiting while he took another gulp of coffee.

"Now, Honey, there might be a chance. It's like you told me last month. You've got yourself a fine home here, an important and respectable job with steady income. You're pretty smart, and I like the way you think"—he pointed at me—"and the mature way you've handled things. And, you know what, maybe Judge Norton might think so too. I'm going to propose we seek your emancipation. Would you like that?"

"Emancipation." I breathed, yearning for it.

"You would no longer need a guardian under the law, and you would be allowed to be on your own. You don't even need your father's permission since he's incarcerated, but of course, it would help and be more respectable if you had it. I will advise you, though, that the courts have been particular about how they grant it."

"Why?" I worried.

"Children, especially those in rural areas, are a valuable commodity to a father who needs farm labor or any help around the homestead without having to pay wages. So goods and service always apply first in the courts."

"But I'm not a commodity, sir."

"No, at the moment you're certainly not. You're working to support yourself. But legally, children are considered the invisible commodity of the father. Let's see." He looked around the room and his eyes landed on the calendar hanging on the wall. "Today's April 6, and I think I can get something drafted in a few weeks. Then I can file an application with the court for the emancipation of Honey Lovett. Hopefully have a court date within the next month or two. I've talked with Mr. Greene, and he feels Social Services shouldn't complain too hard. You're not costing them a nickel being on your own."

"Freedom." I tasted the word, feeling the hope in it.

He grinned. "And under the circumstances, I believe your father will consent, which will make it go smoother. I'll talk with his attorney and start drafting it first thing."

"What about Mama?"

"I can ask her, too, if you like, but the courts only seek a father's permission."

"Mama was in the prison infirmary, sir."

Mr. Morgan wrinkled his brows. "What for? I would need to advise the court if she is ill."

"Doc and I just visited on March 29 after the warden told him the court ordered Mama to undergo sterilization. He thinks the doctors have also been experimenting on her because they're curious about our color. And I saw the lawman who arrested Mama had broken her arm."

Mr. Morgan's eyes hardened. "What the devil—"

"Doc's been helping her out."

"Don't worry, Honey. I'll have Mr. Faust check in on her and tell him to have a talk with the judge and warden."

"I spoke with Papa on the telephone Saturday. He said I couldn't visit, and I believe he was trying to tell me there's a polio outbreak at his prison. Said the men had the fevers."

I could see something fretful darken Mr. Morgan's eyes. "I'll let his attorney know as soon as I get back to my office today." He pushed aside the rest of his coffee and stood. "You let the lawyers worry about your parents, and you focus on your job. Save up those paycheck stubs to show the court."

I followed him to the door. "Mr. Morgan, none of it seems fair."

"What's that, Honey?"

"The laws, sir. The man-made ones about love and marriage. I wanted to ask you when they'll change the miscegenation laws so folk can love who they want to love. Why do they think it's wrong for mine or *any* folk to love another person?" *For me to love who I want.* I swallowed the words, suddenly thinking about

Francis, and any future I might have with a boy snuffed out, then lightly touched my lips. It was still there, fevered and fresh, the same as when he kissed me in the booth.

"Mr. Morgan, they ain't hating, they're loving. Don't seem right the men makin' the laws are ignorin' God's law. Do you think they'll change it, Mr. Morgan?"

He stared at me thoughtfully and, after a long moment, said, "Though it rarely happens fast enough and not near as quick as it should, Honey, I expect like all ugly laws, change will come."

At the outpost, Mr. Taft left a small tin of fresh baked oat cookies for Junia and two poetry books for me, *Harmonium* by Wallace Stevens and Kentuckian Effie Waller Smith's *Rosemary and Pansies* along with the patrons' reads. The minute I spied the collections, I opened them and chewed through the poems, savoring the poets' words and verses, until I realized thirty minutes had passed.

After I'd stacked the old loans and packed up the new ones, I found an envelope with my name on it. Carefully, I opened it. When I saw it was my paycheck, the partial pay for the last weeks of March, I ran out into the yard laughing and twirling in circles, drunk on the joy of receiving my first pay. I waved the letter at Junia.

The ol' girl snorted at my foolishness. I reached inside my sweater pocket and pulled out one of the treats Mr. Taft brought her. So far, the ones I'd baked had worked to keep Junia from running off. She greedily took it, pressing her nose into my palm for more.

"I'm going to make you a bucket of these with this paycheck." I hooted and spun around. Junia wriggled her nose in the air, trying to snatch the paper away.

"It's almost noon, Junia. We'll go to town, and I'll buy you an apple." I rubbed her head, looked at the paycheck again. I'd seen some paychecks for Papa and knew about the deductions the government took out. But I still whistled when I saw the deduction line for federal. "$11.75."

It didn't matter none. I had me $54 and some change after all the taxes, and that was a lot of money for doing something I loved, something that could show the courts I'd earned my freedom.

"Let's go to town, ol' girl."

I tethered Junia to a post behind the Company store and walked around the front.

Bonnie was down on her knees feeding Wrenna's rooster out of the palm of her hand. I watched, fascinated the bad-tempered bird would let her. A few feet away, Perry Gillis and a few other miners laughed. Some of the men yelled at Gillis to leave the girls alone.

Several times, Gillis taunted the young girl by taking a step out into the street toward her. The rooster flew up at him, only to retreat back to Bonnie, but not before Gillis grabbed one of its tail feathers and yelled, "Look, fellers. Bonnie's wanting herself some cock. I got your cock righ' here, girlie." He rubbed the feather over his crotch. Chortles erupted from the small group, but a few men turned away from Gillis, disgusted with the miner's crude display.

Barefoot, Wrenna watched silently from the street, seemingly unmoved.

I stepped around Bonnie and the bird. "Afternoon, Bonnie," I called out a greeting.

"Hey, Honey." She glanced up at me, grinning, ignoring the men's raucous jeers. "Finished your latest. The Undset read. Sure was good. That Vigdis gal was somethin' else. Downright tough."

A fresh bruise darkened her neck along with new scratches. A safety pin was fastened to her overalls, holding the broken straps together.

"Tommie likes my sunflower seeds," she said, pulling out a seed from her bib pocket. "Yessiree, done made myself a new friend...haven't I, Tommie?" The rooster took a seed from her, then sounded an excited *tuck-tuck-tuck*, thinking he'd made a pal too. Bonnie lightly stroked his tall red comb, glided her coal-blackened fingers down his white-feathered back. "You're a handsome boy, Tommie. You watch after Wrenna real good. Maybe you can look after me too...huh, handsome boy?" Bonnie stretched out an arm and tickled his wattle.

Clucking softly to the bird, she dropped a seed onto the ground. The rooster shuffled up to her sideways, preening, brushing his feathers against her hand, then let out a stream of high-pitched *tu-tu-tu*'s and tossed the treat back to her.

Bonnie chuckled and picked up the gift while the miners guffawed.

Wrenna sang out a lilting, "*Coo-coo.*" Tommie startled and made a high-pitched squawk before flying to her side.

I watched as they walked out of town, the rooster herding Wrenna, dipping a spread wing toward her while dashing from one side to the other, circling the young child, leading in front and then nudging from behind, crowing low, guiding her to safety.

Bonnie stared after them, pouring sunflower seeds from one hand to the other. For the first time I saw that beneath her mask of coal dust and hard toil, the young woman was beaming. And a small smile tugged at my lips as I caught my reflection in the shop glass window. I tucked loose hair behind my ear to make myself presentable before going inside.

Eddie stuck his head out the Company store door, and yelled, "Mattie called and said to tell you miners he needs a few boys to cut short their dinner breaks. Says he's got trouble in the hole."

The men grumbled, while a few hurried to their trucks.

"See you Friday," I told Bonnie before I headed into the

store, but she didn't hear. Her eyes were nailed to the girl and her rooster.

Francis waved when I walked by the counter, and I couldn't stop smiling, sneaking sideway glances, seeing his eyes on me as I shopped.

Waiting in line at the cash register, a woman bought butter and flour. The man in front of me said, "Francis, cash my check for me." I watched as Francis counted out Company scrip to the miner in return, knowing that in the end, King Coal owned the Kentucky working man.

Francis gave him a friendly goodbye and reached over to take a bite of something from a bowl, trying to get in his own dinner break during a busy day.

I plunked down an apple and a bag of oats, a fat writing tablet, and a package of envelopes. Pulling out the paycheck, I handed it to him. He sat down the bowl he was eating from and pushed it aside.

"What's this?" He was tanned and looked fit from the early spring sunshine, and he grinned and wiped his mouth with the back of a hand. "Permission letter to date ya from your pa?" he teased.

I could feel the heat rising on my ears and face, his kiss still buzzing on my mouth. "Maybe," I teased back. "I'll let you know soon." I met his smile with a shy, friendly one.

"That'd be real nice," he said.

I pointed to my paycheck. "Miss Foster said I could cash it here."

"Sure thing." He glanced at the paycheck and flipped it over. "See here, Honey." He tapped the signature line, then grabbed an ink pen. "You need to sign it before the store will let me cash it."

"Oh, I was in a hurry and forgot," I said, dismissing it with a wave, wanting to act smart for this man. "Let me take care of it. And that'll be cash, no scrip, Francis." I grabbed the pen and added a fancy signature. After he cashed the check, he handed me back the stub, and I paid for the groceries.

"Anything else for ya today, Honey?"

I looked longingly at a shelf stacked with lipstick, nail polish, rouge, and other cosmetics. Someone came in behind me and took a Coke out of the red Coca-Cola cooler.

The man reached around me, plunked a nickel on the counter, and passed the bottle to Francis. He picked up a church key, opened it for the customer, and put the money into the cash register.

"Filled it just last night," Francis said. "Nice and cold, if you want one, Honey."

It was tempting and I could taste the ice-cold liquid sugar biting at my tongue. I counted my money, then slipped it inside my satchel.

"Anything else I can get ya?"

"I need to buy a headstone, Francis. For Miss Adams."

"Heard she passed." His face grew somber. "Real sorry to hear that. Sears and Roebuck stopped selling them in their catalogs in '49, so you'll need to see Old Man Geary down the road. Let me get you his address." Francis scribbled his name and address down inside a matchbook. "Down on Bridges Road, you go past the county cemetery where you'll see a big barn on the right and Willard's cow pasture on the left. There's a big stone at Geary's entrance."

He grabbed my paper bag and walked around the counter, escorting me to the door. Francis handed me the goods and said, "Wanted to let you know my mama mixes up a delicious bowl of her prized banana pudding for picnic baskets." He pointed to the bowl he'd been eating from. "Right tasty. Matter of fact, the best in Kentucky, the country even," he said, a playfulness in his eyes.

It was daring and a little too bold, but I answered, "Much obliged. I've been fancying some good dessert lately." He passed me the matchbook.

"Well, the delivery driver's waiting on me. Don't *you* wait too long." He stuffed his hand into his pockets, jiggling the coins in his britches, and then hurried to the back of the store.

I slipped out the door and made it a few steps before Perry Gillis blocked me. A few men guffawed, and one other miner chided Gillis, calling him lewd names.

I tried moving in another direction but Gillis stepped in front of me each time, a hardness etched into his face. Then he put a cigarette up to his mouth and pulled out a blackened silver lighter, flicking the toothy wheel once, then twice again, holding the quivering flame inches from my face, slowly circling the lit lighter around my face, the smell of burnt flint and wick stinging my nostrils.

His eyes were cruel, downright deadly, and I thought about Guyla Belle and the broken bottle and the lurking shadows inside her cabin. I wondered what he'd done to her, worried that maybe she had not escaped, but instead, he'd hurt Guyla Belle and locked her up inside their home.

"Mr. Gillis, please let me pass," I said, shaken, lowering my head. "*Please, sir.*"

Suddenly, Bonnie stepped in between us and knocked the lighter out of Gillis's hand. He smacked at her head, and she ducked, yanked me away from him, pulling me to safety.

"Go on with your business, sweet pea," she said a few feet from the Company store, cutting angry eyes to Gillis. "I'll make sure he don't bother ya."

I looked over my shoulder at Gillis's reddening face and shuddered.

Thirty

At Mr. Geary's kitchen table, I counted out $121.23 for the marker, then once again as his wife served a basket of rolls to go with our coffee. After using all Retta's silver coins and what was left of my paycheck, I had 14 cents left.

I was proud, pleased that Retta would have such a fine marker. Earlier, inside Mr. Geary's work building, he'd helped me pick out an angel to perch atop the modest monument, and promised he would have the marble stone polished, lettered, and installed at the Adams cemetery by the end of May. It was the perfect angel, and I ran a palm over the white marble, admiring the craftsmanship and beauty.

We talked about getting my deceased parents a marker, and Mr. Geary said he could do a fine one for $119. After the man tallied up more numbers, he promised to take a $17 deposit, saying I could pay him monthly for the Moffits' tombstone. I told him I would bring back a deposit soon.

Mama had told me a few stories about Angeline, but rarely mentioned Willie, only that they both had a hankering for the books, the learning. And with Angeline being the strength behind it, and wanting the books and book learning for me. I wish I could've met my first parents, could've had more of them.

I rode a tired Junia home as the sun sank in the western skies and a soft rain began to fall. That night as I listened to the pattering of rain hitting the tin roof, I snuggled under the bedcovers and found a contentment, a peace washing over me, grateful for Retta's stone and relieved my parents, Angeline and Willie, would finally have one, too, rather than the small crude rocks that marked their graves.

As I climbed the fire tower, Pearl hollered from above, welcoming me up.

Up in the cab, I dropped the bag on the floor and pulled out Pearl's new loans. I set them next to the Osborne and packed last week's reading material back inside my bag.

Pearl chatted cheerfully as she cut slices of pie and poured us iced tea. When she was through, she sat down.

I leaned across the table. "I've got news."

"I do too!" she exclaimed, and I saw the secret play across her eyes. "You go first, Honey." She put her napkin in her lap and cut into her pie.

I picked up the folded linen and placed it directly on my lap. "Mr. Morgan is going to seek my emancipation with the court."

"What's that?"

"It's where the courts can grant freedom to any minor if they have good reason."

"Freedom... Imagine, no more worries!" Pearl marveled. "I can see more in your eyes." She laughed. "Go on, do tell."

"I met a boy."

Pearl's eyes widened, and she whispered, "I did too. Tell me about your fella first."

"It's Francis down at the Company store."

"Oh, he's cute," she said. "That smile and those dimples."

"He asked me out, but I haven't received permission yet. I might need to call Papa again."

"Anytime. But if you get your freedom, you won't have to."

"Papa will expect me to ask." I took a bite of the pie and chewed. "Francis kissed me." I felt myself reddening.

Pearl sat down her fork, her eyes widened again.

"He stole it," I said secretively.

"Do tell, Honey!"

I laughed. "I let him. Maybe this Saturday I can telephone Papa before we have our pajama party?"

Pearl frowned. "I'm going on a date." She got up and pulled the calendar off the wall and tapped April 11 where it was marked *Party*. "Oh, Honey, I'm sorry I forgot about the invitation. I'll just tell—"

Disappointed, I fibbed, "It's okay. I have chores and a route to make up on Saturday anyway. What's his name?"

"Perry."

My hands flushed suddenly, and I put down my fork. "Hmm, I only know one Perry in these parts."

"He's from here. It's Perry Gillis, the strapping young miner. Has about the biggest arms I've seen anywhere."

I swallowed uneasily, collecting my thoughts. Staring down into my lap, I picked at a loose string alongside the seams of my napkin, then folded it in half and placed the napkin carefully beside my plate, resting my hand across it.

"Perry is Robbie Hardin's cousin," she said. "He's been up here four times in the last six days, trying to make right what his relative did wrong. I turned him down the first three. There was something just off, but I couldn't quite put my finger on it. Something more in those pretty eyes of his. Then Perry explained it was all Robbie's doing and apologized all sweet-like."

When I didn't say anything for the longest time, Pearl said, "What's wrong, Honey?" She glanced at my telling hands. "Go on. Do tell. We've not even had a real date yet, it's not like I'm about to bed or wed him."

My face warmed and I pushed away the pie. I started with the easy—and what I knew to be true. How Gillis punched Francis, taunted Wrenna Abbott and hurt Bonnie Powell. Then I paused, trying to decide what more I should tell.

Pearl flicked her napkin and arranged it neatly back across her lap. "I'll have a talk with him about it. But maybe they were being nasty or did something to him first. Why he even brought me those flowers."

I drew my eyes to the cheerful pot of violets sitting on her chifforobe.

"He's real ornery, Pearl, and his wife, Guyla Belle, has been missing for a while now. And I've been getting an uneasy feeling about it."

"She left him," Pearl quipped.

"No, she's *missing*." I shook my head, sympathetic. "Haven't told a soul, but the more I think about it, the more I'm convinced he's part of it."

She locked disbelieving eyes to mine for a moment.

"Their little boy, Johnnie, fell down the well. I was able to get him out, but…"

"What, Honey? You can tell me." Pearl gripped my coloring palm.

"I'm not so sure that he hasn't hurt Guyla Belle again."

Pearl's eyes narrowed and fear spread across her face. "What about her?"

"Well, I stopped at the nurse's home. Amara was treating their boy for pneumonia. When Perry found out Johnnie had fallen in the well, he hit her in front of us. She had to get stitches."

Pearl stood up and paced the room. "*No.*" Her jaw hardened as she pounded a fist against her leg. "He led me to believe she gave him a divorce and left. *Slick bastard.*"

I looked down at my lap, hating to see the misery in her eyes. "I overhead Perry and his mother talking in the Company store. Robbie was trying to help Perry get your job. They wanted to get rid of Guyla Belle too."

She turned and looked out the windows. "If I don't go, he'll keep coming for my job. I'm guessing he's that kind."

"He's been threatening me over visiting her, and I fear he and Robbie might want to drive you away too." He was the type, and if it meant cozying up with her to get the lookout job, Gillis would. Worse, if he couldn't win Pearl over, no telling what harm he might do to her.

"Honey, he invited me up to his mother's place for dinner with his sister, Ida, and his son."

"I've been stopping by, hoping to see Guyla Belle. But Junia makes an awful fuss, acts skittish. Guyla Belle was supposed to leave a milk bottle on the well along with her loans, to let me know it was safe to visit and that Perry was working. But I found the book I'd loaned her out in the yard, torn. That was definitely Perry's doing. She loved the books and wouldn't have done that," I went on.

"You don't think—" She stopped pacing in front of the windows. "This sounds pretty bad."

"I'm not sure what to think anymore. But I'm worried about her. Maybe they've locked her inside the cabin and she's suffering. He could've hurt her really bad this time. Guyla Belle told me and Amara she'd never leave him. She's from North Carolina, has no family, no money, and nowhere else to go. And the more I think about it, I just know something's bad about it all."

Pearl sat back down, absently playing with her charm bracelet. "My granny always said cowardly men who beat up on females seek out the ones who are all alone. Gives them a bigger power than what they're already born with. I've heard some wife-beaters will take a bride, only to try and move her away so they can break them off from their families—hide their telling misdeeds from the knowing eyes of the female's kin." Pearl took a long drink of her tea, then slammed down the glass. "Dammit." She walked over to her chifforobe and grabbed the pot of flowers, then opened the door to the catwalk and pitched them over the metal rail.

A chill scuttled up, tightening flesh, and I worried about what might be coming at Pearl, and maybe me.

Thirty-One

The morning air was drenched, sweetened with balsam and pine as I lingered on the porch listening to the soft rain hitting the roof. It didn't dampen my spirits, though, because today was April 11, and Pearl had decided to have the pajama party.

Rummaging through a trunk a bit later, I found an old flannel gown and tossed the drab piece aside into the pile of other ugly gowns. Some I'd outgrown, while others were too tattered. *What do I wear to such a party?*

Thumbing through a magazine, I inspected the women's stylish clothing, then set it aside frustrated. In the end I picked the flannel gown, worrying. *I've never attended a party of any kind. Do I wear this to the party, or put it on when I get there, or…? Oh, I couldn't ride over the hills wearing only this. What to do?* "If only Mama was here," I moaned.

I took off my clothes and slipped on the flannel, then put my riding pants and shirt over those, struggling to smooth down the gown. Bulky, but it had to do.

Pearl didn't answer my knock when I arrived earlier than what she'd said, and I huffed at being so impatient to get there, worried where she could be. Again, I rapped on the trapdoor, before climbing back down the stairs.

I sat under the lean-to in the sometimes drizzling rain, then a harder slanting rain, waiting, checking my timepiece. *Where was she?* Junia stiffened her ears and drew her attention to the woods, and I thought I'd caught something red flitter beyond the leaves, certain my eyes were playing tricks.

Tapping a boot on the ground, I ran my palm over my damp hair, aggravated to be stuck out in the cold, my breath billowing into the unshakable drizzle. After an hour, Junia looked toward the path and brayed several warnings.

Pearl slid off Pie and pulled him into the stall. "Honey, I'm sorry I'm late. I forgot the time. You're soaked. Let's get you upstairs."

She took off Pie's saddle and harness and quickly inspected his coat and hooves, then grabbed a bag she'd set down and we trudged up the stairs. Before I stepped inside the cab, I shook the rain off my coat and raked my boots across the metal landing.

Pearl lit the woodstove and dug through her chifforobe for dry clothes for me. "Wear these till I can get yours dry. It's Mother's favorite gown," she said quietly, handing me it along with a pair of socks.

"Obliged. It'll be nice to get warm," I said, a little edgier than I meant to, slipping behind her dressing screen to toss off my coat and damp clothes.

"Looks like the rain's stopping," Pearl said, relieved. "I can see bright skies off to the west."

When I was dressed, I carried my wet clothing over to the stove. Pearl unfolded a wooden quilt rack in front of it. "There, they'll be dry in no time."

She took my coat and stared at the heap of clothing I was holding and laughed. "Who wears pajamas under their clothes to a party?"

Tired, cold, and miserable and a whole lot miffed at waiting in the rain, I lashed back. "Me. I wear pajamas to a party that's called a *pajama party*. Because I've never been before, and my sophisticated friend didn't tell the hill mouse what to wear, nor advised she'd be shivering out in the cold waiting on a party that she'd forgotten."

"Honey, don't be such a pill—"

"*Pill?* Are you calling me difficult?" Everything was building up inside. The loss of my folk and dear Retta, the fear of sneaking around, and Gillis coming at me. And I struggled to tamp it all down.

Pearl shrugged and went to hang up my coat. "Someone's being difficult."

I dropped my stack of clothes and picked up my wet pants, stuffing my legs into them. "This *difficult* girl"—I grabbed my shirt—"showed up in time. I've lost so much, but you'll not poke fun at me and take my dignity, Pearl Grant, and then act hoity-toity—" I stopped, choked back the words that would wound and forever scar. Raw silence batted between us. "I should leave."

For a moment, the stillness was crushing in the small cab. Then Pearl burst into tears.

Feeling small, I wanted to cry, too, but the tears belonged to Pearl, and I had not earned that right; I'd caused them. "I'm sorry, but—" I said, meaning it and wishing I hadn't spoken, knowing better to harness any excuse, and that adding the last word would only diminish the apology. "Forgive me. I'm really sorry, Pearl. Please don't cry."

"Honey." She sniffed and wagged her head. "It's not that. It's Perry Gillis. I went to the store to get eggs for our breakfast. I ran into Perry in the back parking lot and told him I couldn't see him. He got hot about that and knocked the eggs out of my hands." She wiped her eyes and sighed heavily. Reaching for the gown, she held it out to me. "I'm sorry I made you wait. It was thoughtless."

I gasped at the mention of him. "He's dangerous—"

"You're right. He grabbed my arm and started calling me awful names. Finally, Francis and Eddie ran him off." She pulled up her sleeve and rubbed a reddened arm. "I saw it for myself."

I took the gown. "Are you okay? We should put ice on that."

"It's just bruised from him twisting it." She dismissed it with a shake of her head, then inspected her charms closely. "A few days ago, I stopped by Perry's home. The boy was out in the yard alone riding his trike. He came over to me, crying, but I couldn't understand him. Ida ran out the door and snatched him up. She said Perry wasn't home, that he was working a double shift. That was it. She was gone before I could answer."

"Poor Johnnie," I said, slipping back into the borrowed gown.

Pearl picked up a piece of paper off her table and handed it to me. "I chanced leaving the cab unlocked since you were coming, and I planned on being home in time and would've, had I not run into damn Perry. Just in case, I thought you'd go on in and find this note." She handed it to me, and I read her note. *Honey, ran to town for eggs. Be back soon—make yourself comfortable.*

I was surprised that Pearl would leave her cab unlocked, even for a short time.

Pearl pulled down a big colorful tin can off the shelf, pried it open, and pulled out a large bottle of Chicken Cock whiskey and poured a drink. "Sorry. Can you forgive me?"

"Only if you promise to forgive me." I smiled sheepishly, deeply embarrassed by my outburst, worried I would lose her friendship, my *sister*. But Pearl had a generous soul, the words were sincere, her eyes kind, and I didn't think she would be that small to let the riff come between us. "What do you think about Guyla Belle, Pearl?"

"I feel it's bad and we should tell someone about her. Maybe the sheriff?"

"Not sure about the sheriff. He's kin to Perry and Robbie, but we can try."

Pearl shuddered. "If the men at the store hadn't run Perry off, there's no telling what he would've done."

"I know Perry is evil, after seeing him hit Guyla Belle and threatening me."

Pearl sighed loudly. "I think we could both use a drink. And some fun." She handed me the glass of bourbon. "I'm off, my relief is over at the base, and it's time for our party." She raised the bottle with the rooster and pretty flowers on the label, wriggling it. "Only thing better than a fine bottle of Kentucky straight whiskey is having the address of a friendly bootlegger."

I raised my brows, questioning.

Pearl threw back her head and laughed. "I couldn't dare go to Devil John. And it's a dry county, so I asked Francis. He said Devil John won't sell to teenagers. But he pointed me to a discreet fella who used to work with him and dabbles in the bootlegging now and then."

I laughed with her. "Looks like Francis not only steals kisses, but touts prized puddings and good whiskey."

"Go ahead, Honey, have a drink. It'll warm you up, and you've earned some fun."

Hesitant, I sniffed the bourbon, then took my first drink of hard liquor and swallowed, coughing and choking on the burning liquid. My nose burned and eyes watered. Noting the time, I suddenly realized it was too late to call Papa about Francis. "Tell me more about pajama parties," I wheezed and shook my head, tipping back the glass again.

"Well"—she looked at me a little teasingly, trying not to laugh—"you never wear wet ones to a party. Especially to a sleepover. Lest someone think you peed the bed."

I giggled, feeling the whiskey hitting me.

Pearl poured herself another shot. "We should have some music, Honey." She pulled out a small cream-and-red suitcase and another from under her bed and opened the bigger one. It was a new phonograph.

"That looks just like the ones in the magazines," I said over her shoulder, glancing around the cab. "Never seen so many newfangled contraptions, and all in one place." I sat down beside her on the rug.

Pearl handed me the small suitcase beside it. "Here's the carrying case for the 45s. Pick out the records."

I unlatched it to see the records lined between metal racks like the ones advertised in magazines. There had to be twenty, maybe more. Not knowing a lick about music, other than the hymns and ballads Mama taught me, I handed her one that read "The World Is Waiting for the Sunrise" by someone named Les Paul and Mary Ford.

Pearl put it atop the player and sang along to the spirited tune, not missing a word, snapping her fingers, the clinking of charms adding to each beat. I tapped my feet and tried to hum along to the joyful melody.

We played a few more records, and Pearl offered me another drink. It was warm and soothed the aches from somewhere deeper than bruised flesh. I accepted, laughing a little uneasily, knowing my folk wouldn't be so amused. I dug into the record case and pulled out one that said Nat King Cole "Unforgettable" and handed it to her.

Pearl played the lonesome song. Partway through, she said, "Honey, did you ever have a boyfriend?"

"No." I paused a second, wondering why she asked, then took a gulp. "But Carson asked for my hand in March."

Her eyes widened. "*Carson Smith?* Do tell."

"He's a fine friend. And only that. He wanted to save me from the House of Reform."

"I would be tempted because—" Pearl paused, looking a bit uncomfortable.

I cocked my head, waiting.

"Well, one of the boys back home was sent there after he stole some penny candy from Old Man Peyton's store. When he finally made it out, he swore he'd never go back. Said there was a big graveyard hidden on the Reform land for those who got crushed by the rock, died of the fevers, or didn't reform to the rules." Her voice dipped low.

I grew silent a moment, wondering how many didn't make it out.

Pearl rummaged through her records, like she'd said too much.

I brushed away the thought of prison and said, "Carson's really sweet on Greta Clemmons, and I think there'll be a marriage between them. Still, I didn't need anyone's permission to marry at sixteen, and the state would've given the union its blessing. Yet, here I am, fighting for my freedom because I *won't* marry."

"Laws about females never make a lick of sense because they're made and run by men and meant to keep us in bondage. You know, Mother works, but when she went to open a bank account, the banker refused and said she had to get Father's permission first."

"I'm not in any hurry to get married." I sipped on the drink. "And if I ever get my freedom, I'm not going to lose it so easily to just any man." My thoughts went to Francis, and I pressed my lips together, still tasting his kiss.

"I had myself a sweetheart in high school. Dale Clark," Pearl said in a quiet way, looking down. "We'd talked about getting married after we graduated. He was that one *unforgettable*. That boy could kiss you and make you forget to breathe." She put a few records back into the case.

For a moment we listened to the saxophone rise softly between the words of the wistful song.

"What happened?" I finally asked, the bourbon giving me courage.

Pearl shrugged and filled her small glass with more, trying to decide what to tell me. Flicking her wrist, she pressed one of the heart charms between her fingers. I skimmed the room, waiting, wondering if my boldness would be mistaken for prying.

"He gave this one to me." She raised her wrist and tapped the heart charm with her nail.

Leaning over, I studied the fat heart-shaped charm with the double hearts in the middle and a pretty bow etched above them. "Sure is pretty," I said.

She looked into my eyes, searching, then took a breath and in the same quiet voice said, "There was a party a month before graduation in an empty barn down the road from my home.

Everyone was drinking except me." She lifted her jelly-jar glass and took another sip as if to show me.

I blinked, trying to clear my foggy mind, and set the drink down, realizing her secret was a gift and something she thought I had earned.

"It was late. Dale and I had argued about the time, argued about him getting juiced, and argued about him drinking again. He called me a wet rag." Pearl briskly rubbed the charm. "I had a curfew, so I left him there with another couple." She wagged her head bitterly. "There must have been a whole lot more drinking because Dale, Anna, and Eugene never made it down from the loft where they passed out when the barn caught fire. Eugene smoked. They said it was caused by his cigarette. And with all that old straw and bedding in there, well, it went up pretty quick."

Her words were raw, filled with fresh grief like it just happened yesterday.

"What a horrible thing to happen. I'm sorry, Pearl."

She leaned over and put another record on called the "Tennessee Waltz." Then she flopped down in front of me and ran her fingers through her short, dark curls.

The singer was forlorn and sang about her friend stealing her darling. Pearl sang along a minute and then said, "The devil robbed me of my sweetheart that day. Why I finally decided to take the summer job in Big Knob and then landed here. That, and if it was good enough for Hallie Daggett, it was good enough for me."

I shuddered, thinking about her loss and the tragic deaths.

"If I had stayed, I could've saved them." She clenched a fist. "The town thinks so too—"

"No, Pearl. You could've perished like them."

"I'll never know."

"I'm glad you weren't there." I peered into her guilt-ridden eyes, wishing I could lift her somber burden. "You're gonna be fine here watching over the hills," I said softly and took her hand.

"Enough of this gloomy talk." She examined my nails and

raised her brows. "I have the perfect polish for you. And some good cosmetics you can try. Come on, I'll show you."

"Why?" I said, puzzled.

"Well, it's a party, so for fun, and it'll also make you look older if you wear it at your emancipation hearing. We can practice now," Pearl said.

"Oh, older. Yes, that's a good idea." I studied her earrings.

"Would you like me to pierce your ears? Mother did mine. And I bought some potatoes at the Company store just in case." She grinned mischievously, her dimples deepening.

"Potatoes?" I cupped my earlobes, horrified at the thought, scared of the pain. "I don't know, Pearl. And, well, I don't own any earrings."

"You can wear my little pearl ones until you can get a pair. I pierced Jane Scott's ears at my last party, and they turned out perfect."

"Did she cry?"

"Squealed like a stuck pig, but Jane would cry if an ant crawled over her little toe. It doesn't hurt much at all, Honey. C'mon, it'll be fun and you'll be the sophisticated one," she teased as she stood up. "Let's eat something first. I made us some food this morning. I'll just warm the biscuits and get the ham out of the icebox."

We ate and then chatted about books as she applied makeup on me. When she was through, she grabbed a small glass bottle of perfume off her chifforobe and spritzed it on my neck and wrists, perfuming the cab.

While I looked in the mirror, studying my transformation, Pearl got out a skillet, heated and poured corn kernels into it, making us a generous batch of buttery popcorn. Three drinks and an hour later, Pearl sterilized a sewing needle, numbed my flesh with an ice cube, then put a potato behind my ear.

"Don't move, Honey."

I remembered when Mama had ol' Doc inoculate me for smallpox, scarlet fever, and other bad things, and suddenly wanted to run. "Wait, my bladder's full, and I don't want to pee in the chair." I gasped and then escaped, slipping inside her closet to relieve myself on the chamber pot.

Seated back at the table, I gulped down a mouthful of liquor, closed my eyes, and took one deep breath and another, latching onto the wooden seat, gripping it with all my might as she pushed the needle through my flesh.

"There!" she exclaimed, bending down to my face. "Are you okay, Honey? I hope it didn't hurt much."

I exhaled a slow trembling *yes*, relieved it was over so quick. Pearl cleaned my lobe with rubbing alcohol, pushed the small pearl post into my ear before doing the other side. "Don't take them out for about a month—the longer the better. Twist the earrings around every chance you get and keep your skin clean with rubbing alcohol."

I stared into a mirror, admiring her pretty earrings and the cosmetics she'd put on me. "I do look older now. Much obliged, Pearl," I told her, yawning.

It had been a fine pajama party, and we both staggered around giggling as we put away the records, tidied up, and washed the dishes.

Pearl slipped behind the screen and put on a gown. Outside, Junia called out with a long bray. "That doesn't sound good. I better check on her." I reached for the door leading to the catwalk, but Pearl ran over to me and grabbed my arm, pulling me back. "No wandering outside in the dark while drinking. Junia will be fine. She has Pie to keep her company."

I shook my head and tried to shrug off the intoxication. "I'm pie-faced," I admitted, laughing, plopping down on the soft pallet she'd made for me.

Pearl sank down onto her bed and raised the stuffed horse in front of her face. "There you are, dear Mr. Cleveland. Let's giddy-up and get going and outrun the nightmares tonight... C'mon, off to sweet dreamland we go, Mr. Cleveland," she said, the corn-husk mattress chattering into her singsong as she turned over. But her words weren't light or playful; they were stretched out into a tired, woeful plea.

Thirty-Two

Screams broke through my deadened slumber.

Early morning, confused and still reeling from the previous night's spirits, I coughed, the smell of smoke tickling, as I struggled to come fully awake.

"Fire, Honey, *Honey.*" For a moment, I couldn't grip my bearings or who was calling me, and my sluggish mind flitted to my home over in Thousandsticks, then to my small bed at Retta's, and back over to the Carter homestead.

Then I heard her yell again, curse, and jerk on the trapdoor.

Bewildered, I jumped up off the pallet, tangling in the blankets, coughing, stumbling. "Pearl?" I searched around and pulled on my boots. The early morning light streamed into the cab, slashing yellows across the trails of smoke filling inside.

"There's a fire outside this damn trap and we're locked in, Honey."

Cold fear dropped into my belly, souring. "Gillis," I whispered.

"And his cousin Robbie! I heard their footsteps. Hand me the ax, Honey. *Hurry!*" She stomped down on the trapdoor with her boot.

"What about the door that opens to the catwalk?" I said, rushing over to the stove and fetching the ax, ducking low to stay below the smoke.

She coughed and shook her head. "We don't want to be

stuck out there in case it all goes up. Need to get to the metal landings and out of this cab. And the only way down is through this damn trap."

I rubbed my eyes, the smoke blurring my vision. "Should I open the windows?"

"Keep them closed, Honey, so the fire doesn't swoop in on us."

I handed her the ax. Coughing more, she lifted the heavy handle and swung it down. "Quick, wet some towels." Her words were strangled by the smoke.

She dropped the ax onto the trapdoor, but the thick oak board didn't give. Again, she slammed it down, shaking the cab, as I scurried over to the closet, choking, wondering if whoever had set the fire had broken the telephone lines.

Bumping against the washstand, I wet the towels, my face and hair, then passed a soaked one to her, pressing the other to my nose, my eyes and chest. The smoke was thick and darkening, swallowing us.

Down below, Pie whinnied and Junia shrieked.

Pearl struck the door several more times, but it still wouldn't budge. Then she whacked at the hinges and frame, splintering pieces of wood.

The smoke was suffocating, and we coughed and wheezed, gasping for air. I buried my face in the towel and bit down, the panic threatening to erupt into screams, my heart galloping. "*Pearl*," I moaned.

"Don't worry, Honey. I'll get us out." Again, she brought the ax down and I heard a faint crack. "Go ahead and radio R.C. and tell him we've got a fire up here," Pearl said, breathing heavy.

She tried several times more to break the door down, each time the cracks growing louder mangled with her curses. "Dammit, open up!" she yelled while the ax thudded loudly against wood.

I crawled across the room and pulled the radio down, clicked on the button. "Hello, hello?" I coughed. "Help, someone, this is Honey Lovett." Loud static poured through the metal box. "R.C.?" I clicked the button several more times. "R.C., we have a fire at Pearl's cab and we can't get out! R.C.? Anyone? *Fire!*" I stared wildly out the windows into the morning light, yellowed through the cab smoke, the light stretching thinner with each growing second. Any minute now, the smoke would chew up the light and swallow us. "*Pearl?*"

"Keep trying," Pearl hollered. Her blurring face was damp and the short, dark curls were matted to her head as she brought the ax down, trying to cut into and bust the wooden door open.

"R.C., pick up, pick up!" I clicked twice. "*Please, please.*"

"Honey, we copy and I'm on the way," R.C. said in a calm, steady voice.

I crawled over to Pearl, coughing. Pulling myself up, I swayed, the smoke blanketing the cab. "Pearl, I can't see you." I reached out, trying to find her.

"Stay on the floor, Honey," she ordered as she delivered another hard blow, the sound of wood and metal crashing onto the landing platform right below.

Tears stung my eyes as light and smoke poured through the widening crack. "Hang on, Honey, we're almost through. Grab the fire extinguisher."

I felt my way over to the stove, knocking pans and skillets down as I struggled to find it. When I had the extinguisher in my grip, I dropped to my knees, coughing, inching slowly back to her.

Pearl kicked through the wood and finally the door split open. "The bastards had us locked in." She pounded her chest and drew in deep breaths.

I bent over, braced my hands on my legs, coughing and gasping for air. When I finally straightened, I looked over her shoulder and saw the padlock on the stairs and several sets of muddy footprints. Further down, I spotted Gillis's Texaco ball cap lying on one of the steps.

Pearl took the fire extinguisher from me and sprayed the

licking flames that they had set with wood and brush. The smell of gasoline rose in the breeze. They must've carried up the bundle in the early morning hours.

Pearl grabbed her coat off a hook, folded it across her arms, and said, "Let's get downstairs and let the cab air out."

I nodded, wishing I'd had time to dress.

When the fire was nothing more than a smoldering pile, she pulled me across it and down to the next landing where we both hung over the side gasping for fresh air. I looked down at Junia, silently cursing myself. I had been too drunk to go out in the dark when I thought I'd heard the heavy footsteps and the mule's loud warnings earlier. Instead, I had pulled the coverlet over my face and fallen back into a drunken sleep.

The old beast lifted her muzzle and caught my eye and rang out a shivering hee-haw like she was scolding me. I shuddered to think about the men trying to hurt her and Pie and wondered if they'd tried and she'd kicked them away. Wondered what would have happened if I'd tried to stop them. I rubbed my arms.

In a few minutes, we caught our breath and crept slowly down the stairs, inhaling the dewy morning. When we got to the bottom, I sprinted over and inspected Junia while Pearl did the same to her horse.

Pearl bent over and picked up a half-eaten apple core only to throw it angrily back on the ground. I saw small pieces of apple beside Junia. They'd bribed the mounts to keep them quiet. For some reason, Junia had let them. It wasn't like her, and I wondered if Perry's sister had come with them to help quiet the ol' girl and Pie.

When I saw they were fine, I plopped down on the bottom landing, exhausted.

Pearl stroked Pie and then buried her face into his neck. "We could've ended up like Dale and the others." Her shoulders shook, and I stood up and walked over to her. Pressing fingers onto my trembling lips, I looked away, hurting for her.

In a minute, I said quietly, "Pearl, come sit beside me and rest a minute." I hugged her shoulders and led her back over to the landing.

"It was Perry and Robbie," she said, kicking the apple cores away.

"Maybe his sister too since Junia doesn't warm to men easily."

"Makes sense. Otherwise, we would've heard the old apostle fussing earlier."

Pained with guilt, I dropped my gaze to my hands, studying my nails. If I hadn't been so drunk, I would've heard. I coughed several times, the smoke still burning in my lungs. "Perry accused me of breaking them up with the book I'd given Guyla," I said as I sat down beside her. "Said he would go to the law if I wasn't careful."

Pearl flexed tired hands and slipped them over mine. "There's another law in Kentucky, one you won't find in any books. A different justice that comes from our kin and the kin before us. *We take care of our own.*" She squeezed my hand.

I shifted and shrugged my tired body inside the folds of Mrs. Grant's worn gown, aching for Mama's arms.

Pearl looked up at the underside of the cab. "The smoke should be cleared up there in a few minutes, and it'll be safe for you to dress." Pearl wrapped her coat around me and looked straight ahead at the mounts, blowing out a haggard breath.

I pressed my knees to my chest, tucking them under my chin, rocking, looking out to the peaceful forest, the ol' land so strong and beautiful, yet deceptively brutal and imprisoning. My mind drifted to Guyla Belle. Perry Gillis's angry face. The more I pondered it, the more I was convinced he'd done something horribly bad and had locked Guyla Belle somewhere inside.

"*Justice*," I whispered, curling my hand into a fist. "The rule of this ol' land is hard. And it's gonna make it a lot harder for the likes of Perry Gillis and his kind when the Devil comes calling and pushes a mud-rotted fist up from this blood-soaked earth to claim its sinner."

Thirty-Three

Sheriff Buckner arrived with R.C. about twenty minutes later. I ran back up to the cab to get dressed as they rode their horses over to the lookout's stairs. When I returned, Pearl was arguing with the lawman. Junia fussed at the mounts that the men had tethered to the landing.

"You're not going to lock them up? Perry Gillis and his cousin could've killed us," Pearl snapped at the sheriff.

The lawman was a foot taller than Pearl, and I didn't know exactly how he was related to Gillis, but I saw the same bold stance and cruel eyes of Gillis and his kin as he puffed out his chest and hitched his utility belt up over a generous belly, using his harsh voice to keep a woman in her place. Long ago, I'd learned about these types of hardened men from the books I'd read, and they made me mindful to be on alert.

"Done tol' you, Miss Grant," the sheriff said heatedly, his jaw packed with a chaw, "that hat don't mean a damn thing. There's probably fifty men running around this county wearing Texaco ball caps."

She shot out an arm to the stairs. "There's muddy footprints up there, and unless I've magically doubled my shoe size overnight and grown two sets of feet, I say they're Perry Gillis and Robbie Hardin's."

"It could be kids, anyone, Miss Grant. Having themselves some Saturday night fun and it got out of hand. Now I've tol' ya—"

"Your words *done* told me that because they're your kin, you're not going to arrest them, Sheriff," Pearl yelled.

"Watch it, young lady. You're coming close to getting yourself arrested for harassing a lawman." He glared stonily at her, then leaned over into her face and sniffed. "You been drinking, Miss Grant? Maybe you were having yourself some fun up there too? Start that fire yourself?" He sniffed one side of her head, then moved slowly to the other. "I do believe you are drunk."

Scowling, Pearl moved away.

"Hold on there, Sheriff Buckner." R.C. stepped forward, frowning. "Miss Grant has a right to ask that her grievance be recognized. There's been an arson and an attack on her and her home, the Forestry's property."

Pearl lifted her chin. "And what about his wife, Sheriff? What about Guyla Gillis who's gone missing? He could be hiding her after he beat the poor woman up again. Are you going to investigate it after I told you she could be in harm's way or worse?"

"It's true, sir." I stepped off the bottom landing, crossing my arms. "I recognize that ball cap. Perry Gillis had one exactly like it. Same frayed star on the emblem, and his wife is—"

The sheriff stabbed a finger in my direction. "Girl, shut up, not another word!"

I flinched.

"He could have her locked up in her cabin and she's badly injured!" Pearl screamed. "And he's been sneaking out here to my lookout, trying to get me to go out with him—"

"Dammit, lady, I will lock—"

"Buckner, enough!" R.C. yelled, the young ranger's voice bellowing. "I'm the law in this forest, and you're not locking anyone up unless I say so." R.C. glared at him and wiped a damp brow with a curled fist, pushing the copper curls away from his brow and shifting his lanky frame.

"I fear she's hurt or something bad has happened to her," I said quietly.

The sheriff shook his head and snapped, "Perry's done

reported you to me, Miss Lovett, and there *is* a man-made law and God's that forbids the intentional interference with a marital relation. Causing alienation of affection is a serious moral grievance that goes against God's law and Kentucky. And I will arrest you in a Kentucky heartbeat if I find out you've done just that with your foolish, airish books." He chewed on his tobacco and spit the wad close to my feet.

I stepped back. Pearl moved closer to me, our arms touching.

"Now, R.C., I'm headed back to town. If you find real evidence, ya bring it to me." He cut a mean eye toward Pearl and then to me. "Done had my fill of these cockamamie female hysterias for one day." He spit again before ambling off to his mount.

And like that, the Kentucky lawman declared us trite, foolish, and liars, and Guyla Belle the property of her husband to be used as he saw fit.

Pearl and I stood there in silence looking at each other, flattened by the lawman's coldness, the disappointment brimming in our eyes.

"Best go up and have a look," R.C. said, heading toward the landing. "Then I need to find out why your new relief over at the base cab didn't call this in when it happened."

After R.C. inspected the cab, he promised to speak with Robbie Hardin. Swore that if he found out it was him, he'd fire Hardin on the spot. But R.C. admitted that without help from the sheriff, there was little he or the Forestry could do, and their hands were tied. "I'll be back with a new door first thing, Pearl, and we'll make sure the cab and you are protected, and it's safe for you up in there," R.C. promised, apologizing several times for the fire and asking us if we needed anything else before he left.

We sat down on the landing, our voices too hoarse to speak, our lungs tired and achy from the smoke, the shock of the fire settling over our thoughts like a dark thundercloud.

"I'm glad we made it out safe," Pearl said, wiping her eyes, a single tear falling onto her cheek. "That little wooden matchbox could've gone up in flames."

Pearl inhaled a shaky breath and scooted closer. Slipping an arm around my shoulder, she leaned her head against mine and we wept quietly, our cries drifting up into the scarred, cragged bones of grandmother mountains.

Thirty-Four

The child drew her eyes to the rooster when it sounded a piercing *churr*, the shiny hackles jutted out along its neck, a warning swallowed in the bird's waxing plumage. Quietly, Wrenna turned her gaze back to Gillis.

Tired of the coal miner's taunting, I dug out my timepiece. *Already one o'clock. Where was Mr. Morgan?* I snapped the watch shut, dropped it back into my bag, and shifted at the top of the courthouse steps, waiting, sneaking glances down to the town as an older gentleman climbed up the thirty-six stairs toward me. Pressing my earlobes between my fingers, I felt for Pearl's earrings. Satisfied they were safe, I dug out the compact of pressed powder she'd given me and inspected my makeup in the tiny mirror. I had been careful to apply it lightly, but enough to make me appear a bit older. I checked my lipstick, then looked back over my shoulder at the courthouse doors.

Businessmen and attorneys bustled in and out of the stately white building, the scents of stale coffee and smoke-filled corridors haloing before escaping into the sunshine.

I turned back to the town below. Across the street, coal miners loitered outside the Company store, smoking their Camels and Lucky Strikes, drinking ice-cold Cokes, Ale-8-Ones, and harder beverages while bantering after another brutal morning shift. Bonnie saw me standing at the top of the steps and waved, then pulled out seeds from the large breast pocket of her threadbare bib overalls and threw one to Tommie.

But the bird wasn't interested today. Instead, Tommie picked up the sunflower seed, bobbed his head, and shuffled up sideways to Gillis. Clucking deep, hopping excitedly, the bird dropped the kernel at his feet.

Amused, Gillis bent down and flicked the seed back.

Bonnie stood back and smiled thinly.

The men roared, shouting vulgarities. "*Look'a there, fellers, damn bird's done turned Gillis into a fairy boy!*" one of them hollered. "*Baak-bak-bak! Cock-whipped!*" another cackled into the miners' howls.

Reddening, Gillis took a hard puff off his cigarette and swallowed the smoke through clenched teeth before exhaling it out his nostrils.

The day was unbearably warm, and I peeled off my sweaty gloves and stuffed them inside the bag, drying my damp hands on the sides of my dress. Somewhere an automobile door slammed above the distant thrum of rail song from coal trains moving through the pines. I searched for Mr. Morgan in the parking lot below and scanned the storefronts, my eyes resting on Bonnie once more. She scowled at Gillis and said something, then flung another morsel onto the sidewalk. Again, Tommie plucked it up and preened, tidbitting for Gillis before tossing it at him.

Gillis's jaw hardened, and he flicked his cigarette toward Tommie, cursed, and slapped at the rooster, his hands catching only air.

Wrenna silently watched from the street.

The men laughed harder, bursts of hoots and more hollers ringing through town square.

A businessman whisked past me, hurrying down the courthouse steps, a brew of strong coffee, cigar smoke, and spicy cologne hovering, tickling the back of my throat. Coughing, I lifted a hand and fanned my face.

Shop bells jingled greetings as townsfolk went about their

daily business, the warm Kentucky afternoon slowly sweeping into another, the cadences of today folding into yesterday.

I tugged at the collar of my clean dress, wiped a brow. Overhead, a crow cawed across sunny blue skies. Another answered back, its grating bickers swallowed in the hills.

Gillis cursed loudly again and snatched one of Tommie's tail feathers.

"*Damn you, Gillis!*" Bonnie screamed and threw a handful of seeds at the miner.

Tommie scurried to pick them up. Gillis kicked at the bird, and Tommie shrilled and batted his wings, the hackles rising around the neck. Briskly, the rooster hopped up and slashed Gillis's pants leg, the claws ripping into the soiled fabric.

"I'll ring your gawdamn neck, you—" Gillis bent over to grab the bird. Tommie squawked and pecked his hand, sprang upward again, slashing long nails down the miner's other leg.

Gillis kicked and shook Tommie off, then stooped over and swung his arm, knocking the angry bird sideways. Bonnie smacked at Gillis, and he threw back his fist punching her dead square in the jaw. She shrieked and stumbled back against the store, bouncing off the thick shop-glass windows.

Gasping, I pressed a darkening palm over my mouth, and my eyes fell back on Wrenna.

Unmoved, Wrenna stood alone in the street, barefoot, watching Gillis's jeering face. Slowly, she turned to Bonnie and stared a moment before cupping a hand to her cheek and calling out an abrupt, loud *oo-oo*, signaling *hens in danger*.

Pressing my hands over my ears, I stepped back and tumbled into a man rushing out of the courthouse. Annoyed, he shoved me away. I drew my eyes back down to the Company store.

"*Oo-oo*," Wrenna rang out once more.

Tommie stopped, tilted his head toward Wrenna and then back to Bonnie. Suddenly he flew up in a frenzy at Gillis once, twice, and again and again, pecking, clawing, and tearing at flesh, driving his long, sharp spurs into the man's face, eyes, and neck, the blood squirting onto the sidewalk, splattering storefront windows and even the clothing and faces of surprised miners.

The men yelled and cursed, their voices vibrating throughout the town.

Staggering, Gillis turned in circles, stomping and clutching his head, screaming to shed the enraged bird. He dropped to his knees, trying to cradle his face, while the blood trailed down on his hands and arms.

The group of coal miners scattered, some into stores, others to Gillis's side, shouting, slapping, kicking at the furious rooster.

Bonnie shifted her eyes to Wrenna, a mixture of awe and satisfaction in the widow's gaze.

Feeling ill, I turned around and gagged, my bile threatening to escape, the sight of violence and so much blood churning, roiling inside. A hand gripped my elbow, startling me. "Inside, Honey. You don't want to see anymore." Mr. Morgan nudged me over to the courthouse doors.

But it was too late. I heard Wrenna's musical *coo-coo-coo*s. Drawn to the lyrical notes, I glanced back down and saw the blood-smattered bird rapidly toe-hopping away from the man's limp body, racing off nearly in flight toward the young girl.

Wrenna scooped up Tommie, nestled him into the crook of her arm, and marched doggedly away from town.

Thirty-Five

Trembling, I stared up at the judge's empty bench and picked at the fabric on my glove, pulling off a loose string, the horrors of Tommie and Gillis etched in my mind.

Mr. Morgan went out into the hall while I waited inside the courtroom. Except for the clerk, the courtroom was empty. Mr. Morgan was gone for a while, and I watched the clock, waiting. When he returned, the clerk motioned him up to her table, and they talked quietly while looking over papers. He nodded, not saying much, then came back to our table and said, "The judge is filling in for Judge Potter and he's sitting a trial in his courtroom. He'll have to reschedule our hearing."

Disappointed, I could barely shake my head.

"I'll get the new date to you as soon as I get it," Mr. Morgan said outside on the courthouse steps.

I looked down to the Company store. A few men lingered, but there was no sign of Gillis.

"Mr. Morgan, wait. It's about Perry Gillis."

He grimaced. "I bumped into a friend out in the hall, and he said Mr. Gillis was in grave condition. The frontier nurse and one of the coal miners rushed him to the hospital. He's lost a lot of blood. Not sure if the bird punctured the jugular. And now it seems no one can find Mrs. Gillis."

I was troubled by the news, but also filled with a strange calm knowing for the moment, Gillis couldn't hurt me. Not

Guyla Belle, Bonnie, or Pearl, or other women he'd surely tormented.

Unless he recovered.

The thought sank in my belly, souring at what he might do if he pulled through.

In a moment, I swallowed hard and said, "Mr. Morgan, can I walk with you to your automobile? I need to tell you something."

As we walked, I told him what I suspected, talking fast and low wanting to get it all in, but not wanting to catch anyone else's attention. Several times I stopped speaking when a passerby got too close. How little Johnnie fell down the well, and about Gillis beating up Guyla. How Gillis had accused me of breaking them up and threatened to go to his kin lawman. The conversation I'd overheard in the Company store. Then about the sheriff threatening me after the fire at Pearl's. *Everything.* All of it came out like a dam had broke inside me. I paused a minute and touched one of the pearl earrings, then tamped down my urge to tell him about the party.

"Mr. Morgan, I have a feeling Guyla Belle is in a bad way inside that cabin and she needs help." We stood by the lawyer's automobile while he listened, not saying a word.

When I was through, Mr. Morgan rushed me back inside the courthouse and told me to wait on one of the benches out in the hall, then disappeared around the corner. I heard a door squeak open and close.

In a bit, I paced back and forth down the hall, pausing to stop beside closed doors, straining my ears to hear anything. An hour passed before the lawyer came back. He grabbed hold of my arm, hurrying me down the courthouse stairs and back over to his automobile. "Mr. Morgan… What is it, Mr. Morgan?"

"Get in, Honey."

"*Why?*" I took a step back, suddenly afraid. "I've got Junia in the side parking lot."

"She'll be fine for a little while. We're meeting the state police over at the Gillis cabin. They want to hear your recounting of events. Mr. Gillis should be arrested if he's injured his wife, and you can help her by telling your side of the story."

I took one more step back and stood frozen. "But—"

"They won't take you anywhere. I'll be right beside you. Promise."

"Will this hurt my chance of getting emancipation?"

"Not at all. Get in, Honey. You need to help her. And not to do so might hurt you." His eyes were friendly but insistent.

Reluctantly, I climbed in and rolled down the window, the automobile uncomfortably stuffy, the road jarring. A few miles deeper into the wide tree-canopied paths, the air cooled, and the ride became tolerable.

"I hope she's okay," I said softly.

"Don't worry, Honey, they'll find her. If the judge signs the warrant, they'll search every inch of the home. Johnnie needs his mother. Regardless, they'll ask his sister to consent to a search."

"Maybe she won't, if she's helped him."

"They'll get their search warrant one way or another. Oh, almost forgot, Honey. I telephoned the prison about your father and was finally able to speak with him."

"How is Papa?" I turned to him.

"Only spoke with him briefly, barely a minute, but he's doing well." He lifted a hand off the steering wheel. "Sounded good. Sends his love to you and asks that you post letters to him. He said they're still not allowing any visitors. They've placed him and the rest of the prisoners in isolation during the polio outbreak. Then the line went dead."

"Isolation?" I said, miserable at the thought of him being alone and cold in a cramped, dark cell.

"It's not a punishment, Honey. It's for everyone's protection. Good news is, there was an announcement in the papers in March about a vaccine coming soon. The state has said they'll be getting the cure into prisons. Mr. Faust told me he will do everything in his power to see that Jackson gets inoculated. He's well and still has his privileges, and I hear he will be granted outside privileges as soon as he receives the vaccine."

"Yes, sir. What will he do outside?"

"Mr. Faust mentioned he'll be the new groundskeeper for the warden."

"That would suit Papa." I slumped back in my seat and relaxed a bit, thinking of him happy out in the fresh air.

We rode the rest of the way in silence while I fretted about Perry Gillis's revenge and Guyla Belle's whereabouts.

We pulled into the yard just as a state policeman escorted Gillis's sister over to an official automobile. She toted a whimpering Johnnie on her hip, his face tucked tight into her chest. Ida stopped long enough to glare hotly at me, her tears streaked on reddened cheeks. Shuddering, I sank back against the automobile seat.

Another automobile pulled in behind us, and two more followed. Law enforcement officers jumped out and huddled in the yard.

"Come on, Honey. Let's go talk with them."

I snuck another peek at Gillis's sister, her hard eyes boring into mine. We got out and I walked slowly over to the men, my head tucked tight to my chest, the fear dampening my clothes.

"Mr. Morgan?" A tall, redheaded officer approached, and I turned to my lawyer as he extended his hand.

"Mr. Morgan, I'm Sergeant Mattingly. Thanks for coming. We got the warrant signed." He shifted his gaze to me. "You must be Miss Lovett. Thank you for coming. Let's talk on the porch while the men do their job."

A few state police brushed past as they went inside the home. I told Sergeant Mattingly everything I knew, sneaking glances over to Gillis's sister who still stood fuming by the automobile. "Then Perry Gillis and his mama left the Company store. We had a fire at the cab, and I tried to tell the sheriff about Perry and Guyla gone missing. He didn't believe me." I exhaled, wrapping up the events.

An officer walked out of the cabin and hurried over to us.

"Did you find her?" Sergeant Mattingly asked.

I looked at the two men and held my breath.

"No, Sarge, the house is clear."

"Cellar?"

"Yes, sir, all of it," the lawman said.

I exhaled loudly. *Guyla Belle finally left him and was somewhere safe.*

Suddenly, Johnnie escaped Ida and ran up to me bawling, baring a black eye and bruised chin.

I gasped at his swollen face. Johnnie tugged on my skirts, pulled at my arm. "Buk 'uman saved well. Save Ma-ma well!" Johnnie pointed out to the yard, then gripped my hand and jerked harder. "*Ma-ma-ma!*" he wailed.

Confused, I repeated his words. "*Save Mama well?*"

Then Johnnie lifted up his arms to me, pleading. "Save Mama. Ma-ma fall'd down well!"

Tears sprang from my eyes, and with trembling hands, I plucked up the terrified child and held him to my chest, rocking, murmuring soothing words. He pushed his face into my shoulder and wept.

"*Shh, shh*, Johnnie. It's okay. *Shh.*" I pressed kisses to the top of his head and patted his back, knowing nothing would ever be *okay* for this little boy again.

Everyone quieted. The officers looked at the boy, then to one another before suddenly swarming the well.

"Get this boy inside and bust open that damn well!" Sergeant Mattingly bellowed to the men.

A lawman lifted the sobbing boy from my arms and rushed him into the cabin. Another official collected Ida and followed.

Some of the men ran to their automobiles and retrieved axes and picks from their trunks. They chipped at the concrete mouth of the well for a long time while Mr. Morgan and the sergeant chatted somberly about the latest news in these parts.

Over by the well, someone finally shouted, "We got something, Sergeant. Come take a look."

"Wait here," Sergeant Mattingly ordered.

I wrung my hands, praying Guyla Belle had escaped the horrors Gillis made her suffer.

Mr. Morgan took one of my busy hands, placed it in his palm, and patted it.

I looked up at him and in a shaky voice said, "Can I wait inside the automobile, sir?"

"Best we do as the sergeant asked and remain on the porch."

The sergeant walked up to the porch a few minutes later. "I'm sorry to say we found a body. We need help identifying the remains, Miss Lovett. It'll likely be late night before we can retrieve the body from the well. If it's Mrs. Gillis, I would need to go ahead and send one of my men over to the hospital and arrest her husband. Do you think you could come over here and do that?"

"What about his sister?" I asked, afraid.

"We'd like to also have you identify the body, if you could," Sergeant Mattingly pressed.

Mr. Morgan put an arm around my shoulder, and I moaned against his chest. "You've been through a lot today, Honey, but if you could do this, you'd be helping Mrs. Gillis and little Johnnie."

All the men stared at me as I scratched out a *yessir*.

Stepping around busted concrete, I took a breath and leaned over a gaping hole while the men shined their flashlights down into the well, my hands bruised with the blueness.

A blast of putrid odors of rot, mold, and other dark things watered my eyes and crawled down my throat. Choking, I raised my head and tilted it to the sky. Drawing in several ragged breaths, I coughed and dared to look again, squinting as I stared back down.

Again, the men moved their bright flashlights over the dark hole, and then I saw it and gasped at the partially decomposed body, the limbs all crooked and skewed in every direction, draped under her kelly-green dress. Pushing myself away from the well, I feebly called out "It's Guyla Belle" and gagged before running behind an automobile to relieve my twisting innards, the horrors of the day emptying onto the ground.

Wrenna's subtle, sharp warning to Tommie rang in my head and the final lilting *coo-coo* she'd called to him when it was over. Thoughts of Bonnie and the seeds she threw at Gillis and the look of triumph in her eyes after it all. My worries at the court-house table, and now poor Guyla Belle and her young son who somehow saw his mama's murder. I clenched a fist, the deep sorrow and anger stabbing into my indigo-blue palm.

In a few minutes, Mr. Morgan came up behind me. "Sorry you had to witness that, Honey. They'll see to it the county gives Mrs. Gillis a proper burial and arrest Mr. Gillis, thanks to you."

Here I was fighting for my freedom and taking another's away who imprisoned so many. Maybe now, Bonnie, Pearl, Wrenna, and me would finally be shed of the terrifying grip he'd kept us locked in.

Mr. Morgan passed me a clean handkerchief from his back pocket. "Keep it, Honey."

I nodded and wiped my mouth with the linen and looked around. One officer escorted Ida back out of the cabin and questioned her. Several times, she shook her head firmly, talking with broad, sweeping hands. He finally let her go, and she scurried back inside, slamming the door behind her.

Another lawman came out of the home carrying Johnnie. The scared child stretched out his arms for me. "*Buk uman-n-n,*" he blubbered uncontrollably.

I looked away, unable to bear the boy's heartbreak and my own. "What will happen to Johnnie, Mr. Morgan?"

"Relatives will likely take him in after Social Services does its investigation." Mr. Morgan checked his wristwatch. "The sergeant says we can go."

"What will they do to Tommie?"

"Who?" he asked, puzzled.

"Wrenna's rooster."

Looking back at the well, the lawyer scratched his chin. "Well, I imagine the law won't look too hard at the grave injuries of a murderer." He tucked his teeth in a grimace. "Roosters can be damn fickle about family. Downright protective. I saw it with my own aunt Frannie's rooster. And I've seen them fight to the death for their hens."

Hens. My thoughts batted back and forth between Wrenna and Bonnie, Tommie's hens.

"You did a good thing here today, Honey." He cupped his chin, worrying a finger over his knotted lips. "But I would advise you to make yourself as scarce as possible in town, especially around Gillis's kin—and especially the sheriff—until all this dust settles. Even if we win your emancipation, be mindful, you still won't be free. As you know, Honey, your color makes you a target for cruel folks like Gillis and his clan…" He paused, deciding whether to say more, but glimpsed the fear spreading on my face. "Let's get you back to Junia."

Thirty-Six

The bird's wings batted the flames in the fiery air, its long spurs raised dangerously in front of me as the rooster's loud whirring folded into my strangled screams. Tommie haunted my dreams, and he was the last thing I'd see before my eyelids fluttered open, awakening me and leaving me gasping for breath. For nights he appeared, sometimes alone or with Guyla Belle and a crying Johnnie, other times with Wrenna and Bonnie, or Pearl. But the worst was when the rooster showed up with a blood-soaked Perry Gillis and the screams would get locked in my throat, bolting me upright in a drenched, shivery sweat.

The nightmares lingered, draining me during the days, spiraling me into mere restless dozes throughout the long, rough nights.

I'd heard that Gillis was still in the hospital, and I began to worry if they didn't move him to the jail soon, he'd escape or have his kin seek revenge. Soon, I was tormented by other nightmares that had Gillis and the law chasing me through a darkened courthouse while I desperately searched for my freedom. Once I found it, I would raise my hands triumphantly in front of my face, then violently shudder at the stained-blue flesh, suddenly realizing I'd never had it.

Finally, I searched the root cellar, going through Mama's herbs. I found a jar of catnip leaves and some skullcap root and began brewing teas before bed. But somehow, the visitors still broke through, leaving me perspiring and exhausted in the mornings.

Today was no different. Spent, I rode my Monday route letting Junia poke slowly along.

Emma McCain crouched down on her knees, working on a worn upside-down rocker on her porch, her long, frayed skirts bloused around her. "Morn', Book Woman. I'm just felting the rockers for spring. Wrenna keeps walkin' 'em off the porch so I thought I better fix 'em 'fore the chil' breaks a bone." She glued a long, narrow strip of felt onto a curved rocker rail.

"Morning, ma'am. I brought some books for her."

"Sheriff stopped by an' Wrenna took off with Tommie."

"Do you know where she is? I can take the books to her."

"When Wrenna takes off, she's good 'n' gone till she wants to come back." She searched the trees. "Reckon she'll get home sometime."

"Yes, ma'am, I'll just leave these for her," I said, wanting to ask more but not wanting to pry. I wiped my damp brow with a glove, hoping the girl was okay.

"She brung the books with her. Sorry we's late on the loans, Honey." Emma put on the last strip, stood, and wiped her hands on the hem of her apron.

I handed her *The Young and Happy Rooster.* "Wrenna might like this one. And those others aren't due till next week, Mrs. McCain."

She inspected the book, then stooped to pick up a rocker.

"Here, ma'am, let me help you set them upright." I fumbled with the wooden arm and finally turned the heavy rocker over, lifting it up.

"Lookin' a li'l peaked today. Ya ailing, chil'?"

"Just a little tired, ma'am. Been sleeping poorly lately."

She studied me a moment with her ol' eyes, raised the back of her palm to my forehead, then glanced down at my belly. "Chil', have ya been takin' the dick too long?"

I stared at her slacked jaw.

"Ya can tell ol' granny woman inna'thing. I've done heard *and* unheard it all."

"No... *No, ma'am!*" I sputtered.

"Jus' the insomnia?"

I nodded vigorously.

"Wait righ' here." She went inside and returned shortly with a silver dollar–sized ball of resin. "Chew a pinch of this gum opium before bed for the next seven nights. Should pert ya up good as new." She shoved the sticky ball into my hand.

I slept sound that night, better than I had in months using Emma's remedy, and I stuck the gum ball on the headboard to use the next night, and all the bad nights coming.

Breaths of sweet waters saturated the air as I made my way down Troublesome Creek toward the outpost.

Mr. Taft had left an envelope from Mr. Morgan on the table. Quickly, I tore it open to see the lawyer had scheduled the hearing for June 12. That was seven weeks away, and I groaned when I'd read it. Growing frantic, I tried to convince myself that no matter what, it would be more weeks of freedom. But still it was seven more weeks of worrying about Gillis and his kin coming for me and fretting over the sheriff locking me up.

Finding solace in my job, I welcomed the extra folk Miss Foster added to my route, staying away from town as much as I could, and from Gillis's ugly kin. I continued getting the books and material into the hands of my patrons, working for my next pay stub for the court, and nibbling at Emma's gumball to quell the nightmarish dreams.

On my Friday route, I hurried past Guyla Belle's, and Junia was only too happy to do my bidding as she sped by the Gillis yard. Several times I looked back over my shoulder, fearful.

At Amara's cabin, I dropped a newspaper and a tattered romance onto the porch, then rode toward Bonnie's.

The coal miner stepped out her door, smiling, her jaw yellowed with a fading bruise from where Gillis had punched her that day. "Sweet pea, it's good to see ya," she said as I walked across the yard. "Come on up, I just made a fresh pitcher of tea." She went inside to get the drinks, easing the ratty screen door shut so she wouldn't wake up her boy.

I lugged the pannier up to the porch to let her dig through it while I sat on the top step and sipped from my glass.

"I stopped by Loretta's grave and paid my respects. Ran into Mr. Geary. That headstone you picked out is sure pretty."

"Sure is." I nodded, grateful Mr. Geary had it delivered a week earlier than promised, happy that others would pay their respects now.

She took a drink, then rubbed her jaw and grimaced. "Lost a tooth when he attacked me."

"Real sorry to hear that. Does it hurt much?"

"Nah." She set her glass down on the floorboards. "What did ya bring me today, Book Woman?" Bonnie plopped down on Retta's glider and lifted the bag across her lap.

"There's some new storybooks for Joey Jr."

She looked inside. In a few minutes, she lit a cigarette and blew out loudly. The smoke disappeared, ghost-tailing out into the spring sunshine. "The men ain't bothering me no more." Bonnie swatted away a curious bee. "They's actually a little afraid of me." She took a puff off her cigarette, coughed, and laughed hoarsely.

"That's real good they're leaving you alone."

"We women don't always have to work harder than them, jus' *smarter*." Bonnie tapped her temple, then stopped and cocked her head. "Look at ya, sweet pea, getting all grow'd up for a red-heeled Saturday nigh' outing." She poked a slender, black-stained finger toward my earrings.

"Don't own any heels." My face warmed and I touched an ear. "Pearl Grant let me borrow these till I can buy some."

"Real sweet. Joey bought me a pretty pair on our anniversary, but I can't wear 'em down in the mine." Sadness crept in to her eyes for a moment and then she said, "Oh, when Boss Man learned about Perry Gillis, he assigned me an easy job. He said I'll be riding the shuttle cart April 20. I can't wait for this Monday to get here. Pays a nickel more too."

"You deserve it, Bonnie."

She wrinkled her brow, searching inside the pannier, and said quietly, "A few are saying I caused that rooster to attack Perry Gillis."

I stole a glance at the almost-empty mason jar of sunflower seeds beside her foot.

Bonnie tapped her ashes onto the porch and rocked in the glider, staring out into the yard. She dug back through the books, taking out two. "Know what, sweet pea?"

I shook my head and swallowed a sip of the cold, sweetened tea.

"Others say it's an accident, and he got his due." She stood up, dangling the cigarette between her lips. Her eyes grew distant, and she said loudly what others would ponder in soft whispers, "He's a titmouse stunted-dick, that Perry Gillis is. Oh, but that sweet boy, Tommie, sure was something else looking over me like that. Wrenna too, that darlin' li'l hen. And I was mighty pleased an' proud when I heard you led the state police to poor Guyla Belle's body like that, and he was arrested right in his hospital bed." She leaned over and lightly pinched my cheek.

Peeling back my cotton glove, I snuck a peek at my darkening hand, then quickly pulled the fabric over it. "They gave her a decent burial," I said, a little embarrassed but thrilled and appreciative to have earned the young coal miner's grace—more than grateful Guyla Belle had been given a proper burial and Gillis was in custody. I glanced down from the porch at Junia, the scabbard packed on her side with my rifle.

"Thank you, Honey. I think I'll read these again," Bonnie said, a sly grin spreading on her face as she held up Ruth

Krauss's bright-orange children's book, *The Carrot Seed* and Jim
Thompson's *The Killer Inside Me.*

She winked at me, then brushed a fallen ash off the front of
her coal-blackened overalls before heading back inside.

After a rainy April, May brought plenty of sunshine and warmer
weather. The wild dogwoods and fencerow honeysuckle were in
full bloom, fragrant across the spring-soaked mountains. Cabin
windows opened, walls of winter-baked soot were scrubbed, and
more clotheslines appeared, sagging under the weight of fresh-
laundered curtains and spring coverlets.

Last month, I'd stopped by Emma McCain's on my Monday
drops, but Wrenna was never there. Emma said that the girl
would sneak into the cellar and get food but would be gone
before she could catch her. I was hoping May would be more
favorable and I would see my young patron. But when I stopped
by this week, the loans sat untouched on Emma's porch.

The last few weeks I'd worked Saturdays and Sundays because
of the added patrons. Today, I'd caught up and was looking
forward to a free weekend as I rode toward my last drop.

Standing on the wide porch, I waited for Millie to answer the
door so I could give her the books I'd selected and maybe talk to
Doc about Mama. I looked over my shoulder, searching for any
of Gillis's kin, anxious to get my business done and head back
to my holler. Again, I banged on the door knocker, and shortly
Doc swung open the door.

"Honey, come in."

"I have the Friday loans, sir." I held up two novels, *Strangers
on a Train* and *The Heart Is a Lonely Hunter.*

He peered over his spectacles. "Millie will be delighted. She's
gone over to Beauty to visit her brother and his family for the
weekend." He took the books and placed them on the marbled
foyer table and motioned me inside. "You've been asking for

weeks, and I've finally got news on your mother. Get on in here, child." He raised a crooked arm, flapping it twice. "Come in."

I followed him into his library, glancing at all the beautiful shelves. Full of books, they circled up to the ceiling behind his fine oak carved desk and a regal matching chair.

"What is it, Doc? Is she well—"

"Sit down, Honey," he said, pointing to the pretty uphol-stered chair with a delicate fleur-de-lis pattern in front of his large desk.

He scattered a pile of papers, moved journals, and pulled out an envelope, then handed it to me. "From your mother." He sat down behind his desk, pleased.

I turned the envelope over and traced my name.

"I visited her briefly on Wednesday, and she asked that I give this to you."

"How is she, Doc?"

He propped his elbows onto the desk and tapped his fingers against each other. "Doing quite the opposite from the last time you saw her. Her health has greatly improved, and they've assigned her a job."

I let out a breath. "What kind of job?"

Doc pushed a book toward me and tapped, beaming. "The perfect one. I'm sure she'll tell you all about it in her letter. She's thriving, Honey."

I exhaled loudly, relieved she was safe and happy.

"There's more," he said.

I perked, wondering what else.

"Warden Sanders has really taken to her, and she said your mother has also helped many of the prisoners. They've become quite fond of her. She's used her former job and has been instru-mental in teaching and fostering literacy. The warden reported many of the inmates are begging your mother to teach them to read and write. And, the best"—his eyes twinkled—"the governor has promised to grant her a commutation of sentence if she continues to work diligently and stay in the prison's good graces—maybe as early as Thanksgiving."

I jumped up, joyful. "Mama could be coming home in the fall. *The fall*," I savored the words, then ran around the desk and gave Doc a kiss on the cheek. He blushed and cleared his throat.

"That's right, child. Possibly fall, latest the first of the year."

"Much obliged for the news, sir. I'll see myself out."

"You're welcome to join me for supper. Millie left me more than enough."

"Obliged, but I'd like to get home before dark." I couldn't wait to get out the door and read Mama's letter, find out more about her job.

"Wait, Honey. Millie would dish me up a sinner's funeral if I let you leave here without feeding you." He turned and walked down the foyer toward the kitchen. In a moment, he returned with a poke.

I peeked inside the paper bag. "Looks tasty, Doc. Much obliged." It was filled with two apples, a wedge of cheese, figs, a small jar of marmalade and a half loaf of bread. I clutched the sack and letter to my chest, thanking him again.

Opening the door, he said, "Bluet's fine now, child. Ride safe and rest up. Looks like you might be needing some extra."

"Yes, sir," I said, tired of the sleepless nights and nightmares, wondering when they'd ever go away, wondering how long I had to fear Gillis and his kin coming for me or, worse, the leg shackles the state had waiting for me. "Doc." I looked up at him. "Have you heard anything about Perry Gillis?"

"I heard what most know: he's under arrest at the hospital. By the by, you did a brave, kind act, child. And one of the frontier nurses told me in passing just the other day that his eyesight is in question. But the hospital believes they might've stopped all the bleeding for now. I've seen miracles happen before, and he just might recover. And I heard someone say Mr. Gillis's family hired a slick city lawyer from Lexington and he might make bail and—"

Recover. Bail. The thoughts stole my breath, and I bid him a good evening.

No sooner had I made it into the woods than I dropped down off Junia and ripped open the envelope, my eyes lighting over the words, studying Mama's elegant script, the perfect slant and looping letters, a tall elm's fringed flowers casting shadows across the widely spaced lines of a Big Chief school tablet page.

"It's from Mama!"

Junia brayed.

I waved it in front of her. "Hush now and I'll read it to you."

Junia's sleepy eyes widened at the mention of *Mama*, and she wearily lifted her head next to mine as I began to read, my eyes growing wider as I soaked up Mama's words and the long-awaited news from her.

April 26, 1953

My Dearest Daughter,

I hope this letter finds you fit. I'm pleased to write and tell you I am healthy and doing well, and the prison has restored all my privileges.

I was deeply heartbroken to hear that we lost our dear, sweet Loretta, and was greatly troubled to learn you were alone. Mr. Faust advised me about the hearing your lawyer has scheduled, and I am praying for your emancipation and my early freedom as well—for all of us to be free and together again soon.

The warden has kindly assigned me a job as prison librarian. The library is open from 8:00 a.m. to 6:00 p.m. during the week and closes at 2:00 p.m. on Saturdays for the weekend. The library houses a large and varied collection of donated books, and the warden has given me a small budget to purchase new reading material. It's been truly wonderful to work with the books and patrons again. I stay busy and the days seem to fly by quickly.

Doc informed me Troublesome has started a new outreach program akin to the old Pack Horse Library Project, and he said Miss Foster hired you as a librarian assistant to deliver the reading material. I'm thrilled and so proud of you, my darling daughter. It's comforting to know the books will bring you as much joy and comfort as they do me.

It's growing late and I must close for now. Take good care of yourself and Junia.

Write to me soon.

All my love,
Mama

Prison librarian. I reread it all again and once more, then raised the letter and blinked back tears of joy.

"Mama is safe and back with her books." Junia hovered over the page and closed her eyes and blew out a long, contented sigh like she knew it was so.

Inhaling the spring blossoms of awakened tulip trees, I pushed my mind toward fall, ticking off the days until I could see her again.

Junia suddenly brayed and swung her head toward the trees.

I followed her gaze, my hand sliding toward the rifle. I heard something and couldn't be sure but wasn't about to stick around to find out. "Let's hurry, Junia," I said anxious to get back to the safety of our holler.

Thirty-Seven

May 24, 195– Pausing the ink pen on the date, I cocked my head and heard Junia's nervous warnings coming from her stall. Immediately, I bolted upright from the table, sending my parents' letters flying off the table.

I ran across the room for the .22 and slowly cracked open the door. Pennie slipped in and circled around me.

"*Pearl*," I said, surprised, opening the door wider. "It's really good to see you." I let out a breath, shoved the gun back behind the door, and stepped onto the porch.

"Haven't been able to have a good visit since our party," Pearl said, sitting atop Pie, a new scabbard packed to the horse's side. "I was off this Sunday and thought I'd stop by and visit and see if you'd heard the news." She slid off the horse and tethered him, then walked hesitantly up to me.

Puzzled, I searched her eyes for a clue. "What news?"

"R.C. called and told me Perry Gillis passed Friday night. The hospital kept giving him blood but he just grew weaker and the doctors couldn't repair the damage. Developed a raging infection after he lost his eyesight."

I dropped my hand to my belly, almost doubling over, the news feeling more like a release than any grief I could muster for him.

"Nearly did the same, Honey."

We stood there quietly, each of us lost in our thoughts, the news and what comfort it brought mirrored in our eyes. Still, there was his kin, and no telling what they would do to me and Wrenna.

"Come in, come in, Pearl."

"Sure you're up for company? You look a little tired."

"The library added more patrons to my route, and it's been keeping me busy. I was just getting ready to fix some dinner. I'll set an extra plate. Can you stay?"

"Would love to. I've been busy myself. With the weather turning warm, more people are getting out. I had three camp-fires this week alone, and last week I woke up to a sleeping fire from the lightning storm."

"Wondered where you were when I stopped by with the loans."

"I've been out in the forest tracking small fires more than in my cab lately. I thought I'd see if you'd like to show me around like you first offered. That is if you're free?"

"I was looking for an excuse to get out today." Pearl looked a little tired, too, and stretched in the nerves. "How are you doing up there in the cab?"

"Better," she admitted. "R.C. built a new trapdoor, and he also put a rope ladder out on the catwalk that can be released only from the top. Which makes me feel a whole lot better. But nothing better than hearing about the news. I'll sure be sleeping a lot easier now."

I wasn't so sure with Robbie and the sheriff out there.

"How have you been, Honey?" She stepped over the thresh-old, and I scanned the woods before shutting the door.

"It's been hectic, and I haven't been sleeping well either."

"Nightmares?"

I nodded. "Yeah, but the granny woman gave me something, so it's helping." I scrambled to pick up the fallen letters and place them on my bed.

"Mother got me a prescription for Tuinal from our family doctor. But I can only take it on my days off."

I turned back to her and we stared at each other a moment, the weight of the men's misdeeds reflected in our tired eyes, buried deep into our scarred souls. Then Pearl grabbed me and gave me a tight hug. It felt good to see my friend again, and I returned it heartily, a small sob escaping our breaths.

I sniffled and straightened. "I've been thinking. I didn't get to say it, Pearl, at the fire. And although it's small, thank you for saving my life. I couldn't have done what you did and lived through it."

"I couldn't have done what you did either. Leading the law to poor Guyla's horrid grave he dumped her in. I could've been next if you didn't warn me." She plopped down in a chair at the table, pulling Pennie up into her lap.

"It was awful finding out li'l Johnnie had seen his mama being stuffed down that dark cold well." I shivered at the thought.

"Someone should lock that sheriff up for not investigating."

"I just hope Sheriff Buckner doesn't try to get even. I've got my emancipation hearing on June 12. I've been sticking to my route and keeping close to home." I lit the percolator and pulled Retta's teacups down from the shelf, lifted one up to her.

"I'd love some coffee. Mother finally got around to sending my .410, but I've been concerned about the sheriff too. Last week, my uncle telephoned and told me he was going to write a letter to the state police commissioner and report him."

When the coffee had brewed, I handed her a cup. "I told Mr. Morgan and the sergeant about it too."

She put Pennie down, blew on her coffee, and took a sip. "Somebody should investigate that crooked lawman. We could've both been killed."

I chewed on the inside of my cheek, knowing if we had perished, no matter what, the sheriff would've protected his kin.

After I drank a cup of coffee, I made us sandwiches from last night's ham supper and we ate quietly, each of us thinking about Guyla Belle and her husband and how close we came to perishing up there in her cab.

Pearl noticed the envelope and letters on the table and swallowed the food she was chewing. "News about your parents?"

"Mama. She's doing real good. They even made her prison librarian," I said, proud.

"I'm so glad to hear it. With her glowing legacy around here, they would be fools not to. She just better be careful not to do too good of a job or they might keep her longer."

"She may be home in the fall. I was just writing to both of them."

"That soon?"

"Doc said it's a real good chance, or the latest will be after the first of the year."

"Wonderful. I can't wait to meet her. Oh, Mother is coming over in July for a week. She wants us to all have supper together and maybe take in a picture show." She chased down her last bite with the coffee.

"Sounds nice. I'll bring a dessert if I get my emancipation."

Pearl grimaced, reached over, and placed a palm over my hand. "You have to, Honey. Us troublesome women always fight back." She thumped our hands onto the table, knocking the worn wood twice. "Fight, dear *sister*."

"As long as Gillis's kin is out there, I'll have to watch my back. Feuds have been started over less, and Blues have been killed for even lesser grievances. And Mr. Morgan warned me that even if I got my emancipation, I needed to be mindful that it wouldn't free me of being a Blue."

Pearl frowned. Then my thoughts shifted to Bonnie and her fight, and the battle Guyla Belle lost, Pearl's struggle to save us and her job, and Amara's fierce spirit. Suddenly, I realized the women had been teaching me something important: courage. "*Sisters*," I said, grateful, as I began collecting the dishes.

We journeyed alongside the creek, the smell of water and ferns and mud-soaked banks riding the breeze, the scents of wild onions and phlox lifting from our mounts' heavy steps.

Pearl said, "R.C.'s been having me ride the ridges to photograph the terrain and document the topography for a new journal the Forest Service is publishing to aid with fighting the fires." She paused to take note of the contours of the land, the streams and trees, pocketing the information to help her in her job.

"Oh, over there is a good fishing spot. It's where Carson and I used to go hunting for crawdads." I pointed beside a black willow and slid down off Junia. "The Flynns live on the other side. Timmy Flynn's a real nice fella. He was Mama's patron when he was a young boy. Loves the books. He comes home from the University of Kentucky on weekends. He's real smart like that. And if you go down there about a mile, it takes you up to the McCain's cabin. The granny woman and—"

"*Wrenna Abbott*." Pearl climbed off Pie, and we walked beside each other.

"Uh-huh. About three miles north of Emma and Wrenna's place, there's a tiny homestead stitched into the mountain. That's Comfort Marshall's home."

"I heard talk of her in town. Didn't she lose all her babies one year?"

"In 1936," I said solemnly. "Lot of folks died of the pellagra back then. Hunger killed so many of our folk. Mama takes me up there on Decoration Day and we clean the cemetery for her." I tucked stray hair behind my ear, and it snagged one of the earrings. Quickly, I pressed a palm to it, making sure I hadn't lost the precious pearl.

"How are they healing up?" She pointed to my earlobe, touching her own.

"Oh, I best get these back to you. I'm sorry, it's been too long." I started to unscrew the backs and pass them to her.

"Go ahead and keep them, Honey. They're yours."

I'd been saving for my other parents' headstone and didn't

have enough money to buy a pair yet. "I have thread at home I can use. I couldn't—"

"Anyone who's brave enough to suffer my piercings and live through a fire with me is fine enough to have my earrings." She laughed. "Mother bought me two sets. Besides, you'll look real pretty wearing them at your hearing."

"Obliged. They're lovely, Pearl, but I should be giving *you* earrings after you saved me in the fire. I'll take good care of them." It was a generous gift and one I would treasure.

We walked on, enjoying the new bursts of a heavily perfumed spring. Occasionally, I'd stop to point out the names of herbs and flowers, recalling the remedies Mama or Retta used them for. "There's a cluster of ghost pipe. Retta would always make a tonic for her eyes and to help with the stiffness of her ol' bones."

Pearl knelt down and inspected the strange, translucent white stalks with the bell-like blooms that drooped to the ground.

"Oh, Birdie MacKinnon's place is up there at the top," I told Pearl. "She was a Pack Horse librarian like Mama. Her route was mostly along the creeks, and sometimes she'd deliver the books in her small boat. She left for the city to join her husband who'd found factory work, only to return with their son a year later."

"Bet the librarians knew the land better than anyone," Pearl remarked.

Ahead, I spotted a book on the ground and ran over to it. "This is Wrenna's. I've been looking for her on my route." I picked it up.

"*The Doll's House* was one of my favorites," Pearl said. "I just adored Tottie."

I wiped my sleeve over the cover, brushing off a damp leaf. "Doesn't make sense; it's her favorite. She wouldn't leave it out here like this." I scanned the area. "Wrenna?" I called. "Wrenna, it's me, Book Woman." No answer. Pearl glanced around too.

"You know how kids are always losing things. I'm sure she's fine," she said.

I cocked my head, listening, turning slowly around. In a

minute, I heard strange noises over by a cluster of brush and briar. "Did you hear that?" I asked.

"I didn't hear anything."

Junia hawed and pinned her ears straight up like she had.

"There." I nudged my chin to a large cluster of shrubs. The mule snorted as I walked her over. Then she stopped and refused to go any farther. I tugged, she pulled back and all but sat down on her haunches, baring brown-stained teeth and shaking her head.

"Here, Pearl, hold her reins while I check over here behind this brush." But when Junia saw me leaving, she jerked free and hurried to my side. Quickly, I grabbed the reins. Pearl followed closely behind.

Cautiously, I peeked around and startled, jumping back.

The small girl popped up with Tommie in her arms. "*Wrenna*," I said, breathing heavily.

"Ain't getting Tommie!" she screamed, and Junia threw back her head and shrieked.

"Whoa, whoa, easy, Junia. Wrenna, it's me, Book Woman. It's *me*." I raised my hand to Junia and slowly waved it in front of the young girl. "Just me," I said in a soft whisper, the words swallowed into the woodland.

Wrenna tightened her mouth and held Tommie up to her chest. "Ain't touching him," she said, clutching the rooster against her dirt-streaked flour-sack dress. Then she thrust out her arms, holding the bird just inches from my face. A soft, rippling *oo-oo* rose in his throat as he lifted and slowly spread deadly claws. Tommie cocked his head to me, his dark eye locked to mine.

My mouth went dry and I blinked, swallowed hard, and let out a small shaky breath. "Wrenna, *no*."

Pearl choked. "Wren-Wrenna, I'm a friend of Book Woman. No one's going to hurt you or your pet," she said, her voice high.

"Wrenna, this is Pearl Grant, our new lookout. She takes care of our forest and keeps it and all the critters safe. I promise we don't want to take Tommie from you. Here, I'm just returning your book. See, it's *The Doll's House*, your favorite." I tossed her a wobbly smile.

The rooster sounded another *oo-oo*.

Carefully, I set the book on the ground and inched backwards to Junia. "I left some others at your home. *The Young and Happy Rooster* and *Rabbit Hill*, a great tale about critters." The mule toe-hopped nervously, her eyes large, ringed white with terror. I knew she was remembering how our family rooster used to attack her. Still, she shifted closer to me and blew a loud warning over my shoulder.

"Oh, *Rabbit Hill* is wonderful with the brave-hearted little Georgie. And I was just telling Book Woman how much I love Tottie in *The Doll's House*," Pearl said sweetly. "*Don't you, Wrenna?*" Her voice spiked higher.

Wrenna tucked the rooster under her arm and picked up the book, edging slowly backwards, her eyes darting back and forth between Pearl and me. "I thought it was *Perry Gillis*. Perry Gillis and the sheriff so I took off and dropped it. He…" She bit down on her trembling lip. "He's gonna kill me!"

"Perry Gillis is gone now," I said real slow. "He can't hurt you or Tommie anymore. *Promise.*"

"*Lies.*"

"Wrenna, Perry Gillis won't hurt you again."

She narrowed distrustful eyes and wagged her head. "He…he shoved me into his truck last year and, and he—"

My eyes widened.

She turned her face away, shrugged her bony little shoulder to her wet cheek, brushing it hard. Tommie lowly clucked his protests.

"He drove us off the road into them woods up there on 721. Tommie was chasing us an' crow'n up a storm. Said he's gonna kill my rooster and put him in his soup pot if Tommie pecks him again, and after he was done, I was gonna wish he'd killed me too." Tears streaked her dirt-stained cheeks. "He beat on me so hard I wet myself. Then he cursed me for soiling his seat and pushed me out of the truck," she spat out.

"Oh, Wrenna, he can't hurt you anymore. Please let me take you home. Your great-granny will take care of you," I pleaded, stretching out an arm, tears springing to my own eyes. "He won't hurt you, again, Wrenna, no. Don't go. He's *dead*—"

"*No!*" She shook her long, tangled curls, set Tommie down, turned, and bolted into the woods.

"Wrenna, wait!" I called. "*Wait!*"

Tommie ran after her, scattering a string of *caaaw-caaaw*s as he tried to keep up.

"She's gone," Pearl said sadly.

We both stood there helpless, heartbroken for Wrenna. I swiped a dark palm over my face. "She's been running wild and doesn't even realize the monster is dead." I barely breathed.

"You can kill the one under the bed, but there are always a few more in the back of the closet waiting," Pearl said.

I rubbed the rising hairs on my arms, scanning the dense woodlands for the ones walking amongst us in daylight or lurking just beyond the shadow-darkened trees.

Thirty-Eight

The June morning unfolded slowly over the mountains as the fog wound its way through the woods and skated up into the hills. Hours later, we rode into town under a sapphire-shimmered sky.

Resting my cheek against Junia's withers, I gave her an oat cookie and one last stroke before heading into the looming white courthouse for my hearing. Pulling out the photograph of Grandpa Elijah from my dress pocket, I pressed a kiss onto the curling photograph and slipped it back inside, patting the other side that held the paper I'd stuck in there this morning. Calling for strength, I squared my shoulders and took a deep breath. One more and another.

A horse neighed behind me and I turned, surprised to see Pearl riding into the parking lot on Pie. "Honey!" She climbed down and tied the horse to a post. "What? You didn't think I'd let you go to the hearing alone."

I reached for her outstretched hand and gave a grateful squeeze.

"That sure is a pretty scarf."

"I'm so glad to see you. Obliged, and it's one of Retta's." I touched the dangling knot of fabric with my gloved hand, fidgeting. The scarf was comforting, like having a part of her with me today.

From across the street, Francis called out my name and sprinted over.

"Honey, I wanted to ask you something." He glanced at Pearl and looked down at his feet, mumbling, "In private, if you got a minute."

"We can talk over by Junia. I should probably double-check her to make sure she can't get loose."

Pearl raised a brow. "I'll just wait here."

It was good to see him again, and I peeked up at him, sneaking glances. Francis followed beside me, grinning, his eyes warm and cheerful.

"What is it, Francis?" I asked, checking the mule's reins.

He stepped toward me, and Junia nibbled at the air and kicked a warning leg forward.

I raised a hand. "Best stay there, Francis. She's a little feisty with men until she gets to know them."

"I like her already." He shoved both fists into his pants pockets, rocking slightly on the balls of his feet. Concern spread across his face. "Honey, I heard the judge's secretary talking in the store about you having a hearing for your freedom."

Did everyone know? I touched my collar, then locked my hands behind my back. Junia blew and pawed the earth, cautioning him back.

"Steady, Junia," I ordered with a tug to her halter, embarrassed that he knew and now the whole town did too.

"Well, folks were talking and all. Wanted to see if I could help ya."

I didn't want the town talking behind my back, and I didn't want to tell Francis about my troubles. "Obliged, but my lawyer is seeing to my personal family business in a few minutes." I circled around the mule, checking that she was secure. As if on cue, Junia whinnied and I checked my timepiece. "Better get inside." I stepped back, stumbling on a busted brick. Francis caught me, and silently I cursed my feet for betraying me again with him, while Junia rippled out what sounded like soft nickering laughter.

Straightening, I said, "Well, they're waiting."

"Sure thing." He smiled. "I hope you get your freedom, Honey." Francis looked like he wanted to say more, but instead, he said, "Well, see ya later." He pulled out a harmonica and wagged it at the deep blue sky. "Lucky children's moon out today. I just made my wish."

I looked up, couldn't help wondering if it was the same as mine.

He tested a few notes on his harmonica and nodded goodbye, the lyrics of "Old Kentucky Moonlight" climbing up and sweetening the cool pine breezes as he strolled back over toward the Company store.

I remembered Papa playing it on his fiddle during summer evenings. A homesickness swept over me, making me reel, the desperation for my family a breathless ache to my soul, the worry that I'd go to prison and wouldn't see my folk or Francis again for another five years struck me hard.

"Are you going to go out with him?" Pearl asked when I walked up to her.

I pressed a finger over my mouth and tapped, staring after him as he ambled across the road, his notes trembling up into the hills like a psalm yet fevered like fireflies drunk on summer dance.

"Is that a *yes* I see in your eyes, Honey?"

"It might be if I win the emancipation and my feet can stop double-crossing me every time I see him." Cupping a hand over my eyes, I pointed upward. "Children's moon is out today, Pearl. Make a wish."

Devil John and Martha Hannah stood at the bottom of the courthouse steps. The moonshiner raised a flat palm, and I lifted up mine and he gripped it in his hand. "Mr. Morgan said to go on in and he'll be along directly." Martha Hanna hugged me.

Slowly we climbed to the top of the courthouse steps. I looked back down at the town and saw Sheriff Buckner crossing the street and froze when his hardening eyes met mine.

"Let's hurry, Pearl."

"Do you think he'll start trouble?" Pearl saw him, and latched onto my arm, pulling us over to the doors.

"It can't be good."

Inside, I was surprised to find Alonzo waiting by the uni-formed man at the desk. He hobbled over to my side looking dapper in spit-polished shoes.

I searched his clear, weak eyes and glanced down at his clothes. Alonzo wore a clean ready-made dress shirt, his life story bared to all in the two shirt pockets that were stuffed neatly, bulging with his glasses case, several pens, pencils, and banded slips of paper, a small tattered comb, tobacco, matchbooks, a handkerchief, and other things I couldn't make out.

The old man's britches had been pressed, and he was freshly shaven with a track of dried blood dotting his chin from a new razor.

"Honey, losing Auntie's home like that, your home, well, it was bad. So hard, the stiffest whiskey or meanest rock-gut could no longer chase away the disgrace, my own loathing for myself. I had to give it up or die tryin'. She'd want me here for ya. Iffin you'll have me?"

Shocked, I finally uttered, "I'm glad you came, Alonzo." And for some strange reason, I felt Retta near. I looked at him tenderly and pressed my fingers against his crooked, frayed tie, straightening it, then kissed his soap-scrubbed cheek, my heart warming, grateful to see his sober face, wishing Retta was here to witness it too.

With Pearl and Alonzo beside me, I untied my scarf, pulled it off my head and walked slowly inside past the telephone booths, the lawyers' paper-soaked whispers biting at the wires, the hairs on the back of my neck raised, the stagnant whiffs of the tired, lonely, and desperate blanketing the dismal building.

A bailiff stood waiting inside the courtroom doors. Alonzo took a seat in the back behind the railing. Ahead, the Leslie County social worker sat at a table beside a man in a business suit.

I paused and leaned over close to Pearl's ear. "Oh no, it's Mrs. Wallace. She's going to be mad that I tricked her over in Thousandsticks."

"Your lawyer will set her straight, Honey. Don't you worry." Pearl glared at her as I slipped into my chair at the assigned counsel table. "Be right back here," Pearl said and squeezed my shoulder.

I whispered, "If anything happens, can you take care of Junia and Pennie?"

"I promise. But if anything happens, I'm going to claw her eyes out, then march that old apostle girl right in here and let her take care of the rest of *her*." She scowled again at the woman, and I hoped the social worker didn't remember what Junia had done that day over in Thousandsticks.

A woman came in from behind the judge's bench and took a seat at the table below it.

I stared up at the clock, waiting for Mr. Morgan to arrive, twisting my scarf and pulling at the fingertips on my white gloves. Barely five minutes had passed when I heard the door open behind me. I turned. Carrying a briefcase up to our table, Mr. Morgan greeted me with a slight smile.

"How we doing today, Honey?" He pulled out papers and arranged them on the table.

"A bit scared," I said quietly, peeking over my shoulder and hoping Sheriff Buckner had gone somewhere else.

He nodded in a way that said he understood. "Now it'll be just like the last time. If the judge asks you anything, tell the truth. If you don't know, say so. You'll stand when the bailiff announces the judge and stand when the judge asks you anything. Don't interrupt the counselor and his clients over at their table. Don't speak to the spectators in the public gallery behind us. Stay quiet and just follow my lead," he repeated from memory what he'd surely told others hundreds of times. "And—"

We both watched as Sheriff Buckner sidled up and sat down beside the social worker and the attorney.

Terrified, I gripped the scarf as I turned and looked at the empty seat beside me, wishing Retta was still here to hold my hand. Stretching my neck around, my eyes fell on Pearl sitting on the bench in the public gallery, fretfully twisting her charm bracelet. Then I saw Alonzo farther back, shoulders squared, solemn and attentive.

I snapped my head around as the hard click of soles sounded on wooden floors. A new bailiff appeared from an entryway by the judge's bench. "All rise," he ordered. "In the presence of the flags of the United States of America and the State of Kentucky, this court is now in session, the Honorable Judge Norton presiding."

My eyes went to the flags atop the poles flanking each side of the judge's bench, the soft fabrics of the United States and Kentucky state flags slightly ruffling from the whirrs of an overhead fan.

The judge entered and climbed the stairs to his perch.

"Please be seated and come to order," the bailiff instructed before taking a chair over in the corner.

Judge Norton looked down at his papers and then in my direction. A frown passed briefly over his face before he said, "First on the calendar is the matter of Honey Mary-Angeline Lovett's application for emancipation. Please state your appearances."

Mr. Morgan half stood and gave his name and told the judge he was my lawyer. At the other table the man stood and said he was Mr. Vessels and introduced the social worker and sheriff.

The judge peered out into the courtroom, then dropped his eyes back to his papers and said, "I've read all the moving and responding papers and don't need them repeated. I do have one question for Social Services."

Mrs. Wallace stood and waited.

"The state objects to Miss Lovett's emancipation and instead demands she be bound to the Kentucky House of Reform to labor until she is twenty-one years of age. Please state your reason in plain words."

I swallowed hard, rolling and unrolling the scarf in my lap, my gloved hands surely as blue as the square background for the stars on the American flag in front of me. I lifted up a prayer, begging for mercy.

Mrs. Wallace picked up a paper and cleared her throat. "Honey Mary-Angeline Lovett, the sixteen-year-old minor child, is now orphaned after her parents were jailed for violating the anti-miscegenation laws of the Commonwealth of Kentucky and God. We feel it is in the best interest of the state to protect its people against harm and immoral indecency. *This girl*," she spat out, "has lived with the Blue heathens, *criminals*, and has continued to live a sinful, criminal life and is to be remanded to the House of Reform immediately and per Judge Roy Taylor's initial order, dated March 6, 1953, for its own safety and so that no one takes undue advantage of its tender youth."

It, she referred to me again like she'd done in Thousandsticks. I was mortified, and I opened my mouth to protest, but the shame clamped it shut. The room grew stuffy, and miserable, I plucked at my collar and slipped off my gloves, placing them on our table, worriedly rubbing my sweaty palms. Dropping my gaze to my lap, I studied the disgrace seeping into my hands. Mr. Morgan looked at me questioningly, and just as quickly, I pulled my gloves back on.

"Your Honor, I'm prepared to respond," Mr. Morgan said dryly and sat back down.

"Not so fast, Counselor," Judge Norton said. "Mrs. Wallace, do you have any proof that Miss Lovett has committed any crimes or is currently engaged in illegal activities?"

"We do, Your Honor. We have several." Their lawyer stood.

Mr. Morgan leaned over to my ear. "Have you told me everything?"

I looked up wildly at him and feverishly nodded my head.

"Proceed, Mr. Vessels." Judge Norton flicked a wrist in the lawyer's direction.

"On the morning of March 6, 1953, the state witnessed Honey Lovett in the company of Pearl Grant and the notorious John Smith, a known moonshiner. Miss Lovett willfully gave false information to the state and stole the identity of another by claiming she was the moonshiner's daughter just visiting

the home where her parents had holed up before they sur-
rendered, then fled the county. A very serious interference with
an investigation and outright lying to an officer of the law and
a government servant of the people. On the morning of March
30 of this year, the now-deceased Perryman Edwin Gillis visited
Sheriff Buckner to report—"

Mr. Morgan stood and abruptly shouted. I jumped in my
chair. "Objection, your Honor! Hearsay and lack of foundation,
and nowhere in the opposing papers."

"Objection overruled," the judge quipped. "Please continue,
Mr. Vessels."

"Thank you, Your Honor. Mr. Gillis sought to register a
criminal complaint against Miss Lovett for interfering with his
marital relationship after he found Miss Lovett in criminal conversation with his wife, Guyla Belle Gil—"

"Your Honor!" Mr. Morgan jumped up again. "Objections
on the same grounds, particularly from a dead man who we will
never be able to interview or cross-examine."

"Overruled. Please go on, Mr. Vessels," Judge Norton said.

"Miss Lovett insisted that Mrs. Gillis read a censored and
controversial sex-fiction book titled *The Awakening* by known
feminist, Kate Chopin, who supports the disgraceful abandoning of wifely duties and the abandoning of a husband and their
children. Miss Lovett did this in hopes that Mrs. Guyla Belle
Gillis would do just that." He pressed down his drab, stained tie.
"And because of this criminal intent by Miss Lovett to destroy
the sacred sanctity of holy matrimony, we now have *both* parents
deceased and their poor three-year-old son, Jonathan Bailey
Gillis, orphaned. Three lives destroyed by her." He stabbed an
accusing finger toward me, making me recoil.

"I didn't, sir," I hissed into Mr. Morgan's ear. But my heart
grew heavy, and the weight of the deaths and little Johnnie's loss
nearly suffocated me so that I felt I was on trial for them.

Sneering, Mrs. Wallace shot me a tight, satisfied smile.

"Your Honor, I must object to this double hearsay from

a dead man, not to mention a murderer, also totally without foundation and not mentioned in any of Mr. Vessels's papers," Mr. Morgan said as he rose again, casting a concerned eye my way.

The judge leaned over to Mr. Vessels. After a long pause he said, "Mr. Vessels, now that I have the whole claim with no real evidence through witnesses and documents, which you have not presented to this court, I'm hard-pressed to conclude that any single book could cause a failed marriage and or death. Do you have any other real evidence you wish to present, or do you request a continuance to develop evidence?" Judge Norton said.

"Yes, Your Honor, we'd like to present more today, thank you. We are prepared to prove that on April 11 of this year, Sheriff Buckner was then called over to nineteen-year-old Pearl Grant's home, which is the fire tower where she is housed and employed by the state as a fire lookout. Sheriff Buckner here"—he turned, raised an exaggerated flat palm to the lawman sitting on the other side of Mrs. Wallace—"witnessed the drunken outbursts and false accusations by Miss Grant after the two teenagers, she and Miss Lovett, set the government cab on fire during a night of unlawful inebriating and wild parties and—"

"Objection. This is a motion proceeding, and none of this was mentioned in any opposition papers." Mr. Morgan half rose this time.

"Overruled, please proceed," Judge Norton said.

Tittering whispers came from behind, but I was too terrified and embarrassed to turn around, afraid I would see the condemnation in others' eyes. Resting my elbows on the table, I dropped my head into a palm and kneaded my throbbing temples.

"Is this true, Honey?" Mr. Morgan whispered.

"Just the drinking, sir." I barely breathed.

Mr. Morgan bowed his head and cupped his hand over his forehead, shielding his scowl from the judge.

Embarrassed, I hung my head.

"Order," Judge Norton said. "Is there more to your late offer of proof, Mr. Vessels?"

"No, sir, Your Honor. But the court can of course verify everything I have said with Sheriff Buckner here." Mr. Vessels took his seat and smiled satisfied at the sheriff and social worker before raising a contemptuous brow my way.

"Your Honor, if I may speak on behalf of my client—" Mr. Morgan rose.

"Take your seat, Counselor. I have one question for Miss Lovett," Judge Norton declared.

Mr. Morgan leaned over and said, "Stand."

My legs didn't want to. Mr. Morgan stabbed me with a stern look, and I rose, gripping the table.

"Miss Lovett, did you attend a party at Miss Grant's cab where you proceeded to get unlawfully inebriated and set the cab on fire?"

"No, sir. Perry Gillis and his kin set the cab on fire, and when we tried to tell the sheriff, he got real angry."

"Did you attend a party there?" the judge asked.

"Yes, sir, a pajama party."

The judge peered over his glasses. "Speak up, please."

"I-I—"

"Miss Lovett, please answer the question," he demanded.

"Pearl had a pajama party for us two."

From behind, I heard soft laughter.

"Were you drinking, Miss Lovett?" he asked.

"Yes, sir. But we never—"

"Be seated," the judge ordered.

The brisk command felt like a slap, and all I could do was gawk at him.

Mr. Morgan turned slightly and said in a quiet voice. "Take your seat."

Murmurs lifted behind me in the public gallery.

I sank back into my chair, my heart thumping in my ears, drowning out the crowd's energetic whispers skating around the stale, tobacco-soaked weeping walls.

This time, Judge Norton stared in our direction for a long time. He smiled, but it didn't really show in his eyes, nor tug at the corners of his mouth. It was more like a small, troubling gaze. Puzzled, I cast my eyes downward while Mr. Morgan scribbled notes on a pad.

Then the judge said, "This proceeding is somewhat unusual. As it stands, it's the first in this Kentucky court's history where such a request for an emancipation application has been solicited. To save time and get to the bottom of this, I have allowed new evidence, which seems undisputed from Miss Lovett's own mouth. Based on that I am inclined to deny the emancipation application."

Gasps and hisses rose in back of me. Again, I dared not look, lest they see the shame and misery of my unshed tears. The bailiff called out, "Order in the court. No utterances. *Order.*"

Mr. Morgan turned around and fixed his eyes on the people who had made the noises.

Judge Norton leaned back and looked down his long, slender nose at Mr. Morgan. "Counselor, before I rule, do you have any points you wish to raise or any new evidence of your own to offer?"

The lawyer stood. "May I have five minutes, Your Honor? As the court notes, this has been a rather unusual proceeding. I believe with just a few minutes with my client and perhaps others, we can give the court the whole story, not mere snippets."

"Mr. Vessels, I've given you a lot of leeway. It would seem only fair to grant Mr. Morgan's request," the judge said.

Mr. Vessels stood up and, smiling broadly, said, "No objection whatsoever, Your Honor."

"The Court will recess for fifteen minutes. Mr. Morgan, we'll hear from you then." He stepped down and disappeared somewhere in the back, the sound of his long, black robe swishing into the murmurs of those behind us.

Mr. Morgan turned to me. "Stay here, Honey. I see R.C. and a few others back there. Let's see what they know."

Thirty-Nine

Clips of strained conversation rose and fell in the back of the courtroom. Turning partway, I was surprised to see Eula Foster speaking with Mr. Morgan. If she saw my shock, the librarian didn't show it because she barely glanced my way and went right on talking to the lawyer. But the damning was there, and we all knew I'd committed an unforgivable wrong. Several times, Miss Foster shook her head, looking back at me unfavorably.

I was sure I'd be handed my walking papers as they dragged me off to the House of Reform. After all, I was morally indecent, godless, an *It*, and now a criminal in the state's eyes. And soon the town, the whole state of Kentucky even, would declare it true. My eyes landed on the other faces of townsfolk who had slipped in and now filled half the benches. Alonzo's eyes were full of so much pity that I tore my gaze away, saddened to glimpse the sorrow and worriment swallowed in his weathered face.

I turned back to the librarian. Beside Eula stood Amara Ballard. She talked excitedly to Mr. Morgan, her hands flying fast. Pearl and R.C. flanked Mr. Morgan's other side. Once in a while Pearl's troubled eyes fell on mine.

Mr. Morgan came back to the table just as the bailiff said, "All rise."

The judge entered and took the bench. "Are you ready to proceed, Mr. Morgan?"

"Yes, Your Honor. I would like to present real witness testimony on behalf of Miss Lovett."

"How many witnesses and how long do you expect to take, Counselor?"

"Three, Your Honor. It shouldn't take more than a few minutes for each."

Judge Norton rubbed a hand over his clean-shaven jaw and mused on the lawyer's request. "Proceed," he said with a short sigh.

"Thank you, Your Honor. I'd like to call frontier nurse Amara Ballard up to the witness stand."

The judge swore her in, and Mr. Morgan said, "Please tell the court the relationship you have with Miss Lovett."

Amara nodded. "Honey, uh, Miss Lovett hired me to tend to a gravely ill Loretta Adams. I did everything I could medically for Miss Adams, then left her in Honey's good care."

"And did Miss Lovett care for her adequately?" Mr. Morgan asked.

"Not only did she care for her, but she also saw that Miss Adams received a proper burial. And I was told by Mr. Geary that Honey paid for it and the marker with her own earnings."

"Objection, hearsay and irrelevant." Mr. Vessels stood.

"Overruled," the judge said.

"Do you receive books from Honey's outreach program?" Mr. Morgan asked.

"Honey delivers the books to me every Friday." She looked appreciatively at me.

"Can you tell us what you knew about your neighbors, the Gillis family?"

"Objection!" Mr. Vessels called out.

I glanced over and saw the sheriff's eyes flicker as he looked at Mr. Vessels.

"What's the relevance, Mr. Morgan? And is this witness competent on the character of Mr. Gillis?" Judge Norton asked.

"Yes, Your Honor. I plan to show Miss Lovett's true moral

character and dispute the fabricated indecent one the state and sheriff have wrongly presented."

"Overruled. You may continue, Miss Ballard." The judge jabbed his chin her way.

"I treated their son, Johnnie, after he fell down their family well and caught pneumonia. Then I nursed Mrs. Gillis after her husband attacked her in my home. Honey was there and helped with the nursing too. Before Mrs. Gillis left, she told me that Honey climbed down in the well and rescued Johnnie. She saved his life, and her little boy told me this too. Honey also led the state police to Mrs. Gillis. And because of that, her murderer was arrested and the poor soul has now received a proper burial—"

"Objection! Your Honor—" Mr. Vessels called out, incensed.

"Overruled. As it happens, I have the signed statement from the state police in my file," Judge Norton replied. "Please continue your questioning, Counselor."

"No further questions, Your Honor." Mr. Morgan sat down.

"You may cross-examine, Mr. Vessels."

Mr. Vessels stood. "Miss Ballard, you're a frontier nurse who cares for the sick. What type of books did Miss Lovett drop off to you?"

"Fun and entertaining ones that enlighten and educate. There are a lot of people around here who like to read and will read anything. But sadly, there are a few small-minded people in dire need of her service and who would greatly benefit from it. I commend Miss Lovett on her efforts to spread literacy."

I heard a few smothered chuckles behind me.

"So you support and recommend feminism and immoral indecency?" Mr. Vessels said curtly. "These sex—"

"Objection." Mr. Morgan rose.

"Sustained," the judge answered. "Mr. Vessels, please refrain from injecting your manful interpretations onto the lady's reflections."

"Withdrawn. No further questions, Your Honor." Mr. Vessels reddened.

"You may step down, Miss Ballard," the judge said. "Call your next witness, Counselor."

"Forest Ranger R.C. Cole," Mr. Morgan said. After R.C. was seated and sworn in, Mr. Morgan asked if he was acquainted with me. Then he told him to describe what happened the morning of the fire.

"The young ladies were Sunday sober straight. They both tried to explain about the fire, and Honey's suspicions regarding Mrs. Gillis's disappearance to the sheriff. But Sheriff Buckner wouldn't listen. Instead, he shouted and threatened to lock them up on false charges—"

"Objection and irrelevant!" Mr. Vessels shot out an arm to R.C.

"Overruled. Please continue, Mr. Cole." The judge motioned to him with his palm.

"Miss Grant had several property accidents we believed were caused by Mr. Gillis and his relative in the past, but unfortunately we were unable to prove it or get the sheriff's official help on the matter. I learned just yesterday the state police has opened an official investigation into the sheriff's dereliction of duty and—"

"*Objection*, this hearing isn't about Sheriff Buckner," Mr. Vessels said.

"Sustained," the judge ruled.

R.C. glanced disgustedly over at the lawman.

The sheriff looked away. Mr. Vessels leaned close to the sheriff and whispered. The lawman shook his head.

I exhaled, knowing the sheriff would be under the watchful eye of the state police for some time if not longer. I dared to peek back at Pearl, and she shot me a small, satisfied smile, knowing it too.

"Can you speak of Honey Lovett's character, Mr. Cole?" Mr. Morgan asked.

"Know'd her all her life, as well her family. Honorable and decent folks."

After Mr. Morgan concluded, Mr. Vessels looked like he might question R.C. but for some reason didn't.

"Your Honor, I would like to call my last witness, Miss Eula Foster, the director at the Troublesome Creek Library," Mr. Morgan said.

She was sworn in and quickly took her seat.

"Miss Foster, you hired Miss Lovett to deliver reading material on her mule to extend your outreach program, much like your library had with the Pack Horse initiative in the '30s and '40s, is that correct?"

"It is correct," Miss Foster said quietly, not meeting my eyes.

"Is Miss Lovett a good employee?"

"Her work seems satisfactory enough, but"—she glanced over at the other table—"*if* her character and morals were in question, then unfortunately we'd have to let her go."

I heard the jangling and a hiss behind me and knew it came from Pearl. I chanced a glance and saw the misery puddled on her face.

"But her work performance *is* satisfactory, and she currently has a good record in your employment?" Mr. Morgan pressed.

"Yes, so far." Miss Foster darted her eyes to me and then cast them meekly to her lap.

"Your witness," Mr. Morgan told Mr. Vessels.

"Miss Foster, does your library carry Chopin's *The Awakening*?" Mr. Vessels asked.

"I… Well, I didn't know it was still in circulation anywhere."

"Is it banned?"

"I'm unaware of its current status."

"So your library carries and supports and willingly condones sex-fiction books—"

"Objection." Mr. Morgan scowled.

"Overruled," Judge Norton said briskly.

Mr. Vessels pressed his fingertips together as he walked in front of his table. "Miss Foster, as you are probably aware, *The Awakening* was written by a woman with a diseased mind and blackened soul. So I'm asking you, do you carry *The Awakening*, or any other such damnable written works?" He paused and turned to me. "Did you hire librarian Honey Mary-Angeline Lovett to carry dirty books up those rocks?" Mr. Vessels pushed.

Eula pinched her lips together tightly and screwed up her pale face, her taut cheeks blotting red. "No, sir, I most certainly did not! The Troublesome Creek Public Library doesn't carry books that would offend the Kentucky man or ones that would go against the Godly morals and practicing Christian beliefs of decent, God-fearing folks!"

"You are the director, Miss Foster, and if you don't have it, would it be safe to say it was in Miss Lovett's personal collection and that she alone carried those dirty books—"

My teeth began to clatter, and terrified, I pressed a palm over my mouth.

"Objection! Leading the witness and hearsay," Mr. Morgan said harshly.

"*Mr. Morgan.*" I tugged on his sleeve, but he wrote something down on his pad and wouldn't look at me.

"No more questions." Mr. Vessels smiled thinly.

The judge looked down at us and then said, "Mr. Vessels, would you care to call any other witness, briefly, to counter any of this new evidence presented by Mr. Morgan?"

"Just one moment and thank you, Your Honor." Mr. Vessels leaned over to the sheriff, and they whispered together, then, "No, Your Honor. We rest."

"Mr. Morgan?" said the judge.

"No, Your Honor. Applicant rests."

"If you are both through, I would like to conclude this hearing by ruling on the matter today and later I will write a formal letter. Now, I would like to say…" Judge Norton paused and directed his next words to Mr. Vessels. "Mr. Vessels had the opportunity to call Sheriff Buckner as a witness to refute the claim and did not, so I presume there is some truth to it."

Mr. Vessels half stood, plopped back into his seat, then rose again, sputtering, "But, Your Honor, Your—"

"Take your seat, Counselor," the judge said.

A few grumbles came from Mr. Vessels's table.

"Before I rule, I'd like to ask Miss Lovett one last question. Miss Lovett?"

I uttered a *yessir*.

"Stand," Mr. Morgan instructed me.

I rose slowly.

"Miss Lovett," the judge said, "do you have anything you wish to say?"

I was surprised again that he asked my thoughts, the same as in the last hearing. I was hesitant, recalling how Papa whispered to Mama to never go searching for freedom at the feet of others who could strip it away.

But I had to try even if it meant on bended knee. "Yes, Your Honor," I said, my response hoarse, the words raked across a burning throat. "I–I... Well, sir, I had a marriage proposal recently."

Out of the corner of my eye, I could see Mr. Vessels, Mrs. Wallace, and the sheriff leaning over, gawking, stretching their necks, three sets of curious eyes falling to my belly. Mrs. Wallace whispered something to the lawyer and he nodded.

From the public benches, I heard folk squirm in their seats, knowing some were lengthening backsides to get a glimpse.

"Your Honor," I continued, trying to ignore them, "I know many girls around here are allowed to wed young. The law—"

The judge looked up, perplexed, and made me stop talking. "Miss Lovett, how might you know that law? Are you in other trouble...in the family way?"

I pressed my lips together, tasting the stale, waxy Pastel Pink lipstick from the Avon sample that Pearl had given me the night of the party.

"Miss Lovett?" He waited.

Laughter and a few snickers punched from the rear, but I kept my eyes glued to the judge. "*No, sir.* Mr. Morgan told me that's the law in this state. And he said Kentucky would legally honor such a union between a man and a child bride." I paused,

suddenly remembering my mama, Angeline Moffit, and the
marriage certificate that I'd found in one of our trunks long ago.
She was barely thirteen when she married my papa, Willie.

A touch of kindness spread across the judge's face. "There'd
be no need for any of us to be here today if you were soon to
have a husband. Would there?"

"No, sir, Your Honor. But I haven't even had a chance to
go on my first date because the way things are in my life. Have
myself a proper kiss even," I blurted out, unable to stop myself,
and the laughter grew louder.

"*Order*," the bailiff called out.

"I live alone, Your Honor."

"And where is that?"

"At the Carter homestead alongside Troublesome Creek.
Anyone"—I lifted an unsteady gloved hand over to the sheriff
and social worker—"can visit me anytime."

Again, from behind came guffaws, but I couldn't help myself.
"I keep it nice and clean, and feed and care for my critters. *Junia*.
She was my mama's mule."

Judge Norton's eyes grew distant like he was remembering
something or someone from long ago.

"But Junia's mine now. The ol' girl delivered thousands of
books on hundreds of porches for the Pack Horse Library Project
years ago. And she's doing it again with me. I take care of her
and Miss Retta's cat. I take care of myself." I reached inside my
dress pocket, pulled out the folded paycheck stubs and held them
out in front of me, up high. "My pay stubs, Your Honor."

The judge leaned toward me and looked over his glasses,
quietly studying me.

An utterance of disbelief arose from Mrs. Wallace. I placed the
stubs on the table and glanced down at the empty chair where
Retta had sat beside me, suddenly feeling an ache for her presence, her pride and strength.

The sheriff stared at me, bored, like I was no more than the
bother of a housefly, and I saw Gillis's cruel face in his. My mind

pulled to Guyla Belle's suffering, the horrors Gillis had burdened little Wrenna, me, and the other women with, and a surge of blinding fury and power sent quakes to my being. Steadying my sweaty gloved hands on the table, I took a deep breath and tamped down the anger, trying to think *smart*.

"Your Honor, if I don't want to marry, and instead I want to keep house alone, Kentucky will punish me by sending me to the children's prison and lock me in weighted leg chains to work hard labor until I have reached the age of twenty-one. I will soon be seventeen, and I have a home and a respectable government job and the means to support myself. I deliver books and important reading material into these hills, and my patrons need me and the materials. If the law says I'm of marriageable age, old enough to get hitched at twelve or thirteen or sixteen, why can't it declare me an adult when I've been making it on my own the same as fourteen-year-old Byrne McDaniel? Why should I be forced to marry a man to have my freedom, to do what I'm already doing and doing well?"

Attorney Vessels popped up fast and noisily, stopping me. "Objection. Totally irrelevant."

"Overruled. Miss Lovett, are you seeking permission to marry?" The judge looked at me, puzzled.

"No, Your Honor. *No, sir*. I'm seeking the freedom not to!" I sat down, scooted closer to the table and clasped my trembling hands.

The court clerk lifted the pen off her page and glanced at me, a mixture of pity, shock, and admiration fleeting across her eyes before she dropped her gaze back to the task at hand. I looked back to the judge, gleaning an unsettling rising while the clock ticked loudly into Mr. Morgan's fast-shuffling papers.

Judge Norton stared down at me from his perch.

Purring whispers crawled around the warm, oppressive room as I smoothed down my skirts, tasting the heavy, standing air coating my throat.

Mr. Morgan leaned over and uttered something, but I

couldn't hear anything except the heartbeats of terror pounding in my ears.

The judge finally pulled his gaze away. "Why, indeed, Miss Lovett," he said quietly, then announced louder, "Application for the emancipation of Honey Mary-Angeline Lovett is hereby granted. Please approach the bench with your client, Counselor."

"*Scandalous*—" Mrs. Wallace admonished, and Judge Norton banged his gavel twice into her protest.

Gasps and cheers erupted from behind.

At the bench, the judge leaned over to speak with me. "Miss Lovett, it was Napoleon who supposedly said, 'Show me a family of readers, and I will show you the people who move the world.' Not long ago, I was moving down a different path, straight to the House of Reform. Yanking on little girls' braids, fighting in the schoolyard, and sneaking liquor and raising Cain. But your mother changed all that with the books. From the first"—he raised a finger—"*very* first moment I saw her and that old, cranky mule ride into the schoolyard," he mused. "She once said, 'Books are the cornerstone to greater minds.' And I will never forget what a difference the books made after she gave me a few of the Hardy Boys mysteries. They inspired me to pursue a career in law. *Books'll change you like that.*"

He tapped the words onto his table and stepped down off the bench, then turned slowly around. "Hmm," he grunted, knitting his brows. "There's a problem."

"Your Honor?" I said, the apprehension climbing back into my gut.

"I haven't picked up their latest. Do you have it in yet, Miss Lovett?"

Free. I was still free. But the longer I stared at him, the more I glimpsed the mischievous little boy Mama had seen in the schoolyard years ago.

Checking his wristwatch, Mr. Morgan gently cleared his throat.

"Yes, sir, Your Honor. I came across *The Crisscross Shadow* just the other week. I'll make sure to reserve it for you," I said, relieved.

Amara, Pearl, Alonzo, and R.C. flocked to my side, congratulating me, hugging and pecking my flushed cheeks.

Pearl nudged my arm. "Look who's here." My eyes searched the small crowd in the back of the courtroom, and I caught Francis staring at me, a question in his eyes.

He pointed at me and then back to his chest and mouthed, *Go out with me?*

Though free, I had been pressed into early womanhood by the court and Kentucky law and would likely marry and bear children years from now, but for today, this moment, I wanted to be just a girl getting her first date. *Yes*, I mouthed back, bobbing my head, excited to do just that.

Pearl exclaimed, "Oh, Honey, we have to celebrate your freedom. We'll have a party the likes this town has never seen!"

"First, I'm going on a picnic with that boy and eating me a tub of his mama's prized banana pudding." I looked beyond at a grinning Francis.

Miss Foster approached me slowly, hesitant in her steps. I searched her eyes, wondering if she would dismiss me from my job.

"Honey," she said, digging inside her pocketbook, "Mr. Taft asked me to give you this for your personal collection when he heard I was coming today."

"Ma'am." She handed me *The Golden Book of Tagore*.

"Oren said it's a 1931 signed first edition, and there's only 1,500 in the world." Miss Foster lightly tapped her approval on the book with a nail.

Speechless, I marveled over the cover bound in pale-yellow silk, tracing a finger around the embossed red and gold floral design. "It's a treasure," I murmured, studying the spine, noting the raised ticketed leather title.

She folded her hands. "Honey, I need to apologize. Tell you I'm sorry I listened to the lies of the sheriff and that wretched woman. Forgive me, I was an old fool. I didn't realize your steadfast dedication, the vital services you have provided to your patrons. For poor Mrs. Gillis, her son, and others. I'd be honored if you would continue your mother's important legacy with the outreach program. Honey, there's always the thirst. And you and those books are sorely needed and will surely save a lot of people. If you stay."

I glanced up at the judge's empty bench. "Ma'am, I'll need to reserve a book today. Mama grow'd readers out there, Miss Foster. I want to do that too," I said quietly, thinking about her and the patrons.

The librarian squeezed my shoulder. "You truly are the Book Woman's daughter." She released me and walked briskly over to the courtroom door, turning once to nod approvingly before slipping out.

Bonnie peeked inside, holding her tin lunch bucket and wearing dirty bibs and a miner's helmet. Annoyed by her disheveled appearance, the bailiff held up an arm and loudly said, "Only proper attire is allowed, miss." He blocked her from entering. Undaunted, Bonnie glared at him and elbowed his arm away.

Sullen, the bailiff stepped aside.

Hitching a fallen strap up over her shoulder, Bonnie called out to me, "I heard, sweet pea! You be sure an' bring me some more good books come Friday." She tapped her chest where a read jutted out from the large bib pocket. "Just finished your latest loan on my dinner break today."

Leaving the courtroom, Mrs. Wallace paused beside the miner, and a hand flew up to her collar. The social worker gaped at *Lady Chatterley's Lover* poking out from Bonnie's blackened overalls, then turned slowly to me, surprised, silently working her mouth, the disgust and hatred ripening on her pinched face. "*Heathen*," she spat out.

Bold, I lifted a defiant chin and met her burning eyes with triumphant ones.

Mrs. Wallace bumped Bonnie aside with her large pocket-book and stomped out of the courtroom.

Clutching *The Golden Book of Tagore*, I opened it and saw Mr. Taft had left an inscription.

June '53

Honey,

"Faith is the bird that feels the light and sings when the dawn is still dark." As long as you have the books, you'll always have that light.

—*Oren Taft*

Suddenly, I was there beside her again, riding in the ol' blue hills of Kaintuck, our pannier full, and I felt the sting of tears as I reread what Mama had quoted to her patron long ago—knowing that the books had not only saved me, her, and others, but had given us something even bigger and more precious: *Freedom*.

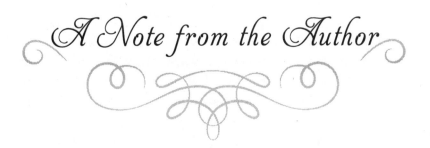

A Note from the Author

Dear Reader,

It's been a tremendous honor to continue the journeys of Honey, Cussy Mary, and Jackson Lovett in this new novel which is both a stand-alone and a sequel. I wanted to explore themes of sisterhood through the brave and indomitable Kentucky women who held uncommon and demanding jobs during a time when males dominated the workforce, and women and children were ruled by patriarchal law.

As a Kentuckian, I've set all my books in my home state, and it's always a privilege when you let me share their stories with you.

Kentucky, especially eastern Kentucky, a land rich in folklore and steeped in tradition, is one of the most beautiful places in the world. The people, my people, are intelligent, proud, and passionate, oftentimes misunderstood, sometimes persecuted, but in their complicated lives and stories you'll find a constant. You'll find dignity.

I was thrilled to revisit the Pack Horse Library Project, honor the pioneering work of these brave librarians, and present more information about the program. For example, in 1913, the Kentucky Federation of Women's Clubs convinced a local coal baron, John C. Mayo, to subsidize a mounted library service to reach eastern Kentucky. Unfortunately, a year later, the program expired when Mayo died.

But the Kentucky women were determined to develop a strong literacy program in Appalachia. Almost twenty years later, they proposed the program to President Franklin D. Roosevelt's Works Progress Administration (WPA), where it was approved as a sole effort to put women to work. Once the program was revived, these literacy pioneers were able to deliver books and reading material on mule and horseback to the poorest and most isolated areas in eastern Kentucky.

Before the mid-1800s, the people of eastern Kentucky lived in isolation except for visits from peddlers and preachers. The Appalachians mined timber and coal, survived off the land, hunted, farmed, and raised livestock. Then came missionaries, churches, government, and coal companies, pushing their ideologies and buying up the Kentucky man's land at dirt-cheap prices, only to leave it destroyed. Many Kentuckians were wary, as well as weary of their new ideas and agendas—especially any ideas modernism might shove on them.

By the time the Pack Horse initiative arrived in 1935, eastern Kentucky was in the midst of its most violent era: the bloody coal-mine wars and the crushing Depression.

The WPA paid the Pack Horse librarians $28 a month. But Roosevelt refused to provide any books and reading materials, or the mounts needed to deliver books, or any housing for the materials.

However, the Pack Horse librarians were clever, and the program flourished when they developed ingenious ways to get the reading material for their routes. Homemade scrapbooks and penny funds were established, and solicitations went out widely to women's clubs, Boy Scouts, and the PTAs in big cities.

I'm grateful for the generosity and dedicated work of Kentuckian Jason Vance, a professor at Middle Tennessee State University, and for his extensive research documenting and photographing many historical scrapbooks during his trips to the FDR Presidential Library and Museum in Hyde Park, NY— where they are held and can be seen today.

The Pack Horse Library Project became an important bridge to education for many who had no access to schools. Literacy offered a break in the cycle of debilitating poverty. More importantly, it gave empowerment and freedom.

The beloved program ran from 1935 until 1943 when funding ceased, more accessible roads were built, and bookmobiles were introduced. Many of the Pack Horse librarians returned to farming, while some sought college to obtain their librarianship and others worked in libraries and for the effort of literacy.

It's been an honor to meet relatives of the Kentucky Pack Horse librarians, their children and grandchildren, and a privilege and joy to know the unique Blue-skinned inhabitants of my home. But any skin color not alabaster-white or farmer-tan brown, or anyone different than most, whether in Appalachia or Anytown USA, suffered harder in an already hard life. And if that skin color was blue brought on by a strange blood disorder, a medical anomaly, families who had it were shunned, shamed, ridiculed, and hunted by news media, pushing them into the darkest holler of Appalachia. The Blues are intelligent, kind, and gracious folks who came over from France and first settled in Kentucky around 1820 when a French orphan claimed a land grant here.

Instead of being lifted up for their uniqueness, the Blues suffered prejudices and isolation and were treated unfairly because of a rare gene. Because I grew up in poverty, spending my first decade in a rural Kentucky orphanage and going on to endure homelessness and other sufferings, it's not hard for me to feel pain deeply. And maybe that is true for anyone who has gone through hardships of their own. It's always my hope to honor, lift up others, and dispel the fear and ignorance that breeds hate and toxicity into cultures.

Congenital methemoglobinemia, a non-life-threatening condition, is due to a deficiency leading to higher-than-normal levels of methemoglobin in the blood—a form of hemoglobin—that overwhelms the normal hemoglobin, which reduces oxygen capacity. Less oxygen in the blood makes it a chocolate-brown color instead of red, causing the skin to appear blue. Doctors can easily diagnose congenital methemoglobinemia because the color of the blood provides the unique clue. The mutation is hereditary and carried in a recessive gene, whereas *acquired* methemoglobinemia is life-threatening and derives from heart disease, airway obstruction, or taking too much of certain drugs.

Once again, I researched fire towers and some of the courageous women who became the country's first lookouts, daring to run these intimidating forest towers while suffering storms, fires, wild creatures, extreme isolation, and more.

Although all my characters are fictional, and events are only inspired by history, I had the pleasure of interviewing several female coal miners. It was an honor to speak with Sara Vance, one young coal miner from West Virginia. Ms. Vance is not related to Professor Vance mentioned above. Sara, a brave, fierce third-generation coal miner, is the daughter of the late Brenda Vance, one of the first female coal miners in the country. Proud of her trade and fellow male colleagues, Sara enjoys her job and for a while worked alongside her mother in the mines. When pregnant and just weeks away from having a baby, Sara continued to work under the watchful eyes of the male miners who worried about her safety working 1,200 feet below the surface.

Years ago, I met the lovely Stephanie Ray Brown, a Kentucky *book woman* in her own right and daughter of another female coal miner. Stephanie introduced me to her retired mother, Rita Ray, who graciously granted me an interview. I learned what it was like for the first female coal miners trying to eke out a living beside male miners, their challenges, dangers, and difficulties.

I love imparting snippets of Kentucky's vital history in my stories. You'll find one of my characters, Amara Ballard, was inspired by the historical Kentucky Frontier Nursing Service founded by Mary Breckinridge in the 1920s. To learn more about these amazing women who were nurses on horseback in eastern Kentucky, I recommend *Wide Neighborhoods* by Mary Breckinridge.

We get a small glimpse into the important historical Moonlight Schools, another of just one of the many prolific and critical Kentucky contributions to the world. The inimitable schools were established in 1911 by Cora Wilson Stewart, to foster literacy among adults. Later, the Moonlight Schools would go on to serve Black and Native American students in other regions of America.

I enjoy exploring authentic Appalachian food in my research travels. Like its music and folklore, Appalachian meals are an intimate celebratory tradition and the very breath of the region and its people. From summer harvests of vine-ripened vegetables to late blackberry and early fall apple picking that shifts quietly into the hog-killing tradition during cold weather, food is church. Fellowship and conversations rise and fall lyrically over and around slow-roasting firepits and inside busy kitchens brimming with large simmering pots and sizzling cast-iron skillets. You'll find twine-pinned walls dangling with leathered fruits, beans, and peppers, tables laden with platters of smoked meats, and shelves stuffed with pickles, relishes, jams, and other delightful assortments of prized canning.

Long ago, I earned a degree in legal studies at the university and have always enjoyed law and research, particularly studying older laws. I was able to interview and pick the astute mind of the Honorable Judge Susan Gibson, who enlightened me with wonderful, thoughtful discussions and shared archaic and revelatory case laws.

Additionally, I couldn't have written the courtroom scenes without the superb suggestions and critical eye of brilliant lawyer and award-winning author G. J. Berger.

As with Junia the mule, Tommie the rooster provided a fun topic for research that sent me delving into newspaper articles, journals, rooster care, and more. Award-winning author Bren McClain was an absolute delight explaining roosters to me while

I listened to her various mocked rooster calls, and we discussed their meanings in between.

People often ask about the region's dialect. As a Kentuckian, I would love to be writing in the vernacular of Kentucky author Harriette Arnow. The language and its literary portrayal and eye phonetics in Arnow's brilliant *The Dollmaker* are music, a gravelly hymnal of haunting songs which I prize. It and the people are clearly inseparable.

I'm a big fan of and appreciate different dialects, whether from north, south, east, west, or across the big ponds, so I find it sad when language gets stripped or lost. But using native language is not always possible because not everyone reading is a native or would be able to follow it easily. It's tricky to find balance when no one set language was in use across all Kentucky lands, especially in the southern mountains of Appalachia.

While most of the archaic language in the southern mountains has Scots-Irish origins, a lot of the turns of phrase and words evolve from the people living here. Yonder becomes *yander* and *poke* is a bag or sack, *tote* means carry, coming and going changes to *a'comin'* and *a'goin'*. *Swarp* and *scrape* mean to fight, hit, or strike, and words like *fire* and *light* drop the *i* and become *far* and *laht*—just a few examples. And to this day, I pronounce *breakfast* as *brehfuss*, but some outsiders laughed so much that I became ashamed to say it and called it the morning meal instead, rarely writing the word in a novel until now. My *wash* sounds like *warsh*, and I had absently titled a novel *The Washed Light Off Ebenezer Road*, only to change it when others poked fun and couldn't understand my pronunciation.

Speech will even vary from town to town and holler to holler. I have a relative who comes from another pocket in Kentucky whose words even I find difficult to pronounce or understand. I've pulled back on some of the language rhythms, but hope you'll understand I couldn't sacrifice all of the local language and have kept some of the authenticity and beauty of it.

I always like to share recommended reads of my longtime

favorite Kentucky authors who wrote unforgettable masterpieces and inspired me. Harriette Simpson Arnow, John Fox Jr., Gwyn Hyman Rubio, Effie Waller Smith, Jesse Stuart, Alex Taylor, and Walter Tevis are just a few. Each one brings the pages to life with rich, evocative landscapes, beautifully told stories, and highly skilled prose.

I am a descendant of Gideon Dyer Cobb, and my cousin Kentuckian Irvin S. Cobb was a celebrated humorist, prolific author, renowned columnist, and reporter whose life and works I found fascinating. Irvin wrote more than sixty-four books and three hundred stories. You'll find some of his books mentioned throughout my works to honor him.

A final note. I'm forever humbled and indebted to you, Dear Reader, for picking up *The Book Woman's Daughter*. I hope you enjoyed reading my latest work as much as I loved writing it for you, and moreso, I pray it entertained and offered you a small respite away from the sadness and messy uncertainties we've all suffered during an exhausting COVID.

As always, my deepest gratitude to the generous, wise librarians and indie booksellers, the dedicated bookwomen and bookmen who work tirelessly to help place mine and other books into the hands and hearts of readers.

Images from the Pack Horse Library Project

Pack Horse librarian.

Natural Resources collection, Archives and Records Management Division—Kentucky Department for Libraries and Archives. Lisa Thompson, Librarian II at Kentucky Department for Libraries and Archives.

Ted Wathen, President's Commission on Coal, National Archives.

Used with permission from Ted Wathen.

Frontier Nursing Service.

Frontier Nursing Service (FNS). 1930. Flahardy, Jason. Frontier Nursing Service photographs, University of Kentucky Special Collections Research Center.

Frontier Nursing Service.

Frontier Nursing Service (FNS). 1930. Flahardy, Jason. Frontier Nursing Service photographs, University of Kentucky Special Collections Research Center.

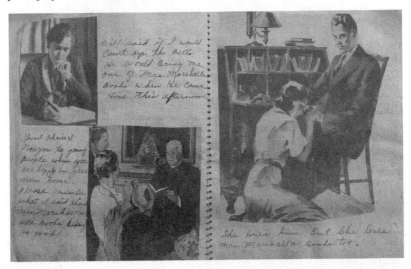

Compiled by Ms. Cleda Wilson of Owsley County, Kentucky, in honor of her "Traveling Librarian" Mrs. Grace Marshall.

Historical Pack Horse Librarians' Scrapbooks. Made by the Kentucky Pack Horse Librarians. Photographed at the Franklin D. Roosevelt Presidential Library by Prof. Jason Vance of Middle Tennessee State University.

An animal-themed scrapbook compiled by the Kentucky Pack Horse Librarians, circa 1938.

Historical Pack Horse Librarians' Scrapbooks. Made by the Kentucky Pack Horse Librarians. Photographed at the Franklin D. Roosevelt Presidential Library by Prof. Jason Vance of Middle Tennessee State University.

A religious scrapbook compiled by the Kentucky Pack Horse Librarians, circa 1938.

Historical Pack Horse Librarians' Scrapbooks. Made by the Kentucky Pack Horse Librarians. Photographed at the Franklin D. Roosevelt Presidential Library by Prof. Jason Vance of Middle Tennessee State University.

Fire tower.

Matt Burton, University of Kentucky College of Agriculture.

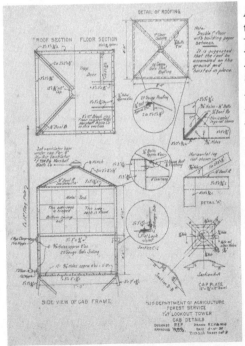

Architectural design for fire tower cab.

Putney Fire Tower, Kentucky. Natural Resources collection, Archives and Records Management Division—Kentucky Department for Libraries and Archives. Lisa Thompson, Librarian II at Kentucky Department for Libraries and Archives.

Female fire tower lookout.

Forest History Society, Durham, NC.

Female fire tower lookout.

Forest History Society, Durham, NC.

Mary Breckinridge, founder of Frontier Nursing Service (FNS) of Kentucky in Eastern Kentucky, 1925.

Frontier Nursing Service (FNS) founder Mary Breckinridge. 1930. Flahardy, Jason., Frontier Nursing Service photographs, University of Kentucky Special Collections Research Center.

Mother and daughter coal miners Brenda Vance and Sara Vance.

Used with permission from Sara Vance.

Woman coal miner Brenda Vance working underground.

Used with permission from Sara Vance.

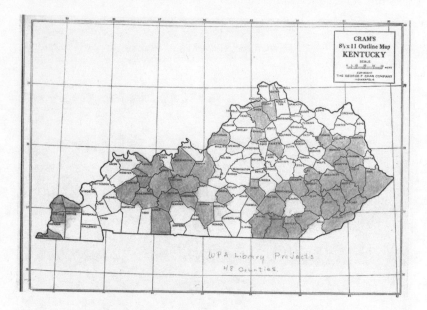

Kentucky Pack Horse librarian map.

Natural Resources collection, Archives and Records Management Division—
Kentucky Department for Libraries and Archives. Lisa Thompson, Librarian II at
Kentucky Department for Libraries and Archives.

Irene Pearl Crisp Stegall (1921–2013) was born in Elliott County, Kentucky. She was fifteen when she began delivering Pack Horse library materials in Elliott County.

Photo donated by Irene's daughter, Janice M. Kreider.

Pack Horse librarian.

Natural Resources collection, Archives and Records Management Division—Kentucky Department for Libraries and Archives. Lisa Thompson, Librarian II at Kentucky Department for Libraries and Archives.

Pack Horse librarian.

Natural Resources collection, Archives and Records Management Division—Kentucky Department for Libraries and Archives. Lisa Thompson, Librarian II at Kentucky Department for Libraries and Archives.

Reading Group Guide

1. Discuss the types of circumstances in which a child, or parent, would ask for a Declaration of Emancipation. Thinking about emancipation and the LeAnn Rimes/Britney Spears issues where the child is earning huge dollars that the parent "manager" is squandering or keeping from the child improperly, what should be put in place to prevent this?

2. Children, especially rural children, were a valuable commodity to families who needed farm labor without having to pay wages. Society continues to be mostly patriarchal, and during the time in which this novel was set, it was the father who could "express" emancipation and consent to his child's emancipation. Discuss patriarchal laws and the role they have played, and continue to play, in shaping women and children's rights and lives.

3. Does prison labor for children still exist like the historical House of Reform in Kentucky? Do children have to work in juvenile facilities as they once did? Should they have to?

4. Dogs are well-known for their protective instincts, but in this book, Junia the mule and Tommie the rooster protect Honey and Wrenna. What other animals have been known to protect their people?

5. Honey's interactions with a far more sophisticated Pearl show a glimpse into innocence and youth, the old land waking up to modernism creeping in, and the mountainfolk caught between their old hard ways and the new advanced world. Though Honey has been well educated by Book Woman Cussy in writing, reading, and more, her isolated life has held her back in other ways. Honey's new friend Pearl is far ahead of her with modern gadgets, young men, parties, and drinking. Discuss their differences, the women's strengths and vulnerabilities, and their adjustments to new environments.

6. Discuss the different jobs Honey, Pearl, Bonnie, and Amara held. What were the dangers they faced? What are unusual jobs women hold today versus years ago?

7. Discuss book banning of long ago and today.

8. Honey's mother, Cussy Mary Lovett, is subjected to forced sterilization while imprisoned for violating Kentucky's anti-miscegenation laws. The American eugenics movement led to this and other atrocities against individuals who were seen as different, including minorities and people with disabilities. Discuss why it is important to remind ourselves of the role eugenics played in America's not-so-distant past.

9. Child marriages are a global problem that can lead to dangerous and devastating consequences. In America, the marriageable age is determined by states. Many still allow child marriages between the ages of fourteen to seventeen with parental or judicial consent. There are some cases where children have married at age twelve and younger. What are the dangers of being a child bride or groom?

10. Choose a character from the novel and imagine what their future would hold.

11. Honey is surprised to find out that Loretta Adams had attended one of Kentucky's Moonlight Schools, which served the uneducated and the elderly. What do you think it would have been like to learn or teach at a Moonlight School?

12. Laws banning interracial marriage in America were first passed in the seventeenth century. They were enacted in many states until they were declared unconstitutional by the U.S. Supreme Court in 1967. Alabama became the last state to remove laws banning interracial marriage from its statutes in the year 2000. Do you know what anti-miscegenation laws your state passed and when they were abolished? Discuss what the history of these laws can tell us about race and marriage in America, both then and now.

13. How do you think Honey, Cussy, and Jackson's lives would unfold over the next two decades? What relevant laws will change, if any?

14. If you were to craft a scrapbook for isolated people, as the Pack Horse librarians did long ago, what would you include?

15. What are popular and favorite recipes of your family and region, and how do they differ or stand out from other families and places?

16. Do you think Honey purposely selected books from her personal collection to empower her women patrons? What books would you select to empower the underserved or disadvantaged in your area, and why?

Acknowledgments

To the generous and gracious book bloggers and first readers: Kristy Barrett, Davida Chazan, Pamela Klinger-Horn, Mary Webber O'Malley, Dawnny Ruby, Kathy Shattuck, Tonya Speelman, Carla Suto, Linda Zagon, The Erudite Bibliophile with Wanderlust, Julie Kaminski and The Walking Book Club, and the countless other bookwomen and bookmen who have helped put my books and others into the hearts of readers. I'm so appreciative and indebted to you, and although it seems small, thank you, all, from the bottom of my heart.

Thank you to Janice Kreider, the daughter of Irene, a Kentucky Pack Horse librarian; Eben Lehman, director of library and archives at Forest History Society, North Carolina; Lisa Thompson, librarian II at Kentucky Department for Libraries and Archives; Professor Jason Vance; coal miner Sara Vance; and photographer Ted Wathen. To all of you for your generous assistance and the use of these gorgeous historical photographs.

To the fabulous foxes: Gary, Karen, and Hyphen at FoxTale Book Shoppe in Woodstock, Georgia; to Chris Wilcox and Eon Alden at City Lights, North Carolina; the darling and supportive Lizz Taylor at Poor Richard's Books in Kentucky; and to all the indie bookstores around the country. Thank you bunches and buckets for connecting books with readers and fostering strong literacy; you are neighborhood treasures we love and cherish.

Small indie bookstores are one of the strongest cornerstones of communities.

I'm incredibly fortunate and eternally grateful to have the many librarians, the wonderful, wise bookwomen and bookmen across the country who offered friendship and bighearted support and who are community lifelines that selflessly serve so many: Kentucky sisters Laura Adams and Tessa Caudill, and a special shout-out and appreciation to friends Brian Shortridge and Teresa Matney of Virginia for your outstanding assistance with my research and helping me track down female coal miners and so much more. Thank you to special librarians and friends Kelly Ann Moore of Texas, Karen O'Connell and Jennifer Wann of Arkansas, Daryl Maxwell in Los Angeles, and Laurie Aitken in New York, just to name a few, for your tremendous support and warm friendships. *I cherish you all.* To the many librarians around the country who invited me into their hometowns for Pandemic Zooms, I loved and treasured each and every virtual visit we shared. Thank you so much.

Sincere thanks, immeasurable admiration, and mad love to all educators, and to name a few: Principal Jack VonHandorph, staff, and students at Notre Dame Academy; Professor Robert Stevens, who assigns *Book Woman* every year, and your wise students (you are so very dear) at University of Texas at Tyler; Kaye Brown and Tonya Northenor of Owensboro Community and Technical College; Nancy Kennedy of Furman University; and so many other educators who've been assigning *Book Woman.* Thank you for entrusting me with your thoughtful, talented, and bright students. It's an honor and privilege and is always humbling speaking with your future leaders.

To my amazing editors, Shana Drehs and Margaret (MJ) Johnston, it's been an honor and tremendous privilege to work with you again, and I'm beholden to you for your patience, wisdom, thoughtful advice, and exceptional edits, which made this book stronger. Much appreciation to my associate managing editor, Heather Hall; my wonderful copy editor, Diane

Dannenfeldt; and my proofreader, Carolyn Lesnick, for their excellent and wise editing. To dearest Margaret Coffee, Valerie Pierce, Broche Fabian, and all the amazing and brilliant Sourcebooks team working diligently and tirelessly behind the scenes for authors—you are the very best of the best.

Much gratitude to book woman Christie Hinrichs for all your generous support connecting my book to readers.

Thank you to Stacy Testa, my dear friend and colleague, for your excellent edits, wise advice, and tremendous support on yet another book journey.

I've been blessed to have my books surrounded by amazing talent: singer extraordinaire Ruby Friedman, thank you for your gorgeous, rich tribute songs, and great appreciation to the remarkably talented actress Katie Schorr, who makes my novels shine and sing with pitch-perfect narration. It's been a privilege working with you both. Masterful wordsmiths and friends Abbott and Sara, I love and thank you for your never-failing support and compassion during the good, bad, and crazy talk-me-off-the-ledge times.

Much love and gratitude to Virginia Berger for your always-generous spirit in lending GJ's keen eyes and valuable insight to my work.

To Joe, my love and a *Tommie* in your own right. For decades, you worked selflessly and tirelessly, helping countless women survivors obtain justice—this one is for *you*—a compassionate man, husband, father, and best friend. As always, you never once wavered when you heard the call of the abrupt *oo-oo*—and I love you always like *salt loves meat* and send out a musical *coo-coo-coo* to your unshakable quest for justice.

About the Author

New York Times, *Los Angeles Times*, and *USA Today* bestselling author Kim Michele Richardson has written five works of historical fiction and a bestselling memoir. Kim Michele was born and raised in Kentucky and lives there with her family and beloved dogs. She is also the founder of Shy Rabbit, a writers' residency and scholarship. To learn more, please visit Kim Michele on her Facebook page or on her website at kimmichelerichardson.com.